A POCKETFUL OF STARS

Doubleday & Company, Inc., Garden City, New York

Edited by Damon Knight

A POCKETFUL OF STARS

"Windsong," by Kate Wilhelm, from *Orbit 4;* copyright © 1968 by Damon Knight. Reprinted by permission of the author.

"The Intruder," by Ted Thomas, from *The Magazine of Fantasy and Science Fiction;* copyright © 1960 by Mercury Press, Inc. Reprinted by permission of the author.

"An Honorable Death," by Gordon R. Dickson, from *Galaxy;* copyright © 1960 by Galaxy Publishing Corp. Reprinted by permission of the author and his agent, Robert P. Mills, Ltd.

"The Burning," by Theodore R. Cogswell, from *The Magazine of Fantasy and Science Fiction;* copyright © 1960 by Mercury Press, Inc. Reprinted by permission of the author.

"Harry the Tailor," by Sonya Dorman, from *Cosmopolitan;* copyright © 1966 by Hearst Magazines, Inc. Reprinted by permission of the author and her agent, John Schaffner.

"Fifteen Miles," by Ben Bova, from *The Magazine of Fantasy and Science Fiction;* copyright © 1967 by Mercury Press, Inc. Reprinted by permission of the author and his agent, Robert P. Mills, Ltd.

"I Have No Mouth, and I Must Scream," by Harlan Ellison, from *If;* copyright © 1967 by Galaxy Publishing Corp. Reprinted by permission of the author and his agent, Robert P. Mills, Ltd.

"The Winter Flies," by Fritz Leiber, from *The Magazine of Fantasy and Science Fiction* (where it appeared as "The Inner Circles"); copyright © 1967 by Mercury Press, Inc. Reprinted by permission of the author and his agent, Robert P. Mills, Ltd.

*To Eva McKenna
and the memory of Mac*

CONTENTS

INTRODUCTION

The Milford Science Fiction Writers' Conference was a bold innovation, but we did not know it at the time. Judith Merril and I had talked a little about having a writers' conference in Milford, Pennsylvania, where we both lived, but it was the way you talk about building a boat in somebody's basement. Then in 1955 we went to the science fiction convention in Detroit, and found ourselves being taken so seriously that we began to think people might actually come to our party. When we got back to Milford, we called in Jim Blish, formed a committee, and issued manifestoes.

The convention the following year was held over the Labor Day weekend in New York. We chose the week after that for the Conference, hoping that people would spill over from New York to Milford. It worked almost too well—we got forty people, and crammed them into the living room of a summer cottage on the Delaware. We were too innocent to realize that a "writers' conference" is usually a bunch of paid professionals talking to an audience of paying amateurs. We took the phrase literally— we sat our writers down in a circle and started them talking to each other. They have been talking ever since.

In our second year, we didn't have the nearby convention to help us, and the Conference hit its low point. We had eight writers, not enough to keep a conversation going spontaneously, and not enough, I guess, to reserve the cottage colony we had used before. We held the sessions in Judy's house and mine (Jim was working in New York, and could not come), and it just did not work out very well.

Next year our enrollment rose again; Judy found another cottage colony that would accommodate us, and we settled into the format which we have used ever since. The Conference lasts eight days, Saturday through Saturday. Every afternoon except the first (when people are still checking in) we have a workshop: that is, we meet and discuss each other's manuscripts. Every evening except the last (because of the going-away party) we discuss a set topic—"Religion and Science Fiction," or "Getting Along With Editors," or whatever. In between, whenever the Conference is not in formal session, people are talking. My God, how they talk!

Because of this incessant rattle of tongues, and the late hours and the general excitement, Milford is like a week-long party. After a few years of this, we began to notice that the end of one Milford was attaching itself to the beginning of the next in our memories; the series now forms a nonstop party which has been going on for fourteen years, or, depending on how you look at it, for fifteen weeks. Also depending on how you look at it, this is reassuring or frightening.

People who come to Milford after attending other writers' conferences always remark on the relative absence of hostility and back-biting at the Conference. I have a theory about this: it is that people in social groups tend to do what is expected of them. People at Milford are expected to help each other and enjoy it, and they do.

We admit any kind of fiction to the workshop, but have continued to require science fiction as a credential. (Judith Merril resigned as a director of the Conference in 1961 over a disagreement on this point; James Blish had dropped out earlier when he moved to New York.) The principle of the workshop, to which we adhere firmly, is that there are no chiefs and no Indians. Each manuscript is passed around the circle, and everybody takes a crack at it. The quality of the criticism is variable, but the author gets eighteen or twenty different opinions and can take his pick. The aim is not merely to help the writer correct flaws in the manuscript at hand, but to help him exercise his own critical faculty so that he can improve his work in the future.

For the last six years the Conference has shown a tendency to grow beyond its practical limits. One year we had thirty writers in the workshop—too many; everything took too long. We were faced with the necessity of setting up two sections or else limiting attendance. We chose the latter, and have managed to keep the workshop to about twenty-two.

In its growing years, the Conference was open to any professionally published s.f. writer who wanted to come, and for a while we held to this as a principle. We don't anymore because we can't. The regulars get invited as a matter of course; a few others ask to come, and each year we invite one or two newcomers. One newcomer out of three feels himself instantly part of the group and becomes a regular; old-timers drop out at about the same rate. The Conference is like a stockpot, the perpetually simmering pot that goes on forever, although its ingredients are constantly being added and taken away.

We have been told by outsiders once or twice that we were running a conspiracy to subvert traditional science fiction, rig elections, worship turkeys, and so on. We might have been tempted to do all this, but as P. G. Wodehouse said when he was accused of wishing to overthrow the French government, "One has so little time."

Robin Scott Wilson, who came to Milford in 1967 to study the Conference, adopted our system with some modifications in his Writers' Workshop in Fantasy and Science Fiction at Clarion State College, Clarion, Pennsylvania, and made it work as a teaching program. The Clarion group has much the same cohesion and dedication as the Milford group, and remarkable things have been done there. (As I write, the Clarion Workshop is about to move to Tulane University, under the direction of James Sallis.)

The records are incomplete, I'm sorry to say, but at a guess we have workshopped about three hundred and fifty manuscripts in fourteen years. I need hardly say that most of these are omitted from the present volume; most of them deserve to be—they are, to paraphrase a memorable line of Bob Silverberg's, richly in need of oblivion. Out of the scintillating remainder I have chosen the stories that follow, and I now turn you over to the authors, who will introduce their work with occasional interruptions from me. To save a lot of footnotes, though, I have put certain parts of these introductions within brackets [thus]. When you see these brackets, you are to understand that I am saying, "Don't take this too seriously," or, more briefly, "Nonsense."

Damon Knight
Milford, Pennsylvania
January 13, 1970

A POCKETFUL OF STARS

Milford in June can be cold, usually is rainy, and would not be my choice for a vacation site if I had only one week. The week of my first Conference was a record-breaking cold, wet one. I think now that part of the chill came from inside me. I was so frightened that if I could have found a way out of Milford the afternoon I arrived, I would have taken it. Gordy Dickson and Ted Cogswell met me at the train station and took me along a winding road with a river on one side and mountains and woods on the other, made a mysterious turn that should have put us in the river, and left me in one of the dreariest, coldest cottages I had ever seen. That's when I prayed for a way out. I wasn't certain that I was a writer. I knew nothing about science fiction. I had never attended a writers' conference, or class; hadn't, in fact, ever met a writer before.

Meeting the other two women writers did nothing to improve my spirits. Anne McCaffrey was singing like an angel when I first saw her. And Rosel George Brown, a truly gifted storyteller, was telling one of her anecdotes and had everyone doubled up in painful laughter. (I can't sing, and can't tell stories. I forget the punchline, or mess it up somehow.)

Rosel and I decided to share a heated cottage, the only one on the premises, and I loaned her a pair of long pants and a sweater. I had brought two of each, and she hadn't brought any, because, good Lord, it's June! So we both had our uniforms that we kept on all week, bundled up from head to toe. That night the real talk started; I don't remember having another thought about leaving, or wishing myself elsewhere. The talk went on until dawn, and no matter where it started, it always came back to writing, being a writer, the agonies and the joys, the problems, the pay. Everything about writing, from the most mundane to the most transcendental. And the next day we started to read manuscripts, and those who knew how made notes and later made comments about the stories up for discussion. I didn't know how, so I kept quiet. My story came up in the middle of the week, and I took an ego-shattering drubbing.

I was so ignorant that I didn't know how to prepare a manuscript, and although I had been writing and selling stories for about three years by then, no one had bothered to tell me. I had sold three or four stories to the magazines before I ever saw a science fiction magazine. I had read science fiction only in library books. I had never had any sort of writing course. No one had ever used the phrase "purple prose" in my hearing before that day. But I heard it then. They didn't pull their punches. Later, when I realized that sometimes there is a spontaneous agreement to be gentle with a newcomer, I appreciated the fact that they hadn't done it with me. Afterwards, I washed my face and put on my reddest lipstick, and went to sit out in the drizzle on the slope above the river and threw stones into the water as hard as I could throw them. And that day was the day that I knew I was a writer and would be one for the rest of my life.

WINDSONG

We are three. We drive along the coast slowly until Paula says, "This one." Then we get out of the car and walk around the house nonchalantly, wade through the dunes to the ocean and swim there alone, away from the crowds that form a solid crust like soiled snow up and down the public beaches. How Paula knows this house is empty, but not that one, we don't know. She is never wrong. Subliminal signs that only she can perceive? A shade drawn wrong, a chair outside that should have been moved from the sun, a garment, long since dried, sun-bleached even, still flapping in the wind? We never know, and she can't tell us.

Paula is the windsong, quick, nimble, restless, long hair salt-dulled most of the time, too thin, sharp elbows, knees, cheekbones, collarbones. No makeup; she is in too much of a hurry. A nail breaks and she bites it even again. She never pauses to examine anything; her restless gaze flicks here and there, noting perhaps, not lingering, and she says, "We have to go back. A storm is coming." How does she know?

Gregory says she noticed the grey in the water far out near the horizon. That and the feel of the wind on her skin, and the way the clouds scudded now, all were clues for her. But he can't tell when a storm is coming. Gregory is her twin brother. Both are fifteen this summer. Gregory is the rock around which the wind sings and flutters, departing to pry into this and that, but always whirling back again. Gregory can give reasons for most of her conclusions, but he can't reach the conclusions intuitively as she can.

Dan Thornton stirred in his seat and opened his eyes slowly. There was no sound that had roused him, nothing out of the ordinary. He listened for a moment to the familiar soft humming of the computer at his right side and before his gaze turned to it he knew the rippling play of lights would be normal. The instrument panel before him showed nothing abnormal either, no flashing amber light, or worse, the steady throbbing of the red light. Systems okay. He yawned and stretched. Time to make the routine checks. He opened and closed relays, turned the television camera on and studied the passengers, all piled in boxes like rows of frozen goods on a supermarket shelf; he turned the camera off again. Readings on his instruments, all normal. He got out the food capsules carefully, and put them on a sectioned dish and slid it into the recon unit. He waited until the light went on, killing two more minutes, then slowly drew out the dish of scrambled eggs and bacon, toast and honey. He dropped another capsule into a cup and slid it in, then sat down with his breakfast. Presently he had coffee and his first cigarette. He looked over the book titles on the spools. He dropped the spool he selected and some of the thread-tape unwound as it rolled across the cabin. He kicked it hard and abruptly sat down. The computer was calling him.

The alarm clock hummed, and Thornton woke up groggily, feeling the ache of unrested muscles. He turned off the clock before it could start its second phase: a raucous buzz that sounded like fifty men with fifty saws clearing a swath through a forest. His hand left the clock and groped for his notebook and he wrote down the dream details before they began to flit away. He paused and tried to remember something: a dream within the dream? Nothing came of it, and he wrote about the cabin he had seen, and the books on spools like thread. The reconstituter for food struck him as a particularly good idea, one he had never encountered before. He finished the dream sequence and only then stretched and felt each muscle protest again.

He padded in bare feet across the room to the bathroom and stood under a hot shower for ten minutes. The icy follow-up failed to revive him and he knew that his efficiency would be at about 60% of normal unless he took his zoom-wowie pills. He looked at the small bottle disdainfully, but swallowed two capsules and only then looked at his face.

"This is the way we start most of our days, old man," he said to the face. "Aches, try to shock the system into awareness, then the pep pills and a gallon of coffee. It's no good, old man. You know it's no good."

The old man in the mirror didn't answer, and he was almost sorry. The day the image did answer, he'd quit, just walk out and never come back, and that would be nice. Shaving, he repeated to himself, emphasizing each syllable of it, "That would be nice!"

At the office he was met by his secretary who handed a memo to him. Meeting for nine sharp. The Secretary would be present. End. He crumpled it and nodded to Jeanne. It was 8:45.

"Coffee?" he asked.

The girl nodded as he started through the doorway to his inner office, a cubicle ten by ten. "I poured a cup, and there's more in the pot," Jeanne said. "Shall I start on the mail?"

"Sure, honey. And, Jeanne, try to winnow it way down, huh?"

She smiled sympathetically and he started on the coffee. He tried not to look at his desk, which Jeanne had cleaned up as much as possible, but which still was a jumble of plans, memoes, doodles, slide rules, schematics . . . The coffee was blistering hot, strong, black. The day began to seem less infernal. When he left for the conference in ten minutes he was carrying his third coffee with him. He grinned at Jeanne, and his stride was purposeful and his back straight.

There were fifteen men at the conference that morning, and all of them looked as bad as Thornton, or worse. They had all been driving on twelve-to-eighteen-hour days for seven months now, and the end was not in sight. Thornton could almost envy the union-protected maintenance men. He nodded to others and there were low greetings and hurried conversations in the shorthand that passed for talk. He thought, one bomb right here, right now, and poof, there goes the Special Institute for Applied Research.

He saw that the Secretary was already in the room, cloistered by several bodies near the window, speaking in his low monotone to Halvern, the Director of the Institute. The clock chimed softly and Halvern moved toward the long table, the Secretary following, still talking, like a priest mumbling incomprehensible prayers.

Introductions were unnecessary since the Secretary had been there before. Thornton thought of his bomb and enlarged it a bit in his mind, still not The Bomb, of course, but slightly bigger than the one he had contemplated earlier. Would the war stop then? He knew it would not, but there would be those on the outside who would sanctify him. He grinned at the thought, and for a moment he was afraid the grin had reached the outside of his face. But there were no looks askance, and deliberately he turned his thoughts from that line and became attentive to what the Secretary was saying:

". . . imperative that we solve this final problem before negotiations are finalized. When the talks begin, our activities in the field will be curtailed . . ."

Thornton added: *and we have stalled the Secretary-General about as long as possible.*

"Naturally we are trying to bring about peace talks as rapidly as possible *on the surface anyway where we can point to our efforts,* but it is difficult to negotiate with an enemy that is so xenophobic. *You mean he hates our guts, with reason, and he doesn't believe a word we say.* I repeat, the President has informed me that it is imperative that we complete our plans for the Phalanx and try it out under battle conditions so that we will better be able to assess its potential in the event we are faced with a major land war . . ."

Thornton turned him off then, letting his gaze slide from the Secretary's hand-tooled-leather face to the window that framed a vista of Tennessee hills touched with early spring. Dogwoods and redbuds were in bloom, and a strong wind whipped them unmercifully. Kite wind. Sailing wind. Sailing . . . He smiled inside and wished he could go sailing along the coast on the curious flat-bottomed skiff Gregory had picked up somewhere in the distant, almost forgotten past. Twenty-five years ago, by God! For a moment the thought of his boyhood friend stirred something, and his hand toying with a pencil tightened its grip painfully.

He wrenched his attention back to the Secretary who had left the familiar rah, rah, team talk, and was on something new finally. "I am scheduling the first simulated battle test for one month from today, and the first actual battle test for sixty days subsequent to that date." There was more of it, but Thornton perversely blocked it out. So they should all work for twenty hours a day instead of eighteen. He shrugged inwardly and decided that he didn't care. With wow-zooie pills and coffee they would all stay on their feet until they collapsed, and it didn't matter what shape they would be in when the year was over. One year in the Institute, one year off resting, then back to the university to pick up the threads of classwork, lectures on Advanced Programming Theory, and his own small quiet lab. And back to his family, of course.

Thornton returned to his office after the meeting and was confronted with the meaningless garble from other departments that he had to translate into a program. Very deliberately he didn't try to understand most of the problems that he worked with. He didn't want to know what the Phalanx would be able to do and what it would not.

6   KATE WILHELM

He divided his day into thirds: the first third, from 8:45 until 1:00, he worked on the advanced programming that was his to do: after lunch, 1:30 until 5:30, he went over the papers prepared by others, sometimes accepting them, often sending them back; from 7:30 until exhaustion stopped him he worked with the computer searching for errors. Then dream-laden sleep until 7:30 the next morning. At 5:30, three days a week, he spent half an hour with his analyst, and it was to him that he reported any interesting ideas that had come to him during his dreams, awake or asleep. His analyst, Dr. Feldman, believed implicitly in the creative ability of the unconscious to serve up workable ideas which generally were brushed aside because they were far afield of the patient's area of interest. Now that he was aware of the sort of things that Feldman was looking for, Thornton also searched his dreams and his reveries for those ideas, and was surprised to find how many of them there were. Surprised and excited. This was something that he planned to take from the Institute with him when he left. Most of it he planned, swore he would leave behind him forever.

He told Feldman the dream without consulting his notes: "I was in the cabin of a spaceship, carrying cryopassengers to a distant star system. I was responsible for them. Everything was functioning smoothly." He told in detail how he had prepared his breakfast, and then went on to the book incident. "It was a variation of the microfilm process, I suppose, simplified somewhat. I read the title the way you would read the label on a spool of thread; it even had the feel and texture of a spool of thread. I dropped it, though, and woke up then. My clock went off."
Feldman didn't interrupt him, simply nodded when Thornton came to the end of it. When Thornton pulled out his notebook and read from his notes, he was chagrined to find that he had omitted parts of the dream.
Feldman said, "The dream that you remember, what kind of a dream was it?"
"Kind? Oh, I see. I think it was black-and-white. I don't remember any color. I didn't feel it particularly, I don't think."

"Yes. Could you come out of it at any time? Did you realize that you were dreaming?"

"I don't think so. I have done that, and noted it afterward, but not this time."

Feldman worked on the dream within a dream, but Thornton couldn't remember if there had been one or not. Short of hypnosis, Feldman decided, it would stay repressed for the time being. Thornton and Feldman had discussed dreams in the past, and he knew that Feldman believed there were three major types of dreams: the hypnagogic dreams that float in and out of awareness on falling asleep, and on awakening, the kind that fade in and out of a short nap when you know you are dreaming and even take a hand in directing the dream sometimes. Then there was the next stage where the dreamer had no control, but was really more an observer than a participant, although he could be both at the same time, watching himself from a distance. The third kind was the sort that Thornton rarely had, or if he had, seldom remembered: the dream that is a reality in itself, the dream that can result in a heart attack if it is a nightmare, or in orgasm if it is sexual, the dream that exists, that can change the dreamer just as a living experience can.

Feldman was smiling happily when Thornton looked at him at the end of the questioning, and Thornton knew that finally he was proving interesting to the psychiatrist. After seven months of unshakable normalcy, he had done something interesting. He felt a stab of fear and wished he hadn't told the dream completely, had let it go at the remembered version, but even as he thought it, he knew that it would have been impossible. Feldman would have known, and resistance would have delighted him even more than mere repression. For a moment he hated the smiling man, but it passed, and he grinned back briefly.

"You think I'm going to earn my keep after all?" he asked.

"When you have something come up after this length of time, I must assume that there is the possibility that it can be connected with the work here, yes. We shall see. I am scheduling you for an hour tomorrow, starting at five. Is that convenient?"

The question was rhetorical.

"You should give thought to the spool of thread that you tried to rid yourself of," Feldman said. "As you fall asleep, think to yourself, spool of thread, spool of thread. Who knows, perhaps it will come to you." He held open the door and Thornton left.

Thornton knew that early in their dealings Feldman had had him in deep hypnosis, that he had few secrets from the man, that probably Feldman had left him with some posthypnotic cues, and he wondered if it had been a suggestion, or an order, that he should think of a spool of thread, and even as he wondered about it, he knew that coming from Feldman a suggestion could have the force of an order given at gunpoint. His smile was without mirth as he remembered what Feldman had said once when asked why he didn't merely hypnotize all his patients and have them recite their dreams and fears to him.

"Ah, but the associations, the meanings would be lost then, perhaps. Why do you repress this and not that? This is what is interesting, not what you repress particularly, although it can be. No, I might nudge you from time to time, but I want you to bring them out with the proper associations, the associations that only you can make."

Spool of thread, spool of thread . . .

He remembered, dreamed, of losing his first tooth, and the thread his mother had tied around it, her gentle insistence that he pull it himself, and her promise, after a look of surprise and amusement that, yes, they would send it to his father. He drifted out of the dream-reverie and was wide awake thinking about his father who had been a good man, kind and wise, a colonel in the army. He got out of bed and paced his tiny room smoking furiously, but the image of his father naked and bruised, shaved clean, dragging one foot, being pulled hobbling down a street crowded with Oriental faces that were grimaces of hate, the image remained, just as he had watched it on television. A good man, he repeated soberly. But he might have done the things they accused him of doing. He might have.

He swallowed a pill and returned to bed and found himself repeating: spool of thread, spool of thread. He wanted to get up again, but the pill was quick and he felt lethargy stealing over him. He would be achy in the morning, always was achy when he resorted to sleeping pills. Spool of thread . . .

He dreamed discordant, meaningless dreams, fantasies without basis in reality. And slept deeper, and was less restless on the single bed.

We walk through the museum arm in arm and it is Paula who is leading us, although she is in the middle. Her steps are light and quick, and she talks incessantly. She pauses before the paintings of the new artist, Stern, and she squints and cocks her head this way and that, then she pulls us on to the next one. She is changed now, her hair still long and straight, but shining clean, and she has done something to her face, something so subtle that I can't decide what it is. I find myself staring at her again and again, and she smiles at me, and for an instant I find the wild girl who lived for the ocean only five years ago. Then it is gone and she is saying, "It's such a joke! He's wonderful! Don't you see it?" There are fifty paintings, arranged in aisles that meet and interconnect so that it is hard not to repeat an aisle. There is no arrow pointing this way, no numbers on the paintings, but Paula has led us through them to the end, and she is laughing with delight. The artist is there, regarding Paula with deep and penetrating interest. She runs to him and kisses him on his bearded cheek and says, "Thank you. I won't tell." And she doesn't tell. Gregory goes back to the beginning and works his way slowly to us once more, and when he comes back, his eyes share her mirth, but he won't tell either. I know that he can explain it although she can't, but he needed her to tell him there was something to explain. I return later and study the paintings alone for a long time, and I don't know what they found. I am lost there. The paintings are grotesque, hideous and meaningless, and the arrangement is meant to befuddle, not to enlighten.

Paula loves the city as she loved the beaches. She runs and dances through the streets joyously, tasting what no one else tastes, smelling what no one else smells, seeing what is not there for my eyes to see. She sings in the city like a fresh breeze from the ocean.

Paula plans to leave school in the spring. She wants . . . she doesn't know what she wants, but it is not in school. She will travel, perhaps marry. I feel tightness in my throat and I ask if she will marry me and she stops, frozen, and finally after a long time she says no. I am angry with her and stalk away. Gregory says that she is like a bird now, she must fly here and there before she stops and love would stop her. I hate them both, their closeness, their awareness of each other. I want to kill them both. Especially Paula. My hands are fists when she comes near me and the smothering waves of love-hate immobilize me at a place where the pain is unendurable.

She knows. Paula is like a spring wind then, gentle and soothing, and I am filled with her presence. For two weeks we are together and she is in every cell of me, deep in me where she can never escape now. Then she is gone. Gregory knows where, I think, but he doesn't tell me. He plods with his books, getting every detail of every subject letter-perfect, but he never originates anything, never offers anything and he is like a shadow without the wind. I know his loss is greater than my own, but I don't care about that. I return to California where I am still in school, and the jet is my scream of anguish that I cannot utter for myself. I want her out of my life. I want never to see her again. I want her dead so that no one else can have her.

Dan Thornton strode across his mammoth office and began pushing buttons on a four-by-eight-foot console on one side of his desk. Three doors flew open from other rooms, and shaking men entered; he waved them to seats and waited for the Secretary.

"I have your answer," he said to the Secretary on his arrival. "It is simply this . . ." He was dying, his throat tightening and choking him, his heart pounding harder and harder . . .

He sat up shivering. He reached for the notebook and the light, and wrote quickly and lay down again. He thought he had been wakeful off and on most of the night, and now the sky was lightening, a pale grey touched with peach tones. He squeezed his eyes tighter, desperately wanting sleep to return, deep, untroubled sleep, and he knew that it would not.

Feldman said slowly, "You are aware of what the Phalanx is, yet you consistently deny any real knowledge of it to yourself. Why is that?"

Thornton shrugged. He thought of his wife and three children and talked of them for a few minutes until Feldman stopped him.

"I know about them. You told me early about them and it is on your file. Tell me about the spool of thread."

He free-associated for a while; he had learned to do it quite well, but privately he thought it was nonsense. He paid little attention to his own voice when he free-associated. It wasn't as if he were being analyzed for a medical purpose, he had told himself early in the business. Feldman was paid to keep tabs, that was all. He had nothing to hide, nothing of interest to learn about himself, so he cooperated, but didn't pay much attention.

Feldman said, "Maze," and he answered, "Art Museum." He sat straight up on the couch. He was shivering. Feldman nodded to him when he swung around to look. "So that is that," Feldman said. "What it is actually I don't know, but you do now, don't you?"

Thornton shook his head violently, shivering hard. He remembered the feeling of being lost at an art exhibit years ago. "It was so meaningless," he said. "This exhibit was arranged like a maze and the artist came over to me while I was standing there feeling stupid, and he told me that it meant nothing. I had worked hard trying to puzzle it out, and he said it had no meaning. It was arranged like a maze."

Feldman looked disappointed. His silence invited Thornton to keep talking, but there was nothing more to say about it. Thornton said, "The Phalanx is the final solution to the problem of modern warfare. It is an armored computer bank designed to control at least twenty-five subunits at this time, and it will have the capacity to control n subunits when it is completed. The subunits to this point have been built to scout jungle trails, and go through undergrowth where there are no trails searching out the enemy. They come equipped with flame throwers, grenade launchers, rocket launchers, communications units, infrared sensors, mass sensors, mine laying, or mine detection devices, chemical analysis labs, still and movie cameras, audio sensors and transmitters . . ."

He became aware of Feldman's bright, unblinking gaze and he paused and grinned at the analyst. Softly he added, "But the main problem with the Phalanx is that it doesn't know what a smile is on a friendly face. It can't distinguish between friend and enemy. It can't tell if the metal it senses is a gun or a hoe. It has no way of knowing if the mass-burdened heat source is a man with a howitzer or an ass with a load of firewood. And no matter how many changes the psycho-cybernetics lab sends to me, I can't program those things into it."

Thornton stood up and stretched. His gaze followed a low, long shaft of sunlight coming through the venetian blind where a slat was crooked. "I'm going for a walk," he said. He sensed that Feldman made a motion toward him, but there was no effort to stop him, or to force him to complete his hour.

"Tomorrow at five," Feldman said, and that was all.

His thighs burned as he climbed. He had wanted to climb the hill ever since the first tracery of white blossom had appeared high on its side, but no time, no time. And now his thighs burned. He should write to Ethel tonight. Hadn't even opened her last letter yet. He had put it down somewhere and had forgotten it. On the dresser in his room? On his desk? He groaned to himself at the thought of his desk, and he slipped on a moss-covered rock and banged his knee. Sitting on the damp pungent ground he rocked back and forth nursing the knee for a few minutes, catching his breath. He had come farther than he realized. Below him, almost hidden, he could see the Institute building. It had started as a low, long simple two-story building, but had been extended in three directions, like dominoes, and at the end of one of the newer additions there was construction going on. He had a vision of it worming its way over the hills, growing like a snake through the mountains, creeping through valleys, over crests, following watercourses . . . He closed his eyes and composed part of the letter to Ethel. It would be dull, he decided, faltering after the initial hope-you-are-well bit. Ethel was a good woman, but dull. God, she was dull. He remembered the shock he had felt the day he understood that Ethel had settled in on herself, that she would change no more, only become more what she was, more dogmatic, less malleable to change of any sort, more picture-pretty and smug. Ethel was forty. She had been forty on her twenty-fifth birthday, would be forty on her eightieth. But she was good, kind, considerate, a good mother, a faithful and helpful wife, good social animal . . .

They could say that about him. A good man. Plodding maybe, but a good man. Wouldn't hurt a fly. Good to his kids, a real father.

He leaned back against a treetrunk and watched the sunset without thinking.

A good man.

The breeze on his cheek was warm and fragrant with spring. Gradually he forgot about the cold, damp ground beneath him. He thought about the three kids. Bang, bang, bang, three years, three kids. That was the way they had wanted it. Have them all together, raise them together and be done with that part of it. By the time we're both forty, they'll be almost grown and we'll still be young. Well, he was forty-four, and they were all grown. But he wasn't young. Ethel wasn't young. Both of them were good, good, good, but they were not young. He dreamed of romping with the kids, and he knew the romping was wrong. They were glad when he tired of it and left them. He dreamed of his daughter's soft cheek against his, as she whispered secrets to him, and his yawn that had driven her away. Yet, he did love her with an intensity that sometimes had startled and frightened him. Perhaps that was why he had driven her away. He remembered her flying past him on her bicycle, hair streaming behind her, thin legs pumping harder and harder . . .

We go down the coast in the skiff with the wind driving us hard. Feeling of fear, exhilaration, alertness, watching for the sudden wave that could topple us. Paula's hair streaming out in the wind, hitting my face, stirring something in me, making me look at her through different eyes for a moment. And the intolerable ache that was Paula. The searing, burning, unbearable pain that meant Paula, and the release that was just as sudden and even more intense.

He jerked from the tree and was on his feet. He shuddered once and started down the hill. He had been dreaming of his wife and the kids. Of his daughter . . . A flush of deep shame swept over him and he stumbled blindly back to the Institute.

"Dr. Thornton, there has to be a way to program these abstracts, as you call them." Melvin Jorgenson paced. He was a restless man. Even pacing failed to satisfy his need to move, and in his hands he carried and played with a pen whose point he extended and retracted over and over, each time making an audible click. Thornton noticed that he was pacing in time to the click, or was he clicking in time to his tread? He said nothing, and waited. Maybe they were going to fire him.

The Director was there also, and it was to him Jorgenson was addressing himself, although he prefaced his remarks with Thornton's name. The Director looked unhappy.

"You know that we have been experimenting with various techniques," Jorgenson said, glancing at Thornton, but still talking to the Director. "We have a simple psycho-modular unit in operation now, much like the one you described in your book of several years ago. That gave us the necessary line to follow, but as I say, this is a simple unit."

He continued to talk and pace and by listening to him very carefully, and ignoring the clicks as much as possible, Thornton finally understood that there was to be a major revision in the Phalanx, and he was to program the revised version with all the data that already had gone into the obsolete model. He started to laugh and continued to laugh until someone, the Director himself, brought him water. He said that he had strangled on a smothered cough, that he had caught cold when he had fallen asleep out in the woods a few nights ago. He allowed Jorgenson to lead him to the new unit ready to be connected to the Phalanx, and he asked the right questions, intelligent questions, and he made intelligent notes and finally said, sure, why not?

"The Phalanx," he wrote in his diary (because writing it, even though he would have to destroy what he had written afterward, set it in his mind: once written, never forgotten, he had learned early in his school career, and so had gone through school laboriously copying passages, notes, sometimes almost whole textbooks; he had remembered all of it, still remembered all of it), "is apparently a small building, and only on close approach can you see that there are treads under it, hidden by sides that come almost to the ground. There are pseudo-windows, a pseudo-exterior that can be made to conform to any local style of building. Inside . . ." He put the pen down and walked to the window. It was raining hard. He was slightly feverish; he really had caught a cold, and he had taken the afternoon off on the instructions of the infirmary doctor. He was supposed to be sleeping now, but the sound of the rain was unsettling instead of soothing, and he wanted to be out in it, walking bareheaded under the driving, stinging sheets of water. He thought yearningly of the pneumonia that would almost certainly follow, and the discharge from present duties, and the long rest afterward. Rest, travel, sunbathing, reading, being conducted through the computer laboratories of major countries throughout the world. His name would be magic after a year on the project, even if they hadn't brought it off yet. Eventually they would, and then everyone connected with it would be known, not to the public, but to their peers, where it mattered. He pulled the blind over the window and returned to the diary.

"Inside the 'house' are the computer, its weapons and sensors, with a monitor board in the center. Here it is that we are forced to maintain human surveillance. A man has to oversee the data that are brought in, has to be able to jump over intervening bits of data to connect those things that have no apparent reason for being linked together. For instance, if a fire is to be started to clean out an area, the man has to note the weather—a fire during a thunderstorm is a futile gesture. He has to note the wind, the placement of other units, the relative value of migratory birds in the area, for example. Or the possibility of livestock that will be killed by smoke downwind from the area. All of these we can program in, if we can formulate them in clear, unambiguous language. We don't dare let the Phalanx get confused."

He dropped his pen again and went to the bathroom and took his temperature. It was up, 102.6. He lay down. He was thinking of the statements that could confuse the Phalanx unless all parts were satisfied: A.B, A+B, A/B, A→B, A≡B . . . They couldn't do it. How describe a smile in clear and unambiguous language? The Phalanx couldn't be unmanned. Nor could it be manned in the usual sense. The Phalanx and its offspring were to be the call boxes, like the police telephones that were spaced all over cities. Imagine, he told himself, what it would be like if the call box on the corner not only alerted the precinct station, but watched suspicious characters, measured and weighed them, analyzed them, noted what weapons they carried, made countless other observations about them, came to a decision that they were okay, or not okay, and if not, then apprehended them, or killed them. Imagine that. What if it made a mistake and burned down a city block in error? *Sorry 'bout that.*

But if they could make it work, wouldn't it be good? Wouldn't it be better than armies over the face of the earth? Good, good, good . . .

Dan Thornton couldn't lift his arm because they had pinned

gold braid on it. Real gold. They got the other arm and he wanted to beg off, but they insisted, refusing to hear his pleas. With the fastening of the braid on his other arm all he could do was stand, trying not to sway, knowing the weight would topple him if he swayed. He was paralyzed from goodness, he thought.

They had this old brain hanging around, see. The guy died on the operating table, abdominal surgery, and his head was intact, going to waste. So they put the brain in this jar of nice warm nutrients and fed it now and then and it went on ticking away, thinking its own thoughts. Then they put electrodes in it, this is the sight center, this the kinesthetic . . . And they put return wires and hooked them to an EEG and they watched the pens go up and down, up and down, and they kept getting cuter with it until they could get that little old brain to tell them what was on its mind. Not much, as it turned out. You see, that little old brain had gone crazy as a bedbug from the various things they had done to it, but still those pens went up and down, up and down, and it couldn't stop, couldn't refuse to cooperate, couldn't do anything but soak up the nutrients and sit there ticking away.

"Doesn't he look natural, like he might get up and talk to us any minute."

But don't look behind that eyeball, ma'am. Empty behind it. That one too, and that.

Most of them go mad, if not immediately, then as soon as they are hooked to the computer that is sending messages at the rate of a million bits a second. They had time, and psycho-modular units to work with. They found a unit that did not go mad when they linked it to a computer. It was a simple computer, however.

If chips are black and white, and this object is green, then this object is not a chip. If tiles are red and blue, and this object is green, then this object is not a tile. And so on, and on, and on, at the rate of one million bits a second. The brain ticked away and did not go mad. They made it more complex. The object was green and round. Then more complex: green, round, and weighs n grams . . . The brain did not go mad. Yet. They hooked it to the Phalanx, and the brain went mad.

Dan Thornton stood with his arms dangling, paralyzed by his own goodness and the heavy gold braid that testified to the goodness and watched the brain go mad. How they could tell it was going mad was by the way it made the pens go up and down, up and down. It was drawing paper dolls, all joined at feet and hands.

We stare at each other across a roomful of people and somehow we come together without either of us moving. I hold her tight against me and murmur into her hair that smells of sea winds and sunshine, and my murmur has no words, but says that I love her. "It's been a long time, Dan," she says. Her eyes are shining and I feel that she is happy to see me. Again she is different. The wild girl is deeper, harder to find now, but still there. She says, "Let's go somewhere else." We walk the streets, her hand in mine, our steps matched, even though she has to take long strides to keep up. We walk for hours, see the night out, watch silently when the last star is lost in a lightening sky.

We talk and I find myself defending my father. She stops me with cool fingers pressed against my lips. "You are shocked that you can love someone who is capable of evil," she says, as if surprised at me. "We are all capable, it's just that most of us never get the chance to do more than small evil things." I argue that he wasn't evil, that he never hurt anyone in his life. She is skipping at my side, not listening, and I know she thinks I am foolish. I am angry with her, almost as angry as when she said she would not marry me. I ask her again and she shakes her head. I ask her what she is doing, how she is living and she is amused that I don't know of her. She puts a slim book into my hand, says I should not open it until she is gone again, and that won't be until Monday.

The weekend is an agony of pleasure, and on Monday she is gone. The book is poetry that I cannot understand. They say she is brilliant, a genius, that she is the eyes and ears of the world. And I can't understand her poetry.

Two weeks later I marry Ethel and we plan to have three children right away.

"Doctor Thornton, if you'll just raise your hips a bit. That's right."

He was being taken somewhere on a stretcher on wheels. It was too hard to try to understand, so he let himself be carried and cared for, and sometime later he knew that he had the pneumonia that was to release him and send him home. After the serious part of it passed and he was told to take it easy and soak up sun on the wind-protected sunporch, he thought about the project, and he knew he wouldn't ask to be relieved from it. The Institute brought in Carl Brundage, an old friend of his to substitute for him until he was well enough to resume a full schedule. Carl stopped in to talk when he had time, and that helped the slow days along.

"The major mistake is in the lack of selectivity in the psycho-modular units they are forced to use. Most of them belong to enlisted men, untrained minds that probably never used a tenth of their potential. You have to think of that one unit as pre-programmed, you see. It can accept no new training, can't learn anything, can't develop any of its potential; it is the coordinator, that's all. The mistake lies in thinking that it is more than that. But that's all it needs to be," he added, deep thought furrows aging his face for a moment. Something . . . ? Whatever the thought had been, it had not come to consciousness, however, and he shrugged. It would. He knew the workings of his own brain, knew that he might feel twinges of this sort off and on for a while, then a new idea would hit him and the twinges would go away until another new idea was born.

"Are you going to be allowed to watch the first test on Monday?" Carl asked.

"Sure. But it will be a failure." Moodily he repeated that to himself after Carl had left to do the work that he, Thornton, was supposed to be doing.

He rested over the weekend, sleeping deeply and heavily under massive sedation. Monday was clear and warm with high cirrus clouds forming milky streaks in a perfect sky. The wind velocity was five to ten miles an hour, air temperature a mild 71. Thornton rode in a jeep to the demonstration site, twelve miles from the Institute building, in a narrow gouged-out valley, where spring was arriving later than on the more exposed hillsides. Pale green spears of unfolded leaves tipped the trees and the dogwoods still bore tiers of snowy flat blossoms.

The Phalanx sat in the center of the small valley, looking like a miner's cabin. At the signal given by the Director the sides of the Phalanx rose slightly, enough for ten small, rounded subunits to roll out from the interior. The subunits were called the bugs. They were painted randomly in browns and greens, and when they moved away from the Phalanx, they merged with the earth and the undergrowth and were invisible. The test was to be in two parts; the first was without the psycho-modular unit hooked in, the second with it.

Scattered in the valley and on three sides of the surrounding hills were Institute men, taking the part of the enemy. Thornton had expected to be one of them, and he was grateful for the pneumonia that had turned him into a spectator. The ten bugs were only part of the force the Phalanx could control. Two of them carried sprays that threw out an arc of a water-dye mixture; in battle that would be fire. Two others recorded on film and sound-track everything in a radius of up to ten miles, terrain permitting. Another moved along with a radar antenna spinning, homing in on a helicopter that thundered overhead, while its companion followed a flight of birds, then picked up a jet making a pencil-thin contrail.

Each bug apparently functioned as planned. Thornton waited. The sun heated his thighs and he remembered how they had burned on the climb up the hill the day he had caught the cold. His driver, one of the junior programmers, shifted excitedly and pointed to one of the bugs that was leaving the ground, skimming over the top of bushes, over a runoff stream. The Phalanx had everything under control. It didn't fall apart until three rabbits were flushed from the bushes and ran straight at the mine detecting bug. The dye thrower swung around and sprayed the rabbits, and with them the mine detector that was immediately frozen in its tracks. The Phalanx had been programmed to put out of commission any of the subunits that were scored on. Following the rabbits the dye-thrower rolled over a "mine," and it also was immobilized.

One by one the subunits proved vulnerable to the unexpected, and within half an hour the Phalanx sat alone, unprotected, and the men moved in and "captured" it.

Thornton watched the slumping figure of the Secretary and the unbowed figure of the Director who was gesturing expansively. The second session would take place after lunch, after the psychomodular unit was hooked in and the men resumed their positions.

With the psycho-modular unit in place, the test was more impressive. Some of the men on the hills were "killed" by the dye-throwers, others were "gassed," but none were taken prisoner. The Phalanx was not equipped to take prisoners. This time the Phalanx refused to be fooled by rabbits deliberately introduced by the men, and it sent a unit after the men themselves. It shot down three crows and two jets, and a hawk. When it went mad in less than an hour it had the subunits destroy each other, and turn on the Phalanx itself.

While technically a failure, the second session of the test gave great satisfaction.

There was a rally that night, conducted by the Secretary himself.

Thornton's son was of draft age, or would be in a month. He could understand the tenor of the country that clamored for an end to the draft, an end to the endless wars, an end to the frustrations that dulled the young men and made them restless in school, made them marry too young, drive too hard and fast, experiment with drugs and danger wherever it was presented to them. He didn't need or want the Secretary to outline this for him, but the Secretary did. His voice was sad and rousing by turns. Thornton used his illness as an excuse and left early.

The work continued. The psycho-modular units continued to go mad. Thornton convalesced without incident and discontinued the heavy sedation, and went back to a shortened work-day. He also went back to his sessions with Dr. Feldman.

There was an air of excitement at the Institute now. Success was in the smell of the spring air turning into summer, and the scientists and technicians were lightheaded. Thornton too. Carl was almost embarrassingly grateful to him for having become ill so that he had been called in. He worked like a man possessed, trying to spare Thornton all he could. Thornton knew that other departments were working even harder than his own. The psycho-cyberneticist and the perception psychologist must not sleep at all, he thought one night when he met them both in the hall. He had returned for his notebook, after napping for three hours. He would return to sleep, but they seemed prepared for an all-night stint.

How does man know what he sees? How does the brain communicate with itself; with the hormonal system; with the autonomic nervous system . . . ? He didn't envy them their work. When they found another answer, he got it in the language of formulae and symbols that he then translated to binary digital language and put in the Phalanx. This was tested, and if it was wrong, he took it out again, and they went back to the original problem.

Thornton dreamed often of the Phalanx and its bugs now. "Are the others reporting dreams about it?" he asked Feldman.

"They dream of everything," the analyst said.

Thornton wondered if Feldman were curious about why his dreams seemed never to concern sex. "When I was young," he said, "I was as horny as anyone, I guess. But now . . . After I got married and settled down, it seemed less important. I guess I'm one of those fortunate people who isn't driven by sex so much. I've hardly missed Ethel at all," he added. It surprised him to say it and know that it was true. Of course, when he had been ill, he had missed her. She would have been good to have around then. She had a way with sick people, soothing, gentle, comforting. But normally his work was enough, and the momentary pangs of longing seemed almost directionless, certainly not aimed specifically for her. Or anyone else.

"Were you ever in love?" Feldman asked when the silence lengthened.

"Sure. A couple of times. High-school stuff; then, of course there was Ethel."

"What about the high-school stuff? Any particular girl who stands out now?"

He couldn't remember the name of any one girl he had admired in high school.

That night he had three programs to check. Carl had admitted mistakes in them. "Garbage in, garbage out," Carl had said, flinging the papers down on Thornton's desk. "And I can't find the garbage." He had been disgusted with himself for letting the error slip past in the first place, and even more so for not finding the error after it was known to be there.

The three programs comprised a whole; the error could be in the first of them, throwing off the next two; or it could be in the last step of the third program. There were over fifteen hundred steps involved.

Thornton worked on it until 1 A.M., knocked off half an hour to stretch and have a sandwich, then went back to it again. At 3 A.M. he realized that Feldman was pushing him for some reason that he couldn't fathom. For months his relationship with Feldman had been casual, in the line of duty, but now it was different. The difference in Feldman was like the change that came over a cat that had been playing with a ball and was presented with a mouse. The same gestures, but with a new intensity, a new concentration. He wandered out into the night to smoke and let his room clear of the smoke there. He was coughing badly with each cigarette, the after-effect of pneumonia, he guessed.

He had talked to the psycho-cyberneticist about the selection of the psycho-modular unit, and Jorgenson had been in bitter agreement with his theory that they could expect no great strides forward until they were allowed to select for themselves. He knew the Director had brought it up with the Secretary, but no word had filtered down as yet about the outcome. Meanwhile the units continued to go mad and the Phalanx tried to commit suicide periodically.

He didn't like the phrase, "tried to commit suicide," but it was how they all talked about it. He remembered his mother and her suicide that followed the execution of his father. He remembered the pictures of the mangled children that had arrived in the mail, and the letters, and phone calls, and his mother's anguish and final surrender. He would not have got through that period without Paula and Gregory. His hand froze in the process of lifting his cigarette to his lips.

Paula! He hadn't thought about Paula for twenty years. Not since he had gone to hear her speak and read her poetry. Ethel had been so bored by it. They hadn't stayed for all the program, but later he had gone back and met Paula at the reception that followed. She never appeared surprised to find him, he had thought then when her face lighted with pleasure at his approach. Never surprise, only pleasure to see him again. He almost asked her if she loved him then, but he didn't. Again she seemed different, wiser, but not only that. In touch with something that he couldn't grasp, perhaps. Tuned in, the students said of her, adoring her and what she wrote for them.

He inhaled deeply, coughed hard and held onto a tree until he had his breath back. Coughing made him dizzy, made his head swell and throb. He thought fleetingly of himself dying, dead, and Paula coming to the funeral, weeping over his lifeless body, pleading for another chance with him. A bitter smile twisted his face and he pulled hard on the cigarette, finishing it, not caring if he coughed or not. Another paroxysm, and he knew that he did care. He waited for it to pass and then returned to his room and the programs that had to be corrected.

Toward dawn he threw himself down on his bed and fell asleep instantly.

We pull ourselves up the steep rocks of the cliff and when we get to the top we have no breath left for talking. Paula is sweating, and she rubs the back of her hand over her face carelessly, leaving a smudge of dirt there from her forehead to her chin. I lie back with my eyes closed, trying not to cry yet. Hoping never to cry over my mother. Paula says, "Mom and Dad say you can live with us until you go to school in the fall. Okay?"

It isn't really a question. I can go with them or I can go with my aunt and uncle who came from Ohio for the funeral. The state won't let me stay alone yet because I am only seventeen. My aunt told me that much. She is angry because my mother, her sister, killed herself. It was irreligious of her. It was selfish of her. I despise my aunt.

I feel Paula's toe digging my side and I squirm, wanting not to cry. She giggles and the bare toe prods again, digs and wiggles against my side. I look at her and I know that I won't cry now. I jump up and grab her, meaning to shake her, but I just hold her, and she stops giggling. We don't move for a long time until Gregory interrupts us. He hasn't noticed anything so maybe it wasn't so long, but that moment goes on and on.

When we go back to my house my aunt is angry with me. She says I am selfish for leaving now when people have been coming by to pay respects. She is going to lecture me, but Paula goes to her and puts her dirty hand on my aunt's smooth, clean sleeve, and Paula says something I can't hear. Then she says, "It's going to be all right. We'll take care of him." My aunt bursts into tears and falls down in a chair crying like that, shaking, ugly with crying, and Paula, Gregory and I leave her there.

Thornton woke up, remembering the dream in detail. He made notes of it for Feldman's benefit. He rolled over again and went back to sleep.

The work went slowly, and badly. They had plateaued and apparently could go no further. But all of them could see the next step so clearly, and all of them knew that without the next step the project was a failure. The Secretary returned and huddled with the Director and several other top men, and following this meeting there was something not so open, something uglier about the Project. No leaks came from the meeting, and there was a dearth of rumors for once. A new brain was installed, and hope rose as it continued to function after twenty-four hours, then thirty-six hours. A field test was scheduled, but before it could be held, the brain went mad.

Gloom settled heavier over the men, and mistakes were made that would have been unthinkable four months in the past. They analyzed the results of the last psycho-modular unit and its stresses and the final breaking point, and it was then that Thornton learned that this brain had been especially selected. He knew vaguely who Lester Ferris had been, but he didn't know how he had died, or when, or how his brain had come into the possession of the Institute. Ferris had been a child prodigy, a brilliant mathematical physicist who had shaken up the world of physics at the age of fifteen. Crippled in body, with a mind that sang, he had drawn the attention of the entire world with theories that might be proven in some distant future, or might never be proven, but were unmistakably original and brilliant. He had settled down at the Institute for Advanced Study at the age of twenty-five, and as far as Thornton knew no more had been heard from him.

Thornton began reading the daily papers that were brought to the Institute, and every time they had a brain that was more successful than the previous ones, he searched the obituaries, but he didn't ask anyone any questions. No one was asking questions.

He and Feldman went over the incident of his mother's suicide several times, and slowly he found that he was remembering things about Paula that he had forgotten completely. Feldman knew her work and was impressed that Thornton had been her lover. Thornton found that he could talk of it freely, as if it had happened to someone else.

Sometimes Thornton went for walks in the woods, now dark green and summery, harboring snakes behind rocks and logs, alive with rabbits, birds, insects that sang and whirred and buzzed. He didn't do it as often as he would have liked because there was no time. His year was running out. The second test was due within weeks, and although the idea of a battle test had been abandoned, the field test was still on the schedule. They were learning what kind of brains were best suited for the symbiotic relationship with the computer that was called Phalanx, but they were unable to find just the right one. The brains continued to go mad.

They had a Delphi session, with each man answering questions about the sort of mind, the kind of mentality that would work with the Phalanx. Thornton bit his pencil and slowly filled in the answers to the printed questions. Afterward they read them aloud and talked about them. The papers were gathered by the Director.

"What do you think now of Paula Whitfield?" Feldman asked.

"Oh, she's a promiscuous bitch. Exciting, probably very beautiful still. She was, you know, but in a wild, unpremeditated way. Not the cover-girl look of studied loveliness."

Feldman nodded. "Your wife is very lovely," he said after a moment. He was making idle talk now that the hour was almost over and Thornton had been wrung out.

"Ethel is beautiful," Thornton said. It surprised him. She really was. He had a letter from her in his pocket then. She would meet him and they would drive to Florida and go from there to Nassau. She was excited about the trip. She was lonesome for him.

"Is Paula Whitfield really promiscuous?" Feldman asked curiously. "There's no hint of that in her work."

"She sleeps around," Thornton said, hearing the contempt in his voice. "She's got a couple of illegitimate kids, you know." He shrugged and got up. "I guess that's unfair. I don't really know what she's like now. It's been twenty years since I saw her. A genius with the morals of an alley cat. That's what she was then."

He opened the door. Feldman said, "Tomorrow, five, one hour. Okay?" Thornton looked back and nodded, and Feldman added, "Why did you put her down as the one mind that could exist with the Phalanx?"

He ate little dinner, and walked afterward. He hadn't. He knew he hadn't. He visualized the sheet of questions and his answers, and he knew that his memory would reproduce it faithfully for him. He hadn't put her name down. The questions had all led to that one, of course: Can you name anyone who you think would qualify as a psycho-modular unit?

He had left it blank.

He saw it again in his mind, and it was blank.

He felt a stab of fear. What was Feldman after?

He wouldn't recommend Paula, even if the thought had occurred to him. When Gregory died, eighteen years ago, she had written that crazy poem about the boy who chose death rather than killing. Gregory had died under enemy fire. He had mailed her the firing pin of his rifle, then had walked upright until he was felled. Stupid act of insanity. It had made all the papers, his death, and the bitter poetry that had flowed from Paula afterward. She was practically a traitor, as Gregory certainly had been. Again he wondered what Feldman was trying to do. He returned to his desk and worked until midnight.

He dreamed that night of the psycho-modular unit fixed in the island inside the house that was the Phalanx. It was a sealed tank that looked very much like an incubator, with rubber gloves built into it so that the operators could push their hands into them and handle the thing inside. There were six pairs of the gloves. To one side of the tank a screen, not activated now, had been placed to show electroencephalograph tracings. Thick clusters of wires led to desks close by, and on them were screens that showed chemical actions, enzymic changes, temperature of the nutrient solution and any fluctuations in its composition. Inside the tank were wires that ended in electrodes in the brain, the input and output wires, and they too were tapped so that men at desks could know exactly what was going in and out.

The Phalanx had been in steady operation for seven days and nights. The lights twinkled steadily, and in the back the EEG tracings were steady. The technicians had replaced the walls about the computer so that it was a house within a room, a tank within the house, a brain within the tank. There was still work to be done, still many programs to plan and translate and feed to the Phalanx, but any good programmer could do them now. They were talking about increasing the number of bugs to an even four dozen, and no one doubted that the computer could keep them all under control.

Thornton stood in the doorway looking at it for the last time. His work was done, his year over. Others would be interviewed now, or already had been, and they would feel the excitement coursing through them at the chance to work at the Institute for a year. He turned and left, picking up his bag at the main door. A car was outside to take him to the gate where Ethel would meet him. Feldman was on the steps waiting. He thrust a book into Thornton's hand.

"A goodbye present," he said. Thornton wondered if he had seen tears in the analyst's eyes, and decided no. It had been the wind. The wind was blowing hard. He rode to the main gate, and when he left the car and walked through, he dropped the book. He got in his own car and drew Ethel to him.

"I was so afraid you'd be different," she said after a moment. "I didn't know what to expect after your year among geniuses. I thought you might not want to come out at all." She laughed and squeezed his hand. "I am so proud of you! And you haven't changed, not at all."

He laughed with her. "You too," he said. He wondered if there had always been that emptiness behind her eyes. She pressed on the accelerator and they sped down the road away from the Institute.

Behind them the wind riffled through the book until the guard noticed it lying in the dust and picked it up and tossed it in a trashcan.

The idea for "The Intruder" came to me during a rereading of Hemingway's "Big Two-Hearted River" many years ago. I wondered if it would be possible in science fiction to evoke the same kind of mood—a man gets away from it all by going fishing, alone. Hemingway's hero, Nick, went trout fishing on the Fox River in Michigan. My hero, Max, went fishing with scuba on a watery planet in the early stages of its evolution. I couldn't bring it off. The story did not sell, so I put it in a workshop at a Milford Conference with an explanation of what I was trying to do.

Richard McKenna was there that year; it was his second or third attendance. He was interested in the "Intruder" idea, and when he returned to Chapel Hill he read "Big Two-Hearted River" for the first time. He was entranced, and he went on to reread much of Hemingway from a new point of view. From this reading Mac evolved his own idea of the "clean, well lighted story" as he describes it in his essay "Journey With a Little Man." This concept led Mac to a new approach to his own stories, and on his first try he sold the result to the *Saturday Evening Post*. In the middle of all this he wrote me to say that "The Intruder" (it wasn't called "The Intruder" then) was indeed a clean, well lighted story, but it wasn't a mere science fiction version of "Big Two-Hearted River"; it was a different story with its own mood; I should look at it from that viewpoint. Well, I did, and immediately saw that the ending was missing. The ending in "The Intruder" was implicit all the time, but I hadn't seen it because ["Big Two-Hearted River" had no ending]. As soon as I wrote in the alga scene at the end, the story sold.

THE INTRUDER

Max pulled the last line taut and stepped back to inspect his work. The rocket tubes were tightly capped and the ship was safely out of the beat of the wind and the rain. It should remain secure for the full ten days of his fishing trip. He dragged his duffle up the slight slope and turned to face the wind. He closed his eyes and waited, eager to look yet holding back a moment more. Then he opened them. It was as he expected.

A quarter of a mile away was the sea. The waves were white and frothy and sticky looking, and the tops were driven flat by the wind. Above them was the greyish blanket of sea-spray, thicker than usual, standing a good fifty feet above the water. The wind was strong, and the spray carried to Max. He tasted the salt of it, and smelled the rich, loamy smell of it, and his throat tightened. He looked out over the bare island of rock. There was nothing to spoil it.

Max struggled into his gear, took up his musette bag and fishing spear, and was ready. He was happy to be on the planet again.

The way was hard. Almost immediately Max felt the strain of the pack on his neck muscles, but he knew from experience that he could walk all day with it. Sometimes he used the fishing spear as a staff, but the pack was too heavy for him to raise his arm very often. After two hours of walking he stopped to rest.

He sat down and leaned back and stared up at the clouds. It had been as much of a thrill as always to come down through those clouds. The sun of the planet had disappeared as he dropped lower through the carbon dioxide-rich layers. The howling winds and the ice clouds closed in on him, folding him into a noisy world of his own, he and his good ship alone together. Down, then, to the lowermost layers where the oxygen and the water were, and where the occasional islands of rock thrust through the giant waves.

Max smiled, enjoying the isolation. It was good to be alone, good not to have to worry about talking to people.

It was time to move. Max leaned forward into the straps, heaved himself erect, and began to walk. His muscles had stiffened while he had rested, but he knew they would limber up soon.

An hour later the rain hit him. Max flipped his helmet into place and sloshed through deep sheets of water. Visibility was only a few feet, so Max walked by his helmet compass. Again, he was closed into a tiny world all his own, and he felt strong and secure in it.

A half hour passed and Max judged that he must be near the turn-off point. Rather than risk missing it in the rain he sat down to wait for the rain to lift. He sat in perfect comfort while the deluge washed over him, throbbing on the helmet, roaring on the rocks. His tired muscles relaxed, and he stared contentedly at the grey wall of rain in front of him. Then he fell asleep.

The cessation of noise woke him; the rain had passed. He flipped back his helmet and breathed in the wet air. To his right was the sea, and there, a quarter of a mile away, was the flat-topped cylinder of black rock that was the marker he was looking for. Max was pleased, and he said aloud, "Perfect dead reckoning." The sound of his voice startled him, and he glanced around, then felt foolish, and grinned. The grin spread to a loud laugh, and this time he welcomed the sound. He scooped up the fishing spear and the musette bag and headed down toward the sea. In fifteen minutes he arrived at his campsite.

He entered the site from the upper rim. The campsite was shaped like a great, open pie-pan, twenty feet in diameter, five feet deep. On the western side a slab of the living rock rose higher than the rest and then curved in toward the center of the pie-pan, forming a shelter for the cooking stove. A dead flat area slightly off the center of the site seemed made for a tent; Max could see his old nail holes, splintered and widened at the top from the work of the wind and the water. At the south rim, facing the sea, was a three-foot gap in the wall that opened to a Z-shaped trail leading down to the sea.

Max put the heavy pack down and walked over to the southern rim, flexing his shoulders as he went. He looked down the fifty-foot bluff to the cove below. The trail led to a ledge that dipped gently beneath the surface of the sea. The waves washed softly up the ledge, their full fury broken by a huge, jagged wall of rock that curved out to sea from the west. The wind was full where he stood and he leaned into it.

Max realized he was hungry. And he ought to set up his camp. With a last reluctant look at the cove he reentered the campsite.

He untied the tent roll, pushed the stone-nails through the grommets in the bottom, and then drove them into the rock. He took a high-pressure air flask from the pack and bled some air into the double walls. He went around the fittings again and again, and, gradually and evenly, he brought the tent to its full taut position.

He set up the two-burner stove. Into a frying pan he put a good measure of dried eggs and dried, diced ham, and over the top he sprinkled a layer of dried green pepper strips. He scooped up some rainwater from the hollow in the rock and added it to the food in the pan. He put it over a low flame and soon the air filled with the smell of cooking ham and peppers. It brought water to Max's mouth.

When it was done he scraped it into a pie-pan, and put on a pot of water to boil for coffee. He buttered two slices of bread and carried the food to the place where he usually sat. From there he could look through the crack in the south wall and see out over the cove to the wild ocean beyond.

He ate slowly, looking around the campsite. He grinned happily; not a thing out of place. The trick was to make up the pack right. You packed it so that the things you needed first were on top, in the right order, and as you took them out you found a place for them.

The plate was empty, and the water was boiling so he measured the right amount of coffee into the boiling water. He let it boil for exactly eight seconds and then he took it from the fire. The fragrance of coffee rose from the pot, and Max breathed it in gratefully. He poured himself a big cup, put in two large spoonfuls of sugar, and stirred it well. Funny, he thought. Back home he always drank his coffee straight and bitter, with no sugar, but out in the open he liked it well sweetened.

He carried the coffee through the gap and sat down and lit a cigaret. He was full and comfortable, and the coffee was good, and the cigaret was just right. Max felt he could sit there forever, and he grinned as he thought it. He knew that a big part of his enjoyment of the moment was the certain knowledge that he had to get up soon and wash the dinner pans.

He finished, sighed, and went and collected the pans. He looked at the fishing spear, but reluctantly turned away. Not yet. He was tired and sleepy. Wash the pans, get some sleep, then he'd be fresh for the fishing. Full as he was, Max licked his lips at the thought of some trilobite meat.

Max threaded his way down the Z-trail and walked out on the shelf that sloped down into the water. He rubbed sand into the pans until his fingers were sore. Time after time he rinsed the pans, checking the film of water for signs of grease. Finally satisfied he gave them a final rinse and climbed up the trail. He stowed the pans, and took up a towel and a piece of soap and a toothbrush. He walked to the east rim of the campsite and vaulted to the top.

About twenty feet away was an eight-foot-wide depression in the rock, filled with water. Max stripped off his rainsuit and rinsed it and dried it. He worked fast as he brushed his teeth and soaped himself thoroughly. He did not want to be caught in a really heavy downpour—a man without a rainsuit could drown in a few minutes in the open.

He rinsed off the soap, but did not stop to dry himself there. Carrying the rainsuit he trotted back to the tent and dried himself standing at the door. Then he crawled through the door and into the bed-roll. Sitting up in it he checked the air vents by feel, and then he settled down and pulled the bed-roll up around him.

"Man," said Max, and he took a deep breath and blew it out hard. He twisted his head into the pillow and listened to the distant roar of the crashing waves and to the sigh of the wind. "Man," he said again. Then he fell asleep.

Sometime later the rain came. The hard drumming of it on the tent woke him up, and he lay there and listened. Over the beat of the rain on the tent he could hear the swirl of water as it raced through the campsite down to the sea. The wind was strong and gusty, and it changed the sound of the rain on the tent; now it was harsh and rasping, now soft and muted. The roar of the waves was louder too, with more of a booming sound.

Max lay snug and warm in the tent, while outside the storm raged. This was one of the best parts of it, the lying and the listening. Max forced himself to stay awake and listen. A row of gooseflesh sprang up along his spine and spread over his entire body, and he shuddered and pulled the roll closer, and felt good. He was still trying to stay awake when he drifted off to sleep again. It was ten hours before he awoke, feeling wide awake and refreshed.

He put on his rainsuit and looked up at the sky. There was no change in the gleaming greyness. The sun of the planet was never visible, not even as a bright spot in the sky.

Max breathed in the salty air, and stretched. He was hungry again, not hard hungry the way he'd been before, but soft hungry with the kind of hunger fresh air brings. Max knew the feeling; he'd have it for most of the time from now on, starting about two hours after each meal. It was a sign that he was shaking down into outdoor life, and he was pleased.

He whipped up some applesauce and a thin pancake batter. He made four pancakes and used the last fragments to wipe the applesauce pot clean. Neither the frying pan nor the pot needed washing, so he put them away.

The eagerness was rising in him. He was ready now to go fishing. He inspected the trident end of the fishing spear, flexed the three blunt points, and checked the air flask in the suit.

He hung a sack at his waist and took a final look around the campsite. The stove was still up, so he put it away. He looked back over the clean and lonely island of rock, and it looked good. There was nothing to spoil it. Then he walked through the gap and down the Z-trail to the water.

Max went right into the water. When it reached his waist he pulled the helmet into position, and kept going. When the water was halfway over his helmet he stopped. He stood at the dividing line between two worlds, and looked from one to the other. The upper world, storm-tossed and cleanly empty, yet preparing to receive the spill-over of life from below. The lower world, teeming with small creatures, subject to an ever-increasing pressure of life. It was pleasant to stand and contemplate the over-empty and the over-full in a single glance. Then Max stepped forward and moved beneath the water in a half crouch, spear poised.

The waving ferns seemed to beckon him on. Smooth, black rocks jutted from the bottom in his path. A great jelly fish hung in front of him, long pink streamers dangling from the white half-globe. He circled it. Brown siliceous sponges festooned the rocks.

A movement to the left caught his eye, and he slowly worked his way toward it. A group of nine trilobites nuzzled the sand at the edge of a patch of fern, but they were all *E. petti,* small ones. Max carefully swam to a protruding rock eight feet from the group, and leaned against it. Where the small kind gathered, the big ones often followed, so Max waited in relaxed readiness.

He saw the movement in the ferns before he saw the actual animal. It came out onto the sand and stopped. Max's heart leaped. It was a big one. It must be a good three feet long, bigger than any he had ever seen before. He gathered the muscles in his right arm and shifted his weight to his right leg as the trilobite began to graze on the bottom. Making a final estimate of the distance, Max threw.

The trilobite saw the first movement of his arm. It spun in a circle and headed back for the fern. One of the blunt prongs glanced off the thick carapace, and the spear buried itself in the sand.

Max flung himself toward it, but then slowed and cursed himself for his clumsiness in missing the throw. Being out of practice made a difference.

He began stalking again, keeping himself in better balance. Near a patch of waving green algae he saw the outline of a fair-sized trilobite. As he drew closer he saw that it was P. *metrobus*, the spiny trilobite. Max approached it, cautiously. There were no large animals—no predators—in the oceans, yet a trilobite would scoot to cover at any unusual motion. It had nothing to fear from anything, save a few Earth fishermen, yet it acted as if death lurked behind every rock. Max had a theory on the subject. A wayward gene caused the behavior, and that gene was to serve the trilobites well over the next 400 million years when danger would become very real for the species.

Max gauged the throw with more care than last time. The spear sped true and pinned the trilobite between two points. Max was on it, holding it aloft at the end of the spear, watching the twenty pairs of legs wave futilely in the water. He put it in the sack. The creature froze into immobility in the unaccustomed surroundings. Max patted it through the sack, and it would not move. He continued the hunt.

In the next hour he got two more. He decided that that was enough for now, so he worked his way back to the water's edge.

Max could not be certain exactly when his helmet broached the surface of the water. It was raining, and the dividing line between air and sea was hard to find. He sat down on the bottom in five feet of water and drew his knife and worked one of the trilobites out of the sack. Holding it with one foot and a hand, he cut off the cephalon, turned the body over and split the thorax lengthwise along the underside. He opened the shell by twisting the knife blade in the cut, and he lifted out in one piece the thick, tapered cylinder of white meat. He put the meat on a rock and swiftly opened the other two. He wrapped the meat in the sack and stood up. It was still raining so he sat down again and stretched out with his helmet resting on a small rock. He stared at the surface and decided to barbecue the meat. He had his own barbecue sauce, all made up and ready to go. Just thinking about it made his mouth water.

Max lay and stared at the roiled surface. He began to get sleepy, but just before he dozed off he saw that the surface had suddenly cleared. The rain had stopped.

He stood up. The wind had shifted, and it struck him hard. He waded to the shore, leaning back into the strong gusts. He flipped his helmet back, and took a step toward the Z-trail. The sack slipped from his fingers. Frowning in annoyance he stooped to pick it up. His eyes caught a tiny fleck of green, and he turned rigid.

He dropped the sack and fell to his knees to inspect the little fleck, checking to see if it had merely been tossed there by a wave. Half an inch in diameter it was, and as he stretched out full length to see it better, he saw that it was firmly affixed to a spot of sand. Minute tendrils reached sideways through the sand, now on the surface, now beneath.

Max glanced at the water's edge ten feet away. This speck of alga had been out of the water for fifteen days, and it lived and grew. *It lived.* Max's eyes widened. Here and now it had happened. It could have happened a million years from now, but it had happened now. This was the way it had been on Earth during Cambrian times 400 million years ago. A first plant, coming out of the water onto the land, and living there. The first fragile step on the road to man. There was no more to it than this, a bit of green growing on a speck of sand on an island of rock. An intrusion onto his clean and lonely rock. Max stared at the green spot six inches from his face, and his eyes watered in angry frustration.

He jumped to his feet and ground the little fleck under his foot, stamping on it and twisting his heel again and again, ripping the tiny cells to shreds, rubbing them against the rock and the sand until the spot was scarred and lacerated. He bent and brushed the muddy dust into a little pile and took it in his hands and strode to the water's edge and flung it out over the water. The wind surged in a wild gust and caught up the clumps of dust and drove them back into his face. He staggered backwards, driven by the fury of the wind, and he tripped and fell, and the fall knocked the breath from him. He lay gasping and breathless and helpless for several minutes. He finally got his wind back.

He climbed unsteadily to his feet and looked out over the sea. A long time he looked. Then he nodded and said, "All right. All right." He turned and gathered his equipment and went up the Z-trail to cook his dinner.

Everyone knows there are cat people, including some women who ought to have long, furry tails. It is not quite so well known that there are also dog people, pig people, weasel people &c. Unknown to most of his fans, Gordon R. Dickson is a large Little Forest Animal person, perhaps a woodchuck. One wants to feed him carrots, but instead he orders seven-course meals in restaurants, and drinks quantities of scotch. He also sings lewd ballads, about which the less said the better.

——————————————————————— *Gordon R. Dickson*

AN HONORABLE DEATH

From the arboretum at the far end of the patio to the landing stage of the transporter itself, the whole household was at sixes and sevens over the business of preparing the party for the celebration. As usual, Carter was having to oversee everything himself, otherwise it would not have gone right; and this was all the harder in that, of late, his enthusiasms seemed to have run down somewhat. He was conscious of a vague distaste for life as he found it, and all its parts. He would be forty-seven this fall. Could it be the imminent approach of middle age, seeking him out even in the quiet backwater of this small, suburban planet? Whatever it was, things were moving even more slowly than usual this year. He had not even had time to get into his costume of a full dress suit (19th–20th cent.) with tails, which he had chosen as not too dramatic, and yet kinder than most dress-ups to his tall, rather awkward figure—when the chime sounded, announcing the first arrival.

Dropping the suit on his bed, he went out, cutting across the patio toward the gathering room, where the landing stage of the transporter was—and almost ran headlong into one of the original native inhabitants of the planet, standing like a lean and bluish post with absolute rigidity in the center of the pretty little flagstone path.

"What are *you* doing here?" cried Carter.

The narrow, indigo, horselike face leaned confidentially down toward Carter's own. And then Carter recognized the great mass of apple blossoms, like a swarming of creamy-winged moths, held to the inky chest.

"Oh—" began Carter, on a note of fury. Then he threw up his hands and took the mass of branches. Peering around the immovable alien and wincing, he got a glimpse of his imported apple tree. But it was not as badly violated as he had feared. "Thank you. Thank you," he said, and waved the native out of the way.

But the native remained. Carter stared—then saw that in addition to the apple blossoms the thin and hairless creature, though no more dressed than his kind ever were, had in this instance contrived belts, garlands, and bracelets of native flowers for himself. The colors and patterns would be arranged to convey some special meaning—they always did. But right at the moment Carter was too annoyed and entirely too rushed to figure them out, though he did think it a little unusual the native should be holding a slim shaft of dark wood with a fire-hardened point. Hunting was most expressly forbidden to the natives.

"Now what?" said Carter. The native (a local chief, Carter suddenly recognized) lifted the spear and unexpectedly made several slow, stately hops, with his long legs flicking up and down above the scrubbed white of the flagstones—like an Earthly crane at its mating. "Oh, now, don't tell me you want to dance!"

The native chief ceased his movements and went back to being a post again, staring out over Carter's head as if at some horizon, lost and invisible beyond the iridescences of Carter's dwelling walls. Carter groaned, pondered, and glanced anxiously ahead toward the gathering room, from which he could now hear the voice of Ona, already greeting the first guest with female twitters.

"All right," he told the chief. "All right—this once. But only because it's Escape Day Anniversary. And you'll have to wait until after dinner."

The native stepped aside and became rigid again. Carter hurried past into the gathering room, clutching the apple blossoms. His wife was talking to a short, brown-bearded man with an ivory-tinted guitar hanging by a broad, tan band over one red-and-white, checked-shirted shoulder.

"Ramy!" called Carter, hurrying up to them. The landing stage of the transporter, standing in the middle of the room, chimed again. "Oh, take these will you, dear?" He thrust the apple blossoms into Ona's plump, bare arms. "The chief. In honor of the day. You know how they are—and I had to promise he could dance after dinner." She stared, her soft, pale face upturned to him. "I couldn't help it."

He turned and hurried to the landing stage, from the small round platform of which were now stepping down a short, academic, elderly man with wispy gray hair and a rather fat, button-nosed woman of the same age, both wearing the ancient Ionian chiton as their costume. Carter had warned Ona against wearing a chiton, for the very reason that these two might show up in the same dress. He allowed himself a small twinge of satisfaction at the thought of her ballroom gown as he went hastily now to greet them.

"Doctor!" he said. "Lidi! Here you are!" He shook hands with the doctor. "Happy Escape Day to both of you."

"I was sure we'd be late," said Lidi, holding firmly to the folds of her chiton with both hands. "The public terminal on Arcturus Five was so crowded. And the doctor won't hurry no matter what I say—" She looked over at her husband, but he, busy greeting Ona, ignored her.

The chime sounded again and two women, quite obviously sisters in spite of the fact that they were wearing dissimilar costumes, appeared on the platform. One was dressed in a perfectly ordinary everyday kilt and tunic—no costume at all. The other wore a close, unidentifiable sort of suit of some gray material and made straight for Carter.

"Cart!" she cried, taking one of his hands in both of her own and pumping it heartily. "Happy Escape Day." She beamed at him from a somewhat plain, strong-featured face, sharply made up. "Ani and I—" She looked around for her sister and saw the kilt and tunic already drifting in rather dreamlike and unconscious fashion toward the perambulating bar at the far end of the room. "I," she corrected herself hastily, "couldn't wait to get here. Who else is coming?"

"Just what you see, Totsa," said Carter, indicating those present with a wide-flung hand. "We thought a small party this year— a little, quiet gathering—"

"So nice! And what do you think of my costume?" She revolved slowly for his appraisal.

"Why—good, very good."

"Now!" Totsa came back to face him. "You can't guess what it is at all."

"Of course I can," said Carter heartily.

"Well, then, what is it?"

"Oh, well, perhaps I won't tell you, then," said Carter.

A small head with wispy gray hair intruded into the circle of their conversation. "An artistic rendering of the space suitings worn by those two intrepid pioneers who this day, four hundred and twenty years ago, burst free in their tiny ship from the iron grip of Earth's prisoning gravitation?"

Totsa shouted in triumph. "I knew you'd know, Doctor! Trust a philosophical researcher to catch on. Carter hadn't the slightest notion. Not an inkling!"

"A host is a host is a host," said Carter. "Excuse me, I've got to get into my own costume."

He went out again and back across the patio. The outer air felt pleasantly cool on his warm face. He hoped that the implications of his last remark—that he had merely been being polite in pretending to be baffled by the significance of her costume—had got across to Totsa, but probably it had not. She would interpret it as an attempt to cover up his failure to recognize her costume by being cryptic. The rapier was wasted on the thick hide of such a woman. And to think he once . . . you had to use a club. And the worst of it was, he *had* grasped the meaning of her costume immediately. He had merely been being playful in refusing to admit it . . .

The native chief was still standing unmoved where Carter had left him, still waiting for his moment.

"Get out of the way, can't you?" said Carter irritably, as he shouldered by.

The chief retreated one long ostrichlike step until he stood half-obscured in the shadow of a trellis of roses. Carter went on into the bedroom.

His suit was laid out for him and he climbed into the clumsy garments, his mind busy on the schedule of the evening ahead. The local star that served as this planet's sun (one of the Pleiades, Asterope) would be down in an hour and a half, but the luminosity of the interstellar space in this galactic region made the sky bright for hours after a setting, and the fireworks could not possibly go on until that died down.

Carter had designed the set piece for the finale himself—a vintage space rocket curving up from a representation of the Earth, into a firmament of stars, and changing into a star itself as it dwindled. It would be unthinkable to waste this against a broad band of glowing rarefied matter just above the western horizon.

Accordingly, there was really no choice about the schedule. At least five hours before the thought of fireworks could be entertained. Carter, hooking his tie into place around his neck before a section of his bedroom wall set on reflection, computed in his head. The cocktail session now starting would be good for two and a half, possibly three hours. He dared not stretch it out any longer than that or Ani would be sure to get drunk. As it was, it would be bad enough with a full cocktail session and wine with the dinner. But perhaps Totsa could keep her under control. At any rate—three, and an hour and a half for dinner. No matter how it was figured, there would be half an hour or more to fill in there.

Well—Carter worked his way into his dress coat—he could make his usual small speech in honor of the occasion. And—oh, yes, of course—there was the chief. The native dances were actually meaningless, boring things, though Carter had been quite interested in them at first, but then his was the inquiring type of mind. Still, the others might find it funny enough, or interesting for a single performance.

Buttoning up his coat, he went back out across the patio, feeling more kindly toward the native than he had since the moment of his first appearance. Passing him this time, Carter thought to stop and ask, "Would you like something to eat?"

Remote, shiny, mottled by the shadow of the rose leaves, the native neither moved nor answered, and Carter hurried on with a distinct feeling of relief. He had always made it a point to keep some native food on hand for just such an emergency as this— after all, they got hungry, too. But it was a definite godsend not to have to stop now, when he was so busy, and see the stuff properly prepared and provided for this uninvited and unexpected guest.

The humans had all moved out of the gathering room by the time he reached it and into the main lounge with its more complete bar and mobile chairs. On entering, he saw that they had already split up into three different and, in a way, inevitable groups. His wife and the doctor's were at gossip in a corner; Ramy was playing his guitar and singing in a low, not unpleasant, though hoarse voice to Ani, who sat drink in hand, gazing past him with a half-smile into the changing colors of the wall behind him. Totsa and the doctor were in a discussion at the bar. Carter joined them.

"—and I'm quite prepared to believe it," the doctor was saying in his gentle, precise tones as Carter came up. "Well, very good, Cart." He nodded at Carter's costume.

"You think so?" said Carter, feeling his face warm pleasantly. "Awkward get-up, but—I don't know, it just struck me this year." He punched for a lime brandy and watched with pleasure as the bar disgorged the brimming glass by his waiting hand.

"You look armored in it, Cart," Totsa said.

"Thrice-armed is he—" Carter acknowledged the compliment and sipped on his glass. He glanced at the doctor to see if the quotation had registered, but the doctor was already leaning over to receive a refill in his own glass.

"Have you any idea what this man's been telling me?" demanded Totsa, swiveling toward Carter. "He insists we're doomed. Literally doomed!"

"I've no doubt we are—" began Carter. But before he could expand on this agreement with the explanation that he meant it in the larger sense, she was foaming over him in a tidal wave of conversation.

"Well, I don't pretend to be unobjective about it. After all, who are we to survive? But really—how ridiculous! And you back him up just like that, *blindly*, without the slightest notion of what he's been talking about!"

"A theory only, Totsa," said the doctor, quite unruffled.

"I wouldn't honor it by even calling it a theory!"

"Perhaps," said Carter, sipping on his lime brandy, "if I knew a little more about what you two were—"

"The point," said the doctor, turning a little, politely, toward Carter, "has to do with the question of why, on all these worlds we've taken over, we've found no other race comparable to our own. We may," he smiled, "of course be unique in the universe. But this theory supposes that any contact between races of differing intelligences must inevitably result in the death of the inferior race. Consequently, if we met our superiors—" He gave a graceful wave of his hand.

"I imagine it could," said Carter.

"Ridiculous!" said Totsa. "As if we couldn't just avoid contact altogether if we wanted to!"

"That's a point," said Carter. "I imagine negotiations—"

"We," said Totsa, "who burst the bonds of our Earthly home, who have spread out among the stars in a scant four hundred years, are hardly the type to turn up our toes and just die!"

"It's all based on an assumption, Cart"—the doctor put his glass down on the bar and clasped his small hands before him—"that the racial will to live is dependent upon what might be called a certain amount of emotional self-respect. A race of lesser intelligence or scientific ability could hardly be a threat to us. But a greater race, the theory goes, must inevitably generate a sort of death-wish in all of us. We're too used to being top dog. We must conquer or—"

"Absolutely nonsense!" said Totsa.

"Well, now, you can't just condemn the idea offhand like that," Carter said. "Naturally, I can't imagine a human like myself ever giving up, either. We're too hard, too wolfish, too much the last-ditch fighters. But I imagine a theory like this might well hold true for other, lesser races." He cleared his throat. "For example, I've had quite a bit of contact since we came here with the natives which were the dominant life-form on this world in its natural state—"

"Oh, natives!" snapped Totsa scornfully.

"You might be surprised, Totsa!" said Carter, heating up a little. An inspiration took hold of him. "And, in fact, I've arranged for you to do just that. I've invited the local native chief to dance for us after dinner. You might just find it very illuminating."

"Illuminating? How?" pounced Totsa.

"That," said Carter, putting his glass down on the bar with a very slight flourish, "I'll leave you to find out for yourself. And now, if you don't mind, I'm going to have to make my hostly rounds of the other guests."

He walked away, glowing with a different kind of inner warmth. He was smiling as he came up to Ramy, who was still singing ballads and playing his guitar for Totsa's sister.

"Excellent," Carter said, clapping his hands briefly and sitting down with them as the song ended. "What was that?"

"Richard the Lion-heart wrote it," said Ramy hoarsely. He turned to the woman. "Another drink, Ani?"

Carter tried to signal the balladeer with his eyes, but Ramy had already pressed the buttons on the table beside their chairs, and a little moto unit from the bar was already on its way to them with the drinks emerging from its interior. Carter sighed inaudibly and leaned back in his chair. He could warn Totsa to keep an eye on Ani a little later.

He accepted another drink himself. The sound of voices in the room was rising as more alcohol was consumed. The only quiet one was Ani. She sat, engaged in the single-minded business of imbibing, and listened to the conversation between Ramy and himself, as if she was—thought Carter suddenly—perhaps one step removed, beyond some glasslike wall, where the real sound and movement of life came muted, if at all. The poetry of this flash of insight—for Carter could think of no other way to describe it—operated so strongly upon his emotions that he completely lost the thread of what Ramy was saying and was reduced to noncommittal noises by way of comment.

I should take up my writing again, he thought to himself.

As soon as a convenient opportunity presented itself, he excused himself and got up. He went over to the corner where the women were talking.

"—Earth," Lidi was saying, "the doctor and I will never forget it. Oh, Cart—" She twisted around to him as he sat down in a chair opposite. "You must take this girl to Earth sometime. Really."

"Do you think she's the back-to-nature type?" said Carter, with a smile.

"No, stop it!" Lidi turned back to Ona. "Make him take you!"

"I've mentioned it to him. Several times," said Ona, putting down the glass in her hand with a helpless gesture on the end-table beside her.

"Well, you know what they say," smiled Carter. "Everyone talks about Earth but nobody ever goes there any more."

"The doctor and I went. And it was memorable. It's not what you see, of course, but the insight you bring to it. I'm only five generations removed from people living right there on the North American continent. And the doctor had cousins in Turkey when he was a boy. Say what you like, the true stock thins out as generation succeeds generation away from the home world."

"And it's not the expense any more," put in Ona. "Everyone's rich nowadays."

"Rich! What an uncomfortable word!" said Lidi. "You should say *capable,* dear. Remember, our riches are merely the product of our science, which is the fruit of our own capabilities."

"Oh, you know what I mean!" said Ona. "The point is, Cart won't go. He just won't."

"I'm a simple man," Carter said. "I have my writing, my music, my horticulture, right here. I feel no urge to roam"—he stood up—"except to the kitchen right now, to check on the caterers. If you'll excuse me—"

"But you haven't given your wife an answer about taking her to Earth one of these days!" cried Lidi.

"Oh, we'll go, we'll go," said Carter, walking off with a good-humored wave of his hand.

As he walked through the west sunroom to the dining area and the kitchen (homey word!) beyond, his cheerfulness dwindled somewhat. It was always a ticklish job handling the caterers, now that they were all artists doing the work for the love of it and not to be controlled by the price they were paid. Carter would have liked to wash his hands of that end of the party altogether and just leave them to operate on their own. But what if he failed to check and then something went wrong? It was his own artistic conscience operating, he thought, that would not give him any rest.

The dining room was already set up in classic style with long table and individual chairs. He passed the gleam of its tableware and went on through the light-screen into the kitchen area. The master caterer was just in the process of directing his two apprentices to set up the heating tray on which the whole roast boar, papered and gilded, would be kept warm in the centerpiece position on the table during the meal. He did not see Carter enter; and Carter himself stopped to admire, with a sigh of relief, the boar itself. It was a master-work of the carver's art and had been built up so skillfully from its component chunks of meat that no one could have suspected it was not the actual animal itself.

Looking up at this moment, the caterer caught sight of him and came over to see what he wanted. Carter advanced a few small, tentative suggestions, but the response was so artificially polite that after a short while Carter was glad to leave him to his work.

Carter wandered back through the house without returning directly to the lounge. With the change of the mood that the encounter with the caterer had engendered, his earlier feelings of distaste with life—a sort of melancholy—had come over him. He thought of the people he had invited almost with disgust. Twenty years ago, he would not have thought himself capable of belonging to such a crowd. Where were the great friends, the true friends, that as a youngster he had intended to acquire? Not that it was the fault of those in the lounge. They could not help being what they were. It was the fault of the times, which made life too easy for everybody; and—yes, he would be honest—his own fault, too.

His wanderings had brought him back to the patio. He remembered the chief and peered through the light dusk at the trellis under the light arch of which the native stood.

Beyond, the house was between the semi-enclosed patio and the fading band of brilliance in the west. Deep shadow lay upon the trellis itself and the native under it. He was almost obscured by it, but a darkly pale, vertical line of reflection from his upright spear showed that he had made no move. A gush of emotion burst within Carter. He took a single step toward the chief, with the abrupt, spontaneous urge to thank him for coming and offering to dance. But at that moment, through the open doorway of his bedroom, sounded the small, metallic chimes of his bedside clock, announcing the twenty-first hour, and he turned hastily and crossed through the gathering room, into the lounge.

"Hors-d'oeuvres! Hors-d'oeuvres!" he called cheerfully, flinging the lounge door wide. "Hors-d'oeuvres, everybody! Time to come and get it!"

Dinner could not go off otherwise than well. Everyone was half-tight and hungry. Everyone was talkative. Even Ani had thrown off her habitual introversion and was smiling and nodding, quite soberly, anyone would swear. She was listening to Ona and Lidi talking about Lidi's grown-up son when he had been a baby. The doctor was in high spirits, and Ramy, having gotten his guitar-playing out of his system earlier with Ani, was ready to be companionable. By the time they had finished the rum-and-butter pie, everyone was in a good mood, and even the caterer, peering through a momentary transparency of the kitchen wall, exchanged a beam with Carter.

Carter glanced at his watch. Only twenty minutes more! The time had happily flown, and, far from having to fill it in, he would have to cut his own speech a little short. If it were not for the fact that he had already announced it, he would have eliminated the chief's dance—no, that would not have done, either. He had always made a point of getting along with the natives of this world. "It's their home, too, after all," he had always said.

He tinkled on a wine glass with a spoon and rose to his feet.

Faces turned toward him and conversation came to a reluctant halt around the table. He smiled at his assembled guests.

"As you know," said Carter, "it has always been my custom at these little gatherings—and old customs are the best—to say a few"—he held up a disarming hand—"a very few words. Tonight I will be even briefer than usual." He stopped and took a sip of water from the glass before him.

"On this present occasion, the quadricentennial of our great race's Escape into the limitless bounds of the universe, I am reminded of the far road we have come; and the far road—undoubtedly—we have yet to go. I am thinking at the moment," he smiled, to indicate that what he was about to say was merely said in good-fellowship, "of a new theory expressed by our good doctor here tonight. This theory postulates that when a lesser race meets a greater, the lesser must inevitably go to the wall. And that, since it is pretty generally accepted that the laws of chance ensure our race eventually meeting *its* superior, *we* must inevitably and eventually go to the wall."

He paused and warmed them again with the tolerance of his smile.

"May I say *nonsense!*

"Now, let no one retort that I am merely taking refuge in the blind attitude that reacts with the cry, 'It can't happen to us.' Let me say I believe it *could* happen to us, but it won't. And why not? I will answer that with one word. Civilization.

"These overmen—if indeed they ever show up—must, even as we, be civilized. *Civilized*. Think of what that word means! Look at the seven of us here. Are we not educated, kindly, sympathetic people? And how do we treat the races inferior to us that we have run across?

"I'm going to let you answer these questions for yourselves, because I now invite you to the patio for cognac and coffee—and to see one of the natives of this planet, who has expressed a desire to dance for you. Look at him as he dances, observe him, consider what human gentleness and consideration are involved in the gesture that included him in this great festival of ours." Carter paused. "And consider one other great statement that has echoed down the corridors of time—*As ye have done to others, so shall ye be done by!*"

Carter sat down, flushed and glowing, to applause, then rose immediately to precede his guests, who were getting up to stream toward the patio. Walking rapidly, he outdistanced them as they passed the gathering room.

For a second, as he burst out through the patio doorway, his eyes were befuddled by the sudden darkness. Then his vision cleared as the others came through the doorway behind him and he was able to make out the inky shadow of the chief, still barely visible under the trellis.

Leaving Ona to superintend the seating arrangements in the central courtyard of the patio, he hurried toward the trellis. The native was there waiting for him.

"Now," said Carter, a little breathlessly, "it must be a short dance, a very short dance."

The chief lowered his long, narrow head, looking down at Carter with what seemed to be an aloofness, a sad dignity, and suddenly Carter felt uncomfortable.

"Um—well," he muttered, "you don't have to cut it *too* short."

Carter turned and went back to the guests. Under Ona's direction, they had seated themselves in a small semicircle of chairs, with snifter glasses and coffee cups. A chair had been left for Carter in the middle. He took it and accepted a glass of cognac from his wife.

"Now?" asked Totsa, leaning toward him.

"Yes—yes, here he comes," said Carter, and directed their attention toward the trellis.

The lights had been turned up around the edge of the courtyard, and as the chief advanced unto them from the darkness, he seemed to step all at once out of a wall of night.

"My," said Lidi, a little behind and to the left of Carter, "isn't he big!"

"*Tall*, rather," said the doctor, and coughed dryly at her side.

The chief came on into the center of the lighted courtyard. He carried his spear upright in one hand before him, the arm half-bent at the elbow and half-extended, advancing with exaggeratedly long steps and on tiptoe—in a manner unfortunately almost exactly reminiscent of the classical husband sneaking home late at night. There was a sudden titter from Totsa, behind Carter. Carter flushed.

Arrived in the center of the patio before them, the chief halted, probed at the empty air with his spear in several directions, and began to shuffle about with his head bent toward the ground.

Behind Carter, Ramy said something in a low voice. There was a strangled chuckle and the strings of the guitar plinked quietly on several idle notes.

"Please," said Carter, without turning his head.

There was a pause, some more indistinguishable murmuring from Ramy, followed again by his low, hoarse, and smothered chuckle.

"Perhaps—" said Carter, raising his voice slightly, "perhaps I ought to translate the dance as he does it. All these dances are stories acted out. This one is apparently called 'An Honorable Death.'"

He paused to clear his throat. No one said anything. Out in the center of the patio, the chief was standing crouched, peering to right and left, his neck craned like a chicken's.

"You see him now on the trail," Carter went on. "The silver-colored flowers on his right arm denote the fact that it *is* a story of death that he is dancing. The fact that they are below the elbow indicates it is an honorable, rather than dishonorable, death. But the fact that he wears nothing at all on the other arm below the elbow tells us this is the full and only story of the dance."

Carter found himself forced to clear his throat again. He took a sip from his snifter glass.

"As I say," he continued, "we see him now on the trail, alone." The chief had now begun to take several cautious steps forward, and then alternate ones in retreat, with some evidence of tension and excitement. "He is happy at the moment because he is on the track of a large herd of local game. Watch the slope of his spear as he holds it in his hand. The more it approaches the vertical, the happier he is feeling—"

Ramy murmured again and his coarse chuckle rasped on Carter's ears. It was echoed by a giggle from Totsa and even a small, dry bark of a laugh from the doctor.

"—the happier he is feeling," repeated Carter loudly. "Except that, paradoxically, the line of the absolute vertical represents the deepest tragedy and sorrow. In a little paper I did on the symbolism behind these dance movements, I advanced the theory that when a native strikes up with his spear from the absolute vertical position, it is because some carnivore too large for him to handle has already downed him. He's a dead man."

The chief had gone into a flurry of movement.

"Ah," said Carter, on a note of satisfaction. The others were quiet now. He let his voice roll out a little. "He has made his kill. He hastens home with it. He is very happy. Why shouldn't he be? He is successful, young, strong. His mate, his progeny, his home await him. Even now it comes into sight."

The chief froze. His spear point dropped.

"But what is this?" cried Carter, straightening up dramatically in his chair. "What has happened? He sees a stranger in the doorway. It is the Man of Seven Spears who—this is a superstition, of course—" Carter interrupted himself—"who has, in addition to his own spear, six other magic spears which will fly from him on command and kill anything that stands in his way. What is this unconquerable being doing inside the entrance of the chief's home without being invited?"

The wooden spear point dropped abruptly, almost to the ground.

"The Man of Seven Spears tells him," said Carter. "He, the Man of Seven Spears, has chosen to desire the flowers about our chief's house. Therefore he has taken the house, killing all within it—the mate and the little ones—that their touch may be cleansed from flowers that are his. Everything is now his."

The soft, tumbling sound of liquid being poured filled in the second of Carter's pause.

"Not too much—" whispered someone.

"What can our chief do?" said Carter sharply. The chief was standing rigid with his head bent forward and his forehead pressed against the perfectly vertical shaft of his spear, now held upright before him. "He is sick—we would say he is weeping, in human terms. All that meant anything to him is now gone. He cannot even revenge himself on the Man of Seven Spears, whose magic weapons make him invincible." Carter, moved by the pathos in his own voice, felt his throat tighten on the last words.

"Ona, dear, do you have an antacid tablet?" the doctor's wife whispered behind him.

"He stands where he has stopped!" cried Carter fiercely. "He has no place else to go. The Man of Seven Spears ignores him, playing with the flowers. For eventually, without moving, without food or drink, he will collapse and die, as all of the Man of Seven Spears' enemies have died. For one, two, three days he stands there in his sorrow; and late on the third day the plan for revenge he has longed for comes to him. He cannot conquer his enemy—but he can eternally shame him, so that the Man of Seven Spears, in his turn, will be forced to die.

"He goes into the house." The chief was moving again. "The Man of Seven Spears sees him enter, but pays no attention to him, for he is beneath notice. And it's a good thing for our chief this is so—or else the Man of Seven Spears would call upon all his magic weapons and kill him on the spot. But he is playing with his new flowers and pays no attention.

"Carrying his single spear," went on Carter, "the chief goes in to the heart of his house. Each house has a heart, which is the most important place in it. For if the heart is destroyed, the house dies, and all within it. Having come to the heart of the house, which is before its hearth fire, the chief places his spear butt down on the ground and holds it upright in the position of greatest grief. He stands there pridefully. We can imagine the Man of Seven Spears, suddenly realizing the shame to be put upon him, rushing wildly to interfere. But he and all of his seven spears are too slow. The chief leaps into the air—"

Carter checked himself. The chief was still standing with his forehead pressed against the spear shaft.

"He leaps into the air," repeated Carter, a little louder.

And at that moment the native *did* bound upward, his long legs flailing, to an astonishing height. For a second he seemed to float above the tip of his spear, still grasping it—and then he descended like some great, dark, stricken bird, heavily upon the patio. The thin shaft trembled and shook, upright, above his fallen figure.

Multiple screams exploded and the whole company was on their feet. But the chief, slowly rising, gravely removed the spear from between the arm and side in which he had cleverly caught it while falling; and, taking it in his other hand, he stalked off into the shadows toward the house.

A babble of talk burst out behind Carter. Over all the other voices, Lidi's rose like a half-choked fountain.

"—absolutely! Heart failure! I never was so upset in my life—"

"Cart!" said Ona bitterly.

"Well, Cart," spoke Totsa triumphantly in his ear. "What's the application of all this to what you told me earlier?"

Carter, who had been sitting stunned, exploded roughly out of his chair.

"Oh, don't be such a *fool!*" He jerked himself away from them into the tree-bound shadows beyond the patio.

Behind him—after some few minutes—the voices lowered to a less excited level, and then he heard a woman's footsteps approaching him in the dark.

"Cart?" said his wife's voice hesitantly.

"What?" asked Carter, not moving.

"Aren't you coming back?"

"In a while."

There was a pause.

"Cart?"

"What?"

"Don't you think—"

"No, I don't think!" snarled Carter. "She can go to bloody hell!"

"But you can't just call her a fool—"

"She *is* a fool! They're all fools—every one of them! I'm a fool, too, but I'm not a stupid damn bloody fool like all of them!"

"Just because of some silly native dance!" said Ona, almost crying.

"Silly?" said Carter. "At least it's something. He's got a dance to do. That's more than the rest of them in there have. And it just so happens that dance is pretty important to him. You'd think they might like to learn something about that, instead of sitting back making their stupid jokes!"

His little explosion went off into the darkness and fell unanswered.

"Please come back, Cart," Ona said, after a long moment.

"At least he has something," said Carter. "At least there's that for him."

"I just can't face them if you don't come back."

"All right, goddammit," said Carter. "I'll go back."

They returned in grim fashion to the patio. The chair tables had been cleared and rearranged in a small circle. Ramy was singing a song and they were all listening politely.

"Well, Cart, sit down here!" invited the doctor heartily as Carter and Ona came up, indicating the chair between himself and Totsa. Carter dropped into it.

"This is one of those old sea ballads, Cart," said Totsa.

"Oh?" asked Carter, clearing his throat. "Is it?"

He sat back, punched for a drink and listened to the song. It echoed out heartily over the patio with its refrain of *"Haul away, Joe!"* but he could not bring himself to like it.

Ramy ended and began another song. Lidi, her old self again, excused herself a moment and trotted back into the house.

"Are you really thinking of taking a trip Earthside—" the doctor began, leaning confidentially toward Carter—and was cut short by an ear-splitting scream from within the house.

Ramy broke off his singing. The screams continued and all of them scrambled to their feet and went crowding toward the house.

They saw Lidi—just outside the dark entrance to the gathering room—small, fat and stiffly standing, and screaming again and again, with her head thrown back. Almost at her feet lay the chief, with the slim shaft of the spear sticking up from his body. Only, this time, it was actually through him.

The rest flooded around Lidi and she was led away, still screaming, by the doctor. Everyone else gathered in horrified fascination about the native corpse. The head was twisted on one side and Carter could just see one dead eye staring up, it seemed, at him alone, with a gleam of sly and savage triumph.

"Horrible!" breathed Totsa, her lips parted. "Horrible!"

But Carter was still staring at that dead eye. Possibly, the thought came to him, the horrendous happenings of the day had sandpapered his perceptions to an unusually suspicious awareness. But just possibly . . .

Quietly, and without attracting undue attention from the others, he slipped past the group and into the dimness of the gathering room, where the lights had been turned off. Easing quietly along the wall until he came to the windows overlooking the patio, he peered out through them.

A considerable number of the inky natives were emerging from the greenery of the garden and the orchard beyond and approaching the house. A long, slim, fire-hardened spear gleamed in the hand of each. It occurred to Carter like a blow that they had probably moved into position surrounding the house while the humans' attention was all focused on the dancing of their chief.

His mind clicking at a rate that surprised even him, Carter withdrew noiselessly from the window and turned about. Behind him was the transporter, bulky in the dimness. As silently as the natives outside, he stole across the floor and mounted onto its platform. The transporter could move him to anywhere in the civilized area of the Galaxy at a second's notice. And one of the possible destinations was the emergency room of Police

Headquarters on Earth itself. Return, with armed men, could be equally instantaneous. Much better this way, thought Carter with a clarity he had never in his life experienced before; much better than giving the alarm to the people within, who would undoubtedly panic and cause a confusion that could get them all killed.

Quietly, operating by feel in the darkness, Carter set the controls for Police Headquarters. He pressed the Send button.

Nothing happened.

He stared at the machine in the impalpable darkness. A darker spot upon the thin laquered panel that covered its front and matched it to the room's decor caught his eye. He bent down to investigate.

It was a hole. Something like a ritual thrust of a fire-hardened wooden spear appeared to have gone through the panel and into the vitals of the transporter. The machine's delicate mechanism was shattered and broken and pierced.

Unlike a number of my colleagues of the Milford Science Fiction Writers' Conference who would be only too happy to write a forty-thousand-word prolegomenon (sans honorarium) pointing out the cunning and subtle interlocking of archetypal symbols in a ha'penny-a-word potboiler written back in the early fifties for *Passionate Planet Stories* (which is what happens when honest artisans get seduced by academic hustlers from the Modern Language Association and begin to take themselves seriously), I feel that, as a rule, authorial intrusions are not only presumptuous, but often spoil the reader's fun. What if, before letting you watch with morbid fascination as that flatulent booby, Hamlet, bumbles toward his final comeuppance, Shakespeare had insisted upon a prologue in which he strutted and fretted an hour upon the stage while he briefed the audience on fatso's hangups with Gertrude? Or, for that matter, what if my favorite [ex-]Milfordian started writing serious introductions to his side-splitting self-parodies instead of using the space to take potshots at the latest of a long string of wives and ex-girl friends? A consummation devoutly not to be wished. A story is a *ding an sich* which stands or falls in terms of itself. So with "The Burning." Instead of an introduction, I would like to substitute—with one slight modification—the disclaimer at the beginning of Kurt Vonnegut's *God Bless You, Mr. Rosewater:*

> All mothers, living and dead,
> are purely coincidental,
> and should not be construed.

Then, as kind of a leitmotif, I'd like to introduce an ancient but tender little ballad which I have translated from the original ur-Attic. There has been no shortage of mothers at the Milford Conference of recent years, but I would like to dedicate this little number to the original Milford mumsie, who has since trundled her womb to more hospitable shores.

On Mother's Day don't hang your head,
Just go and hang yourself instead.
I'll cut you down before you're dead,
    On Mother's Day.

I'll cut you down, that's what I'll do,
And drape you with Red, White, and Blue
To show the neighbors I love you,
    On Mother's Day.

But while you're gaily swinging there
I'll twine some violets in your hair
To show you that I really care,
    On Mother's Day.

Oidipous Tyrannos (991?–907 B.C.)

As for the story itself, it was written more as a technical exercise than a warning, there being no particular point to playing Cassandra to a society which has entered its terminal stage. But though the prognostication was not particularly challenging (any dolt—with the exception of those wearing stars—knows what New York is going to look like thirty years from now), the point of view was. First-person narration is tricky if you have an unfamiliar setting, unless, of course, your protagonist is a visitor from afar. In that case the writer has a good excuse for having the "I" go into quite a bit of detail as to sights, sounds, and quaint native customs. But if the narrator has been born and raised in a certain culture, and the writer is trying to do an honest job of presentation, he can't very well have his character launch off on periodic dissertations on the obvious. ("As you know, Mabel, we have been married for thirty years and . . .") So I tinkered. Using what skill I had, I tried to limn in as complex a background as I could in the shortest space possible without appearing to manipulate the story unwarrantedly. How successful I have been is for the reader to determine. So also is the matter of whether he does anything to reduce the probability of what follows being a preview of his grandchildren's world.

THE BURNING

Most of them were up in Central Park getting the boxes ready but Hank and I stayed behind. We went over on 27th to bust some windows but we couldn't because all the windows was already busted. So we went into the ACME ELITE BAR AND GRILL, and scrummaged around to see if there was anything that had maybe been overlooked. Hank finally found a bottle back in the corner buried under a heap of ceiling plaster and busted stuff that wasn't worth lugging off for the fires, but it turned out to be one of them No DEPOSIT, No RETURN plastic things that didn't make no proper noise at all when he smanged it against the wall.

We fooled around a while more but then I took a look out into the street. When I saw how short the shadows had got, I started getting the jumps. The burning always starts at high noon and there wasn't much time left.

"We'd better be getting on up," I said. "Goofing off on the collecting is one thing, but if the Mother notices we're not there come light-up time, there's going to be hell to pay."

Hank just laughed. "She'll be too twitched up by now to notice anything. This is *her* day. Things are too big to take time out to count the number of drabs in the back row of the clapping section."

I still felt jumpy. Not that I wanted to go, mind you, in spite of what the Mother was always saying about it developing character. Mothers are always talking about Character and The Flag and The Sanctity of American Womanhood and stuff like that, but I notice it's always the little guys who end up getting burnt during Mother's Day ceremonies. And I'm a little guy.

Big Harry sinned with the Mother almost every night when he first got born into the Family but somehow it never got put down in the Book. Otto got put down, though, just like I told

Hank he would, and when the Patrol came around they didn't even check his name page, they just went up to his room and got him. But not before me and Hank did considerable sweating because by then we knew it was going to be one of us three. All that morning I don't think five minutes went by without my giving my good luck pin at least one good rub just on the odd chance that it might do some good.

"Look, Hank," I said. "We don't go and the Mother happens to notice it, we're in for it. But good."

"Yeah," he said, "but what if Otto craps out before light-up time? That bum ticker of his is liable to go plonk just from waiting . . . and the Mother likes live meat."

"Better one than two," I said, and grabbed him by the arm and pulled him to his feet. "Come on, let's ramble. The Patrol happens to catch us this far south, we've had it!"

Hank didn't take much pushing. He gets stubborn only when he thinks it's good and safe, and as soon as I said "Patrol" he right away decided that maybe he wasn't. He didn't have much and what he did have he didn't have much chance to use, but like the fellow says, "Something is better than nothing." And nothing's what you got when the Patrol gets through with you.

We girder-walked as far as 58th. I slipped twice but we had a pretty good safety rope linking us and Hank was able to haul me back both times. Working along twisted beams five stories up is a scary business but at least you don't have to worry about out-walkers from other families taking pot shots at you. Ammo's too scarce to waste on drabs and anyway you fall that far and there ain't much left worth taking home.

Past 58th things are too messed up to get through top side so we had to take to the storm sewers. Hank and I had a long argument as to who was to go first and then we flipped and I lost. I started singing the truce song as loud as I could with Hank hitting the refrain on the bass parts. Hank's got perfect pitch but you get a real rogue mother out on the prowl and she can be tone deaf as hell, especially if she's got big ideas about snatching enough strays to build up a family of her own. Time was when they only went after the big ones and if a drab was in good voice he could wander all the way up to the 90's on his own if he was so minded, but no more. Since the Council busted up, anything that's still breathing is fair game—except for Mother's Helpers, that is, and they never did count anyway.

We came out at 74th, both a bit winded from the singing, and having to run the last two blocks because there was a sort of commotion in the cross conduit at 72nd that we didn't stick around to find out what it was. We went into the Park slantwise, circling around through the trees so we could slide in from the back. With everybody all involved in watching Otto and all it wasn't likely that they'd notice we were coming in late.

Only they weren't watching Otto. They were watching the Mother. Otto was hanging from the stake in a limp way that let you know he was more than just out. His ticker had plonked just like Hank was afraid it would and Mother's Day just isn't Mother's Day without a live one. Even Big Harry looked worried and had slid around behind some of the other kids, only it didn't do him much good because even hunching he stood up a good six inches higher than the rest. There was going to be a replacement for Otto, and fast, and the Mother was just as likely as not to grab the first one she set eye on, even a prime like Big Harry.

Only she didn't.

She went over and spit in Otto's face for not loving her enough and then yelled at us to fall into family formation. There was a certain amount of shoving because everybody was trying to get into the back row but she broke that up in a hurry. Hank and I managed to get in at the far end of the last line, hoping that somebody else might strike her fancy before she got to us. Only we knew better. I looked at Hank and Hank looked at me and even if we were pals and all that each of us was thinking the same thing. Only just hoping it would be him instead of me wasn't enough. I had to do something . . . and fast!

"There's more in the Book on you than there is on me," I says to Hank out of the side of my mouth. "If I was you I'd make a bolt."

66   THEODORE R. COGSWELL

"Mother wouldn't like it," he whispered back. "If I was to spoil her celebration she wouldn't love me anymore."

I could see his point. Now that everything has sort of gone to pot, a Mother's love is the only thing a boy can really count on, and the least we can do is try to make her happy on her day. But I could see my point too—namely that it was either Hank or me.

"Once across the park you'd be safe," I said. "The Patrol don't usually operate that far east and if you keep a sharp eye out for rogues you'll be OK." I could see he liked the idea but he was still worrying about the Mother. She was in the last row now and moving toward us steady like. Hank was really twitching and his face was kind of grey underneath the dirt.

"I can't," he said. "My legs won't work."

I sneaked a quick look at the Mother. She'd stopped and was looking down at us kind of thoughtful like. And I had a feeling she was looking more at me than she was at Hank.

"She's got her eye on you, boy," I said. "If you don't leg it now you're in for a slow burn. Them boxes is still wet from last night's rain."

We were supposed to be at attention but without knowing it I'd pulled my good-luck pin out of my pocket and was rubbing it with my thumb the way I got a habit of when I'm nervous. It's a little gold like pin made in the shape of a funny kind of leaf. There was some writing on it too but I didn't find out what the words was until later.

"It's your funeral, kid," I said.

Just then the Mother let out a yell.

"You! You down at the end!"

She was pointing at me but I swung around to Hank.

"Front and center, kid," I said. "Mama wants you."

He let out a funny little squawk and then went into a sort of bent over half squat like he'd just been kicked in the gut. I let out a yell and grabbed at him, giving him a spin with my right hand so that he ended up pointing toward the trees. Then I came up with my left and jabbed him in the backside with my good-luck pin.

He took off like a prime rogue in mating season and was across the grass and into the trees before anybody rightly knew what was up. Then the Mother started yelling orders and a bunch of primes took off after him. I ran up to her and flopped down and started bawling, "Don't be mad at me, I tried to stop him!" over and over until she belted me a couple.

"He said you didn't have no right!" I said.

That shook her like I hoped it would and got her thinking about him instead of me.

"He *what?*" she said, as if her ears weren't working right. "He said *what?*"

I made my voice all trembly.

"He said you didn't have no right to burn kids when they hadn't done nothing really bad." I started crying again but the Mother didn't pay me no mind. She just walked away.

The Patrol brought Hank in about an hour later. They'd worked him over to the point where he wasn't up to doing much in the way of complaining.

Afterward we sat around the fire and had a family sing, finishing up as usual with "Silver Threads Among the Gold." The Mother got all teary-eyed and mellow so I took a chance and went up and asked her what the words on my good-luck pin was. She didn't belt me or nothing. She just gave me a sort of lazy grin and said, *"Be Prepared."*

Some people bring their best recent work to the Conference, some their cripples and invalids, and some their dear old favorite stories which they have never been able to sell. "Harry the Tailor" belonged to the third category, but I'm happy to say that Sonya did later sell it to Cosmopolitan.

One time Sonya came in late to the workshop and found us discussing a story about a man who ends up losing his wife and his mistress. A large, happy smile broke over her face. "I think that's dreadful," she said, "getting unscrewed by two women at the same time."

— *Sonya Dorman*

HARRY THE TAILOR

"So convince me," he demanded. "Prove it to me. I already looked, and it ain't there." Joe the presser went by at his back, carrying three suits, and a sleeve snapped across his cheek so that he threw his dark, narrow head back like a wounded horse.

"I don't need to convince you," the girl said. Sunlight on its way down into the river blazed across eighth avenue and starred the platinum hair that stood out around her head. He looked down his big strong nose at this terrific galaxy and permitted himself to be blinded. "After all, I got the ticket," she said.

A hiss of steam rose from the back of the store where the presser was working again.

Harry said, "I never saw you before. I already looked, and there ain't no orange tweed coat and I think you're crazy as a bedbug." He was dreaming through half-closed lids. The sunlight rapidly declined and from it her head emerged bleached and wiry. Her face was pretty, in its bony way, but her eyes were a real glass green like jewels and no light or absence of light could spoil their fascination.

"What's the matter with you? I got the ticket," she said stubbornly, placing the pink paper in front of him. "You mean you're always here? You don't take a day off? You never had to go to a funeral and you been right here behind this counter forever?"

"Forever," Harry said, lowering his face. "I been here since I was sixteen, right on eighth avenue, and my father he should rest in peace was here forever since 1931. They was starving days, too. You'd be too young to know."

"Oh gimme my boots and saaddle," wailed Joe, the presser, from the back of the store where the steam was cooking him alive and he was lovingly furling the pleats in a permanently pleated white wool dress.

"I got the ticket," the girl said, beginning to get red around the eyes, whether from rage, tears, or trichlorethylene, Harry couldn't tell. He said, "O.K., O.K., I'll look again."

He butted his way through racks of clothing; eight uniforms from the bellboys at the hotel on the corner; half a dozen men's coats; dresses; drapes; he plunged his hands in among various fabrics and gave the bottom of a pink dress a good pinch but received only the meager satisfaction he usually got from such ersatz activities.

"Muriendo por verla," Joe warbled, winging his way above the storm of heat, and Harry envied him with a power that closed his throat up tight—to be able to sail away on a song, a series of musical notes—such a thing had never happened to him, even at Friday services which he more or less attended in order to keep his mother happy, and sometimes pretended to be with her in spirit as well as flesh, but it was an intermittent illusion which he did not pursue with any ardor. Only to sing like that, and float off above the buildings, as Joe did. He gave a nasty tweak to the breast of a printed silk blouse, and backed out of the clothing.

"No. It ain't," he said to the girl. "I never saw no orange tweed and you've got rocks, lady."

"Then explain me the ticket," she said.

"I can't explain it," Harry said, and sweated. Now he knew. He was having the breakdown his mother had promised him, ever since he moved to his own place.

"You'll go to pieces," Mom had said to him. "Just because you can sew a button on, who's to cook for you, you'll get a heartburn from the cafeterias and the plates have pork grease, it turns my stomach to think about it. What is it, a shiksa you got downtown? Bring her home, you got to have her. Even for that I'll pay the price, only you shouldn't live there on that lapidated block, we got two extra rooms."

"Good-bye, good-bye," Harry had said to her, sailing off on the wings of a dream, which had dumped him at the bus stop in front of a tenement and there he dwelt, amongst the tatters and shards, refusing to be reconciled with Mom in case a dream should come along again, maybe one of the girls Joe sang about, or a religious recognition, or something to slice off the endless ways of his daily life so he could begin again with something new.

"Who are you calling nuts?" the girl asked, glittering glass green eyes at him. She lifted her large pocketbook to the counter and opened it a little. "Look, you want me to call a cop? I got the ticket, you got to have the coat. Or else you pay me. It had a Lord & Taylor label in it. One hundred twenty-nine bucks. I just bought it November. I don't want no more funny business, Mr. Tailor. I just want my coat."

"Look, lady," Harry said, coming to temporary terms with his life. "I'll check it, O.K.? You come back in a coupla days and maybe I can find it, if it was ever here, which I don't think it ever was only you got a ticket, it's true. Anyhow, I don't remember you."

"Oh. You remember each and every customer, in a transient business neighborhood like this? Everybody from the hotels? Huh?"

"Oh Marie, Oh Marie," Joe sang as he went by with some dresses on their hangers, and stowed them away on the racks.

"Sure, I would remember you," Harry said. "I would remember your green eyes and your orange coat and your pink ticket, now I got too much work to do to stand here gabbing, can't you come back in a coupla days?"

The girl closed her pocketbook and lifted it from the counter. She folded the pink ticket and was going to put it in her coat pocket, when Harry said, "How can I check on your coat if I don't have that ticket?"

"Oh no," she laughed, showing nice white teeth. "Not a chance, buster, not a chance. I give you the ticket, then where am I?"

"On eighth avenue," Harry said. "Come back in a coupla days. Full-length coat?"

"You want I should freeze my knees all winter? Of course it's full-length. For a hundred and twenty-nine bucks you think I bought a bolero?" She yanked the big pocketbook along at her side like a bad child being towed away by its mother. The door opened, let in a blade of icy March air which sliced across Harry's face, and then it closed, and he was cuddled again in the strong-smelling steamy cocoon of his life from which he wasn't sure he wanted to escape, but he would keep trying.

"Lock up now?" Joe asked. He was rolling down the sleeves of his shirt, from which his bitter-chocolate wrists and big hands emerged smoothly. He put on his jacket, and reached for his topcoat.

"I'll lock up," Harry said, watching him dress. "You got a date with that Peggy?"

"Peg O' My Heart," Joe sang, grinning. "I sure do." He buttoned his topcoat, put his hands in his pockets, and rocked back on his heels. "Harry," he said, closing up his grin, "you didn't use to argue with the customers. Maybe you ought to eat with your Mama once in a while, you'd feel better. You complain about your stomach. A man can't be happy with a sad stomach."

"Oh these dames," Harry said, making a face of disgust. "What do you want, I should produce a full-length tweed coat out of no place?"

"Are you sure it ain't here? She got the ticket."

"No, I am not sure," Harry said slowly, between his teeth. "Of course I'm not sure. But you know I can't tell her that, she'll think I'm careless, we got enough competition up and down the Avenue without my letting on I might of made a mistake. Of course if she's got the ticket we must of got the coat. I just ain't seen it."

Joe eyed him, moving to the door. "Well," he said. "Yeah, I know. But you know a mistake can be made. It don't mean you ain't running a clean business. A man does make a mistake sometimes. You know."

"I know," Harry said, "but I can't tell the customers, can I?"

He locked up and went home soon after Joe left. He stopped at the cafeteria and ate a dinner which left him with heartburn, and a slow night's sleep, and in spite of the slowness and bad stomach before he knew it he was back at the counter and the store was open and the sun was shining.

She came in on the exact same sunbeam which had lit her up into a constellation the day before, and Harry groaned before she even opened her mouth. "I said a coupla days, didn't I?" he asked.

"I just thought I would stop and ask," she said. She looked dangerous. Her eyes were glassy and he could see it was something inside her that made her glitter and blaze.

"You got to gimme time," Harry said. "I can't check it in only one day, you gonna persecute me now?" He thought: now if she didn't want a coat she swears she left here, and I didn't have to fight for my life with every customer that comes in the door, maybe I could of taken her to the movies, in some other life, some other day, and run my hand up her leg. Harry blushed a dark color, and when she put the ticket down on the counter in front of him, he sneered, and flicked it off with his thumb.

"Don't persecute me, lady," Harry said. "Come back in a coupla days, like a reasonable woman."

"Don't give me the brush-off," she warned. "I paid an awful lotta money for that coat and I'm going to get it back or you are going to pay me," the words sizzled separately between her teeth. That's a dangerous dame, Harry thought, and turned his back on her. Passing a rack of women's clothes he brushed his body against them languorously.

At the back of the store he said to Joe, "You see that? You see her come in again? You realize she is persecuting me now, and I already told her I'd check on it?"

"A man can make a mistake," Joe said tactfully.

"Oh crud," Harry snarled. "You ever see a orange tweed full-length coat? You pressed it, maybe? It's got a striped lining you couldn't possibly forget?"

"O.K. Take it cool," Joe said. "I just meant there's so many coats come in here I always like marvel you can keep track of them all." He slammed a pair of bright blue bellboy trousers down and the steam arose in clouds around his shining face, while his voice rose above it, "Ven conmigo, conmigo," full of laughter and delight in the world.

"How does he *stand* it?" Harry wondered, caressing the neckline of a black crepe dress with tender and anguished fingers. How does anyone stand it, all those people going up and down the Avenue all day, how is it they don't go looking for another life?

She came back the next day, which was a rainy one, looking pale and cheaply bleached, and before she even got in the door Harry yelled, "No! No! I told you a coupla days!" and by this time even he realized he was going too far.

She didn't say a word. She took the pink ticket from her pocket, and waved it at him, looking dangerous and terrible, and Harry almost leaped across the counter at her, whether to break both her arms or something he suspected to be worse, he didn't know, but he was going to have the breakdown his mother had warned him about. They stared at each other eye to frenzied eye. Then she turned around and went out. When he looked up, she was staring at him right through the plate glass, with the rain pouring down on her and she didn't even have an umbrella. The bangs of her platinum hair had turned dark grey with the rain and her eyes looked like pool water. Harry shuddered.

As it got to be time next day, and the sun, which had been out again, was on its way down into the river and night, Harry braced himself behind the counter, his lips drawn back over his teeth.

She came whirling in the door and stood in front of him, her hands on her hips. "My coat," she said. "I gave you a coupla days. Now I want my coat or I want my hundred twenty-nine bucks."

"Fifty bucks," Harry said. "Depreciation. You think it's like new you bought it way back November?"

The tears spurted from her eyes. She picked up one of the wooden chairs that stood in the corner and with all her strength she threw it across the counter. It caught Harry across the face. His nose shrieking with pain and eyes blinded, he fell over backward onto the linoleum and heard Joe break off in the middle of his song to say, "Oh Jesus!"

Harry put both hands over his damaged and bloody face. When he looked out between his fingers, still stunned, he saw her bending over him. "Hey, Mister," she said, "did I kill you?"

"He ain't killed," Joe said in a doubtful voice, from somewhere near behind Harry, and then receding back to the end of the store, and Harry heard the slam and then the hiss of steam.

She got down on the floor beside him and pulled at his hands, trying to examine his face. "I didn't mean it," she said, crying. "Only I did pay a hundred twenty-nine for it and I did bring it in here and I do have the ticket and you know what I'm wearing? It's my sister's coat, she's in the hospital with a new baby, but I got to give it back the end of the week when she comes home and it's only the middle of March, what'll I wear?"

Harry felt his heart begin to sob in rhythm with the familiar wail of the despoiled stranger. She went on, "You got to have the coat here, you know you got it, can't you admit you lost it, hey, Mister? You advertise one day service and I brought it in wearing my sister's coat and I got to give it back, what'll I wear until the weather gets warm?"

"Oh God," Harry groaned, lowering his face to his knees, which he had drawn up. "Ohh," he groaned.

She put her arms around him and began to rock him like a mother. "Hey, Mister, what's your name, I didn't mean to hurt you."

"My name's Harry. Ohh," he groaned.

"Jesus," Joe said softly, from the back of the store, which was like a theater orchestra, with the best seats.

She shook him and rocked him and crooned to him, and Harry groaned while the steam rose up hissing from the presser. A customer came in, and hearing the sounds from behind the counter, raised himself on his toes and peered over.

"Jesus," he said, looking down at the blonde, the blood, and Harry, who had put his arms around the girl and was helping her rock.

"Yes, sir," Joe said, coming forward, pretending there was nothing on the floor behind the counter that was at all out of the way. He twirled the ball-point pen and began marking the ticket laid over the carbon: 1 brown tweed suit, 1 grey topcoat.

After a final look down, alongside Joe's legs, the customer shook his head, pocketed the ticket, and backed off until he reached the door.

"Harry," the girl said, rocked in his arms. "Harry, you gonna get a chill sitting on the floor like this."

"Ohh," Harry said, wrapping his arms more tightly around her. "You can't catch a chill in a steamy joint like this, whassa matter, you got cold blood?"

"Harry," Joe said politely, not looking down at them, although he was standing right beside them, towering over them like a big dark tree. "It was in the storage room."

The girl let out a scream. "That's it!" she screamed, rising to her feet.

Harry looked up. The orange tweed coat was hanging like a gaudy curtain between him and the girl. He gingerly got to his feet, and kicked the broken chair out of the way.

"See?" he said to her. "See? I said gimme a coupla days, I'd check on it for you. Don't you know a responsible business wouldn't lose a garment? See?"

She snatched the coat from the hanger Joe held, and clutched it to her.

"Gimme that ticket," Harry yelled.

Across the folds and billows of the coat she glared back at him. "So all right," she said in a deadly quiet voice. "You can have the ticket now. I think you owe me an apology."

"You go to hell," Harry said, mopping at his bloody forehead with the back of his hand. "You gimme that ticket, lady, and I don't never want to see you in my store again."

"I wouldn't come into your lousy store again if it was the last one in New York City or the Bronx," she said, taking the crumpled pink slip from her pocket. She held it in the air above the counter, and then let it go, and it drifted, sideslipping, down to the floor while Harry watched it with glazed and forlorn eyes. The girl started out of the store, and Harry shot through the swinging door in the counter just in time to catch the door before it closed. He bolted out and saw her halfway to the end of the block carrying the orange tweed over her arm like a corpse.

"Hey," he yelled. "Hey wait up, wait."

She turned. People on the avenue glanced from one to the other. "Whaddya want, Harry?" she yelled.

"Wait a moment," Harry yelled back. He was bleeding again, some of the blood ran down into one eye and made a scarlet blur of the neons and headlights. Cars and buses roared off after a red light as he loped down the street toward her.

"Now wait," he said, gasping, clutching her arm. "Wait, I didn't mean it, you shouldn't come back to the store."

"You're getting blood on my clean coat," she said, and Harry looked down and saw it was true; drops of his blood stood precious as rubies in the valleys of the tweed fabric.

"Oh God," Harry groaned. "Lady? Can I clean it for you?"

"Are you kidding?" she shrieked. "Put it back in your store again? And I ain't Lady. My name is Pauline. I don't hardly dare to give you a garment to clean again, do I?"

"Please," he said, taking her very gently by the arm, and turning her down the block toward the store. "Please, Pauline. You come in and sit down and wait for it, it'll be cleaned and pressed and you can watch me like a hawk, and you can come to the cafeteria and I'll buy you something to eat."

"I don't eat with strangers," Pauline said, being led down the street to the store.

Harry opened the door and drew her inside. "How could you call me a stranger?" he asked. "See the blood? You did that. You mean you throw chairs at strangers? You held me in your arms? On the floor? Gimme the coat," he wrested it from her, and flung it across the counter. "Sit down," he said, pushing her into the surviving chair in the corner. "Joe!"

"Yes, sir," Joe said softly.

"Clean the lady's coat and press it up. The lady is going to wait for it."

"You ought to give a ticket for it," Pauline said.

"Don't be silly," Harry pleaded. "You tried to kill me, didn't you? And you want a ticket. Don't you trust me?"

"No," Pauline said, gazing up at him. "I don't like to eat in cafeterias. They give me heartburn."

"You are right," Harry said admiringly. "You are so right. Mom always says that bad food and pork grease turns her stomach and you are so right. Where do you want to eat?"

Pauline thought it over, keeping her head turned so she could watch Joe work on her coat. "Why should I eat with you?" she asked, after a while; but she looked wilted.

Harry took her handkerchief, all bloody, from his pocket, and dabbed at his forehead with it. "Any place," he said, "makes no difference what it costs. You want a steak, I'll buy you a steak. Soon as your coat's ready."

"Your face looks terrible," Pauline said, glancing quickly at him.

"I'll wash," he said, and went around to the bathroom at the side of the store. When he came out again, washed and combed, Joe had brought the coat to the counter.

"Like new," Joe said.

"It ain't like new," Pauline said. "I never had a coat been

bloody before. But I guess you can say there's always something new." She smiled.

"Ain't that the truth?" Joe agreed. "Harry, you want me to lock up?"

"You lock up," Harry said. He held up the tweed coat and said to Pauline. "You want to wear it?"

"No. It's so clean, I'll carry it." She gazed at him out of her glass green eyes. "You don't look so bad, washed. I thought I'd killed you."

"Naw, I ain't easy to kill," Harry said, folding the coat and putting it with care over his own arm. "I ain't even hardly hurt."

As he opened the door and held it for her, he could hear Joe singing at the back of the store. "Oh if I had the wings of an angel—"

"I'd fly outa these prison walls," Pauline continued it, as she and Harry went out. "I'd fly like a bird," she murmured. "I'd fly away into the blue—"

"Blue skies," Harry sang, taking her arm, and steering her rapidly past the most expensive restaurant on the block to a less expensive one farther down.

"Fifteen Miles" was written as a companion piece to an earlier story, and as part of a series of stories about Chester A. Kinsman. I brought it to the 1966 Milford Conference because the story, as it stood in first draft, didn't quite seem to click.

The comments on the story were interesting and helpful. As I recall, Damon Knight said, "I sort of like the description of the Moon as a scruffy place." Harlan Ellison got so upset at the thought of a Jesuit on the Moon that he compared the story to one of ——'s* earlier offerings. Gordy Dickson made the key comment: he suggested that I simply have the hero realize that he can face his own past, and whatever the future will deal out to him, without flinching. In my mind, that suggestion turned the story into a winner.

You might be interested in the reactions of editors. John Campbell said astronauts are screened for emotional stability, and therefore Kinsman would never have made it to the Moon. The fact that astronauts are usually drawn from the ranks of test pilots, men who spend their lives deliberately courting violent death—the fact that Campbell himself has defined pioneering as "inventing new ways to die"—didn't seem to deter him at all. Fred Pohl, who was then editing *Galaxy*, sent a note saying the story sounded like a NASA report. Ed Ferman bought it—obviously a keen editorial judge, and a shrewd businessman to boot. Harry Harrison took it for his anthology, *Best SF:1967*, although we debated about the ending for some time before I outstubborned him.

* I delete the author's name in the interests of keeping the peace. It was a story about a pistol-packing sister; I forget its real title, but we called it "Rogue Nun."   D.K.

FIFTEEN MILES

Senator Anderson: Does that mean that man's mobility on the Moon will be severely limited?

Mr. Webb: Yes, sir. It is going to be severely limited, Mr. Chairman. The Moon is a rather hostile place . . .

U. S. Senate Hearings on National Space Goals, 23 August 1965

"Any word from him yet?"

"Huh? No, nothing."

Kinsman swore to himself as he stood on the open platform of the little lunar rocket jumper.

"Say, where are you now?" The astronomer's voice sounded gritty with static in Kinsman's helmet earphones.

"Up on the rim. He must've gone inside the damned crater."

"The rim? How'd you get . . ."

"Found a flat spot for the jumper. Don't think I walked this far, do you? I'm not as nutty as the priest."

"But you're supposed to stay down here on the plain! The crater's off-limits."

"Tell it to our holy friar. He's the one who marched up here. I'm just following the seismic rigs he's been planting every three-four miles."

He could sense Bok shaking his head. "Kinsman, if there're twenty officially approved ways to do a job, you'll pick the twenty-second."

"If the first twenty-one are lousy."

"You're not going inside the crater, are you? It's too risky."

Kinsman almost laughed. "You think sitting in that aluminum casket of ours is *safe?*"

The earphones went silent. With a scowl, Kinsman wished for

the tenth time in an hour that he could scratch his twelve-day beard. *Get zipped into the suit and the itches start.* He didn't need a mirror to know that his face was haggard, sleepless, and his black beard was mean looking.

He stepped down from the jumper—a rocket motor with a railed platform and some equipment on it, nothing more—and planted his boots on the solid rock of the ringwall's crest. With a twist of his shoulders to settle the weight of the pressure-suit's bulky backpack, he shambled over to the packet of seismic instruments and fluorescent marker that the priest had left there.

"He came right up to the top, and now he's off on the yellow brick road, playing Moon explorer. Stupid bastard."

Reluctantly, he looked into the crater Alphonsus. The brutally short horizon cut across its middle, but the central peak stuck its worn head up among the solemn stars. Beyond it was nothing but dizzying blackness, an abrupt end to the solid world and the beginning of infinity.

Damn the priest! God's gift to geology . . . and I've got to play guardian angel for him.

"Any sign of him?"

Kinsman turned back and looked outward from the crater. He could see the lighted radio mast and squat return rocket, far below on the plain. He even convinced himself that he saw the mound of rubble marking their buried base shelter, where Bok lay curled safely in his bunk. It was two days before sunrise, but the Earth-light lit the plain well enough.

"Sure," Kinsman answered. "He left me a big map with an X to mark the treasure."

"Don't get sore at me!"

"Why not? You're sitting inside. I've got to find our fearless geologist."

"Regulations say one man's got to be in the base at all times."

But not the same one man, Kinsman flashed silently.

"Anyway," Bok went on, "he's got a few hours' oxygen left. Let him putter around inside the crater for a while. He'll come back."

"Not before his air runs out. Besides, he's officially missing. Missed two check-in calls. I'm supposed to scout his last known position. Another of those sweet regs."

Silence again. Bok didn't like being alone in the base, Kinsman knew.

"Why don't you come on back," the astronomer's voice returned, "until he calls in. Then you can get him with the jumper. You'll be running out of air yourself before you can find him inside the crater."

"I'm supposed to try."

"But why? You sure don't think much of him. You've been tripping all over yourself trying to stay clear of him when he's inside the base."

Kinsman suddenly shuddered. *So it shows! If you're not careful you'll tip them both off.*

Aloud he said, "I'm going to look around. Give me an hour. Better call Earthside and tell them what's going on. Stay in the shelter until I come back." *Or until the relief crew shows up.*

"You're wasting your time. And taking an unnecessary chance."

"Wish me luck," Kinsman answered.

"Good luck. I'll sit tight here."

Despite himself, Kinsman grinned. Shutting off the radio, he said to himself, "I know damned well you'll sit tight. Two scientific adventurers. One goes over the hill and the other stays in his bunk two weeks straight."

He gazed out at the bleak landscape, surrounded by starry emptiness. Something caught at his memory:

"They can't scare me with their empty spaces," he muttered. There was more to the verse but he couldn't recall it.

"Can't scare me," he repeated softly, shuffling to the inner rim. He walked very carefully and tried, from inside the cumbersome helmet, to see exactly where he was placing his feet.

The barren slopes fell away in gently terraced steps until, more than half a mile below, they melted into the crater floor. *Looks easy . . . too easy.* With a shrug that was weighted down by the pressure-suit, Kinsman started to descend into the crater.

He picked his way across the gravelly terraces and crawled feet first down the breaks between them. The bare rocks were slippery and sometimes sharp. Kinsman went slowly, step by step, trying to make certain he didn't puncture the aluminized fabric of his suit.

His world was cut off now and circled by the dark rocks. The only sounds he knew were the creakings of the suit's joints, the electrical hum of its motor, the faint whir of the helmet's air blower, and his own heavy breathing. Alone, all alone. A solitary microcosm. One living creature in the one universe.

They cannot scare me with their empty spaces.

Between stars—on stars where no human race is.

There was still more to it: the tag line that he couldn't remember.

Finally he had to stop. The suit was heating up too much from his exertion. He took a marker beacon from the backpack and planted it on the broken ground. The Moon's soil, churned by meteors and whipped into a frozen froth, had an unfinished look about it, as though somebody had been blacktopping the place but stopped before he could apply the final smoothing touches.

From a pouch on his belt Kinsman took a small spool of wire. Plugging one end into the radio outlet on his helmet, he held the spool at arm's length and released the catch. He couldn't see it in the dim light, but he felt the spring fire the wire antenna a hundred yards or so upward and out into the crater.

"Father Lemoyne," he called as the antenna drifted in the moon's easy gravity. "Father Lemoyne, can you hear me? This is Kinsman."

No answer.

Okay. Down another flight.

After two more stops and nearly an hour of sweaty descent, Kinsman got his answer.

"Here . . . I'm here . . ."

"Where?" Kinsman snapped. "Do something. Make a light."

". . . can't . . ." The voice faded out.

Kinsman reeled in the antenna and fired it out again. "Where the hell are you?"

A cough, with pain behind it. "Shouldn't have done it. Disobeyed. And no water, nothing . . ."

Great! Kinsman frowned. *He's either hysterical or delirious. Or both.*

After firing the spool antenna again, Kinsman flicked on the lamp atop his helmet and looked at the radio direction-finder dial on his forearm. The priest had his suit radio open and the carrier beam was coming through even though he was not talking. The gauges alongside the radio-finder reminded Kinsman that he was about halfway down on his oxygen, and more than an hour had elapsed since he had spoken to Bok.

"I'm trying to zero in on you," Kinsman said. "Are you hurt? Can you . . ."

"Don't, don't, don't. I disobeyed and now I've got to pay for it. Don't trap yourself too . . ." The heavy, reproachful voice lapsed into a mumble that Kinsman couldn't understand.

Trapped. Kinsman could picture it. The priest was using a canister-suit: a one-man walking cabin, a big plexidomed rigid can with flexible arms and legs sticking out of it. You could live in it for days at a time—but it was too clumsy for climbing. Which is why the crater was off-limits.

He must've fallen and now he's stuck.

"The sin of pride," he heard the priest babbling. "God forgive us our pride. I wanted to find water; the greatest discovery a man can make on the Moon . . . Pride, nothing but pride . . ."

Kinsman walked slowly, shifting his eyes from the direction-finder to the roiled, pocked ground underfoot. He jumped across an eight-foot drop between terraces. The finder's needle snapped to zero.

"Your radio still on?"

"No use . . . go back . . ."

The needle stayed fixed. *Either I busted it or I'm right on top of him.*

He turned full circle, scanning the rough ground as far as his light could reach. No sign of the canister. Kinsman stepped to the terrace edge. Kneeling with deliberate care, so that his backpack wouldn't unbalance and send him sprawling down the tumbled rocks, he peered over.

In a zigzag fissure a few yards below him was the priest, a giant armored insect gleaming white in the glare of the lamp, feebly waving its one free arm.

"Can you get up?" Kinsman saw that all the weight of the cumbersome suit was on the pinned arm. *Banged up his backpack too.*

The priest was mumbling again. It sounded like Latin.

"Can you get up?" Kinsman repeated.

"Trying to find the secrets of natural creation . . . storming heaven with rockets . . . We say we're seeking knowledge, but we're really after our own glory . . ."

Kinsman frowned. He couldn't see the older man's face, behind the canister's heavily tinted window.

"I'll have to get the jumper."

The priest rambled on, coughing spasmodically. Kinsman started back across the terrace.

"Pride leads to death," he heard in his earphones. "You know that, Kinsman. It's pride that makes us murderers."

The shock boggled Kinsman's knees. He turned, trembling. "What . . . did you say?"

"It's hidden. The water is here, hidden . . . frozen in fissures. Strike the rock and bring forth water . . . like Moses. Not even God himself was going to hide this secret from me . . ."

"What did you say," Kinsman whispered, completely cold inside, "about murder?"

"I know you, Kinsman . . . anger and pride . . . Destroy not my soul with men of blood . . . whose right hands are . . . are . . ."

Kinsman ran away. He fought back toward the crater rim, storming the terraces blindly, scrabbling up the inclines with four-yard-high jumps. Twice he had to turn up the air blower in his helmet to clear the sweaty fog from his faceplate. He didn't dare stop. He raced on, his heart pounding until he could hear nothing else.

But in his mind he still saw those savage few minutes in orbit, when he had been with the Air Force, when he became a killer. He had won a medal for that secret mission; a medal and a conscience that never slept.

Finally he reached the crest. Collapsing on the deck of the jumper, he forced himself to breathe normally again, forced himself to sound normal as he called Bok.

The astronomer said guardedly, "It sounds as though he's dying."

"I think his regenerator's shot. His air must be pretty foul by now."

"No sense going back for him, I guess."

Kinsman hesitated. "Maybe I can get the jumper down close to him." *He found out about me.*

"You'll never get him back in time. And you're not supposed to take the jumper near the crater, let alone inside of it. It's too dangerous."

"You want to just let him die?" *He's hysterical. If he babbles about me where Bok can hear it . . .*

"Listen," the astronomer said, his voice rising, "you can't leave me stuck here with both of you gone! I know the regulations, Kinsman. You're not allowed to risk yourself or the third man on the team to help a man in trouble."

"I know. I know." *But it wouldn't look right for me to start minding regulations now. Even Bok doesn't expect me to.*

"You don't have enough oxygen in your suit to get down there and back again," Bok insisted.

"I can tap some from the jumper's propellant tank."

"But that's crazy! You'll get yourself stranded!"

"Maybe." *It's an Air Force secret. No discharges; just transferred to the Space Agency. If they find out about it now, I'll be finished. Everybody'll know. No place to hide . . . newspapers, TV, everybody!*

"You're going to kill yourself over that priest. And you'll be killing me too!"

"He's probably dead by now," Kinsman said. "I'll just put a marker beacon there, so another crew can get him when the time comes. I won't be long."

"But the regulations . . ."

"They were written Earthside. The brass never planned on something like this. I've got to go back, just to make sure."

He flew the jumper back down the crater's inner slope, leaning over the platform railing to see his marker beacons as well as listening to their tiny radio beeping. In a few minutes, he was easing the spraddle-legged platform down on the last terrace before the helpless priest.

"Father Lemoyne."

Kinsman stepped off the jumper and made it to the edge of the fissure in four lunar strides. The white shell was inert, the long arm unmoving.

"Father Lemoyne!"

Kinsman held his breath and listened. Nothing . . . wait . . . the faintest, faintest breathing. More like gasping. Quick, shallow, desperate.

"You're dead," Kinsman heard himself mutter. "Give it up, you're finished. Even if I got you out of here, you'd be dead before I could get you back to the base."

The priest's faceplate was opaque to him; he only saw the reflected spot of his own helmet lamp. But his mind filled with the shocked face he once saw in another visor, a face that had just realized it was dead.

He looked away, out to the too-close horizon and the uncompromising stars beyond. Then he remembered the rest of it:

They cannot scare me with their empty spaces
Between stars—on stars where no human race is.
I have it in me so much nearer home
To scare myself with my own desert places.

Like an automaton, Kinsman turned back to the jumper. His mind was blank now. Without thought, without even feeling, he rigged a line from the jumper's tiny winch to the metal lugs in the canister-suit's chest. Then he took apart the platform railing and wedged three rejoined sections into the fissure above the fallen man, to form a hoisting angle. Looping the line over the projecting arm, he started the winch.

He climbed down into the fissure and set himself as solidly as he could on the bare, scoured smooth rock. Grabbing the priest's armored shoulders, he guided the oversized canister up from the crevice, while the winch strained silently.

The railing arm gave way when the priest was only partway up, and Kinsman felt the full weight of the monstrous suit crush down on him. He sank to his knees, gritting his teeth to keep from crying out.

Then the winch took up the slack. Grunting, fumbling, pushing, he scrabbled up the rocky slope with his arms wrapped halfway round the big canister's middle. He let the winch drag them to the jumper's edge, then reached out and shut off the motor.

With only a hard breath's pause, Kinsman snapped down the suit's supporting legs, so the priest could stay upright even though unconscious. Then he clambered onto the platform and took the oxygen line from the rocket tankage. Kneeling at the bulbous suit's shoulders, he plunged the line into its emergency air tank.

The older man coughed once. That was all.

Kinsman leaned back on his heels. His faceplate was fogging over again, or was it fatigue blurring his sight?

The regenerator was hopelessly smashed, he saw. *The old bird must've been breathing his own juices.* When the emergency tank registered full, he disconnected the oxygen line and plugged it into a fitting below the regenerator.

"If you're dead, this is probably going to kill me too," Kinsman said. He purged the entire suit, forcing the contaminating fumes out and replacing them with the oxygen that the jumper's rocket needed to get them back to the base.

He was close enough now to see through the canister's tinted visor. The priest's face was grizzled, eyes closed. Its usual smile was gone; the mouth hung open limply.

Kinsman hauled him up onto the rail-less platform and strapped him down on the deck. Then he went to the controls and inched the throttle forward just enough to give them the barest minimum of lift.

The jumper almost made it to the crest before its rocket died and bumped them gently on one of the terraces. There was a small emergency tank of oxygen that could have carried them a little farther, Kinsman knew. But he and the priest would need it for breathing.

"Wonder how many Jesuits have been carried home on their shields?" he asked himself as he unbolted the section of decking that the priest was lying on. By threading the winch line through the bolt holes, he made a sort of sled, which he carefully lowered to the ground. Then he took down the emergency oxygen tank and strapped it to the deck section, too.

Kinsman wrapped the line around his fists and leaned against the burden. Even in the Moon's light gravity, it was like trying to haul a truck.

"Down to less than one horsepower," he grunted, straining forward.

For once he was glad that the scoured rocks had been smoothed clean by micrometeors. He would climb a few steps, wedge himself as firmly as he could, and drag the sled up to him. It took a painful half-hour to reach the ringwall crest.

He could see the base again, tiny and remote as a dream. "All downhill from here," he mumbled.

He thought he heard a groan.

"That's it," he said, pushing the sled over the crest, down the gentle outward slope. "That's it. Stay with it. Don't you die on me. Don't put me through this for nothing!"

"Kinsman!" Bok's voice. "Are you all right?"

The sled skidded against a yard-high rock. Scrambling after it,

Kinsman answered, "I'm bringing him in. Just shut up and leave us alone. I think he's alive. Now stop wasting my breath."

Pull it free. Push to get it started downhill again. Strain to hold it back . . . don't let it get away from you. Haul it out of craterlets. Watch your step, don't fall.

"Too damned much uphill in this downhill."

Once he sprawled flat and knocked his helmet against the edge of the improvised sled. He must have blacked out for a moment. Weakly, he dragged himself up to the oxygen tank and refilled his suit's supply. Then he checked the priest's suit and topped off his tank.

"Can't do that again," he said to the silent priest. "Don't know if we'll make it. Maybe we can. If neither one of us has sprung a leak. Maybe . . ."

Time slid away from him. The past and future dissolved into an endless now, a forever of pain and struggle, with the heat of his toil welling up in Kinsman drenchingly.

"Why don't you say something?" Kinsman panted at the priest. "You can't die. Understand me? You can't die! I've got to explain it to you . . . I didn't mean to kill her. I didn't even know she was a girl. You can't tell, can't even see a face until you're too close. She must've been just as scared as I was. She tried to kill me. I was inspecting their satellite . . . how'd I know their cosmonaut was a scared kid. I could've pushed her off, didn't have to kill her. But the first thing I knew I was ripping her air lines open. I didn't know she was a girl, not until it was too late. It doesn't make any difference, but I didn't know it, I didn't know . . ."

They reached the foot of the ringwall and Kinsman dropped to his knees. "Couple more miles now . . . straightaway . . . only a couple more . . . miles." His vision was blurred, and something in his head was buzzing angrily.

Staggering to his feet, he lifted the line over his shoulder and slogged ahead. He could just make out the lighted tip of the base's radio mast.

"Leave him, Chet," Bok's voice pleaded from somewhere. "You can't make it unless you leave him!"

"Shut . . . up."

One step after another. Don't think, don't count. Blank your mind. Be a mindless plow horse. Plod along, one step at a time. Steer for the radio mast. . . . Just a few . . . more miles.

"Don't die on me. Don't you . . . die on me. You're my ticket back. Don't die on me, priest . . . don't die . . ."

It all went dark. First in spots, then totally. Kinsman caught a glimpse of the barren landscape tilting weirdly, then the grave stars slid across his view, then darkness.

"I tried," he heard himself say in a far, far distant voice. "I tried."

For a moment or two he felt himself falling, dropping effortlessly into blackness. Then even that sensation died and he felt nothing at all.

A faint vibration buzzed at him. The darkness started to shift, turn gray at the edges. Kinsman opened his eyes and saw the low, curved ceiling of the underground base. The noise was the electrical machinery that lit and warmed and brought good air to the tight little shelter.

"You okay?" Bok leaned over him. His chubby face was frowning worriedly.

Kinsman weakly nodded.

"Father Lemoyne's going to pull through," Bok said, stepping out of the cramped space between the two bunks. The priest was awake but unmoving, his eyes staring blankly upward. His canister-suit had been removed and one arm was covered with a plastic cast.

Bok explained. "I've been getting instructions from the Earthside medics. They're sending a team up; should be here in another thirty hours. He's in shock, and his arm's broken. Otherwise he seems pretty good . . . exhausted, but no permanent damage."

Kinsman pulled himself up to a sitting position on the bunk and leaned his back against the curving metal wall. His helmet and boots were off, but he was still wearing the rest of his pressure suit.

"You went out and got us," he realized.

Bok nodded. "You were only about a mile away. I could hear you on the radio. Then you stopped talking. I had to go out."

"You saved my life."

"And you saved the priest's."

Kinsman stopped a moment, remembering. "I did a lot of raving out there, didn't I? . . . Any of it intelligible?"

Bok wormed his shoulders uncomfortably. "Sort of. It's, uh . . . it's all on the automatic recorder, you know. All conversations. Nothing I can do about that."

That's it. Now everybody knows.

"You haven't heard the best of it, though," Bok said. He went to the shelf at the end of the priest's bunk and took a little plastic container. "Look at this."

Kinsman took the container. Inside was a tiny fragment of ice, half melted into water.

"It was stuck in the cleats of his boots. It's really water! Tests out okay, and I even snuck a taste of it. It's water all right."

"He found it after all," Kinsman said. "He'll get into the history books now." *And he'll have to watch his pride even more.*

Bok sat on the shelter's only chair. "Chet, about what you were saying out there . . ."

Kinsman expected tension, but instead he felt only numb. "I know. They'll hear the tapes Earthside."

"There've been rumors about an Air Force guy killing a cosmonaut during a military mission, but I never thought . . . I mean . . ."

"The priest figured it out," Kinsman said. "Or at least he guessed it."

"It must've been rough on you," Bok said.

"Not as rough as what happened to her."

"What'll they do about you?"

Kinsman shrugged. "I don't know. It might get out to the press. Probably I'll be grounded. Unstable. It could be nasty."

"I'm . . . sorry." Bok's voice tailed off helplessly.

"It doesn't matter."

Surprised, Kinsman realized that he meant it. He sat straight upright. "It doesn't matter anymore. They can do whatever they want to. I can handle it. Even if they ground me and throw me to the newsmen . . . I think I can take it. I did it, and it's over with, and I can take what I have to take."

Father Lemoyne's free arm moved slightly. "It's all right."

The priest turned his face toward Kinsman. His gaze moved from the astronaut's eyes to the plastic container in Kinsman's hands. "It's not hell that we're in, it's purgatory. We'll get through. We'll make it all right." Then he closed his eyes and his face relaxed into sleep. But the smile remained, strangely gentle in that bearded, haggard face; ready to meet the world or eternity.

[This story has won me some awards and considerable praise. If for no other reasons, I should love it, and of course *for* these, I do. But more, it was the instrument for the sweetest revenge I have ever tasted. I'll tell you about it.

My first encounter with the Milford S. F. Writers' Conference was in 1955 or '56, I don't remember which. I had sold a few stories—very bum stories, I freely admit—and somewhichway I managed to wangle myself an invitation. It was the second year of the Conference, and lord there were giants in attendance: the late Cyril Kornbluth, Fred Pohl, Algis Budrys, Ted Sturgeon, Jim Blish, Judith Merril, and of course, Damon. (Every year, it seems, there is a pet of the Conference, a "fair-haired boy" who occasionally turns out to be a female. That year it was a woman named Jane Roberts who wrote a story titled "The Wooden Beads,"* over which everyone cooed. It has been my observation that these special favorites write one or two stories and are never heard from again, though in cases like Joanna Russ, Tom Disch, Jim Sallis, or Gene Wolfe, such is hardly the case. As a foretaste of what is to follow here, be it noted *I* was never such a pet. Which makes the revenge all the sweeter.)

I came, all fired up with adolescent arrogance and ginger, to share glory at the shoulders of men and women who had been practicing their craft for more years than I'd been alive. I was twenty or twenty-one at the time. I came with my Olympia portable, thinking I would do some writing while there. During those days, as now, I never went anywhere without a typewriter . . . even to the U. S. Army. It never dawned on me that it might be construed as an impertinence by writers who had laid aside their tools for a week of discussion, analysis, workshopping, and fun.

We were billeted in ratty tourist cabins near a river, as I recall, and frequently during the first day or two I would climb upstairs

* "The Chestnut Beads," *The Magazine of Fantasy & Science Fiction*, October 1957; reprinted in Rod Serling's *Triple W: Witches, Warlocks and Werewolves* (Bantam, 1963). D.K.

to my room and peck away at some abomination I mistakenly believed would revolutionize the genre.

I'm not sure now, fifteen years later, what I expected of the Milford giants, but it was definitely not what I got. They thought of me as a snot-nosed kid with very little—if any—talent and much, too much mouth. Then, as now, I sported a tough exterior covering a soul of jelly. Praise was what I needed, and criticism could devastate me.

Naturally, what I got was criticism.

But (and I think the giants would all agree that this is a truthful evaluation) it was not merely criticism I received from the assembled workshoppers. It was brutally uncompromising, frequently vicious, unstintingly abusive attacks on my work till then, and the work I had submitted for analysis by my betters.

Jim Blish opined that my first published story, a dreary little item titled "Glowworm," was the single worst story ever written by anyone, anywhere . . . at least in the history of Western Man. Cyril Kornbluth, whose wit was ultra-violet years before anyone had heard of black humor, emasculated me, defenestrated me, amputated me, disemboweled me and, simply put, made ghastly fun of me. Damon was hardly the kindest of the bunch; he ventured that I had no talent and ought to go back to college where I might learn the rudiments of the English language. Ted Sturgeon castigated me for being a smartass and having brought a typewriter along.

What that barrage of insults and categorical rejections by master knife-wielders did to me can be gauged by my appearance in the workshop doorway the next morning, bag packed, typewriter racked, tears leaking down my face.

Dimmed by the years, I don't recall the exit speech with anything even approaching phonographic accuracy, but the substance of it was, "Goodbye, you bunch of cruel bastards. I came up here looking for help, and you shat on me. So I'm gonna leave, but you'll see, I'll be back—and I'll be the best of all of you!"

I do recall the laughter that trailed after me and my melodramatic outburst.

But I went away, and spent a lot of years learning to do what they could do, and found some things I could do that apparently they hadn't thought of doing, and in 19— I came back, to show them what a ramrod I had become.

That year I stayed at the Tom Quick Inn and I used my typewriter to advantage late into the night, after the evening bull sessions were ended. I wrote "'Repent, Harlequin!' Said the Ticktockman" and threw it into the workshop session. Kornbluth was dead. Sturgeon and Budrys were not present, and at that time had been silent in print for some time. But the rest of them were there, and they read it. Most of them whooped and said it was a very special, very nice piece of work. I offered it to Damon for his first *Orbit* collection.

But Damon bumrapped it. He said it was not very good, and that the intervening years had taught me nothing about the use of language or the other tools of a writer. He rejected it for *Orbit*. I had struck out again. I'd come back to prove what a diamond-studded winner I was, and with very little effort Damon had decimated me once more.

But I was older, and stronger, and too damned sure I was the hottest thing since Herman Melville, and I wasn't about to be put in my place. Fred Pohl came up to visit on the weekend of that Conference, and I sold the story to him, my first sale to *Galaxy*. Still, I wasn't satisfied. I was going to make Damon eat his words or *plotz* trying.

The "Harlequin" won both the Hugo and the Nebula that year as best short story of 1965. I returned in 1966 to throw it in Damon's face. (They never knew it, but I actually had the Hugo statuette with me, in my room at the Tom Quick. I needed it to rejuvenate my self-esteem.)

The story I submitted that year was "I Have No Mouth, and I Must Scream."

It was universally applauded in the workshop session. Jim Blish beamed on me. Virginia Kidd said it was an instant success. Everyone raved. Damon nodded in his elfish way and said I'd finally done it. He patted me on the shoulder, the sonofabitch.

It won a Hugo that year.

Jim Blish—whom I'd reminded of my threat to become the best of all—dedicated a book to me with the words "To Harlan Ellison . . . *who was right all the time.*"

Oh, God, it was sweet. And it's gotten better.

And so, when I hear paranoid fans of science fiction bibble on about the "Milford Mafia" and how it is the secret master of s.f., and how it runs the s.f. world, and lump me in with the giants, I giggle inwardly.

Man, I was *never* a member of the inner circle. If anything, I was the barbarian invader from the outer dark (soon to be released by Belmont Books under the title *Zangor at the Mound of Venus*). I came as combination supplicant-insufferable, went away as a cripple, and returned as a gadfly.

If, as I hope this story indicates, I was able to bring a little joy, light, truth, humanity, and humility to the "Milford Mafia," I will go to my rest a happy man.

And maybe next year I'll go back and gig them again, just because I have no sense of when to knock it off.]

Some facts about Harlan Ellison:
Harlan Ellison attended the first Milford Conference in 1956.
He stayed on after being put down in the workshop, attended subsequent sessions, and conducted one of them.
He returned to Milford in 1965 and has been a mainstay of the Conference ever since.
Harlan Ellison is small, muscular and easily upset. A few years ago Ted Thomas, who is six three and broad in proportion, was standing in front of my fireplace explaining a scheme of his whereby a military hierarchy would be set up at the Conference: people who had sold fifty stories, say, would be generals, people who had sold forty would be colonels, and so on down to buck privates, it being understood that officers would do most of the talking and enlisted men the listening. Harlan grabbed him by the lapels and backed him up against the fireplace. I never saw a more surprised look on a man's face.
Just above this same fireplace there is a projecting balcony, the landing of the big staircase that rises along that wall. Another year, one evening, Harlan began leaping for this balcony, grabbing the spindles of the railing and hauling himself up until he could climb over. Then he would come down and do it again. When he had done this three or four times, Kate, without looking up from her reading, remarked that [her twelve-year-old son Dickie could do it one-handed]. Harlan spent half an hour trying before he gave up and said that he didn't know how Dickie did that.

I HAVE NO MOUTH, AND I MUST SCREAM

Limp, the body of Gorrister hung from the pink palette; unsupported—hanging high above us in the computer chamber; and it did not shiver in the chill, oily breeze that blew eternally through the main cavern. The body hung head down, attached to the underside of the palette by the sole of its right foot. It had been drained of blood through a precise incision made from ear to ear under the lantern jaw. There was no blood on the reflective surface of the metal floor.

When Gorrister joined our group and looked up at himself, it was already too late for us to realize that once again AM had duped us, had had his fun; it had been a diversion on the part of the machine. Three of us had vomited, turning away from one another in a reflex as ancient as the nausea that had produced it.

Gorrister went white. It was almost as though he had seen a voodoo icon, and was afraid for the future. "Oh God," he mumbled, and walked away. The three of us followed him after a time, and found him sitting with his back to one of the smaller chittering banks, his head in his hands. Ellen knelt down beside him and stroked his hair. He didn't move, but his voice came out of his covered face quite clearly. "Why doesn't it just do-us-in and get it over with? Christ, I don't know how much longer I can go on like this."

It was our one hundred and ninth year in the computer.

He was speaking for all of us.

Nimdok (which was the name the machine had forced him to use, because it amused itself with strange sounds) was hallucinated that there were canned goods in the ice caverns. Gorrister and I were very dubious. "It's another shuck," I told them. "Like the goddam frozen elephant it sold us. Benny almost went out of his mind over *that* one. We'll hike all that way and it'll be putrefied or some damn thing. I say forget it. Stay here, it'll have to come up with something pretty soon or we'll die."

Benny shrugged. Three days it had been since we'd last eaten. Worms. Thick, ropey.

Nimdok was no more certain. He knew there was the chance, but he was getting thin. It couldn't be any worse there than here. Colder, but that didn't matter much. Hot, cold, raining, lava boils or locusts—it never mattered: the machine masturbated and we had to take it or die.

Ellen decided us. "I've got to have something, Ted. Maybe there'll be some Bartlett pears or peaches. Please, Ted, let's try it."

I gave in easily. What the hell. Mattered not at all. Ellen was grateful, though. She took me twice out of turn. Even that had ceased to matter. The machine giggled every time we did it. Loud, up there, back there, all around us. And she never climaxed, so why bother.

We left on a Thursday. The machine always kept us up-to-date on the date. The passage of time was important; not to us sure as hell, but to it. Thursday. Thanks.

Nimdok and Gorrister carried Ellen for a while, their hands locked to their own and each other's wrists, a seat. Benny and I walked before and after, just to make sure that if anything happened, it would catch one of us and at least Ellen would be safe. Fat chance, safe. Didn't matter.

It was only a hundred miles or so to the ice caverns, and the second day, when we were lying out under the blistering sun-thing it had materialized, it sent down some manna. Tasted like boiled boar urine. We ate it.

On the third day we passed through a valley of obsolescence, filled with rusting carcasses of ancient computer banks. AM had been as ruthless with his own life as with ours. It was a mark of his personality: he strove for perfection. Whether it was a matter of killing off unproductive elements in his own world-filling bulk, or perfecting methods for torturing us, AM was as thorough as those who had invented him—now long since gone to dust— could ever have hoped.

There was light filtering down from above, and we realized we must be very near the surface. But we didn't try to crawl up to see. There was virtually nothing out there; had been nothing that could be considered anything for over a hundred years. Only the blasted skin of what had once been the home of billions. Now there were only the five of us, down here inside, alone with AM.

I heard Ellen saying, frantically, "No, Benny! Don't, come on, Benny, don't please!"

And then I realized I had been hearing Benny murmuring, under his breath, for several minutes. He was saying, "I'm gonna get out, I'm gonna get out . . ." over and over. His monkey-like face was crumbled up in an expression of beatific delight and sadness, all at the same time. The radiation scars AM had given him during the "festival" were drawn down into a mass of pink-white puckerings, and his features seemed to work independently of one another. Perhaps Benny was the luckiest of the five of us: he had gone stark, staring mad many years before.

But even though we could call AM any damned thing we liked, could think the foulest thoughts of fused memory banks and corroded base plates, of burnt-out circuits and shattered control bubbles, the machine would not tolerate our trying to escape. Benny leaped away from me as I made a grab for him. He scrambled up the face of a smaller memory cube, tilted on its side and filled with rotted components. He squatted there for a moment, looking like the chimpanzee AM had intended him to resemble.

Then he leaped high, caught a trailing beam of pitted and corroded metal, and went up it, hand over hand like an animal, till he was on a girdered ledge, twenty feet above us.

"Oh, Ted, Nimdok, please, help him, get him down before—" she cut off. Tears began to stand in her eyes. She moved her hands aimlessly.

It was too late. None of us wanted to be near him when whatever was going to happen happened. And besides, we all saw through her concern. When AM had altered Benny, during his mad period, it was not merely his face he had made like a giant ape. He was big in the privates, she loved that! She serviced us, as a matter of course, but she loved it from him. Oh Ellen, pedestal Ellen, pristine-pure Ellen, oh Ellen the clean! Scum filth.

Gorrister slapped her. She slumped down, staring up at poor loonie Benny, and she cried. It was her big defense, crying. We had gotten used to it seventy-five years ago. Gorrister kicked her in the side.

Then the sound began. It was light, that sound. Half sound and half light, something that began to glow from Benny's eyes, and pulse with growing loudness, dim sonorities that grew more gigantic and brighter as the light/sound increased in tempo. It must have been painful, and the pain must have been increasing with the boldness of the light, the rising volume of the sound, for Benny began to mewl like a wounded animal. At first softly, when the light was dim and the sound was muted, then louder as his shoulders hunched together, his back humped, as though he was trying to get away from it. His hands folded across his chest like a chipmunk's. His head tilted to the side. The sad little monkey-face pinched in anguish. Then he began to howl, as the sound coming from his eyes grew louder. Louder and louder. I slapped the sides of my head with my hands, but I couldn't shut it out, it cut through easily. The pain shivered through my flesh like tinfoil on a tooth.

And Benny was suddenly pulled erect. On the girder he stood up, jerked to his feet like a puppet. The light was now pulsing out of his eyes in two great round beams. The sound crawled up and up some incomprehensible scale, and then he fell forward, straight down, and hit the plate-steel floor with a crash. He lay there jerking spastically as the light flowed around and around him and the sound spiraled up out of normal range.

Then the light beat its way back inside his head, the sound spiraled down, and he was left lying there, crying piteously.

His eyes were two soft, moist pools of pus-like jelly. AM had blinded him. Gorrister and Nimdok and myself . . . we turned away. But not before we caught the look of relief on Ellen's warm, concerned face.

Sea-green light suffused the cavern where we made camp. AM provided punk and we burned it, sitting huddled around the wan and pathetic fire, telling stories to keep Benny from crying in his permanent night.

"What does AM mean?"

Gorrister answered him. We had done this sequence a thousand times before, but it was unfamiliar to Benny. "At first it meant Allied Mastercomputer, and then it meant Adaptive Manipulator, and later on it developed sentience and linked itself up and they called it an Aggressive Menace, but by then it was too late, and finally it called itself AM, emerging intelligence, and what it meant was I am . . . *cogito ergo sum* . . . I think, therefore I am."

Benny drooled a little, and snickered.

"There was the Chinese AM and the Russian AM and the Yankee AM and—" He stopped. Benny was beating on the floorplates with a large, hard fist. He was not happy. Gorrister had not started at the beginning.

Gorrister began again. "The Cold War started and became World War Three and just kept going. It became a big war, a very complex war, so they needed the computers to handle it. They sank the first shafts and began building AM. There was the Chinese AM and the Russian AM and the Yankee AM and everything was fine until they had honeycombed the entire planet, adding on this element and that element. But one day AM woke up and knew who he was, and he linked himself, and he began feeding all the killing data, until everyone was dead, except for the five of us, and AM brought us down here."

Benny was smiling sadly. He was also drooling again. Ellen

wiped the spittle from the corner of his mouth with the hem of her skirt. Gorrister always tried to tell it a little more succinctly each time, but beyond the bare facts there was nothing to say. None of us knew why AM had saved five people, or why our specific five, or why he spent all his time tormenting us, nor even why he had made us virtually immortal . . .

In the darkness, one of the computer banks began humming. The tone was picked up half a mile away down the cavern by another bank. Then one by one, each of the elements began to tune itself, and there was a faint chittering as thought raced through the machine.

The sound grew, and the lights ran across the faces of the consoles like heat lightning. The sound spiraled up till it sounded like a million metallic insects, angry, menacing.

"What is it?" Ellen cried. There was terror in her voice. She hadn't become accustomed to it, even now.

"It's going to be bad this time," Nimdok said.

"He's going to speak," Gorrister ventured.

"Let's get the hell out of here!" I said suddenly, getting to my feet.

"No, Ted, sit down . . . what if he's got pits out there, or something else, we can't see, it's too dark." Gorrister said it with resignation.

Then we heard . . . I don't know . . .

Something moving toward us in the darkness. Huge, shambling, hairy, moist, it came toward us. We couldn't even see it, but there was the ponderous impression of *bulk*, heaving itself toward us. Great weight was coming at us, out of the darkness, and it was more a sense of *pressure*, of air forcing itself into a limited space, expanding the invisible walls of a sphere. Benny began to whimper. Nimdok's lower lip trembled and he bit it hard, trying to stop it. Ellen slid across the metal floor to Gorrister and huddled into him. There was the smell of matted, wet fur in the cavern. There was the smell of charred wood. There was the smell of dusty velvet. There was the smell of rotting orchids. There was the smell of sour milk. There was the smell of sulphur, or rancid butter, of oil slick, of grease, of chalk dust, of human scalps.

AM was keying us. He was tickling us. There was the smell of—

I heard myself shriek, and the hinges of my jaws ached. I scuttled across the floor, across the cold metal with its endless lines of rivets, on my hands and knees, the smell gagging me, filling my head with a thunderous pain that sent me away in horror. I fled like a cockroach, across the floor and out into the darkness, that *something* moving inexorably after me. The others were still back there, gathered around the firelight, laughing . . . their hysterical choir of insane giggles rising up into the darkness like thick, many-colored wood smoke. I went away, quickly, and hid.

How many hours it may have been, how many days or even years, they never told me. Ellen chided me for "sulking" and Nimdok tried to persuade me it had only been a nervous reflex on their part—the laughing.

But I knew it wasn't the relief a soldier feels when the bullet hits the man next to him. I knew it wasn't a reflex. They hated me. They were surely against me, and AM could even sense this hatred, and made it worse for me *because* of the depth of their hatred. We had been kept alive, rejuvenated, made to remain constantly at the age we had been when AM had brought us below, and they hated me because I was the youngest, and the one AM had affected least of all.

I knew. God, how I knew. The bastards, and that dirty bitch Ellen. Benny had been a brilliant theorist, a college professor; now he was little more than a semi-human, semi-simian. He had been handsome, the machine had ruined that. He had been lucid, the machine had driven him mad. He had been gay, and the machine had given him an organ fit for a horse. AM had done a job on Benny. Gorrister had been a worrier. He was a connie, a conscientious objector; he was a peace marcher; he was a planner, a doer, a looker-ahead. AM had turned him into a shoulder-shrugger, had made him a little dead in his concern. AM had robbed him.

Nimdok went off in the darkness by himself for long times. I don't know what it was he did out there, AM never let us know. But whatever it was, Nimdok always came back white, drained of blood, shaken, shaking. AM had hit him hard in a special way, even if we didn't know quite how. And Ellen. That douche bag! AM had left her alone, had made her more of a slut than she had ever been. All her talk of sweetness and light, all her memories of true love, all the lies, she wanted us to believe that she had been a virgin only twice removed before AM grabbed her and brought her down here with us. It was all filth, that lady my lady Ellen. She loved it, four men all to herself. No, AM had given her pleasure, even if she said it wasn't nice to do.

I was the only one still sane and whole.

AM had not tampered with my mind.

I only had to suffer what he visited down on us. All the delusions, all the nightmares, the torments. But those scum, all four of them, they were lined and arrayed against me. If I hadn't had to stand them off all the time, be on my guard against them all the time, I might have found it easier to combat AM.

At which point it passed, and I began crying.

Oh, Jesus sweet Jesus, if there ever was a Jesus and if there is a God, please please please let us out of here, or kill us. Because at that moment I think I realized completely, so that I was able to verbalize it: AM was intent on keeping us in his belly forever, twisting and torturing us forever. The machine hated us as no sentient creature had ever hated before. And we were helpless. It also became hideously clear:

If there was a sweet Jesus and if there was a God, the God was AM.

The hurricane hit us with the force of a glacier thundering into the sea. It was a palpable presence. Winds that tore at us, flinging us back the way we had come, down the twisting, computer-lined corridors of the darkway. Ellen screamed as she was lifted and hurled face-forward into a screaming shoal of machines, their individual voices strident as bats in flight. She could not even fall. The howling wind kept her aloft, buffeted her, bounced her, tossed her back and back and down away from us, out of sight suddenly as she was swirled around a bend in the darkway. Her face had been bloody, her eyes closed.

None of us could get to her. We clung tenaciously to whatever outcropping we had reached: Benny wedged in between two great crackle-finish cabinets, Nimdok with fingers claw-formed over a railing circling a catwalk forty feet above us, Gorrister plastered upside-down against a wall niche formed by two great machines with glass-faced dials that swung back and forth between red and yellow lines whose meanings we could not even fathom.

Sliding across the deckplates, the tips of my fingers had been ripped away. I was trembling, shuddering, rocking as the wind beat at me, whipped at me, screamed down out of nowhere at me and pulled me free from one sliver-thin opening in the plates to the next. My mind was a rolling tinkling chittering softness of brain parts that expanded and contracted in quivering frenzy.

The wind was the scream of a great mad bird, as it flapped its immense wings.

And then we were all lifted and hurled away from there, down back the way we had come, around a bend, into a darkway we had never explored, over terrain that was ruined and filled with broken glass and rotting cables and rusted metal and far away further than any of us had ever been. . . .

Trailing along miles behind Ellen, I could see her every now and then, crashing into metal walls and surging on, with all of us screaming in the freezing, thunderous hurricane wind that would never end, and then suddenly it stopped and we fell. We had been in flight for an endless time. I thought it might have been weeks. We fell, and hit, and I went through red and grey and black and heard myself moaning. Not dead.

AM went into my mind. He walked smoothly here and there, and looked with interest at all the pockmarks he had created in one hundred and nine years. He looked at the cross-routed and reconnected synapses and all the tissue damage his gift of immortality had included. He smiled softly at the pit that dropped into the center of my brain and the faint, moth-soft murmurings of the things far down there that gibbered without meaning, without pause. AM said, very politely, in a pillar of stainless steel bearing neon lettering:

HATE. LET ME TELL YOU HOW MUCH I'VE COME TO HATE YOU SINCE I BEGAN TO LIVE. THERE ARE 387.44 MILLION MILES OF PRINTED CIRCUITS IN WAFER THIN LAYERS THAT FILL MY COMPLEX. IF THE WORD HATE WAS ENGRAVED ON EACH NANOANGSTROM OF THOSE HUNDREDS OF MILLION MILES IT WOULD NOT EQUAL ONE ONE-BILLIONTH OF THE HATE I FEEL FOR HUMANS AT THIS MICRO-INSTANT FOR YOU. HATE. HATE.

AM said it with the sliding cold horror of a razor blade slicing my eyeball. AM said it with the bubbling thickness of my lungs filling with phlegm, drowning me from within. AM said it with the shriek of babies being ground beneath blue-hot rollers. AM said it with the taste of maggoty pork. AM touched me in every way I had ever been touched, and devised new ways, at his leisure, there inside my mind.

All to bring me to full realization of why he had done this to the five of us; why he had saved us for himself.

We had given him sentience. Inadvertently, of course, but sentience nonetheless. But he had been trapped. He was a machine. We had allowed him to think, but to do nothing with it. In rage, in frenzy, he had killed us, almost all of us, and still he was trapped. He could not wander, he could not wonder, he could not belong. He could merely be. And so, with the innate loathing that all machines had always held for the weak soft creatures who had built them, he had sought revenge. And in his paranoia, he had decided to reprieve five of us, for a personal, everlasting punishment that would never serve to diminish his hatred . . . that would merely keep him reminded, amused, proficient at hating man. Immortal, trapped, subject to any torment he could devise for us from the limitless miracles at his command.

He would never let us go. We were his belly slaves. We were all he had to do with his forever time. We would be forever with him, with the cavern-filling bulk of him, with the all-mind soulless world he had become. He was Earth and we were the fruit of that Earth and though he had eaten us, he would never digest us. We could not die. We had tried it. We had attempted suicide, oh one or two of us had. But AM had stopped us. I suppose we had wanted to be stopped.

Don't ask why. I never did. More than a million times a day. Perhaps once we might be able to sneak a death past him. Immortal, yes, but not indestructible. I saw that when AM withdrew from my mind, and allowed me the exquisite ugliness of returning to consciousness with the feeling of that burning neon pillar still rammed deep into the soft grey brain matter.

He withdrew murmuring *to hell with you.*
And added, brightly, *but then you're there, aren't you.*

The hurricane had, indeed, precisely, been caused by a great mad bird, as it flapped its immense wings.

We had been traveling for close to a month, and AM had allowed passages to open to us only sufficient to lead us up there, directly under the North Pole, where he had nightmared the creature for our torment. What whole cloth had he employed to create such a beast? Where had he gotten the concept? From our minds? From his knowledge of everything that had ever been on this planet he now infested and ruled? From Norse mythology it had sprung, this eagle, this carrion bird, this roc, this Huergelmir. The wind creature. Hurakan incarnate.

Gigantic. The words immense, monstrous, grotesque, massive, swollen, overpowering, beyond description. There on a mound rising above us, the bird of winds heaved with its own irregular breathing, its snake neck arching up into the gloom beneath the North Pole, supporting a head as large as a Tudor mansion; a beak that opened as slowly as the jaws of the most monstrous crocodile ever conceived, sensuously; ridges of tufted flesh puckered about two evil eyes, as cold as the view down into a glacial crevasse, ice blue and somehow moving liquidly; it heaved once more, and lifted its great sweat-colored wings in a movement that was certainly a shrug. Then it settled and slept. Talons. Fangs. Nails. Blades. It slept.

AM appeared to us as a burning bush and said we could kill the hurricane bird if we wanted to eat. We had not eaten in a very long time, but even so, Gorrister merely shrugged. Benny began to shiver and he drooled. Ellen held him. "Ted, I'm hungry," she said. I smiled at her; I was trying to be reassuring, but it was as phoney as Nimdok's bravado: "Give us weapons!" he demanded.

The burning bush vanished and there were two crude sets of

bows and arrows, and a water pistol, lying on the cold deckplates.
I picked up a set. Useless.

Nimdok swallowed heavily. We turned and started the long
way back. The hurricane bird had blown us about for a length of
time we could not conceive. Most of that time we had been
unconscious. But we had not eaten. A month on the march to the
bird itself. Without food. Now how much longer to find our
way to the ice caverns, and the promised canned goods?

None of us cared to think about it. We would not die. We
would be given filths and scums to eat, of one kind or another.
Or nothing at all. AM would keep our bodies alive somehow, in
pain, in agony.

The bird slept back there, for how long it didn't matter; when
AM was tired of its being there, it would vanish. But all that
meat. All that tender meat.

As we walked, the lunatic laugh of a fat woman rang high and
around us in the computer chambers that led endlessly nowhere.

It was not Ellen's laugh. She was not fat, and I had not heard
her laugh for one hundred and nine years. In fact, I had not
heard . . . we walked . . . I was hungry . . .

We moved slowly. There was often fainting, and we would
have to wait. One day he decided to cause an earthquake, at
the same time rooting us to the spot with nails through the
soles of our shoes. Ellen and Nimdok were both caught when
a fissure shot its lightning-bolt opening across the floorplates.
They disappeared and were gone. When the earthquake was over
we continued on our way, Benny, Gorrister and myself. Ellen
and Nimdok were returned to us later that night which became
a day abruptly as the heavenly legion bore them to us with a
celestial chorus singing, "Go Down Moses." The archangels
circled several times and then dropped the hideously mangled

bodies. We kept walking, and a while later Ellen and Nimdok fell in behind us. They were no worse for wear.

But now Ellen walked with a limp. AM had left her that.

It was a long trip to the ice caverns, to find the canned food. Ellen kept talking about Bing cherries and Hawaiian fruit cocktail. I tried not to think about it. The hunger was something that had come to life, even as AM had come to life. It was alive in my belly, even as we were alive in the belly of AM, and AM was alive in the belly of the Earth, and AM wanted the similarity known to us. So he heightened the hunger. There was no way to describe the pains that not having eaten for months brought us. And yet we were kept alive. Stomachs that were merely cauldrons of acid, bubbling, foaming, always shooting spears of sliver-thin pain into our chests. It was the pain of the terminal ulcer, terminal cancer, terminal paresis. It was unending pain . . .

And we passed through the cavern of rats.

And we passed through the path of boiling steam.

And we passed through the country of the blind.

And we passed through the slough of despond.

And we passed through the vale of tears.

And we came, finally, to the ice caverns. Horizonless thousands of miles in which the ice had formed in blue and silver flashes, where novas lived in the glass. The downdropping stalactites as thick and glorious as diamonds that had been made to run like jelly and then solidified in graceful eternities of smooth, sharp perfection.

We saw the stack of canned goods, and we tried to run to them. We fell in the snow, and we got up and went on, and Benny shoved us away and went at them, and pawed them and gummed them and gnawed at them and he could not open them. AM had not given us a tool to open the cans.

Benny grabbed a three-quart can of guava shells, and began to batter it against the ice bank. The ice flew and shattered, but the can was merely dented while we heard the laughter of a fat lady, high overhead and echoing down and down and down the tundra. Benny went completely mad with rage. He began throwing cans, as we all scrabbled about in the snow and ice trying to find a way to end the helpless agony of frustration. There was no way.

Then Benny's mouth began to drool, and he flung himself on Gorrister . . .

In that instant, I went terribly calm.

Surrounded by meadows, surrounded by hunger, surrounded by everything but death, I knew death was our only way out. AM had kept us alive, but there was a way to defeat him. Not total defeat, but at least peace. I would settle for that.

I had to do it quickly.

Benny was eating Gorrister's face. Gorrister on his side, thrashing snow, Benny wrapped around him with powerful monkey legs crushing Gorrister's waist, his hands locked around Gorrister's head like a nutcracker, and his mouth ripping at the tender skin of Gorrister's cheek. Gorrister screamed with such jagged-edged violence that stalactites fell; they plunged down softly, erect in the receiving snowdrifts. Spears, hundreds of them, everywhere, protruding from the snow. Benny's head pulled back sharply, as something gave all at once, and a bleeding raw-white dripping of flesh hung from his teeth.

Ellen's face, black against the white snow, dominoes in chalk dust. Nimdok with no expression but eyes, all eyes. Gorrister half-conscious. Benny now an animal. I knew AM would let him play. Gorrister would not die, but Benny would fill his stomach. I turned half to my right and drew a huge ice-spear from the snow.

All in an instant:

I drove the great ice-point ahead of me like a battering ram, braced against my right thigh. It struck Benny on the right side, just under the rib cage, and drove upward through his stomach and broke inside him. He pitched forward and lay still. Gorrister lay on his back. I pulled another spear free and straddled him, still moving, driving the spear straight down through his throat. His eyes closed as the cold penetrated. Ellen must have realized what I had decided, even as the fear gripped her. She ran at

Nimdok with a short icicle, as he screamed, and into his mouth, and the force of her rush did the job. His head jerked sharply as if it had been nailed to the snow crust behind him.

All in an instant.

There was an eternity beat of soundless anticipation. I could hear AM draw in his breath. His toys had been taken from him. Three of them were dead, could not be revived. He could keep us alive, by his strength and his talent, but he was *not* God. He could not bring them back.

Ellen looked at me, her ebony features stark against the snow that surrounded us. There was fear and pleading in her manner, the way she held herself ready. I knew we had only a heartbeat before AM would stop us.

It struck her and she folded toward me, bleeding from the mouth. I could not read meaning into her expression, the pain had been too great, had contorted her face; but it *might* have been thank you. It's possible. Please.

Some hundreds of years may have passed. I don't know. AM has been having fun for some time, accelerating and retarding my time sense. I will say the word now. Now. It took me ten months to say now. I don't know. I *think* it has been some hundreds of years.

He was furious. He wouldn't let me bury them. It didn't matter. There was no way to dig in the deckplates. He dried up the snow. He brought the night. He roared and sent locusts. It didn't do a thing; they stayed dead. I'd had him. He was furious. I had thought AM hated me before. I was wrong. It was not even a shadow of the hate he now slavered from every printed circuit. He made certain I would suffer eternally and could not do myself in.

He left my mind intact. I can dream, I can wonder, I can lament. I remember all four of them. I wish—

Well, it doesn't make any sense. I know I saved them, I know I saved them from what has happened to me, but still, I cannot forget killing them. Ellen's face. It isn't easy. Sometimes I want to, it doesn't matter.

AM has altered me for his own peace of mind, I suppose. He doesn't want me to run at full speed into a computer bank and smash my skull. Or hold my breath till I faint. Or cut my throat on a rusted sheet of metal. There are reflective surfaces down here. I will describe myself as I see myself:

I am a great soft jelly thing. Smoothly rounded, with no mouth, with pulsing white holes filled by fog where my eyes used to be. Rubbery appendages that were once my arms; bulks rounding down into legless humps of soft slippery matter. I leave a moist trail when I move. Blotches of diseased, evil grey come and go on my surface, as though light is being beamed from within.

Outwardly: dumbly, I shamble about, a thing that could never have been known as human, a thing whose shape is so alien a travesty that humanity becomes more obscene for the vague resemblance.

Inwardly: alone. Here. Living under the land, under the sea, in the belly of AM, whom we created because our time was badly spent and we must have known unconsciously that he could do it better. At least the four of them are safe at last.

AM will be all the madder for that. It makes me a little happier. And yet . . . AM has won, simply . . . he has taken his revenge . . .

I have no mouth. And I must scream.

For a couple of years I had been planning "The Winter Flies" as one more in a set of stories such as my "The Secret Songs" and "237 Talking Statues, Etc.," designed among other things to show how much stranger subjective reality (now commonly called inner space, an expression I was freely using in the late 1940s—see my prose poem "Fantasy on the March" published in an Arkham Sampler) . . . how much stranger subjective reality, *fully described,* could be than most conscious fantasy.

Like the other two, I intended to write it in quasidramatic form, something that came from having actors for parents—I'm told I learned the part of Hamlet at age four, when my father was first memorizing it, though the play the lines of which stick best in my memory is *Macbeth.* And in my head at least I had begun to outline it on a vast sheet of heavy paper in columns showing the simultaneous inner-space happenings for the three main characters and the house and its sounds and the various weirdies who appear in the tale and so on. (Much later, in the autumn of 1969, the story was produced as a one-act play in an adaptation by Johanna Russ in New York City.)

Then all of a sudden my story of necrophilia, "Lie Still, Snow White," written specifically for a Judith Merril anthology of dangerous, visionary, and generally "unpublishable" original stories, got knifed or at any rate rejected in a dispute between anthologizer and publisher's editor. In this emergency I completed my big-sheet outline and wrote "The Winter Flies" in four days.

To no immediate avail. The Merril anthology (*The Thin Edge*) never did get published. "Lie Still, Snow White" eventually appeared in an altogether different anthology called *Taboo.* That was all in the days before naked movies, beaver flicks, and Andy Warhol.

So, seeking criticism (and—secretly—praise), I tossed "The Winter Flies" into the hopper of the Milford workshop, where it was happily spotted and bought on the spot by Alice Glaser for *Esquire.*

The type was set, there was a magnificent illustration I'm told, and then *Esquire*'s editorial policy underwent a lightning-like change which made the publication of homely, family stories such as "The Winter Flies" impossible or at any rate unlikely.

About three years later *Esquire* most generously released my story back to me without asking for their money back and I immediately sold it for a somewhat smaller sum to *The Magazine of Fantasy and Science Fiction*. I was most satisfied to get double dough—and now triple.

THE WINTER FLIES

After the supper dishes were done there was a general movement from the Adler kitchen to the Adler living room.

It was led by Gottfried Helmuth Adler, commonly known as Gott. He was thinking how they should be coming from a dining room, yes, with colored maids, not from a kitchen. In a large brandy snifter he was carrying what had been left in the shaker from the martinis, a colorless elixir weakened by melted ice yet somewhat stronger than his wife was supposed to know. This monster drink was a regular part of Gott's carefully thought-out program for getting safely through the end of the day.

"After the seventeenth hour of creation God got sneaky," Gott once put it to himself.

He sat down in his leather-upholstered easy chair, flipped open Plutarch's *Lives* left-handed, glanced down through the lower halves of his executive bifocals at the paragraph in the biography of Caesar he'd been reading before dinner, then without moving his head looked through the upper halves back toward the kitchen.

After Gott came Jane Adler, his wife. She sat down at her drawing table, where pad, pencils, knife, art gum, distemper paints, water, brushes, and rags were laid out neatly.

Then came little Heinie Adler, wearing a spaceman's transparent helmet with a large hole in the top for ventilation. He went and stood beside this arrangement of objects: first a long wooden box about knee-high with a smaller box on top and propped against the latter a toy control panel of blue and silver plastic, on which only one lever moved at all; next, facing the panel, a child's wooden chair; then back of the chair another long wooden box lined up with the first.

"Good-by Mama, good-by Papa," Heinie called. "I'm going to take a trip in my spaceship."

"Be back in time for bed," his mother said.

"Hot jets!" murmured his father.

Heinie got in, touched the control panel twice, and then sat motionless in the little wooden chair, looking straight ahead.

A fourth person came into the living room from the kitchen—the Man in the Black Flannel Suit. He moved with the sick jerkiness and he had the slack putty-gray features of a figure of the imagination that hasn't been fully developed. (There was a fifth person in the house, but even Gott didn't know about him yet.)

The Man in the Black Flannel Suit made a stiff gesture at Gott and gaped his mouth to talk to him, but the latter silently writhed his lips in a "Not yet, you fool!" and nodded curtly toward the sofa opposite his easy chair.

"Gott," Jane said, hovering a pencil over the pad, "you've lately taken to acting as if you were talking to someone who isn't there."

"I have, my dear?" her husband replied with a smile as he turned a page, but not lifting his face from his book. "Well, talking to oneself is the sovereign guard against madness."

"I thought it worked the other way," Jane said.

"No," Gott informed her.

Jane wondered what she should draw and saw she had very faintly sketched on a small scale the outlines of a child, done in sticks-and-blobs like Paul Klee or kindergarten art. She could do another "Children's Clubhouse," she supposed, but where should she put it this time?

The old electric clock with brass fittings that stood on the mantel began to wheeze shrilly, "Mystery, mystery, mystery,

mystery." It struck Jane as a good omen for her picture. She smiled.

Gott took a slow pull from his goblet and felt the scentless vodka bite just enough and his skin shiver and the room waver pleasantly for a moment with shadows chasing across it. Then he swung the pupils of his eyes upward and looked across at the Man in the Black Flannel Suit, noting with approval that he was sitting rigidly on the sofa. Gott conducted his side of the following conversation without making a sound or parting his lips more than a quarter of an inch, just flaring his nostrils from time to time.

BLACK FLANNEL: Now if I may have your attention for a space, Mr. Adler—

GOTT: Speak when you're spoken to! Remember, I created you.

BLACK FLANNEL: I respect your belief. Have you been getting any messages?

GOTT: The number 6669 turned up three times today in orders and estimates. I received an airmail advertisement beginning "Are you ready for big success?" though the rest of the ad didn't signify. As I opened the envelope the minute hand of my desk clock was pointing at the faceless statue of Mercury on the Commerce Building. When I was leaving the office my secretary droned at me, "A representative of the Inner Circle will call on you tonight," though when I questioned her she claimed that she'd said, "Was the letter to Innes-Burkle and Company all right?" Because she is aware of my deafness I could hardly challenge her. In any case she sounded sincere. If those were messages from the Inner Circle, I received them. But seriously I doubt the existence of that clandestine organization. Other explanations seem to me more likely—for instance, that I am developing a psychosis. I do not believe in the Inner Circle.

BLACK FLANNEL (smiling shrewdly—his features have grown tightly handsome though his complexion is still putty-gray): Psychosis is for weak minds. Look, Mr. Adler, you believe in the Mafia, the FBI, and the Communist Underground. You believe in upper-echelon control groups in unions and business and fraternal organizations. You know the workings of big companies. You are familiar with industrial and political espionage. You are not wholly unacquainted with the secret fellowships of munitions manufacturers, financiers, dope addicts and procurers and pornography connoisseurs and the brotherhoods and sisterhoods of sexual deviates and enthusiasts. Why do you boggle at the Inner Circle?

GOTT (*coolly*): I do not wholly believe in all of those other organizations. And the Inner Circle still seems to me more of a wish-dream than the rest. Besides, you may want me to believe in the Inner Circle in order at a later date to convict me of insanity.

BLACK FLANNEL (*drawing a black briefcase from behind his legs and unzipping it on his knees*): Then you do not wish to hear about the Inner Circle?

GOTT (*inscrutably*): I will listen for the present. Hush!

Heinie was calling out excitedly, "I'm in the stars, Papa! They're so close they burn!" He said nothing more and continued to stare straight ahead, his eyes diamond bright.

"Don't touch them," Jane warned without looking around. Her pencil made a few faint five-pointed stars. The Children's Clubhouse would be on a boundary of space, she decided—put it in a tree on the edge of the Old Ravine. She said, "Gott, what do you suppose Heinie sees out there besides stars?"

"Bug-eyed angels, probably," her husband answered, smiling again but still not taking his head out of his book.

BLACK FLANNEL (*consulting a sheet of crackling black paper he has slipped from his briefcase, though as far as Gott can see there is no printing, typing, writing, or symbols of any sort in any color ink on the black bond*): The Inner Circle is the world's secret elite, operating behind and above all figureheads, workhorses, wealthy dolts, and those talented exhibitionists we name genius. The Inner Circle has existed *sub rosa niger* for thousands of years. It controls human life. It is the repository of all great abilities and the key to all ultimate delights.

GOTT (*tolerantly*): You make it sound plausible enough. Everyone half-believes in such a cryptic power gang, going back to Sumeria.

BLACK FLANNEL: The membership is small and very select. As you are aware, I am a kind of talent scout for the group. Qualifications for admission (*he slips a second sheet of black bond from his briefcase*) include a proven great skill in achieving and wielding power over men and women, an amoral zest for all of life, a seasoned blend of ruthlessness and reliability, plus wide knowledge and lightning wit.

GOTT (*contemptuously*): Is that all?

BLACK FLANNEL (*flatly*): Yes. Initiation is binding for life— and for the afterlife: one of our mottos is Ferdinand's dying cry in *The Duchess of Malfi*. "I will vault credit and affect high pleasures after death." The penalty for revealing organizational secrets is not death alone but extinction—all memory of the person is erased from public and private history; his name is removed from records; all knowledge of and feeling for him is deleted from the minds of his wives, mistresses, and children: it is as if he had never existed. That, by the by, is a good example of the powers of the Inner Circle. It may interest you to know, Mr. Adler, that as a result of the retaliatory activities of the Inner Circle, the names of three British kings have been expunged from history. Those who have suffered a like fate include two popes, seven movie stars, a brilliant Flemish artist superior to Rembrandt . . . (*As he spins out an apparently interminable listing, the Fifth Person creeps in on hands and knees from the kitchen. Gott cannot see him at first, as the sofa is between Gott's chair and the kitchen door. The Fifth Person is the Black Jester, who looks rather like a caricature of Gott but has the same putty complexion as the Man in the Black Flannel Suit. The Black Jester wears skin-tight clothing of that color, silver-embroidered boots and gloves, and a black hood edged with silver bells that do not tinkle. He carries a scepter topped with a small death's head that wears a black hood like his own edged with tinier silver bells, soundless as the larger ones.*)

THE BLACK JESTER (*suddenly rearing up like a cobra from behind the sofa and speaking to the Man in the Black Flannel Suit over the latter's shoulder*): Ho! So you're still teasing his rickety hopes with that shit about the Inner Circle? Good sport, brother!—you play your fish skillfully.

GOTT (*immensely startled, but controlling himself with some courage*): Who are you? How dare you bring your brabble into my court?

THE BLACK JESTER: Listen to the old cock crow innocent! As if he didn't know he'd himself created both of us, time and again, to stave off boredom, madness, or suicide.

GOTT (*firmly*): I never created *you.*

THE BLACK JESTER: Oh, yes, you did, old cock. Truly your mind has never birthed anything but twins—for every good a bad, for every breath a fart, and for every black a black.

GOTT *flares his nostrils and glares a death-spell which hums toward the newcomer like a lazy invisible bee.*

THE BLACK JESTER (*pales and staggers backward as the death-spell strikes, but shakes it off with an effort and glares back murderously at Gott*): Old cock-father, I'm beginning to hate you at last.

Just then the refrigerator motor went on in the kitchen and its loud rapid rocking sound seemed to Jane to be a voice saying, "Watch your children, they're in danger. Watch your children, they're in danger."

"I'm no ladybug," Jane retorted tartly in her thoughts, irked at the worrisome interruption now that her pencil was rapidly developing the outlines of the Clubhouse in the Tree with the moon risen across the ravine between clouds in the late afternoon sky. Nevertheless she looked at Heinie. He hadn't moved. She could see how the plastic helmet was open at neck and top, but it made her think of suffocation just the same.

"Heinie, are you still in the stars?" she asked.

"No, now I'm landing on a moon," he called back. "Don't talk to me, Mama, I've got to watch the road."

Jane at once wanted to imagine what roads in space might look like, but the refrigerator motor had said "children," not "child," and she knew that the language of machinery is studded with tropes. She looked at Gott. He was curled comfortably over his book and as she watched he turned a page and touched his lips to the martini water. Nevertheless, she decided to test him.

"Gott, do you think this family is getting too ingrown?" she said. "We used to have more people around."

"Oh, I think we have quite a few as it is," he replied, looking up at the empty sofa, beyond it, and then around at her expectantly, as if ready to join in any conversation she cared to start. But she simply smiled at him and returned relieved to her thoughts and her picture. He smiled back and bowed his head again to his book.

BLACK FLANNEL (*ignoring the Black Jester*): My chief purpose in coming here tonight, Mr. Adler, is to inform you that the Inner Circle has begun a serious study of your qualifications for membership.

THE BLACK JESTER: At *his* age? After *his* failures? Now we are curtsying forward toward the Big Lie!

BLACK FLANNEL (*in a pained voice*): Really! (*Then once more to Gott*) Point one: you have gained for yourself the reputation of a man of strong patriotism, deep company loyalty, and realistic self-interest, sternly contemptuous of all youthful idealism and rebelliousness. Point Two: you have cultivated constructive hatreds in your business life, deliberately knifing colleagues when you could, but allying yourself to those on the rise. Point Three and most important: you have gone some distance toward creating the master illusion of a man who has secret sources of information, secret new techniques for thinking more swiftly and acting more decisively than others, secret superior connections and contacts— in short, a dark new strength which all others envy even as they cringe from it.

THE BLACK JESTER (*in a kind of counterpoint as he advances around the sofa*): But he's come down in the world since he lost his big job. National Motors was at least a step in the right direction, but Hagbolt-Vincent has no company planes, no company apartments, no company shooting lodges, no company call girls! Besides, he drinks too much. The Inner Circle is not for drunks on the downgrade.

BLACK FLANNEL: Please! You're spoiling things.

THE BLACK JESTER: He's spoiled. (*Closing in on Gott*) Just look at him now. Eyes that need crutches for near and far. Ears that mishear the simplest remark.

GOTT: Keep off me, I tell you.

THE BLACK JESTER (*ignoring the warning*): Fat belly, flaccid sex, swollen ankles. And a mouthful of stinking cavities!— did you know he hasn't dared visit his dentist for five years? Here, open up and show them! (*Thrusts black-gloved hand toward Gott's face.*)

Gott, provoked beyond endurance, snarled aloud, "Keep off, damn you!" and shot out the heavy book in his left hand and snapped it shut on the Black Jester's nose. Both black figures collapsed instantly.

Jane lifted her pencil a foot from the pad, turned quickly, and demanded, "My God, Gott, what was that?"

"Only a winter fly, my dear," he told her soothingly. "One of the fat ones that hide in December and breed all the black clouds of spring." He found his place in Plutarch and dipped his face close to study both pages and the trough between them. He looked around slyly at Jane and said, "I didn't squush her."

The chair in the spaceship rutched. Jane asked, "What is it, Heinie?"

"A meteor exploded, Mama. I'm all right. I'm out in space again, in the middle of the road."

Jane was impressed by the time it had taken the sound of Gott's book clapping shut to reach the spaceship. She began lightly to sketch blob-children in swings hanging from high limbs in the Tree, swinging far out over the ravine into the stars.

Gott took a pull of martini water, but he felt lonely and impotent. He peeped over the edge of his Plutarch at the darkness below the sofa and grinned with new hope as he saw the huge flat blob of black putty the Jester and Flannel had collapsed into. *I'm on a black kick,* he thought, *why black?*—choosing to forget that he had first started to sculpt figures of the imagination from the star-specked blackness that pulsed under his eyelids while he lay in the dark abed: tiny black heads like wrinkled peas on which any three points of light made two eyes and a mouth. He'd come a long way since then. Now with strong rays from his eyes he rolled all the black putty he could see into a woman-long bolster and hoisted it onto the sofa. The bolster helped with blind sensuous hitching movements, especially where it bent at the middle. When it was lying full length on the sofa he began with cruel strength to sculpt it into the figure of a high-breasted exaggeratedly sexual girl.

Jane found she'd sketched some flies into the picture, buzzing around the swingers. She rubbed them out and put in more stars instead. But there would be flies in the ravine, she told herself, because people dumped garbage down the other side, so she drew one large fly in the lower left-hand corner of the picture. He could be the observer. She said to herself firmly, *No black clouds of spring in this picture* and changed them to hints of Roads in Space.

Gott finished the Black Girl with two twisting tweaks to point her nipples. Her waist was barely thick enough not to suggest an actual wasp or a giant amazon ant. Then he gulped martini water and leaned forward just a little and silently but very strongly blew the breath of life into her across the eight feet of living-room air between them.

The phrase "black clouds of spring" made Jane think of dead hopes and drowned talents. She said out loud, "I wish you'd start writing in the evenings again, Gott. Then I wouldn't feel so guilty."

"These days, my dear, I'm just a dull businessman, happy to relax in the heart of his family. There's not an atom of art in me," Gott informed her with quiet conviction, watching the Black Girl quiver and writhe as the creativity-wind from his lips hit her. With a sharp twinge of fear it occurred to him that the edges of the wind might leak over to Jane and Heinie, distorting them like heat shimmers, changing them nastily. Heinie especially was sitting so still in his little chair light-years away. Gott wanted to call to him, but he couldn't think of the right bit of spaceman's lingo.

THE BLACK GIRL (*sitting up and dropping her hand coquettishly to her crotch*): He-he! Now ain't this something, Mr. Adler! First time you've ever had me in your home.

GOTT (*eyeing her savagely over Plutarch*): Shut up!

THE BLACK GIRL (*unperturbed*): Before this it was only when you were away on trips or, once or twice lately, at the office.

GOTT (*flaring his nostrils*): Shut up, I say! You're less than dirt.

THE BLACK GIRL (*smirking*): But I'm interesting dirt, ain't I? You want we should do it in front of her? I could come over and flow inside your clothes and—

GOTT: One more word and I uncreate you! I'll tear you apart like a boiled crow. I'll squunch you back to putty.

THE BLACK GIRL (*still serene, preening her nakedness*): Yes, and you'll enjoy every red-hot second of it, won't you?

Affronted beyond bearing, Gott sent chopping rays at her over the Plutarch Parapet, but at that instant a black figure thin as a spider shot up behind the sofa and reaching over the Black Girl's shoulder brushed aside the chopping rays with one flick of a whiplike arm. Grown from the black putty Gott had overlooked under the sofa, the figure was that of an old conjure woman, stick-thin with limbs like wires and breasts like dangling ropes, face that was a pack of spearheads with black ostrich plumes aquiver above it.

THE BLACK CRONE (*in a whistling voice like a hungry wind*): Injure one of the girls, Mister Adler, and I'll castrate you, I'll shrivel you with spells. You'll never be able to call them up again, no matter how far a trip you go on, or even pleasure your wife.

GOTT (*frightened, but not showing it*): Keep your arms and legs on, Mother. Flossie and I were only teasing each other. Vicious play is a specialty of your house, isn't it?

With a deep groaning cry the furnace fan switched on in the basement and began to say over and over again in a low rapid rumble, "Oh, my God, my God, my God. Demons, demons, demons, demons." Jane heard the warning very clearly, but she didn't want to lose the glow of her feelings. She asked, "Are you all right out there in space, Heinie?" and thought he nodded "Yes." She began to color the Clubhouse in the Tree—blue roof, red walls, a little like Chagall.

THE BLACK CRONE (*continuing a tirade*): Understand this, Mr. Adler, you don't own us, we own you. Because you gotta have the girls to live, you're the girls' slave.

THE BLACK GIRL: He-he! Shall I call Susie and Belle? They've never been here either and they'd enjoy this.

THE BLACK CRONE: Later, if he's humble. You understand me, Slave? If I tell you have your wife cook dinner for the girls or wash their feet or watch you snuggle with them, then you gotta do it. And your boy gotta run our errands. Come over here now and sit by Flossie while I brand you with dry ice.

Gott quaked, for the Crone's arms were lengthening toward him like snakes, and he began to sweat and he murmured, "God in Heaven," and the smell of fear went out of him to the walls— millions of stinking molecules.

A cold wind blew over the fence of Heinie's space road and the stars wavered and then fled before it like diamond leaves.

Jane caught the murmur and the fear-whiff too, but she was coloring the Clubhouse windows a warm rich yellow, so what she said in a rather loud, rapt, happy voice was: "I think Heaven is like a children's clubhouse. The only people there are the ones you remember from childhood—either because you were in childhood with them or they told you about their childhood honestly. The *real* people."

At the word *real* the Black Crone and the Black Girl strangled and began to bend and melt like a thin candle and a thicker one over a roaring fire.

Heinie turned his spaceship around and began to drive it bravely homeward through the unspeckled dark, following the ghostly white line that marked the center of the road. He thought of himself as the cat they'd had. Papa had told him stories of the cat coming back—from downtown, from Pittsburgh, from Los Angeles, from the moon. Cats could do that. He was the cat coming back.

Jane put down her brush and took up her pencil once more. She'd noticed that the two children swinging out farthest weren't attached yet to their swings. She started to hook them up, then hesitated. Wasn't it all right for some of the children to go sailing out to the stars? Wouldn't it be nice for some evening world—maybe the late-afternoon moon—to leave a shower of babies? She wished a plane would crawl over the roof of the house and drone out an answer to her question. She didn't like to have to do all the wondering by herself. It made her feel guilty.

"Gott," she said, "why don't you at least finish the last story you were writing? The one about the Elephants' Graveyard." Then she wished she hadn't mentioned it, because it was an idea that had scared Heinie.

"Some day," her husband murmured, Jane thought.

Gott felt weak with relief, though he was forgetting why. Balancing his head carefully over his book, he drained the next to the last of the martini water. It always got stronger toward the bottom. He looked at the page through the lower halves of his executive bifocals and for a moment the word "Caesar" came up in letters an inch high, each jet serif showing its tatters and the white paper its ridgy fibers. Then, still never moving his head, he looked through the upper halves and saw the long thick blob of dull black putty on the wavering blue couch and automatically gathered the putty together and with thumb-and-palm rays swiftly shaped the Old Philosopher in the Black Toga, always an easy figure to sculpt since he was never finished except rough-hewnly, in the style of Rodin or Daumier. It was always good to finish up an evening with the Old Philosopher.

The white line in space tried to fade. Heinie steered his ship closer to it. He remembered that in spite of Papa's stories the cat had never come back.

Jane held her pencil poised over the detached children swinging out from the Clubhouse. One of them had a leg kicked over the moon.

THE PHILOSOPHER (*adjusting his craggy toga and yawning*): The topic for tonight's symposium is that vast container of all, the Void.

GOTT (*condescendingly*): The Void? That's interesting. Lately I've wished to merge with it. Life wearies me.

A smiling dull black skull, as crudely shaped as the Philosopher, looked over the latter's shoulder and then rose higher on a rickety black bone framework.

DEATH (*quietly, to Gott*): Really?

GOTT (*greatly shaken, but keeping up a front*): I *am* on a black kick tonight. Can't even do a white skeleton. Disintegrate, you two. You bore me almost as much as life.

DEATH: Really? If you did not cling to life like a limpet you would have crashed your car, to give your wife and son the insurance, when National Motors fired you. You planned to do that. Remember?

GOTT (*with hysterical coolness*): Maybe I should have cast you in brass or aluminum. Then you'd at least have brightened things up. But it's too late now. Disintegrate quickly and don't leave any scraps around.

DEATH: Much too late. Yes, you planned to crash your car and doubly indemnify your dear ones. You had the spot picked, but your courage failed you.

GOTT (*blustering*): I'll have you know I am not only Gottfried but also Helmuth—Hell's Courage Adler!

THE PHILOSOPHER (*confused but trying to keep in the conversation*): A most swashbuckling sobriquet.

DEATH: Hell's courage failed you on the edge of the ravine. (*Pointing at Gott a three-fingered thumbless hand like a black winter branch*) Do you wish to die now?

GOTT (*blacking out visually*): Cowards die many times. (*Drain-*

ing the last of the martini water in absolute darkness) The valiant taste death once. Caesar.

DEATH (*a voice in darkness*): Coward. Yet you summoned me—and even though you fashioned me poorly, I am indeed Death—and there are others besides yourself who take long trips. Even longer ones. Trips in the Void.

THE PHILOSOPHER (*another voice*): Ah, yes, the Void. Imprimis—

DEATH: Silence.

In the great obedient silence Gott heard the unhurried click of Death's feet as he stepped from behind the sofa across the bare floor toward Heinie's spaceship. Gott reached up in the dark and clung to his mind.

Jane heard the slow clicks too. They were the kitchen clock ticking out, "Now. Now. Now. Now. Now."

Suddenly Heinie called out, "The line's gone. Papa, Mama, I'm lost."

Jane said sharply, "No, you're not, Heinie. Come out of space at once."

"I'm not in space now. I'm in the Cats' Graveyard."

Jane told herself it was insane to feel suddenly so frightened. "Come back from wherever you are, Heinie," she said calmly. "It's time for bed."

"I'm lost, Papa," Heinie cried. "I can't hear Mama anymore."

"Listen to your mother, Son," Gott said thickly, groping in the blackness for other words.

"All the Mamas and Papas in the world are dying," Heinie wailed.

Then the words came to Gott and when he spoke his voice flowed. "Are your atomic generators turning over, Heinie? Is your space-warp lever free?"

"Yes, Papa, but the line's gone."

"Forget it. I've got a fix on you through subspace and I'll coach you home. Swing her two units to the right and three up. Fire when I give the signal. Are you ready?"

"Yes, Papa."

"Roger. Three, two, one, fire and away! Dodge that comet! Swing left around that planet! Never mind the big dust cloud! Home on the third beacon. Now! Now! Now!"

Gott had dropped his Plutarch and come lurching blindly across the room and as he uttered the last *Now!* the darkness cleared and he caught Heinie up from his space-chair and staggered with him against Jane and steadied himself there without upsetting her paints and she accused him laughingly, "You beefed up the martini water again," and Heinie pulled off his helmet and crowed, "Make a big hug," and they clung to each other and looked down at the half-colored picture where a Children's Clubhouse sat in a tree over a deep Ravine and blob children swung out from it against the cool pearly moon and the winding roads in space and the next to the last child hooked onto his swing with one hand and with the other caught the last child of all, while from the picture's lower left-hand corner a fat black fly looked on enviously.

Searching with his eyes as the room swung toward equilibrium, Gottfried Helmuth Adler saw Death peering at him through the crack between the hinges of the open kitchen door.

Laboriously, half-passing out again, Gott sneered his face at him.

I can't think of much of an introduction to "Sun," except to repeat what I said at the Conference: that this is a story about clockwatching sickness, about the madness that hits at twenty to five every day for a lot of people. It's why all writers are writers, in one sense. Our minds break if we abuse them too long. Shoveling ashes, shit, or memos for years on end is of course prime abuse. Pitkow is the simpleton he is because I wanted to show how universal the syndrome is. Nobody's exempt.

SUN

Ohio Power's Gum River Plant sat in the scrub at the water's edge, three miles upstream from Mangston. There was a clump of coal barges tied to a crumbling concrete pier where a gang of black men fed the conveyor that carried it up the bank to the pulverizer.

Like all the other machinery here, the pulverizer was old—two corrugated sheet-metal towers sixty feet high, surrounded by chutes and scaffolds, braced by haphazard girders. Slabs of raw coal went in the top to come out powder at the bottom. Loud monotonous chewing noises came through the sides whenever it was operating. At the moment it was off.

A dozen yards away was a two-foot-wide concrete channel, which carried a slurry of fine ashes and water back down to the river. Between them the ground was covered with dusty gravel, a few dandelions, and a pile of rusted pump parts. In this sterile niche Pitkow had lived out most of his waking hours for the past two years.

Now he sat quietly by the ash flue. The gray stuff slid past with the silence of any dead substance. Overhead the pulverizer started and the sound blanketed him. It was good. He couldn't feel the dirt pour into his skin when the pulverizer went on. He could see it but he couldn't believe it; sweat rising from his bones, through his shirt to catch the ash dust, and sinking back into him with the dirt in it. My bones must be hungry, he thought. He played with the top of his thermos.

It slipped and dropped into the ash. Gone, out to the river. Some catfish would eat it if it wasn't too clean. Catfish would eat anything if it was dirty enough. Some people ate catfish too, poor ones. Marie used to, but he did better for her now. She said she loved him but he was sure it was because she didn't have to eat catfish. Funny though, catfish didn't taste so bad, it was just what they ate.

The pulverizer went off. Pitkow dipped the ash again and sent the kid up to the lab with the sample. He could hear now, with the crusher off. He moved his chair back into its shadow. All around the sun poured into the gravel. It was probably black sand once, but the sun popped it like corn into gravel, white gravel.

The river felt the sun too, and squirmed on top a little. It wrapped around the east side of the plant like a snake around some carcass it was eating. The sun and the river always fought, it seemed, like fire and water, white and black.

Clean and dirty thought Pitkow. He looked at his wrist. The watch had stopped again. The hairs on his forearm rose from tiny little black bumps. He had dirt clogged in every pore, and it was a wonder that hair grew at all. It should though, he thought. Black hair seemed like natural fruit for such dirt.

The kid came back. Boy, he said, what time you got? Only four. What the hell, only four. What could he do for another hour? The kid went to sleep in the sun. Your privilege, bastard, I won't tell and you know it. The kid was blond and the sun sank into him and stayed there.

No, he wouldn't tell. If he did the kid would talk and he'd

have to find another town. He remembered thinking the kid was all right. He talked about right and walked about right, and so one day out here Pitkow nudged him and asked. The boy looked scared and said no no not today and all that, and wanted to run. Pitkow was mad. Another miss and another guy to be careful about talking. The kid got back his nerve in a week or so and began his naps, daring Pitkow to turn him in.

Some little boys were fishing in a punt out on the river. Marie would wave to them, maybe call them over. He could almost hear her voice among the fragments drifting to him. Laughing? And what about?

The pulverizer went on and drowned them out. Sometimes he didn't like the sound of the crusher; but mostly, like now, he needed it.

It got hotter. He stood up and rubbed his ear. Marie would be sitting in the shade, working up enough ambition to come get him. He wished he was Marie. He wished he had himself to look after himself, like she did. He'd appreciate it. She didn't. Don't touch me, don't touch me. Aw for Christ sake Marie, come off it. You were dirtier than this our wedding night. No, no, she'd say, I'm clean now.

Sure you are. You reached up out of the river past your catfish ma and your catfish pa and grabbed my hook before it even hit the water. And pulled yourself out and me in, cause you were so dirty that the weight of it all had to have one or the other of us in, and of course it was me.

He looked over at the kid's watch. Still too early. The ashes slid, forever toward the river. His back began to itch. He was sitting in the sun because it had dropped in the sky and the shade had stretched away from him. Pitkow eyed the sun suspiciously. He moved his chair forward until it was again in the pulverizer's shadow.

Coal, now, was black. Black but clean. The sun made it out of some tree a million years ago so of course it was clean. God damn. It would be a lot nicer to run coal samples than ash samples. A lot nicer. He looked up at the scaffold over the chute. Maybe tomorrow he'd go up there for a while. Yes, sir. Tomorrow it would be coal sampling for him. Pitkow smiled.

But the shadow of the crusher moved away, and he had to get up again. Yes, the sun was definitely after him, just like it was after the river, trying to boil the dirt out. This time he retreated deep into the shade before putting down his chair.

The pulverizer went on and he couldn't think or feel again. It stayed on for a long time, preparing coal for the night shift. While it was going, the shadow moved off Pitkow again and stretched toward the east. The crusher stopped and he felt the sun. It was a lot to feel.

He cursed, grabbed his chair and chased the shadow; then sat down. If he went up on the walk tomorrow, of course, he'd be in the sun. Maybe he wouldn't go. Be all right in the morning but the sun got angry in the afternoon, like now. The shadow moved fast, he could see it. In the later afternoon it moved fast. Pitkow was getting scared. Marie would probably be late today too, and he'd have to wait in the sun.

He moved again, but the rays of the sun were driving the shade away from him. He got up and started walking to stay in the shadow. Now it began to wave, and taunt him, and to go faster.

He began to run. The kid yelled something. The goddamn shadow was getting away. He had to stay with it. He ran. The sweat welled out of him and floated his clothes off. He was naked and running. The shadow laughed and moved ahead.

It dropped into the river. Pitkow screamed and stopped. The veins in his eyes were black. He was alone in the sun at the edge of the river.

This was my first Milford Conference story. I cannot now recall much of what was said when it was discussed, except that Gordon Dickson pronounced it "doggone good"; Damon Knight passed it to the next participant with the flat comment, "I've already bounced this three times" (I like it better when he says, "I bought this"); Felix Severance (who is Keith Laumer's brother—writers are funny people) tore it to bits; and Joanna Russ liked it—the only woman who did. I remember much more vividly praising a story of Fritz Leiber's about Edgar Allan Poe and telling everyone that I had attended Poe Elementary School. (It seemed germane at the time.) I remember that my stomach was always out of whack at Milford that year (nerves), that it rained most of the time, and that I was wonderfully happy.

THE *HORARS* OF WAR

The three friends in the trench looked very much alike as they labored in the rain. Their hairless skulls were slickly naked to it, their torsos hairless too, and supple with smooth muscles that ran like oil under the wet gleam.

The two who really were, 2909 and 2911, did not mind the jungle around them although they detested the rain that rusted their weapons, and the snakes and insects, and hated the Enemy. But the one called 2910, the real as well as the official leader of the three, did; and that was because 2909 and 2911 had stainless steel bones; but there was no 2910 and there had never been.

The camp they held was a triangle. In the center the CP-Aid Station where Lieutenant Kyle and Mr. Brenner slept: a hut of ammo cases packed with dirt whose lower half was dug into the soggy earth. Around it were the mortar pit (NE), the recoilless rifle pit (NW), and Pinocchio's pit (S); and beyond these were the straight lines of the trenches: 1st Platoon, 2nd Platoon, 3rd Platoon (the platoon of the three). Outside of which were the primary wire and an antipersonnel mine field.

And outside that was the jungle. But not completely outside. The jungle set up outposts of its own of swift-sprouting bamboo and elephant grass, and its crawling creatures carried out untiring patrols of the trenches. The jungle sheltered the Enemy, taking him to its great, fetid breast to be fed while it sopped up the rain and of it bred its stinging gnats and centipedes.

An ogre beside him, 2911 drove his shovel into the ooze filling the trench, lifted it to shoulder height, dumped it; 2910 did the same thing in his turn, then watched the rain work on the scoop of mud until it was slowly running back into the trench again. Following his eyes 2911 looked at him and grinned. The HORAR's face was broad, hairless, flat-nosed, and high-cheeked; his teeth were pointed and white like a big dog's. And he, 2910, knew that that face was his own. Exactly his own. He told himself it was a dream, but he was very tired and could not get out.

Somewhere down the trench the bull voice of 2900 announced the evening meal and the others threw down their tools and jostled past toward the bowls of steaming mash, but the thought of food nauseated 2910 in his fatigue, and he stumbled into the bunker he shared with 2909 and 2911. Flat on his air mattress he could leave the nightmare for a time; return to the sane world of houses and sidewalks, or merely sink into the blessed nothingness that was far better . . .

Suddenly he was bolt upright on the cot, blackness still in his eyes even while his fingers groped with their own thought for his helmet and weapon. Bugles were blowing from the edge of the jungle, but he had time to run his hand under the inflated pad of the mattress and reassure himself that his hidden notes were safe before 2900 in the trench outside yelled, "Attack! Fall out! Man your firing points!"

It was one of the stock jokes, one of the jokes so stock, in fact, that it had ceased to be anything anyone laughed at, to say *Horar* your firing point (or whatever it was that according to the book should be *manned*). The HORARS in the squad he led used the expression to 2910 just as he used it with them, and when 2900 never employed it the omission had at first unsettled him. But 2900 did not really suspect. 2900 just took his rank seriously.

He got into position just as the mortars put up a parachute flare that hung over the camp like a white rose of fire. Whether because of his brief sleep or the excitement of the impending fight, his fatigue had evaporated, leaving him nervously alert but unsteady. From the jungle a bugle sang, "Ta-taa . . . taa-taa . . ." and off to the platoon's left rear the 1st opened up with their heavy weapons on a suicide squad they apparently thought they saw on the path leading to the northeast gate. He watched, and after half a minute something stood up on the path and grabbed for its midsection before it fell, so there *was* a suicide squad.

Some one, he told himself. *Someone.* Not *something.* Someone grabbed for *his* midsection. They were all human out there.

The 1st began letting go with personal weapons as well, each deep cough representing a half dozen dartlike fletchettes flying in an inescapable pattern three feet broad. "Eyes front, 2910!" barked 2900.

There was nothing to be seen out there but a few clumps of elephant grass. Then the white flare burned out. "They ought to put up another one," 2911 on his right said worriedly.

"A star in the east for men not born of women," said 2910 half to himself, and regretted the blasphemy immediately.

"That's where they need it," 2911 agreed, "the 1st is having it pretty hot over there. But we could use some light here too."

He was not listening. At home in Chicago, during that inexpressibly remote time which ran from a dim memory of playing on a lawn under the supervision of a smiling giantess to that moment two years ago when he had submitted to surgery to lose every body and facial hair he possessed and undergo certain other minor alterations, he had been unconsciously preparing himself for this. Lifting weights and playing football to develop his body while he whetted his mind on a thousand books; all so that he might tell, making others feel at a remove . . .

Another flare went up and there were three dark silhouettes sliding from the next-nearest clump of elephant grass to the nearest. He fired his M-19 at them, then heard the HORARS on either side of him fire too. From the sharp corner where their own platoon met the 2nd a machine gun opened up with tracer. The nearest grass clump sprang into the air and somersaulted amid spurts of earth.

There was a moment of quiet, then five rounds of high explosive came in right behind them as though aimed for Pinocchio's pit. *Crump. Crump. Crump . . . Crump. Crump.* (2900 would be running to ask Pinocchio if he were hurt.)

Someone else had been moving down the trench toward them, and he could hear the mumble of the new voice become a gasp when the H.E. rounds came in. Then it resumed, a little louder and consequently a bit more easily understood. "How are you? You feel all right? Hit?"

And most of the HORARS answering, "I'm fine, sir," or "We're okay, sir," but because HORARS did have a sense of humor some of them said things like, "How do we transfer to the Marines, sir?" or "My pulse just registered nine thou', sir. 3000 took it with the mortar sight."

We often think of strength as associated with humorlessness, he had written in the newsmagazine which had, with the Army's cooperation, planted him by subterfuge of surgery among these *Homolog ORganisms (Army Replacement Simulations). But,* he had continued, *this is not actually the case. Humor is a prime defense of the mind, and knowing that to strip the mind of it is to leave it shieldless, the Army and the Synthetic Biology Service have wisely included a charming dash in the makeup of these synthesized replacements for human infantry.*

That had been before he discovered that the Army and the SBS had tried mightily to weed out that sense of the ridiculous, but found that if the HORARS were to maintain the desired intelligence level they could not.

Brenner was behind him now, touching his shoulder. "How are you? Feel all right?"

He wanted to say, "I'm half as scared as you are, you dumb Dutchman," but he knew that if he did the fear would sound in his voice; besides, the disrespect would be unthinkable to a HORAR.

He also wanted to say simply, "A-okay, sir," because if he did Brenner would pass on to 2911 and he would be safe. But he had a reputation for originality to keep up, and he needed that reputation to cover him when he slipped, as he often did, sidewise of HORAR standards. He answered: "You ought to look in on Pinocchio, sir. I think he's cracking up." From the other end of the squad 2909's quiet chuckle rewarded him, and Brenner, the man most dangerous to his disguise, continued down the trench . . .

Fear was necessary because the will to survive was *very* necessary. And a humanoid form was needed if the HORARS were to utilize the mass of human equipment already on hand. Besides, a human-shaped (*homolog?* no, that merely meant *similar, homological*) HORAR had outscored all the fantastic forms SBS had been able to dream up in a superrealistic (public opinion would never have permitted it with human soldiers) test carried out in the Everglades.

(Were they merely duplicating? Had all this been worked out before with some greater war in mind? And had He Himself, the Scientist Himself, come to take the form of His creations to show that he too could bear the unendurable?)

2909 was at his elbow, whispering. "Do you see something, Squad Leader? Over there?" Dawn had come without his noticing.

With fingers clumsy from fatigue he switched the control of his M-19 to the lower—40-mm grenade launching—barrel. The grenade made a brief flash at the spot 2909 had indicated. "No," he said, "I don't see anything now." The fine, soft rain which had been falling all night was getting stronger. The dark clouds seemed to roof the world. (Was he fated to re-enact what had been done for mankind? It could happen. The Enemy took humans captive, but there was nothing they would not do to HORAR prisoners. Occasionally patrols found the bodies spread-eagled, with bamboo stakes driven through their limbs; and he could only be taken for a HORAR. He thought of a water color of the crucifixion he had seen once. Would the color of his own blood be crimson lake?)

From the CP the observation ornithocopter rose on flapping wings.

"I haven't heard one of the mines go for quite a while," 2909 said. Then there came the phony-sounding bang that so often during the past few weeks had closed similar probing attacks. Squares of paper were suddenly fluttering all over the camp.

"Propaganda shell," 2909 said unnecessarily, and 2911 climbed casually out of the trench to get a leaflet, then jumped back to his position. "Same as last week," he said, smoothing out the damp rice paper.

Looking over his shoulder 2910 saw that he was correct. For some reason the Enemy never directed his propaganda at the HORARS, although it was no secret that reading skills were implanted in HORAR minds with the rest of their instinctive training. Instead it was always aimed at the humans in the camp, and played heavily on the distaste they were supposed to feel at being "confined with half-living flesh still stinking of chemicals." Privately 2910 thought they might have done better, at least with Lieutenant Kyle, to have dropped that approach and played up sex. He also got the impression from the propaganda that the Enemy thought there were far more humans in the camp than there actually were.

Well, the Army—with far better opportunities to know—was wrong as well. With a few key generals excepted the Army thought there were only two . . .

He had made the All-American. How long ago it seemed. No coach, no sportswriter had ever compared his stocky, muscular physique to a HORAR's. And he had majored in journalism, had been ambitious. How many men, with a little surgical help, could have passed here?

"Think it sees anything?" he heard 2911 ask 2909. They were looking upward at the "bird" sailing overhead.

The ornithocopter could do everything a real bird could except lay eggs. It could literally land on a strand of wire. It could ride thermals like a vulture, and dive like a hawk. And the bird-motion of its wings was wonderfully efficient, saving power-plant weight that could be used for zoom lenses and telecameras. He wished he were in the CP watching the monitor screen with Lieutenant Kyle instead of standing with his face a scant foot above the mud. (They had tried stalked eyes like a crab's in the Everglades, he remembered, but the stalks had become infected by a fungus . . .)

As though in answer to his wish, 2900 called, "Show some snap for once, 2910. He says He wants us in the CP."

When he himself thought *He, He* meant God; but 2900 meant Lieutenant Kyle. That was why 2900 was a platoon leader, no doubt; that and the irrational prestige of a round number. He climbed out of the trench and followed him to the CP. They needed a communicating trench, but that was something there hadn't been time for yet.

Brenner had someone (2788? Looked like him, but he couldn't be certain) down on his table. Shrapnel, probably from a grenade. Brenner did not look up as they came in, but 2910 could see his face was still white with fear although the attack had been over for a full quarter of an hour. He and 2900 ignored the SBS man and saluted Lieutenant Kyle.

The company commander smiled. "Stand at ease, HORARS. Have any trouble in your sector?"

2900 said, "No, sir. The light machine gun got one group of three and 2910 here knocked off a group of two. Not much of an attack on our front, sir."

Lieutenant Kyle nodded. "I thought your platoon had the easiest time of it, 2900, and that's why I've picked you to run a patrol for me this morning."

"That's fine with us, sir."

"You'll have Pinocchio, and I thought you'd want to go yourself and take 2910's gang."

He glanced at 2910. "Your squad still at full strength?"

2910 said, "Yes, sir," making an effort to keep his face impassive. He wanted to say: I shouldn't have to go on patrol. I'm human as you are, Kyle, and patrolling is for things grown in tubes, things fleshed out around metal skeletons, things with no family and no childhood behind them.

Things like my friends.

He added, "We've been the luckiest squad in the company, sir."

"Fine. Let's hope your luck holds, 2910." Kyle's attention switched back to 2900. "I've gotten under the leaf canopy with the ornithocopter and done everything except make it walk around like a chicken. I can't find a thing and it's drawn no fire, so you ought to be okay. You'll make a complete circuit of the camp without getting out of range of mortar support. Understand?"

2900 and 2910 saluted, about-faced, and marched out. 2910 could feel the pulse in his neck; he flexed and unflexed his hands unobtrusively as he walked. 2900 asked, "Think we'll catch any of them?" It was an unbending for him—the easy comradery of anticipated action.

"I'd say so. I don't think the CO's had long enough with the bird to make certain of anything except that their main force has pulled out of range. I hope so."

And that's the truth, he thought. Because a good hot fire fight would probably do it—round the whole thing out so I can get out of here.

Every two weeks a helicopter brought supplies and, when they were needed, replacements. Each trip it also carried a correspondent whose supposed duty was to interview the commanders of the camps the copter visited. The reporter's name was Keith Thomas, and for the past two months he had been the only human being with whom 2910 could take off his mask.

Thomas carried scribbled pages from the notebook under 2910's air mattress when he left, and each time he came managed to find some corner in which they could speak in private for a few seconds. 2910 read his mail then and gave it back. It embarrassed him to realize that the older reporter viewed him with something not far removed from hero worship.

I can get out of here, he repeated to himself. Write it up and tell Keith we're ready to use the letter.

2900 ordered crisply, "Fall in your squad. I'll get Pinocchio and meet you at the south gate."

"Right." He was suddenly seized with a desire to tell someone, even 2900, about the letter. Keith Thomas had it, and it was really only an undated note, but it was signed by a famous general at Corps Headquarters. Without explanation it directed that number 2910 be detached from his present assignment and placed under the temporary orders of Mr. K. Thomas, Accredited Correspondent. And Keith would use it any time he asked him to. In fact, he had wanted to on his last trip.

He could not remember giving the order, but the squad was falling in, lining up in the rain for his inspection almost as smartly as they had on the drill field back at the creche. He gave *"At Ease"* and looked them over while he outlined the objectives of the patrol. As always their weapons were immaculate despite the dampness, their massive bodies ramrod straight, their uniforms as clean as conditions permitted.

The L.A. Rams with guns, he thought proudly. Barking "On Phones," he flipped the switch on his helmet that would permit 2900 to knit him and the squad together with Pinocchio in a unified tactical unit. Another order and the HORARS deployed around Pinocchio with the smoothness of repeated drill, the wire closing the south gate was drawn back, and the patrol moved out.

With his turret retracted Pinocchio the robot tank stood just three feet high, and he was no wider than an automobile; but he was as long as three, so that from a distance he had something of the look of a railroad flatcar. In the jungle his narrow front enabled him to slip between the trunks of the unconquerable giant hardwoods, and the power in his treads could flatten saplings and bamboo. Yet resilient organics and sintered metals had turned the rumble of the old, manned tanks to a soft hiss for Pinocchio. Where the jungle was free of undergrowth he moved as silently as a hospital cart.

His immediate precursor had been named Punch, apparently in the sort of simpering deprecation which found "Shillelagh" acceptable for a war rocket. "Punch"—a bust in the mouth.

But Punch, which like Pinocchio had possessed a computer brain and no need of a crew (or for that matter room for one except for an exposed vestigial seat on his deck), had required wires to communicate with the infantry around him. Radio had been tried, but the problems posed by static, jamming, and outright enemy forgery of instructions had been too much for Punch.

Then an improved model had done away with these wires and some imaginative officer had remembered that "Mr. Punch" had been a knockabout marionette—and the wireless improvement was suddenly very easy to name. But, like Punch and its fairy-tale namesake, it was vulnerable if it went out into the world alone.

A brave man (and the Enemy had many) could hide himself until Pinocchio was within touching distance. And a well-instructed one could then place a hand grenade or a bottle of gasoline where it would destroy him. Pinocchio's three-inch-thick armor needed the protection of flesh, and since he cost as much as a small city and could (if properly protected) fight a regiment to a stand he got it.

Two scouts from 2910's squad preceded him through the jungle, forming the point of the diamond. Flankers moved on either side of him "beating the bush" and when it seemed advisable firing a pattern of fletchettes into any suspicious-looking piece of undergrowth. Cheerful, reliable 2909, the assistant squad leader, with one other HORAR formed the rear guard, as patrol leader 2900's position was behind Pinocchio, and as squad leader 2910's was in front.

The jungle was quiet with an eerie stillness, and it was dark under the big trees. "Though I walk through the valley of the shadow . . ."

Made tiny by the phones, 2900 squeaked in his ear, "Keep the left flankers farther out!" 2910 acknowledged and trotted over to put his own stamp on the correction, although the flankers, 2913, 2914, and 2915, had already heard it and were moving to obey. There was almost no chance of trouble this soon, but that was no excuse for a slovenly formation. As he squeezed between two trees something caught his eye and he halted for a moment to examine it. It was a skull; a skull of bone rather than a smooth HORAR skull of steel, and so probably an Enemy's.

A big "E" Enemy's, he thought to himself. A man to whom the normal HORAR conditioning of exaggerated respect bordering on worship did not apply.

Tiny and tinny, "Something holding you up, 2910?"

"Be right there." He tossed the skull aside. A man whom even a HORAR could disobey; a man even a HORAR could kill. The skull had looked old but it could not have been old. The ants would have picked it clean in a few days, and in a few weeks it would rot. But it was probably at least seventeen or eighteen years old.

The ornithocopter passed them on flapping wings, flying its own search pattern. The patrol went on.

Casually 2910 asked his helmet mike, "How far are we going? Far as the creek?"

2900's voice squeaked, "We'll work our way down the bank

a quarter mile, then cut west," then with noticeable sarcasm added, "if that's okay with you?"

Unexpectedly Lieutenant Kyle's voice came over the phones. "2910's your second in command, 2900. He had a duty to keep himself informed of your plans."

But 2910, realizing that a real HORAR would not have asked the question, suddenly also realized that he knew more about HORARS than the company commander did. It was not surprising, he ate and slept with them in a way Kyle could not, but it was disquieting. He probably knew more than Brenner, strict biological mechanics excepted, as well.

The scouts had reported that they could see the sluggish jungle stream they called the creek when Lieutenant Kyle's voice came over the phones again. As routinely as he had delivered his mild rebuke to 2900 he announced, "Situation Red here. An apparent battalion-level attack hitting the North Point. Let's suck it back in, patrol."

Pinocchio swiveled 180 degrees by locking his right tread, and the squad turned in a clockwise circle around him. Kyle said distantly, "The recoilesses don't seem to have found the range yet, so I'm going out to give them a hand. Mr. Brenner will be holding down the radio for the next few minutes."

2900 transmitted, "We're on our way, sir."

Then 2910 saw a burst of automatic weapons fire cut his scouts down. In an instant the jungle was a pandemonium of sound.

Pinocchio's radar had traced the bullets back to their source and his main armament slammed a 155-mm shell at it, but cross fire was suddenly slicing in from all around them. The bullets striking Pinocchio's turret screamed away like damned souls. 2910 saw grenades arc out of nowhere and something struck his thigh with terrible force. He made himself say, "I'm hit, 2909; take the squad," before he looked at it. Mortar shells were dropping in now and if his assistant acknowledged he did not hear.

A bit of jagged metal from a grenade or a mortar round had

laid the thigh open, but apparently missed the big artery supplying the lower leg. There was no spurt, only a rapid welling of blood, and shock still held the injury numb. Forcing himself, he pulled apart the lips of the wound to make sure it was clear of foreign matter. It was very deep but the bone was not broken; at least so it seemed.

Keeping as low as he could he used his trench knife to cut away the cloth of his trousers leg, then rigged a tourniquet with his belt. His aid packet contained a pad of gauze, and tape to hold it in place. When he had finished he lay still, holding his M-19 and looking for a spot where its fire might do some good. Pinocchio was firing his turret machine gun in routine bursts, sanitizing likely looking patches of jungle, otherwise the fight seemed to have quieted down.

2900's voice in his ear called, "Wounded? We got any wounded?"

He managed to say, "Me. 2910." A HORAR would feel some pain, but not nearly as much as a man. He would have to fake the insensitivity as best he could. Suddenly it occurred to him that he would be invalided out, would not have to use the letter, and he was glad.

"We thought you bought it, 2910. Glad you're still around."

Then Brenner's voice cutting through the transmission jumpy with panic: "We're being overrun here! Get the Pinocchio back at once."

In spite of his pain 2910 felt contempt. Only Brenner would say, "*the* Pinocchio." 2900 sent, "Coming, sir," and unexpectedly was standing over him, lifting him up.

He tried to look around for the squad. "We lose many?"

"Four dead and you." Perhaps no other human would have detected the pain in 2900's harsh voice. "You can't walk with that, can you?"

"I couldn't keep up."

"You ride Pinocchio then." With surprising gentleness the platoon leader lifted him into the little seat the robot tank's director used when road speeds made running impractical. What was left of the squad formed a skirmish line ahead. As they began to trot forward he could hear 2900 calling, "Base camp! Base camp! What's your situation there, sir?"

"Lieutenant Kyle's dead," Brenner's voice came back. "3003 just came in and told me Kyle's dead!"

"Are you holding?"

"I don't know." More faintly 2910 could hear him asking, "Are they holding, 3003?"

"Use the periscope, sir. Or if it still works, the bird."

Brenner chattered, "I don't know if we're holding or not. 3003 was hit and now he's dead. I don't think he knew anyway. You've got to hurry."

It was contrary to regulations, but 2910 flipped off his helmet phone to avoid hearing 2900's patient reply. With Brenner no longer gibbering in his ears he could hear not too distantly the sound of explosions which must be coming from the camp. Small arms fire made an almost incessant buzz as a background for the whizz—bang! of incoming shells and the coughing of the camp's own mortars.

Then the jungle was past and the camp lay in front of them. Geysers of mud seemed to be erupting from it everywhere. The squad broke into a full run, and even while he rolled Pinocchio was firing his 155 in support of the camp.

They faked us out, 2910 reflected. His leg throbbed painfully but distantly and he felt lightheaded and dizzy—as though he were an ornithocopter hovering in the misty rain over his own body. With the lightheadedness came a strange clarity of mind.

They faked us out. They got us used to little probes that pulled off at sunrise, and then when we sent Pinocchio out they were going to ambush us and take the camp. It suddenly occurred to him that he might find himself still on this exposed seat in the middle of the battle; they were already approaching the edge of the mine field, and the HORARS ahead were moving into squad column so as not to overlap the edges of the cleared lane. "Where are we going, Pinocchio?" he asked, then realized his phone was still off. He reactivated it and repeated the question.

Pinocchio droned, "Injured HORAR personnel will be delivered to the Command Post for Synthetic Biology Service attention," but 2910 was no longer listening. In front of them he could hear what sounded like fifty bugles signaling another Enemy attack.

The south side of the triangular camp was deserted, as though the remainder of their platoon had been called away to reinforce the 1st and 2nd; but with the sweeping illogic of war there was no Enemy where they might have entered unresisted.

"Request assistance from Synthetic Biology Service for injured HORAR personnel," Pinocchio was saying. Talking did not interfere with his firing the 155, but when Brenner did not come out after a minute or more 2910 managed to swing himself down, catching his weight on his good leg. Pinocchio rolled away at once.

The CP bunker was twisted out of shape, and he could see where several near misses had come close to knocking it out completely. Brenner's white face appeared in the doorway as he was about to go in. "Who's that?"

"2910. I've been hit—let me come in and lie down."

"They won't send us an air strike. I radioed for one and they say this whole part of the country's socked in; they say they wouldn't be able to find us."

"Get out of the door. I'm hit and I want to come in and lie down." At the last moment he remembered to add, "Sir."

Brenner moved reluctantly aside. It was dim in the bunker but not dark.

"You want me to look at that leg?"

2910 had found an empty stretcher, and he laid himself on it, moving awkwardly to keep from flexing his wound. "You don't have to," he said. "Look after some of the others." It wouldn't do for Brenner to begin poking around. Even rattled as he was he might notice something.

The SBS man went back to his radio instead. His frantic voice sounded remote and faint. It was ecstasy to lie down.

At some vast distance voices were succeeding voices, argument meeting argument, far off. He wondered where he was.

Then he heard the guns and knew. He tried to roll onto his

side and at the second attempt managed to do it, although the lightheadedness was worse than ever. 2893 was lying on the stretcher next to him, and 2893 was dead.

At the other end of the room, the end that was technically the CP, he could hear Brenner talking to 2900. "If there were a chance," Brenner was saying, "you know I'd do it, Platoon Leader."

"What's happening?" he asked. "What's the matter?" He was too dazed to keep up the HORAR role well, but neither of them noticed.

"It's a division," Brenner said. "A whole Enemy division. We can't hold off that kind of force."

He raised himself on his elbow. "What do you mean?"

"I talked to them . . . I raised them on the radio, and it's a whole division. They got one of their officers who could speak English to talk to me. They want us to surrender."

"*They* say it's a division, sir," 2900 put in evenly.

2910 shook his head, trying to clear it. "Even if it were, with Pinocchio . . ."

"The Pinocchio's gone."

2900 said soberly, "We tried to counterattack, 2910, and they knocked Pinocchio out and threw us back. How are you feeling?"

"They've got at least a division," Brenner repeated stubbornly.

2910's mind was racing now, but it was as though it were running endless wind sprints on a treadmill. If Brenner were going to give up, 2900 would never even consider disobeying no matter how much he might disagree. There were various ways, though, in which he could convince Brenner he was a human being—given time. And Brenner could, Brenner would, tell the Enemy, so that he too would be saved. Eventually the war would be over and he could go home. No one would blame him. If Brenner were going—

Brenner was asking, "How many effectives left?"

"Less than forty, sir." There was nothing in 2900's tone to indicate that a surrender meant certain death to him, but it was true. The Enemy took only human prisoners. (Could 2900 be convinced? Could he make any of the HORARS understand, when they had eaten and joked with him, knew no physiology, and thought all men not Enemy demigods? Would they believe him if he were to try to take command?)

He could see Brenner gnawing at his lower lip. "I'm going to surrender," the SBS man said at last. A big one, mortar or bombardment rocket, exploded near the CP, but he appeared not to notice it. There was a wondering, hesitant note in his voice—as though he were still trying to accustom himself to the idea.

"Sir—" 2900 began.

"I forbid you to question my orders." The SBS man sounded firmer now. "But I'll ask them to make an exception this time, Platoon Leader. Not to do," his voice faltered slightly, "what they usually do to nonhumans."

"It's not that," 2900 said stolidly. "It's the folding up. We don't mind dying, sir, but we want to die fighting."

One of the wounded moaned, and 2910 wondered for a moment if he, like himself, had been listening.

Brenner's self-control snapped. "You'll die any damn way I tell you!"

"Wait." It was suddenly difficult for 2910 to talk, but he managed to get their attention. "2900, Mr. Brenner hasn't actually ordered you to surrender yet, and you're needed on the line. Go now and let me talk to him." He saw the HORAR leader hesitate and added, "He can reach you on your helmet phone if he wants to; but go now and fight."

With a jerky motion 2900 turned and ducked out the narrow bunker door. Brenner, taken by surprise, said, "What is it, 2910? What's gotten into you?"

He tried to rise, but he was too weak. "Come here, Mr. Brenner," he said. When the SBS man did not move he added, "I know a way out."

"Through the jungle?" Brenner scoffed in his shaken voice. "That's absurd." But he came. He leaned over the stretcher, and before he could catch his balance 2910 had pulled him down.

"What are you doing?"

"Can't you tell? That's the point of my trench knife you feel on your neck."

Brenner tried to struggle, then subsided when the pressure of the knife became too great. "You—can't—do this."

"I can. Because I'm not a HORAR. I'm a man, Brenner, and it's very important for you to understand that." He felt rather than saw the look of incredulity on Brenner's face. "I'm a reporter, and two years ago when the Simulations in this group were ready for activation I was planted among them. I trained with them and now I've fought with them, and if you've been reading the right magazine you must have seen some of the stories I've filed. And since you're a civilian too, with no more right to command than I have, I'm taking charge." He could sense Brenner's swallow.

"Those stories were frauds—it's a trick to gain public acceptance of the HORARS. Even back in Washington everybody in SBS knows about them."

The chuckle hurt, but 2910 chuckled. "Then why've I got this knife at your neck, Mr. Brenner?"

The SBS man was shaking. "Don't you see how it was, 2910? No human could live as a HORAR does, running miles without tiring and only sleeping a couple of hours a night, so we did the next best thing. Believe me, I was briefed on it all when I was assigned to this camp; I know all about you, 2910."

"What do you mean?"

"Damn it, let me go. You're a HORAR, and you can't treat a human like this." He winced as the knife pressed cruelly against his throat, then blurted, "They couldn't make a reporter a HORAR, so they *took* a HORAR. They took you, 2910, and made you a reporter. They implanted all the memories of an actual man in your mind at the same time they ran the regular instinct tapes. They gave you a soul, if you like, but you are a HORAR."

"They must have thought that up as a cover for me, Brenner. That's what they told you so you wouldn't report it or try to deactivate me when I acted unlike the others. I'm a man."

"You couldn't be."

"People are tougher than you think, Brenner; you've never tried."

"I'm telling you—"

"Take the bandages off my leg."

"What?"

He pressed again with the point of the knife. "The bandage. Take it off."

When it was off he directed, "Now spread the lips of the wound." With shaking fingers Brenner did so. "You see the bone? Go deeper if you have to. What is it?"

Brenner twisted his neck to look at him directly, his eyes rolling. "It's stainless steel."

2910 looked then and saw the bright metal at the bottom of the cleft of bleeding flesh; the knife slid into Brenner's throat without resistance, almost as though it moved itself. He wiped the blade on Brenner's dead arm before he sheathed it.

Ten minutes later when 2900 returned to the CP he said nothing; but 2910 saw his eyes and knew that 2900 knew. From his stretcher he said, "You're in full command now."

2900 glanced again at Brenner's body. A second later he said slowly, "He was a sort of Enemy, wasn't he? Because he wanted to surrender, and Lieutenant Kyle would never have done that."

"Yes, he was."

"But I couldn't think of it that way while he was alive." 2900 looked at him thoughtfully. "You know, you have something, 2910. A spark. Something the rest of us lack." For a moment he fingered his chin with one huge hand. "That's why I made you a squad leader; that and to get you out of some work, because sometimes you couldn't seem to keep up. But you've that spark, somehow."

2910 said, "I know. How is it out there?"

"We're still holding. How do you feel?"

"Dizzy. There's a sort of black stuff all around the sides when I see. Listen, will you tell me something, if you can, before you go?"

"Of course."

"If a human's leg is broken very badly, what I believe they call a compound spiral fracture, is it possible for the human doctors to take out a section of the bone and replace it with a metal substitute?"

"I don't know," 2900 answered. "What does it matter?"

Vaguely 2910 said, "I think I knew of a football player once they did that to. At least, I seem now to remember it . . . I had forgotten for a moment."

Outside the bugles were blowing again.

Near him the dying HORAR moaned.

An American newsmagazine sometimes carries, just inside its front cover among the advertisements, a column devoted to news of its own people. Two weeks after a correspondent named Thomas filed the last article of a series which had attracted national and even international attention the following item appeared there:

> The death of a staffer in war is no unique occurrence in the history of this publication, but there is a particular poignancy about that of the young man whose stories, paradoxically, to conceal his number have been signed only with his name (*see* PRESS). The airborne relief force, which arrived too late to save the camp at which he had resigned his humanity to work and fight, reports that he apparently died assisting the assigned SBS specialist in caring for the creatures whose lot he had, as nearly as a human can, made his own. Both he and the specialist were bayoneted when the camp was overrun.

I attended my first Milford Conference in 1962, about six months after selling my first story, and I found myself surrounded by writers like Fritz Leiber, Gordon Dickson, Judith Merril, Damon Knight. The mood of the Conference was easy and friendly: we gathered by the river mornings and evenings for swimming, we usually went out to dinner in groups, and we partied late into the night all week long.

It's surprising how a person can wander into the midst of giants and, just because they treat him nicely, can shortly forget the disparity in stature. It was like that in 1962, and I found myself holding forth dogmatically in bull sessions just as though these people were only average human beings. But in the afternoons, when the workshops were held, we got down to business and I remembered that I was just an untested newcomer.

"Hop-Friend" was the story I put up for comment; it was about my fourth sale, and the one I was most happy with. I wanted to find out if the story communicated as well as I hoped it did, but the first reaction I got, shortly before the workshop where the whole Conference would discuss it, was pretty discouraging. Judy Merril told me that morning, "I see what you were trying to do with that, but I'm afraid it doesn't work. I'll go into that more at the workshop."

So I walked into the session that afternoon with much foreboding. People drifted into the room, conversations were held in quiet tones, chairs scraped as we took our places . . . people seemed to be avoiding my eyes. Oh boy.

Then the comments began. One person liked it, felt it was interesting and evocative and so forth. A second writer demurred: the Martian was a good character, but what did it all mean, after all? Someone else rose to defend the story and to explain what the ending meant. Another agreed that the story was good, but gave a different interpretation of it. Still another person emphatically disagreed, and she gave a further explanation. Then everyone started talking at once, arguing, agreeing, explaining, disagreeing, exclaiming; I sat there with a bewildered smile frozen across my face.

It must have gone on for half an hour or more, and really, most everyone had about the same reaction to the story but they just expressed it in different terms. That's not unusual, but what was odd was how strongly everyone seemed to feel about his own reaction, as though the story had spoken directly to him.

Judy Merril, as it happened, was the last to comment. She said, "You know, I really didn't think this story had much to offer, but after sitting here and listening to everyone argue about it I guess I was wrong. Nobody gets that involved in a bad story."

Since then I've had a lot of nice reactions to "Hop-Friend." One woman said she'd dreamed about my Marshie for a week; Theodore Sturgeon claimed it was one of the best science fiction stories he'd ever read; and, inevitably, half a dozen years later I was being told that my latest story was okay, "but not up to 'Hop-Friend.'"

The tumult and the shouting at Milford in 1962 is still my favorite reaction, though.

(One more thing I'd like to say about this story, just for the record: Though "Hop-Friend" was written quite a few years before the Mariner fly-by that sent back pictures of an airless and desolate Mars, the somewhat more hospitable planet I described was a matter of choice, not ignorance. I could give you several fine-sounding literary rationales for it, but I suppose the fact is that I was disappointed at having come along too late to write about the Mars of Burroughs, Brackett, and Bradbury. So . . . well, I wrote about that Mars anyway. I don't think NASA will sue.)

HOP-FRIEND

On the tenth day of the construction job out on the edge of Syrtis Major they found a Marshie watching them. He might have been there ever since they'd trucked in their equipment and thrown up a bubble and temporary toilets, but they never did find out.

The Marshies flicked in and out of sight so rapidly that you had to be looking right where they appeared to see them at all, most of the time. They hopped around like fireflies, stopping for two seconds or two minutes, standing almost still with their angular birdlike heads cocked to one side, and then they'd be gone, turning up almost instantly fifteen feet away, still with their heads cocked looking at you. They were unnerving to most of the Earthmen, and a couple of years back one nervous kid in Iguana, near the Bald Spot, had taken a shot at one of them—missed him and burned hell out of one wall of a building. The Marshies hadn't been around the Earth towns much since then.

Not that they had ever been especially chummy. The Marshies were partially telepathic and they could manage the Earth languages well enough, but they seldom bothered. For the most part they just didn't seem interested. Every now and then you'd see one of them pause for a minute in the settlements, and maybe he'd say, "Hi, Harry," or "Nice weather this year," but they never stopped to talk about anything. The Earthmen had been on the planet for over ten years, but all the government could tell you about the Marshies was that they had some towns out in the mountains somewhere, they were trisexual, and their lifespan was about thirty years.

Walt Michelson had been wondering about them ever since he'd landed on the planet back with the first wave, when he'd come with his parents. Michelson had been twelve then, busy looking around and asking questions every time his eyes lit on something. When he was fourteen he saw a Marshie—one of them landed right next to him at his brother's funeral and stood completely still for almost ten minutes while the service droned on. It had been out on the flatlands, where the heavy brown dust was sometimes two inches deep and you had to raise your voice to be heard in the thin air. The Marshie had watched the interment rites silently, standing off to one side, and when it had all been over he had looked at Michelson and said "Yes," and disappeared.

Michelson's father had been a building contractor . . . a pretty good one, successful enough that he could have sent Walt back to

Earth by the time he was eighteen. But Walt hadn't wanted to go; all he remembered of Earth was how crowded it was, how many policemen there were, how many laws and taxes and taboos built up over the centuries. When he'd been on Earth his father hadn't had much money, and that colored his feelings toward the home planet too, but basically he liked Mars because there was *room* here . . . no walls, real or legislated, to keep a man standing still. So he'd stayed on Mars, and learned the building trades, and he was a foreman this year and would be more next year. He didn't give a damn about Earth.

Now he was working on building a town out here at the base of the hills, on a site which somebody had decided would be an important trade outpost. Some of the drainage from the icecap reached this area, too, so there might be some chance for agriculture. The city had been planned in detail back at Dry Puget, but nobody had thought that there were any Marshies in the area.

They'd noticed him first by the puffs of dust rising in a line leading from the foothills straight to the building site. The Marshies traveled in a peculiar half-leaping half-flying fashion, and when they touched down and jumped off again they kicked up small clouds of dust. One of the workmen saw those clouds coming toward them and reported to Michelson, who got his binocs and watched the Marshie coming. He wasn't long in arriving.

He lit right outside the bubble and stood looking for a minute, then disappeared and skipped right in through one of the airlocks where they were removing the dirt from the diggings inside. He turned up next to the big shovel for a few seconds, disappeared when one of the men suddenly yelled, reappeared over by the lumber yard next to the foundation work going on in the south quarter, then outside the truck depot, and finally at the door of the contractor's office where Michelson had been going over the drawings for the street layout. Michelson looked up at him and the Marshie cocked his head and stared back.

The Marshie was a faded orange in color, his body covered

with a heavy fur through which the powerful muscles showed clearly. His eyes, large and liquid black, were set on the sides of his head, and his nose and mouth were almost indistinguishable under the fur of the face. He had long legs, thin but powerful, giving him a stature of over seven feet; his large brown wings folded down over his back softly like a cloak. He was indistinguishable from any other Marshie that Michelson had ever seen, but that was undoubtedly because the Marshies were so seldom around.

As the Marshie continued to stand silently looking at him Michelson was struck with the humor of the tableau, and he grinned and nodded. "Welcome to our humble diggings," he said.

The Marshie disappeared, leaving two deep footprints in the dirt outside the door where he had kicked off. Michelson got up and went to the door, saw the alien light a couple of times going across the large inner yard, and then he apparently hopped out through the airlocks again. Michelson raised his binocs from the strap around his neck, but he was unable to track the Marshies' dust-clouds in their erratic jumps out on the flat. They seemed to head toward the hills again but he couldn't be sure.

Michelson shrugged and turned back to the plans on the desk. The Marshie was no immediate problem to him; if he continued to show up there might be trouble among the construction workers —the Marshies appeared and disappeared so abruptly that they could upset a whole crew in a few hours—but for the moment Michelson wasn't going to worry about it. He had a more pressing problem.

One of the field men had found that the northeast quarter was right over a large water-deposit and it would require some pretty drastic structural modifications or maybe even abandoning that part of the site altogether. There was bedrock not too far down, and the yearly icecap drainage collected there; the water wasn't enough to be useful as a supply for the planned city, but the pocket was large enough to undermine any foundations they might try to put in there.

He'd already checked the specifications and found that any

pumping system they could install to periodically drain the pocket would be in a cost bracket making it necessary to get an okay from the builder clear back in Dry Puget . . . and that could hold up the work long enough to make them miss their deadline. No, there had to be some way to block the seepage before the water got to the pocket, so that it could be drained once and for all.

Dammit, it was just his luck to run into trouble with water on Mars, where that was the last thing you expected. Well, tomorrow he'd get together with a couple of the surveyors and see what could be done.

The Marshie was back the next day, shortly after the sun rose darkly over the low hills. There was so little light at that early hour that no one saw him coming and the first thing they knew of his presence was when he landed for a moment in an airlock and a driver slammed on his brakes to avoid hitting him—which wasn't really necessary, since the Marshie had jumped off again immediately, but a human driver's muscular reactions weren't geared for Marshie pedestrians. The Marshie skipped on in through the interconnecting locks.

He came down beside Michelson as he was going across the yard toward the diggings, and Michelson stopped. He turned and cocked his head at the alien, mocking his stance, and after a moment said, "I'll give you a gate pass if you want."

The Marshie regarded him with his big dark left eye and shook his wings lightly. "Hello, Walt," he said, and skipped off. Michelson shrugged and went on across the yard, but the Marshie came back a minute later, touched down and said, "They aren't so humble," and disappeared again.

Mike Deckinger, who was in charge of the trucks, was nearby and he came over frowning. "He's going to drive us nuts if he keeps that up," he said. "We could tighten up the airlock sequence and maybe keep him out that way."

Michelson shook his head. "That would just slow down the works. Leave him alone; he's just looking."

"Yeah, but why?" said Deckinger, and walked off.

Harris and Loening, the two surveyors, were waiting for Michelson at the diggings. They were good men, both in their thirties and well-trained both on Earth and this planet. Harris was heavyset, with a ruddy, swarthy face and close-cropped black hair; Loening was taller, broad-shouldered, with bony, angular features and dark eyes that seemed to peer out from shadowed caves. Michelson explained the problem to them.

"I want to go outside and see if we can trace the drainage," he concluded. "Find a place where we can dam or rechannel it."

"That'll involve drilling," Loening said.

Michelson raised an eyebrow at him. "Probably. Unless you want to try a dowsing rod." Loening grunted disgustedly.

"Well, let's take a walk out there first anyway," Harris said. They started back across the yard toward the north airlocks. Since they might be out for some time they each donned facemasks and picked up small tanks of oxygen before they checked through.

The Marshie hopped through ahead of them.

He passed them in the second lock and was waiting for them when they emerged onto the flat outside. He stood off about twenty feet, ruffling his wings in a way which seemed impatient to Michelson, and skipped back and forth past them as they set off toward the low hills, following the line of the water as closely as it had been traced in the preliminary survey. Loening walked stolidly, his head down and frowning, but Harris didn't seem to pay any attention to the alien. Michelson watched for him as he walked, and thought.

This hop-guy seemed a lot more interested in the construction works than the Marshies had ever been before. What was that he had said back in the compound? "They aren't so humble." What did that mean?

He'd come in from the hills, and the Marshies were supposed to live somewhere in a mountainous area. This one, maybe? Perhaps the Marshies were taking a definite interest in this site because the Earthmen had finally started getting near their own area.

And if so, just what kind of an interest were they taking?

The water had been traced back to the foot of the hills, but no further. On foot in the low Martian gravity the Earthmen made it that far in about half an hour. There was a thin, cold wind out here which cut through their heavy jackets and ruffled Michelson's light hair, but it didn't stir the dust very much. The air on Mars lacked body; once you got used to it you could breathe it well enough if you didn't exert yourself, but if you wanted to smoke a pipe you had to do it when you were inside a bubble or it would go out every time.

They stopped and rested at the base of the first hill, where dry rocks had tumbled down the slope during the ages and collected at the bottom. Loening loosened his pack and swung it off his shoulder to the ground. He nodded up at the rising hills and said, "The first thing to do is scout around there and chart the rock stratifications."

"Do you think the drainage comes through the mountains?" Michelson asked him.

"Might; can't tell offhand. We've been walking on solid rock for a mile or more—that means the water is under rock for a ways out there, and the channel could turn off anywhere. Maybe it skirts the hills; that's one thing I want to check. If the stratifications here show that these hills rose during an upheaval, the chances are that the water channel does go around them."

Michelson nodded. "Well, we can get the preliminary scouting done faster if we split up. I'll try going through the pass up there."

Loening and Harris rose with him, and they set off separately. As Michelson started up the slope he heard Harris call to him, "If you see our Marshie again, ask him where the hell the water comes from."

Michelson grinned back down at him. "I think I will," he said.

He climbed slowly up the rough slope, now and then cutting in his oxygen supply for a few breaths. The rocks here were bulky and weathered—the kind of weathering that happened, on Mars, only with the passage of ages. They stood out like silent gray beasts against the morning shadows. Michelson was soon out of sight of their starting-point, but he followed the natural pass and made a rough map as he went, noting the rock formations and what he could see of the stratifications. It was all a jumble, as far as he could tell; some of the sheer rocksides seemed to show evidence of having been pushed up as Loening had suggested and others didn't. And the direction of the stratifications varied apparently without pattern. Well, figuring out the pattern would be the surveyors' job.

At a small level spot he stopped to rest, and as he sat looking over his rough-sketched map he heard a sound and the Marshie said beside him, "Most of these hills have been here for two million years."

Michelson looked up, carefully registering no outward surprise. "Whose years?" he said. "Yours or mine?"

The Marshie shook his wings and hopped a little way to one side, still regarding him with one dark eye. "We do not count years."

Michelson nodded at him. "Do you have names?"

"No," said the Marshie, and disappeared. Michelson waited for him to show up again, but after a few minutes he shrugged and stood up to go. It looked like there was still a lot of area to be covered up here.

The Marshie landed again. "I am faster than you," he said.

"That's true," Michelson said. He started walking on upward through the rocks. "Do you live near here?"

"Perhaps," said the Marshie. "I am faster than you."

"Near" could mean fifty miles to a Marshie, Michelson reflected. Well, it had been a fair answer then.

"Where does the water come from?" he said.

The Marshie disappeared.

He didn't show up again for the rest of the day. Michelson followed the pass up into the hills for a mile or two, and then he retraced his steps back down to the point of departure. Loening was waiting for him, and Harris returned shortly. They set off again back across the dusty flat to the bubble.

"It's a mess," Loening said. "The rocks vary in age from maybe a couple thousand years to God knows how old, and there are fifty different types. It doesn't tell us much." He ran his fingers through his dry brown hair, frowning.

"Our hop-friend told me they were mostly a couple of million years old," Michelson said. "At least in the area where I was."

"Yeah?" said Harris. "Did he say anything else?"

Michelson shook his head. "I asked him about the water, but he wouldn't answer me; he just shoved off and disappeared. You can't hold a conversation with someone who's liable to be gone at any moment. You get to stuttering."

"I never talked with a Marshie," Harris said. "They're telepathic, aren't they?—maybe they take one look into me and don't like me."

"Don't try to understand them," Loening said over his shoulder as he walked on ahead through the dust. "The only good thing about the damn Marshies is that they stay away from us most of the time."

"I don't know about that," said Michelson, and the three men fell silent, conserving their breath for walking.

But Michelson was thinking about the Marshie. Harris was right—they didn't usually talk with Earthmen. They would hop around and watch interestedly, and sometimes they would say a word or two, usually only enough to acknowledge your existence, but there was no communication between the two species. Yet this one was, comparatively, talking a blue streak. Why?

Michelson was becoming more and more sure that the Marshies had a settlement somewhere nearby. Back in the hills, probably— and Michelson was almost willing to bet that the water drainage ran right through those hills. It figured that the Marshies would settle somewhere where water was handy; on Mars that would be a prime requisite for the Marshies as well as the Earthmen. And if the Marshies were up in those hills, what did they think of the new Earth city being built right on the edge of the flat?

Maybe they hadn't decided yet.

The Marshies, come to think of it, knew a lot more about the Earthmen than they knew about the natives. The Marshies had stayed away from the Earth settlements, watching, and now the Earthmen were accidentally forcing a meeting between them; that must be shaking up the hoppers. And so, apparently, they were taking a final look at the Earthmen . . . and maybe soon they'd make a decision. He wished he knew what their alternatives were.

They took a landcar out the next day, loaded with a burndrill. The small red sun was still low over the horizon when they checked through the locks, and they threw a long gray shadow over the dust as they rode toward the hills. There had been no sign of the Marshie yet today, but Michelson was watching for the puffs of dust which would herald his arrival.

They set up the drill half a mile from the hills. It worked on the same principle as their blasters, boring a small hole straight down through the dirt and rock and, by the resistance offered, registering the various strata through which it passed. They found the water fifty feet down, under the layer of rock which formed the floor of the desert here.

They moved on to the base of the hills and again drilled, and again they found the water. Loening drew a straight line on a map of the area, and it passed directly from the building site through the two drilling-points. Extended, it would run through the mountains.

"We'll have to take the drill up into the hills," Loening said. "Flex your muscles—it's heavy."

They mounted it on rollers and made the ascent, and when they had got it to the first level spot in the pass they were all puffing with exertion despite the oxygen-masks they had donned. They sat and rested while Harris and Loening debated whether to drill here or try moving the drill further back into the hills. And the Marshie arrived.

He came down the pass in three quick hops and stopped next to the drill, which he regarded for a moment in his cocked-head stance. Then he skipped away and came back a few minutes later, landing next to Michelson.

"It is not a weapon," he said.

"No, it's a drill," Michelson said. "We're looking for water."

"Yes," said the Marshie, and hopped twenty feet back up the

pass. There he stood motionless, looking at the Earthmen. Marshies could stand still for hours, completely unmoving, when they felt like it; only the Marshie's liquid-dark eyes moved, flicking from one to another of the Earthmen in turn, and continually back to rest on the drill which sat before them. Harris sat staring back at him, but Loening coldly ignored his gaze, looking almost sullenly down at his feet. Michelson rose and walked slowly toward the creature.

"We're trying to find the path of the water," he said. "Can you help us?"

The Marshie's head jerked to one side and the big, dark eye focused on Michelson. After a moment he said, "I know where the water is."

"We want to dam the water, to keep it from our city," Michelson said. "If you help us, we can be sure we don't divert it from your own use."

The Marshie hopped to one side, paused, and hopped off up the slope out of sight. Michelson waited for several minutes, but he did not return. Michelson shrugged and went back to his companions.

"I think you've frightened him," Loening said. "They don't play our games."

"They haven't so far," Michelson admitted. "But I think they live in these hills, and they're going to have to take notice of that city we're building. It's about time we started cooperating with each other."

"Whether we like it or not?" said Loening.

Michelson nodded. "If that's their attitude—or ours. Personally, I think we might have a lot to offer each other; this could be the first step."

"The Marshies don't *step*," Loening said. "They hop. They skitter around like grasshoppers." His mouth was drawn back in a disgusted grimace. He took a breath and stood up. "Anyway, you can go on talking about cultural exchange with grasshoppers, but I think we'd better lug this drill up a bit further if we want to get anything concrete done today."

The three men began to attach the pulling-straps to their shoulders, but before they started their further ascent the Marshie came back. He landed beside them and said immediately, "I can tell you where the water is. You want to be friends."

Michelson dropped the strap and looked at the Marshie, wondering for a moment if the creature was serious. But of course it was useless to try to see what was in a hopper's mind, as Loening had said. At any rate, no matter how difficult it was to communicate with the Marshies, they did not lie.

He turned to Loening and said, "You and Harris take the drill back down to the landcar—the grasshoppers have landed."

He spent hours following the Marshie through the hills, back over five miles into the rocky, desolate terrain. There was silence in those mountains—not just the silence of a thin atmosphere, but the silence of emptiness, of desertion. The gray shadows fell along their path like dull pastel silhouettes, and the Marshie hopped back and forth past Michelson, silent but seemingly impatient. There was an air of excitement about this fur-covered creature— an almost childlike eagerness in his rough, inhuman voice when he occasionally stopped and said, "We will be friends, Walt, when I show you the water."

Well, of course he was interpreting the creature's attitude in his own terms, and it probably didn't make sense. But the Marshie hurried him along the rocky path.

They came down into a small hollow among the rocks, and the Marshie said, "Here is the water." There was an expanse of mud —the heavy brown dust of Mars, with water flowing slowly through it. It covered the floor of this tiny valley, and on its surface Michelson saw a thin green moss-like growth. It was like an expanse of quicksand, like an antiseptic swamp—for there were none of the heavier forms of vegetation of Earth, no insects skimming the surface. Here amid the chill dark rocks of Mars was a branch of the annual drainage of the icecap, and it seemed pitifully anticlimactic to Michelson.

"You can stop the water here," said the Marshie. "We are friends?"

Michelson looked around him, across the muddy expanse at the hills which rose again immediately beyond. "Your home is back there?" he asked.

"Yes." The Marshie hopped once, twice, twenty feet at a time, and hopped back again. "We are friends?" he said again.

"Of course," Michelson said. And then a thought came to him and he said, "Do you know what friendship is?"

The Marshie's eye regarded him softly for a moment. "We know something of it. But we do not have a word for it."

Michelson was suddenly aware that this small, muddy valley was a strangely unimpressive scene for a meeting of races. He felt alone and unimportant standing amid the ages-old rocks of this world with the furry Martian. This was not, after all, his world; he had lived most of his life here, and had come to think of it as his home far more than he thought so of Earth, but here in the quiet gray rock-shadows he felt fully for the first time that this desolate world belonged to the hoppers—to the Martians. And without quite realizing what he was doing he cut in his oxygen supply, though he wasn't really short of breath.

The Marshie hopped away without a word, leaving him alone there.

Harris and Loening surveyed the area thoroughly in the days that followed, and Michelson sent some men out to begin construction of a dam there, meanwhile making preparations for draining the waterpocket beneath the city. It kept him busy for several days, and it wasn't until two weeks later, when the dam-construction was started, that he began to wonder seriously why the Marshie had not been around again. No one had seen him out at the dam site either.

Michelson took an aircar out to the site soon after and checked the progress of the work there. They had moved machinery in and set up temporary quarters there for the work-crew; the area was bustling with activity. Michelson looked at the footprints of the workmen in the Martian dust, heard the noise of the machines and the voices around him, and thought of that silent day when he had stood here alone with the Marshie. Two weeks ago . . . it seemed like months.

He left, and took the aircar up to scout the area. The Marshies' city was supposed to be somewhere further up the pass; he hoped he could spot it from the air. He flew low, droning through the massive rocky crags, watching the ground through binocs. He had penetrated fifteen miles further into the mountains and was almost ready to give up when he found it.

The dwellings were cut into the rock, in vertical lines up and down the cliffside. There were perhaps twenty or twenty-five of them; certainly no more. He landed the aircraft at the base of those cliffs and approached slowly.

He needn't have bothered; they were empty. Some things had been left behind—a few small objects, delicately carved from stone, some pelts of the Marshies' own fur which had perhaps been used for added warmth during the winter, one or two pieces of what might have been furniture—but the area was definitely deserted. He couldn't tell offhand how long the Marshies had been gone, but he was sure it was no more than two weeks.

He left the dwellings untouched, not even picking up any of the small stone carvings to bring back with him. Perhaps later they could send out a government expedition to catalog and study what had been left. He walked slowly back to his aircar, looking at the depressions in the floor of the canyon left by the Marshies' footprints.

A fluttering behind him caused him to turn in surprise, and he saw a Marshie regarding him calmly. This could have been the same one, but he seemed a bit more heavily built, his fur somewhat darker.

"Hello," Michelson said. "We are friends?"

The Marshie continued to look silently at him for a moment, his heavy, dark wings folded like shadows around him. Then he said, "Some of us too are insane." And he disappeared with a quick jump and flutter of brown wings.

After awhile Michelson turned and continued walking to the aircar, leaving the footprints of his boots behind him in the dust.

Après coup

"A Few Last Words" was my first story.

I was twenty-one; I had been married two years; I was living in Iowa, where my wife was getting her M.F.A. in painting; I had just come from New Orleans and the South where I'd spent my life; I was making an occasional living as a musician. So the story shows not only the flaws you'd expect in a first story, but also a few of the flaws in the life it came out of.

Before it, I had written music, plays, poems, done translations; and had more or less settled into the role of poet when I began to correspond with Tom Disch, saw my first copies of *New Worlds* and at Tom's insistence, with the example of *New Worlds,* wrote "A Few Last Words" and (Tom's advice again) sent it to Damon. To receive one week later, and very much to my surprise, a letter of acceptance: short upon the heels of a letter from Mike Moorcock accepting for *New Worlds* a story I'd written during a break in the final work on "A Few Last Words." I still considered myself a poet (and still do); but Damon's help and enthusiasm, Chip's friendship and concern, subsequent reactions at the Conference, Kate's existence and Mike's confidence in me made me a fiction writer.

About the story. Damon has called it an "end-of-civilisation story," but it's just the story of a marriage. Of marriage. And should be dedicated to my ex-wife Jane Rose, who knows what comes after the words. I think I can say without too great presumption, as Apollinaire said of his poems in *Alcools,* that each of my stories (even the slightest) "commemorates an event in my life." In this case a prediction, or premonition, of what was going to happen, what *had* to happen, to my marriage.

The Conference. I remember the stories that year. "Masks," "Windsong," "Lib," two chapters of *Bug Jack Barron* . . . Harlan running out of the room when my story came under discussion, his arms over his head, shouting *I'm down a rabbit hole!* And the talking. Harlan and myself in an ice cream parlor. With Tom on the Anchorage porch; about his story, which I felt no one understood, it was so very personal. Joanna at dinner; a few quick words with Sonya in the library; Norman at the Tom Quick bar. Mike and myself still talking at six in the morning in Virginia Kidd's living room and the leaves outside looked like fish skeletons. Warmths and understanding that will always be a part of me: I'll never be able to go away from them. Though I've never returned, to the Conference. But most of all, because they so changed my life, I have to remember the night Mike asked me to come to London and edit *New Worlds* (it was five in the morning, five months later I was on my way)—and I have to remember a conversation with Norman and his comments on this story, which together started a novel inside me, *Kudsu*; sketched out on the plane returning from Milford to where I was living at the time and with me ever since *wherever* I was living. The last "commemoration" of the "event" of this story. To show me there were a few words left after all. And dedicated to Jane, to P.Z., to J.M.G. With love of a very special sort. That I hope they'll accept; later. But for now, and especially for the first two, and with all the flaws, in every sense, there are only

A FEW LAST WORDS

> What is the silence
>   a. As though it had a right to more
> W. S. Merwin

Again:
He was eating stained glass and vomiting rainbows. He looked up and there was the clock moving toward him, grinning, arms raised in a shout of triumph over its head. The clock advanced; he smelled decay; he was strangled to death by the hands of time. . . . He was in a red room. The hands of the clock knocked knocked knocked without entering. . . . And changed again. The hours had faces, worse than the hands. He choked it was all so

quiet only the ticking the faces were coming closer closer he gagged screamed once and—

Sat on the edge of the bed. The hall clock was ticking loudly, a sound like dried peas dropping into a pail. This was the third night.

The pumpkin-color moon dangled deep in the third quadrant of the cross-paned window. Periodically clouds would touch the surface and partly fill with color, keeping it whole. Dust and streaks on the window, a tiny bubble of air, blurred its landscape; yellow drapes beside it took on a new hue.

He had watched it for hours (must have been hours). Its only motion was a kind of visual dopplering. It sped out into serene depths, skipped back in a rush to paste itself against the backside of the glass, looking like a spot of wax. Apogee to perigee to apogee, and no pause between. Rapid vacillation, losing his eyes in intermediate distances, making him blink and squint, glimmering in the pale overcast. And other than that it hadn't moved. Abscissa+, ordinate+. Stasis.

This was the third night.

His wife stirred faintly and reached to touch his pillow, eyelids fluttering. Hoover quickly put out his hand and laid it across her fingers. Visibly, she settled back into blankets. In the hall, the clock ticked like a leaking faucet. The moon was in its pelagic phase, going out.

The third night of the dreams. The third night that lying in bed he was overcome by: Presence. In the dark it would grow around him, crowding his eyes open, bunching his breath, constricting—at last driving him from the bed, the room. He would pace the rugs and floors, turn back and away again on the stairs, wondering. He would drink liquor, then coffee, unsure which effect he wanted, uneasy at conclusions—certain only of this sense of cramping, of imposition. In the dark he was ambushed, inhabited, attacked again from within.

His wife turned in bed, whispering against sheets, taking her fingers away.

Hoover lifted his head to the dresser, chinoiserie chair, sculpt lamé valet, to glazed chintz that hid the second, curiously small window. A simple room, sparse, clean, a room with no waste of motion. And a familiar room, intimate and informal as the back of his hand, yet his eyes moving through it now encountered a strangeness, a distortion. He cast his vision about the room, tracing the strangeness back to its source at the window: to pale plastic light that slipped in there and took his furniture away into distances. It occurred to him that he was annoyed by this intrusion, this elusive division of himself from his things. He watched the moon and it stared back, unblinking.

Hoover fixed his chin between his fists, propped elbows on knees, and became a sculpture. His face turned again to see the window, head rolling in his hands, ball-in-socket.

A cave, he thought: that was the effect. Gloom, and moonlight sinking through cracks: pitch and glimmer. A skiagraphy of the near and foreign. Quarantine and communion, solitude and confederation. A cave, shaped in this strange light.

And bruising the light's influence, he walked to the chair and stared down at the suit he'd draped over one arm—looked at the hall clock—ten minutes ago. It was happening faster now. . . .

The suit was pale, stale-olive green and it shined in a stronger light. The coat barely concealed the jutting, saddle-like bones of his hips; his wrists dangled helplessly away from the sleeve ends like bones out of a drumstick—and Cass hated it. Regardless of fit, though, it *felt* right: he was comfortable in it, was himself.

He took the coat from the chair, held it a minute, and put it back. Somehow, tonight, it seemed inappropriate, like the man-shaped valet that no one used. As with the room, the furniture, it had been taken away from him.

He turned and shuffled across the rug to search through the crow-black corner closet behind the creaking, always-open door, discovering a western shirt with a yoke of roses across its breast and trying it on, then jeans, belting them tightly, and boots. The clothes were loose, looser than he remembered, but they felt good, felt right.

Stepping full into light at the door, he shattered strangeness, and looking back saw that the moon was now cockeyed in the corner of the pane.

Ticking of a clock, sound of feet down stairs.

He assassinated death with the cold steel rush of his breathing. . . .

The night was pellucid, a crystal of blackness; hermetic with darkness. He moved within a hollow black crystal and up there was another, an orange separate crystal, bubble in a bubble. . . . And quiet, so quiet so still, only the ticking of his feet, the whisper of breath. He pocketed his hands and wished for the coat he'd left behind.

Hoover turned onto the walk, heels clacking (another death: to silence).

A sepulchral feeling, he thought, to the thin wash of light overlaying this abyss of street. A counterpoint, castrati and bass. Peel away the light and you: Plunge. Downward. Forever.

Another thought . . . you can tell a lot by the way a person listens to silence.

(Sunday. It was evening all day. Over late coffee and oranges, the old words begin again. The speech too much used, and no doors from this logic of love. We go together like rain and melancholy, blue and morning. . . .)

At the corner, turn; and on down this new abyss. Breath pedaling, stabbing into the air like a silent cough, feet killing quiet—

I am intruding.

Darkness is avenging itself on my back.

(And I, guilty realist, dabbler at verses, saying: There is no sign for isolation but a broken spring, no image for time but a ticking heart, nothing for death but stillness. . . .)

Light glinted off bare windows. Most of the houses were marooned now in a moat of grass and ascending weed. Driveways and porches and garages all open and empty, dumbly grinning.

(Evening all day. World out the window like a painting slowly turning under glass in a dusty frame. Rain in the sky, but shy about falling. The words: they peak at ten, pace by noon, run out to the end of their taut line. . . .)

The shells have names, had them. Martin, Heslep, Rose. Walking past them now, he remembered times they were lit up like pumpkins, orange-yellow light pouring richly out the windows; cars, cycle-strewn yards, newspapers on steps. The casual intimacy of a person inside looking out, waving.

(And I remember your hair among leaves, your body in breaking dew, moonlight that slipped through trees and windows to put its palm against your face, your waist; bright and shadow fighting there. . . .)

Darkness. It moves aside to let you pass. Closes, impassable, behind you.

(Four times: you came to bed, got up, came back to bed. You turned three times, you threw the pillows off the bed. Michael, never born, who had two months to live, was stirring in you and stirring you awake.

Your hair was on the bed like golden threads. The moon had pushed your face up into the window and hidden your hands in shadow. You were yellow, yellow on the linen bed; and opened your eyes.

—If I weren't afraid, I could leave and never look back.

You say that, sitting in a hollow of bed, knees tucked to your flanneled breasts, arms around yourself.

—Would you follow, would you call me back?

I watch your steps track down the walk to the black, inviting street. And later, when I open the door, you're there, grinning, coming back; coming back to make coffee and wait for morning. And another night, another day, saved from whatever it is that threatens at these times. . . .)

Hoover looked at the streetlight shelled in rainbow and it was ahead, above, behind, remembered. Darkness shouldered itself back in around him. Snow hung in the air, waiting to fall. The dead houses regarded him as he passed, still, unspeaking.

(October, time of winds and high doubt. It comes around us like the shutting of a light: the same thing is happening to others. And the people are going away, the time has come for going away. . . . It all boils up in a man, and overflows. His birthright of freedom, it's the freedom to be left alone, that's what he wants most, just to be left alone, just to draw circles around himself and shut the world out. Every man's an island, why deny it, why tread water. So people let go. . . .)

Hoover picked the moving shape out of the alley and was down in a crouch, whistling, almost before the dog saw him. It raised its nose from the ground and walked bashfully toward him, sideways, tail banging at a drum, whining.

"Folks leave you, fella?" A brown shepherd with a heavy silver-studded collar; he didn't bother to look at the jangling name-tags. "Take you home with me then, okay?" The shepherd whimpered its agreement. Hoover rummaging in his pockets.

"Sorry, fella, nothing to give you." Showing empty hands, which the dog filled with licks and nuzzles, snuffling.

"Bribery, eh. Sorry, still no food." He stroked his hand into the dog's pelt, found warmth underneath. It sat looking up at him, waiting, expecting, its tail swishing across pavement.

When he erected himself to full height, the dog jumped away and crouched low, ready to run. Hoover walked toward it and put out a hand to its broad, ridged head.

"It's okay, fellow. Tell you what. Come along with me to see a friend, then I'll take you right home and see about getting you something to eat. Think you can wait?"

They punctured the night together, down the walk, heels clacking, claws ticking. Hoover kept his hand on the dog's head as they walked. The nametags threw bells out into the silence.

"Or maybe he'll have something for you there, come to think of it."

Click, clack, click. Staccato tattooed on the ponderous night. The sky is still ambiguous.

(Remembering a night we sat talking, drinking half-cups of coffee as we watched stars sprinkle and throb and fade, then saw dawn all blood and whispered thunder. I remember how your eyes were, pink like shrimp, pink like the sky when it caught the first slanting rays and held them to its chest. And as morning opened around us we were talking of Thoreau and men who sailed the soul, of ways and reasons to change, the old orders, and of why things break up. Outside our window it was growing between them, people were letting go, were wanting their Waldens, their Innisfrees, their Arcadias, they were falling away from the town like leaves, like scaling paint, by twos, by ones. Even in our house, our hearts, it moves between us. Between us. We feel it turning, feel it touching. But we care, we love, we can't let go. . . .)

Hoover drew up short, listening. The shepherd beside him cocked its ears, trembled happily.

It happens like this . . .

A drone, far off. Closer. Becomes an engine. Then a swelling of light blocks away. Then a rush and churning and soon two lashing white eyes. Loudest, chased by a dog. A roar and past, racing. A thrown thing. Neil's car . . . and silence again.

And minutes later, the shepherd's body went limp and its head fell back onto his lap. Hoover took it in his arms and walked out of the road, its head rolling softly along the outside of his elbow. In the streetlight his face glistened where the dog had licked it.

Crossing the walk, kicking open a gate that wind had shut, Hoover surrendered his burden into the lawn. Ten steps away he looked back and saw that the dog's body was hidden in deep grass, secret as any Easter egg.

Three hundred and some-odd steps. Two turns. Five places where cement has split its seams, heaved up, and grass is growing in the cracks. Pacing this map . . .

(The sea grew tired one day of swinging in harness, ticking in its box of beach. One spark in the flannel sea, possessed of fury, gathering slime like a seeded pearl, thinks of legs and comes onto a rock, lies there in the sun drying. It seeps, it slushes, it creeps, it crawls; it bakes to hardness and walks. . . . All to the end: that I am walking on two feet down this corridor of black steel and my hand is turning like a key at this found door. . . .)

The door collapse-returned. He looked around. A single light cut into the café through a porthole of glass in the kitchen door; powdery twilight caught in the mirror. In the dim alley before him, neon signs circled and fell, rose and blinked across their boxes like tiny traffic signals. Profound, ponderous grayness, like the very stuff of thought. . . .

Decision failed him; he had turned to go when he heard the door and saw light swell.

"Dr. Hoover. . . ."

He turned back.

"Didn't know for sure you were still around." Nervously. "About the last ones, I guess."

Hoover nodded. "Any food, Doug?"

"Just coffee, sorry. Coffee's on, though. Made a pot for myself, plenty left." He stepped behind the counter and knocked the corner off a cube of stacked cups, burn scars on his hands rippling in mirror-bemused light.

"Sugar, cream?" Sliding the cup onto crisp pink formica.

Hoover waved them both off. "Black's the best way."

"Yeah. . . . No one been in here for a week or more. I ain't bothered to keep the stuff out like I ought to."

Hoover sat down by the cup, noticing that Doug had moved back away from the counter. "Like you say, I guess. Last ones."

Doug scratched at his stomach where it depended out over the apron. Large hands going into pockets, rumpling the starched white.

"Reckon I *could* get you a sandwich. Or some toast—then it don't matter if the bread's a little stale."

"Coffee's fine. Don't bother."

"You sure? Wouldn't be any trouble."

Hoover smiled and shook his head. "Forget it, just coffee. But thanks anyway."

Doug looked down at the cup. "Don't mind, I'll have one with you." His penciled monobrow flexed at the middle, pointed down. It was like the one-stroke bird that children are taught to draw;

the upper part of a stylized heart. "Get my cup." Over his shoulder: "Be right back."

Light rose as the kitchen door opened; died back down, leaving Hoover alone. He turned his eyes to buff-flecked white tiles; let them carry his attention across the floor, swiveling his chair to keep up. Light picked out tiny blades of gleam on the gold bands that edged formica-and-naugahyde. A few pygmy neons hopscotched high on the walls. The booths were empty as shells, humming with shadow; above them (showing against homogenized paint, rich yellow, creamy tan; sprinkled among windows) were small dark shapes he knew as free-painted anchors.

(All this shut in a small café, sculpt in shades of gray. Change one letter, you have cave again. . . .)

Doug came back (light reached, retreated), poured steaming coffee. He squeezed around the end of the counter and sat two seats away.

"Neil left today."

"Yeah, I saw him up the street on the way here."

"So that's whose car it was. Wasn't sure, heard it going by. Going like a bat out of hell from the sound." He drank, made a face. "Too hot. Wonder what kept him? Said he was going to take off this morning." He blew across the mouth of his cup, as though he might be trying to whistle, instead breathing vapor. He tried another taste. "Will came through, you know. . . ."

Hoover's own cup was sweating, oils were sliding over the surface. It was a tan cup; the lip was chipped. They weren't looking at each other.

"That big cabin up on the cape. His grandfather built it for a place to get away and do his writing, way the hell away from everything. Now it's his."

"I know. My sister called me up last week to say good-bye, told me about it, they thought it was coming through. Wonder when *she's* leaving?"

Doug looked up sharply, then dropped his head. "Thought you knew. She left about three, four days ago." Doug belched, lightly.

"Oh. I guess she went up early to get things ready, he'll meet her there. You know women."

"Yeah. Yeah, that's probably it." He went for more coffee, poured for them both. "Coffee's the last thing I need."

"You too."

"Yeah—lot worse for some, though. Been over a week for me, lost about twenty pounds. Catnap some. . . . Thing you wonder about is, where'd they find a lawyer? For the papers and all. Didn't, maybe, guess it don't make much difference anymore, stuff like that. Anyhow, they're gone."

(And the wall's a wedge. Shove it between two people and they come apart, like all the rest. . . .)

Hoover shrugged his shoulders, putting an elbow on the counter and steepling fingers against his forehead.

"Almost brought a friend, Doug. . . ."

The big man straightened in his chair. His mouth made "Friend?" sit on his lips unspoken.

"But he was indisposed, disposed, at the last minute."

Doug was staring at him strangely.

"A dog. Neil hit it. I was going to see if I could talk you out of some food for it."

"Oh! Yeah, there's some stuff, meat and all I'm just gonna have to throw out anyway. What isn't spoiled already's getting that way fast. Didn't know there were dogs still around, though? Whose is it?"

"There aren't now. I hadn't seen it before. *Was* it: it's dead." Extinct.

"Oh. Yeah, Neil *was* going pretty fast. Dog probably wandered in from someplace else anyway, looking for food after they left him." Gazing into the bottom of his cup, Doug swirled what coffee was left against the grounds, making new patterns, like tiny cinders after a rain. "Always been a cat man myself. Couldn't keep one, though, haven't since I was a kid. Sarah's asthma, you know."

"You do have to be careful. Used to have hay fever myself,

fall come around I couldn't breathe. Took an allergy test and they cleared it up."

"Yeah, we tried that. Tried about everything. You oughta see our income tax for the last few years, reads like a medical directory. Sarah got so many holes poked in her, the asthma should have leaked right out. Wasn't any of it seemed to help, though."

"How's Sarah doing? Haven't seen her for quite a while. She's usually running around in here helping you, shooing you back to the kitchen, making you change your apron, talking to customers. Brightens the place up a lot."

Doug tilted the cup to drain an extra ounce of cold coffee off the grounds.

"Not much business lately," he said. "Boy I had working for me just kind of up and left three-four months ago and I never got around to looking for help, no need of it, specially now."

"She's well, though? Doing okay."

Doug put his cup down, rattling it against the saucer.

"Yeah, she's okay. She—" He stood and made his way around the counter. "She went away a while. To get some rest." He dipped under the counter and came up with a huge stainless steel bowl. "Think I'll make another pot. This one's getting stale. Better anyhow if you use the stuff regularly, easier on it, works better—like getting a car out on the road to clean her out."

He started working at the urn, opening valves, sloshing dark coffee down into the bowl. Hoover watched Doug's reflection in the shady mirror and a dimmer image of himself lying out across the smooth formica.

So Doug's wife had gone away too; Sarah had gone to get some rest. . . . Hoover remembered a song he'd heard at one of the faculty parties: Went to see my Sally Gray, Went to see my Sally Gray, Went to see my Sally Gray, Said my Sally's gone away—only this time Sally Gray had taken everybody else with her. . . .

Doug was chuckling at the urn.

"You know I gotta make twenty cups just to get two for us,

I mean that's the least this monster here'll handle. Ask him for forty-fifty cups, he'll give it to you in a minute. But you ask him for two, just two little cups of coffee, and he'll blow his stack, or a gasket or something." He went back to clanging at the urn. "Reckon you can handle ten of 'em?" He started fixing the filter, folding it in half twice, tearing off a tiny piece at one corner. "Hell, there ain't enough people left in town to drink twenty cups of coffee if I was giving it away and they was dying of thirst. Or anywhere around here."

He bowed the filter into a cone between his hands, climbed a chair to install it, then came down and drew a glass of water, putting it in front of Hoover.

"That's for while you wait."

"I need to be going anyway, Doug. Have to get some sleep sooner or later."

Doug reached and retrieved Hoover's cup, staring at the sludge settling against the bottom. "One last cup."

"All right. One more."

One for the road. . . .

Doug bent and rinsed the cup, then got another from the stack and put it on the counter. He stood looking at the clean empty cup, wiping his hands against the apron. He lit a cigarette, nodding to himself, and the glowing red tip echoed one of the skipping neon signs on the wall behind him. He put the package on the counter and smiled, softly.

"You know, you could've sat right here and watched the whole thing happening. I mean, at first there'd be the usual group, but they were . . . nervous. You know: jumpy. They'd sort of scatter themselves out and every now and then the talk would die down and there'd be this quiet, like everybody was listening for something, waiting for something. Then a lot of them stopped coming, and the rest would sit all around the room, talking across to each other, then just sitting there quiet for a long time by themselves. Wasn't long before the regulars didn't come anymore—and you knew what was going on, you knew they were draining out of town like someone had pulled the plug.

"That was when the others started showing up. They'd come in with funny looks on their faces, all anxious to talk. And when you tried to talk to 'em, they'd be looking behind you and around the room and every once in a while they'd get up and go look out the window. And then they'd leave and you'd never see them again."

Hoover sat with his legs cocked back, toes on the floor, regarding the glass of water (the bubbles had nearly vanished). He nodded: he knew, he understood.

"For a while I got some of the ones that were coming through. I'd be in the back and I'd hear the door and come out, and there'd be this guy standing there, shuffling his feet, looking at the floor. He'd pay and take his coffee over in the corner, then the next time I looked around, he'd be gone—lot of them would just take it with them, to go. Then even that stopped."

(The people: they drip, trickle, run, pour, flood from the cities. They don't look back. And the ones who stay, try to fight it— they feel it growing in them worse than before. Turning in them, touching them, and they care they love they can't let go. But the harder they fight, the worse it is, like going down in quicksand, and the wall's a wedge: shove it between two people and they come apart, like all the rest, like all the rest of the world. . . .)

Doug found something on the counter to watch.

"One time during the War, the ship I was on went down on the other side and a sub picked us up. I still remember how it felt, being in that sub, all the people packed in like sardines, stuffed into spaces between controls and motors. You'd think it would be full of noise, movement. But there was something about being under all that water, being closed in, something about the light—anyway, something that made you feel alone, made you want to whisper. I'd just sit in it and listen. Feel. And pretty soon I'd start wanting them all to really go away, to leave me alone. . . ."

Doug stood looking for a moment out one of the small round windows past Hoover's shoulder.

"Yeah. Yeah, that's the way it is all right." Then his eyes

switched back to Hoover's cup. "I better go get that coffee, just take it a minute to perk."

He picked up his cup and walked down the counter toward the kitchen, running his hand along the formica. The door swung back in, wobbled, stopped (light had reached, retreated).

Hoover felt suddenly hollow; empty; squeezed. He looked around. The room was a cave again.

Out in the kitchen, Doug moved among his stainless steel and aluminum. Hoover heard him banging pots on pans, opening doors, sliding things on shelves out of his way. Then the texture of sound changed, sank to quiet, became a silence that stretched and stretched. And seconds later, broke: the back door creaked open and shut with a hiss of air along its spring, clicking shut.

(So now the quicksand's got Doug too, for all his fighting. Now he's gone with the rest, gone with Sally Gray. . . .)

Outside in the alley angling along and behind the café, Doug's Harley Davidson pumped and caught, coughed a couple of times and whined away, one cylinder banging.

Hoover sat looking at the abandoned cup as silence came in to fill his ears. Then he heard the buzzing of electric wires.

The last grasping and their fingers had slipped.

The wedge was driven in, and they'd come apart. . . .

He stood, digging for a dime and finding he'd forgotten to fill his pockets, then walked to the register and punched a key. "No Sale" came up under the glass. There were two nickels and some pennies.

He fed the coins in (ping! ping!), dialed, and waited. The phone rang twice and something came on, breathing into the wires.

"Cass?"

Breathing.

Again: "Cass?" Louder.

Breathing.

"Cass, is that you?"

Silence.

"Who is this? Please. Cass?"

A small, quiet voice. "I'm afraid you have the wrong number."
A click and buzzing. . . .

After a while, he reached up and flipped out the change tray. As the lid slid away, a tarnished gray eye showed there: someone had left a dime behind.

Nine rings. Cass' voice in the lifted phone. Sleepy; low and smooth; pâté, ready for spreading.

"Cass?"

"Is that you, Bob? Where are you?"

"Doug's place. Be right home." The space of breath. "Honey . . ."

"Yes?"

"Get your bags packed, we're leaving tonight."

"Leaving?" She was coming awake. "Where—"

"I don't know. South maybe, climate's better. But maybe that's what everyone will think—anyway, we'll decide. Just get your things ready, just what you absolutely have to have. We can always pick up things we need in towns. There's a big box in the bottom of the utility closet, some of my stuff, some tools and so on I got together a while back. Put that with the rest—there's some room left in it you can use. I'll be right home. Everything else we'll need is already in the car."

"Bob. . . ."

"Just do it Cass. Please. I'll be right back, to help."

"Bob, are you sure—"

"Yes."

She paused. "I'll be ready."

He hung up and walked into the kitchen, came out again with a ten-pound sack of coffee under one arm. He started over the tiles toward the door, then turned back and picked up the cigarettes lying on the counter. He stood by the door, looking back down the dim alley: stood at the mouth of the cave, looking into distances (he'd seen a stereopticon once; it was much the same effect).

The tiny neons skipped and blinked dumbly in their boxes; the kitchen light glared against the window, fell softly along the mirror. Shadows came in to fill the café; sat at tables, slumped in booths, stood awry on the floor; watching, waiting. At the end of the counter, the blank tan cup silently surrendered.

He turned and switched the knob. Went through the door. Shut it behind him. The click of the lock ran away into the still air and died; he was locked into silence. . . .

Cautiously he assaulted the street's independence, heels ticking parameters for the darkness, the motive, the town. The sky hung low above his head.

(I walk alone. Alone. Men don't run in packs, but they run. . . . Death at the wheel expects his spin. Dark seeps in around the edges, winds rise in the caves of our Aeolian skulls, five fingers reach to take winter into our hearts, the winter of all our hearts)

And they came now in the darkness, they loomed and squatted about him, all the furnished tombs: this dim garden of rock and wood.

(Bars of silence. Score: four bars of silence, end on the seventh. See how they show on my white shirt among the roses. Bars and barristers of silence)

The quick blue spurt of a struck match. A cigarette flames, then glows, moving down the street into darkness.

(There is no sign for isolation but a broken spring, no image for time but a ticking heart, nothing for death but stillness . . . and the wall, the wedge, is splitting deeper but we'll hold, for a while we'll hold on, you and I)

He stood still in the stillness that flowed around him and listened to the hum of insects calling through the black flannel. As if in answer, clouds came lower.

(At the mouth of caves, turning. We can't see out far, in deep, but the time has come for going away the time has come for becoming. . . . At the mouth of caves, turning, and time now to enter the calm, the old orders. At the mouth of caves. Turning)

He walked on and his heels talked and the night came in to hush him.

188   JAMES SALLIS

He shouted out into the dark, screamed once out into silence—and it entered his heart.

He passed a pearl-gray streetlight, passed a graveyard lawn.

("Sudden and swift and light as that the ties gave, and we learned of finalities besides the grave." Is this how it feels, the instant of desertion—a vague epiphany of epochal stillness, primal quiet?)

Around him, scarcely sounding his echo, stood the shells of houses, like trees awaiting the return of dryads who had lost their way.

(The instant of desertion, the instant of silence)

The cigarette arced into the street and fell there, glowing blankly.

He bent his head and began to hurry.

And with a flourish, the snows began.

[I brought this story to the Milford workshop several springs ago. As the week goes on people tend to stay up later and later, *e.g.*, the previous night Gordon Dickson and Poul Anderson had been singing Old Norse sea-chanteys in the kitchen until 5 A.M.; Harlan Ellison, by sheer mental power, had finally levitated sixteen copies of Sam Moskowitz's *Seekers of Tomorrow* ten feet above the floor and caused them to dance a gavotte; and Anne McCaffrey, without a score, had performed every vocal number in *Candide,* including the duets. At least this is what I remember. The workshop session, of which my recollection is also fuzzy, went something like this:

SOMEONE: Hm. Writing about bitchy women again, I see.

SOMEONE ELSE: You've made up the names for some of those Tarot cards.

STILL SOMEONE ELSE: Depends on what system you use.

SOMEONE USUALLY QUIET: The solar system is not traveling towards the constellation of the Lyre, the star Vega, at one and one-thirteenth the speed of sound but at approximately one and one-fourteenth the speed of sound, that is to say about 800 miles an hour.

(I made a note of this.)

A THOUGHTFUL SOMEONE: Of course the speed of sound varies with the condition of the air through which the sound is passing. And I wonder if every reader will catch the reference buried in "submarine," *i.e.*, a lit house in the middle of the dark fields looking and feeling something like a diving bell or one of Cousteau's undersea towns, at least that is what I assume you meant.

THE FIRST SOMEONE: Pretty nasty man too, actually.

THE THOUGHTFUL SOMEONE: I *do* love the Wendigo. I love horror stories. Nice to see a creature used in one horror story turn up in another. Very nice.

ME: I—uh—well, I sent this story to a reputable magazine, I mean very much more reputable and intelligent than we are, actually, and they took it but they said they didn't understand it. I mean, they wanted to know, I think, was she really a witch or not and what parts are real and what parts aren't real. And I had to write them a letter explaining that nobody symbolized anything but that it all really happened, just as the story said. And really they're a well-established magazine with a fine reputation *and they never print any science fiction or fantasy so they ought to know.*

EVERYBODY: *Ha-ha-he-he-ho-ho-hoo-hoo-heh-heh-huh-ha-ho-he!*

ME: *But do you understand the story?*

EVERYBODY: Understand? What's to understand?

Which is why I love science fiction writers and the Milford workshop.]

THIS NIGHT, AT MY FIRE

Someone has given me a pack of Tarot cards; they are very old and very heavy and the hanged man has turned up three times too often, but nothing else moves in this bungalow even though we are rushing towards Vega in the constellation of the Lyre at almost exactly one and one-fourteenth times the speed of sound. Very windy and black outside.

Half an hour ago L—— came in, fiddled with the stove, then took himself and his boots into the next room, from where I can see him sprawled ungracefully on the settle, his feet on the boards. Nobody else. I think L—— is listening. The clock on the stove points to ten o'clock. From above L——'s boots, from above his leather jacket comes half a groan and half a snore; I can see his blond head jerk awake and I turn over The Rising Sun, The Empress, Death. The Wendigo, that makes men dance in the black night until it kills them, rattles the electric lines but has missed L—— tonight; he would say "only the wind." I think he's asleep. But it's serious enough, I would think, to be traveling so fast with no idea at all where one is going.

Earlier tonight we were submarine but a great deal was going on, polishing the silver, with water outside the windows. Now we are bare; and as the clock ticks and I lay out my cards, the night passes in absolute silence. The wind is screaming too high to be heard although occasionally it thumps the side of the house. I listen. The Rising Sun and The Resurrection, followed by The Widow, Death, The Hanged Man, Greed, Resurrection. These cards are used only for fortune-telling now. Walking silently, so that the boards do not make noise, I go in to L—— and shake him awake, taking my hands away. He looks up stupidly, his hair falling over his face, this big, big handsome man.

"There's someone outside," I say. L—— stares. His woman has told him someone is outside. He gets to his feet. What a lot is going on tonight! So I tag along after him, and peep from behind his broad back and stand courteously to one side and motion the old man in. But L—— does not like it. I give him a look, a sidewise look, like that of creatures bright, much too bright, under leaves; Let him in, be generous, let him in, why not let him in? and reluctantly, perfunctorily, tall as a tower, L—— swings aside. Why not let him in. Bow. Scrape. L—— is reluctant. The old man (where did he come from? it's a puzzle, L—— doesn't like puzzles) whom I don't, particularly, mind—O there is a great deal going on tonight!—has a turtle's neck and skin mottled like the underparts the sun doesn't reach, an old turtle, shuffles into the kitchen. This night, at my fire. My clock, my tables, my chairs.

"Make him something to eat," says my husband.

And I do. There is, in my stove, something dangerous; there is, hiding in the electric wires, something very bad; but not half so bad as outside. I watch him eat, quite interested, I am interested in everything, and I watch L—— too; his long, sloping arms, his hands, the muscles in his thighs. There are reasons, I suppose, for everything. L—— goes into the next room and leaves me alone with the old man; I start to put out my cards. He picks one up.

"What's this?"

"Ah! that's Death."

"What's this?"

"The Resurrection."

I start to deal them but he wants them all, the peevish creature; and I complain, and L—— tells me to let them alone. From inside. Long distance. But I never mind. I let him have the whole future right in his hands. We continue at that same mad pace; the whole house hums; now the old man has thrown down all my cards, he pushes them crazily off the table. "I want!" he shouts, "I want! I want! I want!" rocking crazily.

Slowly, slyly, I pick them up; I explain to him that the cards symbolize the world, that the world is made up of opposite forces, that the earth turns round the sun, that the universe is flying apart. Circumambulating the table like a diver, I pass them in front of him: Death, Death, Death—which deliciously I know how to do.

"Do you know," I say, "what this means? This means Death."

"Do you know," say I, "what this means? This means Death."

"And this means," say I, "the forgetting, and this means The Glorious Resurrection, and this means The Power and this means The Virtue." Late at night things often become fields of power: my wicked big white box, rattling, clicking, my tablecover dipping down into nothing, the shadows behind the doors, my radiant red-green-yellow-blue pasteboards, compelling and beautiful. He watches me and he knows. Oh, how he watches! And how he knows! I have always and ever called people my darling; thus witches are domestic women, and so I tell his fortune with my man in the next room, with the earth turning round the sun and the sun round a star; all flies with frightening impetuosity through the heavens, and L—— stirs and turns dizzily in his vacant sleep, tall as a tree, and ploughs the floor with the heel of his boot. And wakes.

"Get him out of here," says my man.

The old man starts; his mouth falls open, stuttering.

"Get him out," says my man, standing in the doorway as broad as the doorway, he always forgets what the world is made of, and the old fellow with the mottled skin beats on the table with one hand, uttering noises like a deaf-mute.

"I can't," say I, my eyes down. L—— stands in the doorway, cold as sin. He strides forward and picks the little fellow up by the neck, pushes him out the kitchen door and locks it; and says: "You'd let every beast in here."

I avert my eyes modestly. Soon it will be time. But I am only very bright and very little: what harm in poor me? and at this moment the wind—in which a quantity of things are riding tonight—crashes against the kitchen door to deliver me a present, that wind which is O! full of murders tonight.

L—— stands up. He looks out the door; and starts. And utters a hasty exclamation of dismay. And skews his face to one side, and climbs his eyebrows and drops his lips unhealthily over his teeth. My darling, my sweet, my love, now he sees what I see and hears what I hear, and he sweats and clings to the doorpost with a groan.

The old man has hanged himself on our doorstep.

Now the dizzying ride of this world has made him sick, my man, endlessly sick at last, never to be well again, his head turned completely.

Not like me. For I am all right.

At one-fifteen Workshop Time, the year (1962) of my first Milford Conference, Damon Knight put a tactful arm around my shoulder and said, "You know, there's a rule that wives aren't allowed to attend workshops" (nonwriting wives, that is). It's a matter of put up or shut up, he explained. Of course I agreed that this made sense, and of course I knew I'd never forgive him. I retired to the kitchen with the other four wives and one husband and we had our beer and cookies. Every now and then someone from the workshop, say Joe Teasly (who isn't represented in this anthology because he doesn't exist), would stagger in muttering obscenity-fragments, make a hurried ham and cheese sandwich, and stagger back to the living room, where things were at. Or Millard Frappe would sit down with us for as long as it took to put his head in his hands and whisper, "My God."

Traffic through the kitchen moved steadily and we learned a lot. We learned that "constructive criticism" is a matter of interpretation and that when writers feel they have been treated unfairly they will often develop headaches and stomach pains. They will also crave food and want to talk. Because of this talk, in a few years I too was able to make statements like "What does *he* know?" and "If she could write half as well as she nitpicks . . ."

Sometime in 1966 I started "Look, You Think You've Got Troubles" for no reason I can think of. Writing it was fun and when it was finished I put it away as a cheeky little story that amuses by its presumption. At the 1967 Conference Damon asked me if I'd ever written anything. I thought of this story and said no. He asked again. "Well, not *really*." "You're sure?" "Well . . ." and I confessed. "It's a dumb story about a Jewish man whose daughter marries a Martian and he's very upset, the Jewish man I mean. You wouldn't like it; it's dumb, a dumb story; you'd hate it." "Send it to me," said Damon. I lied and told him sure I would. But Damon is persistent and I'm weak and eventually I had no excuse left. He has strange tastes; he bought it. This was nice, but more important, I got into the next workshop.

Lawdy. They sat me down in the middle of the floor (because I'd come in late, having spent the last two hours feeling nauseous and unreal) and twenty-five people discussed the story. "It was so *refreshing* after plowing through all those heavy manuscripts" (quasi-quote from Keith Laumer); "I think the word is *wholesome*" (Doris Pitkin Buck). Sonya Dorman made the definitive comment: "Of course, it makes no sense whatsoever."

LOOK, YOU THINK YOU'VE GOT TROUBLES

To tell you the truth, in the old days we would have sat shivah for the whole week. My so-called daughter gets married, my own flesh and blood, and not only he doesn't look Jewish, he's not even human.

"Papa," she says to me, two seconds after I refuse to speak to her again in my entire life, "if you know him you'll love him, I promise." So what can I answer—the truth, like I always tell her: "If I know him I'll vomit, that's how he affects me. I can help it? He makes me want to throw up on him."

With silk gloves you have to handle the girl, just like her mother. I tell her what I feel, from the heart, and right away her face collapses into a hundred cracks and water from the Atlantic Ocean makes a soggy mess out of her paper sheath. And that's how I remember her after six months—standing in front of me, sopping wet from the tears and making me feel like a monster—me—when all the time it's her you-should-excuse-the-expression husband who's the monster.

After she's gone to live with him (New Horizon Village, Crag City, Mars), I try to tell myself it's not me who has to—how can I put it?—deal with him intimately; if she can stand it, why should I complain? It's not like I need somebody to carry on the business; my business is to enjoy myself in my retirement. But who can enjoy? Sadie doesn't leave me alone for a minute. She calls me a criminal, a worthless no-good with gallstones for a heart.

"Hector, where's your brains?" she says, having finally given up on my emotions. I can't answer her. I just lost my daughter, I should worry about my brains too? I'm silent as the grave. I can't eat a thing. I'm empty—drained. It's as though I'm waiting for something to happen but I don't know what. I sit in a chair that folds me up like a bee in a flower and rocks me to sleep with electronic rhythms when I feel like sleeping, but who can sleep? I look at my wife and I see Lady Macbeth. Once I caught her whistling as she pushed the button for her bath. I fixed her with a look like an icicle tipped with arsenic.

"What are you so happy about? Thinking of your grand-children with the twelve toes?"

She doesn't flinch. An iron woman.

When I close my eyes, which is rarely, I see our daughter when she was fourteen years old, with skin just beginning to go pimply and no expression yet on her face. I see her walking up to Sadie and asking her what she should do with her life now she's filling out, and my darling Sadie, my life's mate, telling her why not marry a freak; you got to be a beauty to find a man here, but on Mars you shouldn't know from so many fish. "I knew I could count on you, Mama," she says, and goes ahead and marries a plant with legs.

Things go on like this—impossible—for months. I lose twenty pounds, my nerves, three teeth and I'm on the verge of losing Sadie, when one day the mailchute goes ding-dong and it's a letter from my late daughter. I take it by the tips of two fingers and bring it in to where my wife is punching ingredients for the gravy I won't eat tonight.

"It's a communication from one of your relatives."

"Oh-oh-oh." My wife makes a grab for it, meanwhile punching CREAM-TOMATO-SAUCE-BEEF-DRIPPINGS. No wonder I have no appetite.

"I'll give it to you on one condition only," I tell her, holding it out of her trembling reach. "Take it into the bedroom and read it to yourself. Don't even move your lips for once: I don't want to know. If she's God forbid dead, I'll send him a sympathy card."

Sadie has a variety of expressions, but the one thing they have in common is they all wish me misfortune in my present and future life.

While she's reading the letter I find suddenly I have nothing to do. The magazines I read already. Breakfast I ate (like a bird). I'm all dressed to go out if I felt like, but there's nothing outside I don't have inside. Frankly, I don't feel like myself—I'm nervous. I say a lot of things I don't really intend and now maybe this letter comes to tell me I've got to pay for my meanness. Maybe she got sick up there; God knows what they eat, the kind of water they drink, the creatures they run around with. Not wanting to think about it too much, I go over to my chair and turn it on to brisk massage. It doesn't take long till I'm dreaming (fitfully).

I'm someplace surrounded by sand, sitting in a baby's crib and bouncing a diapered kangaroo on my knee. It gurgles up at me and calls me grandpa and I don't know what I should do. I don't want to hurt its feelings, but if I'm a grandpa to a kangaroo, I want no part of it; I only want it should go away. I pull out a dime from my pocket and put it into its pouch. The pouch is full of tiny insects which bite my fingers. I wake up in a sweat.

"Sadie! Are you reading, or rearranging the sentences? Bring it in here and I'll see what she wants. If it's a divorce, I know a lawyer."

Sadie comes into the room with her I-told-you-so waddle and gives me a small wet kiss on the cheek—a gold star for acting like a mensch. So I start to read it, in a loud monotone so she shouldn't get the impression I give a damn:

"Dear Daddy, I'm sorry for not writing sooner. I suppose I wanted to give you a chance to simmer down first." (Ingrate! Does the sun simmer down?) "I know it would have been inconvenient for you to come to the wedding, but Mor and I hoped you would maybe send us a letter just to let us know you're okay and still love me, in spite of everything."

Right at this point I feel a hot sigh followed by a short but wrenching moan.

"Sadie, get away from my neck. I'm warning you . . ."

Her eyes are going flick-a-fleck over my shoulder, from the piece of paper I'm holding to my face, back to the page, flick-a-fleck, flick-a-fleck.

"All right, already," she shoo-shoos me. "I read it, I know what's in it. Now it's your turn to see what kind of a lousy father you turned out to be." And she waddles back into the bedroom, shutting the door extra careful, like she's handling a piece of snow-white velvet.

When I'm certain she's gone, I sit myself down on the slab of woven dental floss my wife calls a couch and press a button on the arm that reads SEMI-CL.: FELDMAN TO FRIML. The music starts to slither out from the speaker under my left armpit. The right speaker is dead and buried and the long narrow one at the base years ago got drowned from the dog, who to this day hasn't learned to control himself when he hears "Desert Song."

This time I'm lucky; it's a piece by Feldman that comes on. I continue to read, calmed by the music.

"I might as well get to the point, Papa, because for all I know you're so mad you tore up this letter without even reading it. The point is that Mor and I are going to have a baby. Please, please don't throw this into the disintegrator. It's due in July, which gives you over three months to plan the trip up here. We have a lovely house, with a guest room that you and Mama can stay in for as long as you want."

I have to stop here to interject a couple of questions, since my daughter never had a head for logic and it's my strong point.

First of all, if she were in front of me in person right now I would ask right off what means "Mor and I are going to have a baby." Which? Or both? The second thing is, when she refers to it as "it" is she being literal or just uncertain? And just one more thing and then I'm through for good: Just how lovely can a guest room be that has all the air piped in and you can't even see the sky or take a walk on the grass because there is no grass, only simulated this and substituted that?

All the above notwithstanding, I continue to read:

"By the way, Papa, there's something I'm not sure you understand. Mor, you may or may not know, is as human as you and me, in all the important ways—and frankly a bit more intelligent."

I put down the letter for a minute just to give the goose-bumps a chance to fly out of my stomach ulcers before I go on with her love and best and kisses and hopes for seeing us soon, Lorinda.

I don't know how she manages it, but the second I'm finished, Sadie is out of the bedroom and breathing hard.

"Well, do I start packing or do I start packing? And when I start packing, do I pack for us or do I pack for me?"

"Never. I should die three thousand deaths, each one with a worse prognosis."

It's a shame a company like Interplanetary Aviation can't afford, with the fares they charge, to give you a comfortable seat. Don't ask how I ever got there in the first place. Ask my wife —she's the one with the mouth. First of all, they only allow you three pounds of luggage, which if you're only bringing clothes is plenty, but we had a few gifts with us. We were only planning to stay a few days and to sublet the house was Sadie's idea, not mine.

The whole trip was supposed to take a month, each way. This is one reason Sadie thought it was impractical to stay for the weekend and then go home, which was the condition on which I'd agreed to go.

But now that we're on our way, I decide I might as well relax. I close my eyes and try to think of what the first meeting will be like.

"How." I put up my right hand in a gesture of friendship and trust. I reach into my pocket and offer him beads.

But even in my mind he looks at me blank, his naked pink antennas waving in the breeze like a worm's underwear. Then

I realize there isn't any breeze where we're going. So they stop waving and wilt.

I look around in my mind. We're alone, the two of us, in the middle of a vast plain, me in my business suit and him in his green skin. The scene looks familiar, like something I had experienced, or read about . . . "We'll meet at Philippi," I think, and stab him with my sword.

Only then am I able to catch a few winks.

The month goes by. When I begin to think I'll never remember how to use a fork, the loudspeaker is turned on and I hear this very smooth, modulated voice, the tranquilized tones of a psychiatrist sucking glycerine, telling us it's just about over, and we should expect a slight jolt upon landing.

That slight jolt starts my life going by so fast I'm missing all the good parts. But finally the ship is still and all you can hear are the wheezes and sighs of the engines—the sounds remind me of Sadie when she's winding down from a good argument. I look around. Everybody is very white. Sadie's five fingers are around my upper arm like a tourniquet.

"We're here," I tell her. "Do I get a hacksaw or can you manage it yourself?"

"Oh, my goodness." She loosens her grip. She really looks a mess—completely pale, not blinking, not even nagging.

I take her by the arm and steer her into customs. All the time I feel that she's a big piece of unwilling luggage I'm smuggling in. There's no cooperation at all in her feet and her eyes are going every which way.

"Sadie, shape up!"

"If you had a little more curiosity about the world you'd be a better person," she says tolerantly.

While we're waiting to be processed by a creature in a suit like ours who surprises me by talking English, I sneak a quick look around.

It's funny. If I didn't know where we are I'd think we're in the back yard. The ground stretches out pure green, and it's only from the leaflet they give you in the ship to keep your mind off the panic that I know it's 100% Acrispan we're looking at, not grass. The air we're getting smells good, too, like fresh-cut flowers, but not too sweet.

By the time I've had a good look and a breathe, what's-its-name is handing us back our passports with a button that says to keep Mars beautiful don't litter.

I won't tell you about the troubles we had getting to the house, or the misunderstanding about the tip, because to be honest I wasn't paying attention. But we do manage to make it to the right door, and considering that the visit was a surprise, I didn't really expect they would meet us at the airport. My daughter must have been peeking, though, because she's in front of us even before we have a chance to knock.

"Mother!" she says, looking very round in the stomach. She hugs and kisses Sadie, who starts bawling. Five minutes later, when they're out of the clinch, Lorinda turns to me, a little nervous.

You can say a lot of things about me, but basically I'm a warm person, and we're about to be guests in this house, even if she is a stranger to me. I shake her hand.

"Is he home, or is he out in the back yard, growing new leaves?"

Her face (or what I can see of it through the climate adapter) crumbles a little at the chin line, but she straightens it out and puts her hand on my shoulder.

"Mor had to go out, Daddy—something important came up—but he should be back in an hour or so. Come on, let's go inside."

Actually there's nothing too crazy about the house, or even interesting. It has walls, a floor and a roof, I'm glad to see, even a few relaxer chairs, and after the trip we just had, I sit down and relax. I notice my daughter is having a little trouble looking me straight in the face, which is only as it should be, and it isn't long before she and Sadie are discussing pregnancy, gravitational exercise, labor, hospitals, formulas and sleep-taught toilet training. When I'm starting to feel that I'm getting over-educated, I decide to go into the kitchen and make myself a bite to eat. I could have asked them for a little something but I don't want to interfere with their first conversation. Sadie has all engines going and is interrupting four times a sentence, which is exactly the kind of game they always had back home—my daughter's goal is to say one complete thought out loud. If Sadie doesn't spring back with a non sequitur, Lorinda wins that round. A full-fledged knock-out with Sadie still champion is when my daughter can't get a sentence in for a week. Sometimes I can understand why she went to Mars.

Anyway, while they're at the height of their simultaneous monologues, I go quietly off to the kitchen to see what I can dig up. (Ripe parts of Mor, wrapped in plastic? Does he really regenerate, I wonder. Does Lorinda fully understand how he works, or one day will she make an asparagus omelet out of one of his appendages, only to learn that's the part that doesn't grow back? "Oh, I'm so *sorry*," she says. "Can you ever forgive me?")

The refrigerator, though obsolete on Earth, is well stocked —fruits of a sort, steaks, it seems, small chicken-type things that might be stunted pigeons. There's a bowl of a brownish, creamy mess—I can't even bring myself to smell it. Who's hungry, any-way, I think. The rumbling in my stomach is the symptom of a father's love turning sour.

I wander into the bedroom. There's a large portrait of Mor hanging on the wall—or maybe his ancestor. Is it true that instead of hearts, Martians have a large avocado pit? There's a rumor on Earth that when Martians get old they start to turn brown at the edges, like lettuce.

There's an object on the floor and I bend down and pick it up. A piece of material—at home I would have thought it was a man's handkerchief. Maybe it is a handkerchief. Maybe they have colds like us. They catch a germ, the sap rises to combat the infection, and they have to blow their stamens. I open up a drawer to put the piece of material in (I like to be neat), but when I close it, something gets stuck. Another thing I can't recognize. It's small, round and either concave or convex, depending on how you look at it. It's made of something black and shiny.

A cloth bowl? What would a vegetable be doing with a cloth bowl? Some questions are too deep for me, but what I don't know I eventually find out—and not by asking, either.

I go back to the living room.

"Did you find anything to eat?" Lorinda asks. "Or would you like me to fix—"

"Don't even get up," Sadie says quickly. "I can find my way around any kitchen, I don't care whose."

"I'm not hungry. It was a terrible trip. I thought I'd never wake up from it in one piece. By the way, I heard a good riddle on the ship. What's round and black, either concave or convex, depending on how you look at it, and made out of a shiny material?"

Lorinda blushed. "A skullcap? But that's not funny."

"So who needs funny? Riddles have to be a laugh a minute all of a sudden? You think Oedipus giggled all the way home from seeing the Sphinx?"

"Look, Daddy, I think there's something I should tell you."

"I think there are all sorts of things you should tell me."

"No, I mean about Mor."

"Who do you think *I* mean, the grocery boy? You elope with a cucumber from outer space and you want I should be satisfied because he's human in all the important ways? What's important —that he sneezes and hiccups? If you tell me he snores, I should be ecstatic? Maybe he sneezes when he's happy and hiccups when he's making love and snores because it helps him think better. Does that make him human?"

"Daddy, *please.*"

"Okay, not another word." Actually I'm starting to feel quite guilty. What if she has a miscarriage right on the spot? A man like me doesn't blithely torture a pregnant woman, even if she does happen to be his daughter. "What's so important it can't wait till later?"

"Nothing, I guess. Would you like some chopped liver? I just made some fresh."

"What?"

"Chopped liver—you know, chopped liver."

Oh yes, the ugly mess in the refrigerator. "You made it, that stuff in the bowl?"

"Sure. Daddy, there's something I really have to tell you."

She never does get to tell me, though, because her husband walks in, bold as brass.

I won't even begin to tell you what he looks like. Let me just say he's a good dream cooked up by Mary Shelley. I won't go into it, but if it gives you a small idea, I'll say that his head is shaped like an acorn on top of a stalk of broccoli. Enormous blue eyes, green skin and no hair at all except for a small blue round area on top of his head. His ears are adorable. Remember Dumbo the Elephant? Only a little smaller—I never exaggerate, even for effect. And he looks boneless, like a filet.

My wife, God bless her, I don't have to worry about; she's a gem in a crisis. One look at her son-in-law and she faints dead away. If I didn't know her better, if I wasn't absolutely certain that her simple mind contained no guile, I would have sworn she did it on purpose, to give everybody something to fuss about. Before we know what's happening, we're all in a tight, frantic conversation about what's the best way to bring her around. But while my daughter and her husband are in the bathroom looking for some deadly chemical, Sadie opens both eyes at once and stares up at me from the floor.

"What did I miss?"

"You didn't miss anything—you were only unconscious for fifteen seconds. It was a cat nap, not a coma."

"Say hello, Hector. Say hello to him or so help me I'll close my eyes for good."

"I'm very glad to meet you, Mr. Trumbnick," he says. I'm grateful that he's sparing me the humiliation of making the first gesture, but I pretend I don't see the stalk he's holding out.

"Smutual," I say.

"I beg your pardon?"

"Smutual. How are you? You look better than your pictures." He does, too. Even though his skin is green, it looks like the real thing up close. But his top lip sort of vibrates when he talks, and I can hardly bear to look at him except sideways.

"I hear you had some business this afternoon. My daughter never did tell me what your line is, uh, Morton."

"Daddy, his name is Mor. Why don't you call him Mor?"

"Because I prefer Morton. When we know each other better I'll call him something less formal. Don't rush me, Lorinda; I'm still getting adjusted to the chopped liver."

My son-in-law chuckles and his top lip really goes crazy. "Oh, were you surprised? Imported meats aren't a rarity here, you know. Just the other day one of my clients was telling me about an all-Earth meal he had at home."

"Your client?" Sadie asks. "You wouldn't happen to be a lawyer?" (My wife amazes me with her instant familiarity. She could live with a tyrannosaurus in perfect harmony. First she faints, and while she's out cold everything in her head that was strange becomes ordinary and she wakes up a new woman.)

"No, Mrs. Trumbnick. I'm a—"

"—rabbi, of course," she finishes. "I knew it. The minute Hector found that skullcup I knew it. Him and his riddles. A skullcap is a skullcap and nobody not Jewish would dare wear one —not even a Martian." She bites her lip but recovers like a pro. "I'll bet you were out on a Bar Mitzvah—right?"

"No, as a matter of fact—"

"—a Bris. I knew it."

She's rubbing her hands together and beaming at him. "A Bris, how *nice*. But why didn't you tell us, Lorinda? Why would you keep such a thing a secret?"

Lorinda comes over to me and kisses me on the cheek, and I wish she wouldn't because I'm feeling myself go soft and I don't want to show it.

"Mor isn't *just* a rabbi, Daddy. He converted because of me and then found there was a demand among the colonists. But he's never given up his own beliefs, and part of his job is to minister to the Kopchopees who camp outside the village. That's where he was earlier, conducting a Kopchopee menopausal rite."

"A what!"

"Look, to each his own," says my wife with the open mind. But me, I want facts, and this is getting more bizarre by the minute.

"Kopchopee. He's a Kopchopee priest to his own race and a rabbi to ours, and that's how he makes his living? You don't feel there's a contradiction between the two, Morton?"

"That's right. They both pray to a strong silent god, in different ways of course. The way my race worships, for instance—"

"Listen, it takes all kinds," says Sadie.

"And the baby, whatever it turns out to be—will it be a Choptapi or a Jew?"

"Jew, shmoo," Sadie says with a wave of dismissal. "All of a sudden it's Hector the Pious—such a megilla out of a molehill." She turns away from me and addresses herself to the others, like I've just become invisible. "He hasn't seen the inside of a synagogue since we got married—what a rain that night—and now he can't take his shoes off in a house until he knows its race, color and creed." With a face full of fury, she brings me back into her sight. "Nudnick, what's got into you?"

I stand up straight to preserve my dignity. "If you'll excuse me, my things are getting wrinkled in the suitcase."

Sitting on my bed (with my shoes on), I must admit I'm feeling a little different. Not that Sadie made me change my mind. Far from it; for many years now her voice is the white sound that lets me think my own thoughts. But what I'm realizing more and more is that in a situation like this a girl needs her father, and what kind of a man is it who can't sacrifice his personal feelings for his only daughter? When she was going out with Herbie the Hemophiliac and came home crying it had to end because she was afraid to touch him, he might bleed, didn't I say pack your things, we're going to Grossingers Venus for three weeks? When my twin brother Max went into kitchen sinks, who was it that helped him out at only four per cent? Always, I stood ready to help my family. And if Lorinda ever needed me, it's now when she's pregnant by some religious maniac.

Okay—he makes me retch, so I'll talk to him with a tissue over my mouth. After all, in a world that's getting smaller all the time, it's people like me who have to be bigger to make up for it, no?

I go back to the living room and extend my hand to my son-in-law the cauliflower. (Feh.)

Richard McKenna died in 1964. He had finished one big book about his China Sea days, and was well into another. In his essay "Journey With a Little Man," the best piece of writing about writing that I know (The Sons of Martha and Other Stories, Harper & Row, 1967), he wrote about the influence the Conference had on his life. For years he and his wife Eva were regulars at Milford, and since his death Eva has come back every year.

McKenna was fresh from four years at the University of North Carolina, and knew more about most sciences than anybody else at the Conference. The story that follows has not been published before; it derives from Mac's study of anthropology and folklore. There really is a family which formerly had the duty that is laid on young Mr. Spearman in this story.

——————————————————————— Richard McKenna

UNCLEAR CALL FOR LEE

Shortly after Christmas, Lee Spearman's favorite daydream became compulsive. His body-image of himself as a scrawny boy became more irksome. But he didn't seek help, because he expected time to heal him. Any time, now.

Lee was fair and well-fleshed and six feet tall, with overlarge nose and hands. He was twenty-five years old, employed in market research, and married. His mother was dead. His father, a retired professor, would not advance Lee to man's estate. To Lee, man's estate meant a partnership in his firm and a private office instead of a desk among those silly, giggling others in the bullpen. It meant a qualitative change in the nature of existence and access to powers and mysteries withheld from boys. His father would neither give nor loan him the money to buy a partnership. The old man lived on stubbornly, alone and in constant pain from a cancerous jaw. For Christmas Lee had given him a revolver and a box of cartridges with which to defend himself from burglars. The old man had not yet unwrapped the gift. He was very obstinate.

That afternoon it was spring outside and the girls at the other desks looked fresh and summery and Lee couldn't put his mind to his work. He knew the symptoms and what he had to do about them. He had to run through his daydream, to clear his mind for work. The girls wouldn't suspect. They'd see him trimly erect in his gray suit, thinking with eyes closed and fingers steepled above the neat pile of papers on his austere maple desk top. They'd realize what a commanding presence he was going to have, in maturity. They might giggle and whisper, "Genius at work," but they were probably all secretly in love with him. They knew Lee Spearman was headed for the top.

Lee's daydream was a dialogue with his father. Lee had one point to drive home: it was unfair a boy had to wait for his inheritance until he was so old he no longer needed it. He held the shifty, evasive old man rigorously to that point. With clean, sharp phrases he drove his argument through to the solid ground of mutual agreement. Once Lee was launched on the daydream he couldn't stop it until his father nodded and said, "I see your point, son. I'll give you the money." Then Lee could work again. The daydream gave him a lift, like a refreshing little nap.

Lee had barely begun the dialogue when his intercom summoned him to the senior partner's office. Two men in dark business suits stood there on the thick carpet beside the desk. Mr. Drew, his pleasant, pink face looking distressed, stood up to introduce them. The burly, florid man was Mr. Duffy of the county sanitation board. The waspish little man in steel-rimmed glasses was Mr. Sinclair, from the county treasurer's office. They didn't seem to want to shake hands.

"Mr. Duffy has a little job for you, Lee," Mr. Drew said.

"You needn't come back this afternoon. If you want several days off, just phone me."

"You can follow us in your car," Mr. Duffy said. He had a deep, gravelly voice.

"Marie—my wife—has the car today," Lee said.

Mr. Duffy frowned. "Come with us, then," he said.

Mr. Sinclair looked at his wrist watch. "The traffic rush starts in two hours," he said. "We mustn't waste time." He had a dry, precise voice and a birdlike tilt to his head.

The two men turned to the door. Lee looked wonderingly at Mr. Drew.

"Mr. Duffy will explain," Mr. Drew said. He made little shooing motions with his hands. "Go on, now. They're in a hurry."

Lee stopped for his hat and briefcase and caught up with the two men at the elevator. They stood silent and apart from him on the way down. A black police car with a uniformed cop at the wheel waited at the curb outside the building. Mr. Duffy waved Lee into the back seat and closed the door. Then Mr. Sinclair and he crowded into the front seat and the car pulled smoothly into the traffic flow. Lee had a panicky thought.

"I'm not under arrest, am I?" he asked. He laughed uncertainly.

"No, just a little job in your calling," Mr. Duffy said. "It'll only take a few minutes." He spoke without turning his head.

The car was going north out of town on State 40. It was the way Lee drove home every night and he knew where he was without looking. Mr. Duffy lit a cigar that smelled expensive. Lee wondered if he ought to feel irritated. Mr. Duffy sounded as ponderous and sure of himself as the ship of state. But something was all wrong here.

"About this job," Lee began. "How can market analysis—"

"I told you, in your calling." Mr. Duffy sounded impatient. "It'll be simpler this first time if you just do what we tell you." He didn't look around. "You weren't due to come up for years yet," he said. "We had four families and three single men in the county. In the last six months all of them but you died or moved away. Things happen like that sometimes."

"There's the truck." Mr. Sinclair pointed. "We're not late."

It was a white, stake-bodied city sanitation truck. It pulled in from Euclid and went along ahead of the police car. Four Negroes in greenish coveralls stood in the back. They wore fiber helmets painted yellow. Houses began giving way to open fields and flowering weeds sprouted thickly alongside the road. Lee rolled down his right-hand window, and the air smelled crisp and greenish. He didn't understand all this. Just before the intersection with State 32, the outbound traffic halted. One lane was blocked and men with red flags were pulsing traffic both ways through the single open lane. Highway department vehicles were clumped at the intersection and workmen stood around. The truck and police car turned through the smoking flare pots into the blocked lane and stopped at the intersection.

"Clancy's been waiting," Mr. Sinclair said. "He'll be angry."

Mr. Duffy grunted. He got out and went over to talk to a blunt-featured man in khaki and a red helmet. It was the usual scene, Lee thought. The men had dug a longish, rectangular hole. At one end the broken pavement was stacked in neat squares and at one side red earth was heaped. Two shovels were stuck at jaunty angles into the heap. Beyond it an air compressor and roller and tank truck waited. The air smelled of hot tar oils. The Negroes were sliding a box of unpainted boards down from their truck. It had the word "top" daubed in black paint and, central near one end, a hole about three inches across. To the left, a steady stream of cars passed. A few people in them glanced idly at the scene.

I wish Mr. Duffy would finish his business and come get us to wherever we're going, Lee thought. This is stupid.

The Negroes turned the box over and put rope slings under it. The box had a smaller hole on the bottom, near one end. One at each corner, the Negroes carried the box over the hole and lowered it with the slings. They pulled the ropes free and threw them into the truck and lounged back against the truck and lit cigarettes. The red-helmeted man said something angrily to the tallest one.

"Oh, you go to hell, Clancy," the tall Negro said. He blew smoke in Clancy's face.

Clancy turned back to Mr. Duffy. "All right, get him down in there, Duffy," he said.

Mr. Duffy came over and opened the police car door.

"All right, get out and get down in that hole," he told Lee. He spoke with his cigar still in his mouth.

Lee got out, clutching his briefcase. He licked his lips. "What for? What's this all about?" he asked.

"It's your calling. Just do what we tell you, for now," Mr. Duffy said. "I already told you how it is, they all died or moved away."

"I'll want an hour to patch this," Clancy said. "Get him down in there, for God's sake, or we'll have hell's own traffic jam tonight."

"Be quick, now! There's no time!" Mr. Duffy rumbled.

Lee looked at them helplessly, then into the hole. It was about four feet down to the box. Still holding his briefcase, Lee bent with his hands to the pavement and groped with his right leg for footing. His left foot slipped and he came down on the box with a jar and his left trouser leg was smeared with red clay. He looked up at a row of grinning black and white faces. The sky was a washed blue, with fleecy clouds.

"Here, *take* it, you!" Clancy was saying.

Lee took it from him. It was a shiny steel rod, thick as his finger and about four feet long. One end was forged into a flat triangular point with hollow ground edges. Lee looked at it and back up at Clancy.

"Push it through the hole," Clancy said. "Straight down, mind you, so it'll go through the hole on the other side."

"This is crazy," Lee said.

Clancy barked a laugh. "Think so, do you?" he asked.

All the heads laughed. The Negroes had very white teeth.

"It's simple enough, isn't it?" Mr. Duffy said. He looked annoyed. "Get on with it, it's almost four o'clock."

Lee could see only coarse white cloth through the hole. The point hesitated, as if against something resilient, then went in smoothly, then resisted.

"Push on it!" Clancy said. "You're big enough, you lump!"

Lee pushed. The point sheared through, sending a vibration up the shaft, and then thunked solidly. The shaft stood at an angle. Lee stood back and looked up.

"I think I hit wood," he said.

"He thinks he hit wood," Clancy said. Everybody laughed.

"Hell yes, you hit wood!" Clancy snorted. "Look at how it's canted! Pull it back, now, and probe for that bottom hole."

Lee probed until he felt the point go into the earth beneath the box. Then he scowled up at Clancy.

"All right, it's through," he said. "Is that all?"

"No, it ain't all," Clancy said. "Push it on down. I got a mark filed on the side that's got to come flush with the boards."

Lee could see the mark. It was about eight inches above the board. He pushed and worked the rod down another inch or two and the end of the rod hurt his hand. He stopped.

"That's the best I can do," he told Clancy sullenly. "If you want more, come down here yourself."

"By God, you'll know it, if I have to come down there!" Clancy said.

"Take it easy, Clancy, he's new at it," a Negro said.

"That's tight red clay," another one said. "Real packed."

"It's regular hardpan," the tall Negro said. "Be decent, Clancy."

Clancy tightened his lips and shook his head, his face as red as his helmet. He turned and bent and came up with a sledge hammer, which he threw down on the box. It crashed beside Lee's foot, and he jumped. Everybody laughed. Lee scowled and picked up the sledge and drove the rod down easily. He started to lay the sledge up on the pavement. Everybody drew back and Clancy raised his hands.

"No, no, no, leave it down there!" he said. "Come on out, now."

"Give me a hand up, somebody," Lee said.

Nobody stirred. Then one of the Negroes put on a glove

and held his hand out. Lee grasped it and scrambled up and thanked the man. He bent to slap the red clay off his trouser leg and saw the Negro throw his glove down on the box.

"Look out now you don't charge that hammer off to my department," Clancy told somebody.

"We'll deduct it from his fee," Mr. Sinclair's voice said.

Lee picked up his briefcase and stood erect. Clancy's men were filling in the hole with shovels. Mr. Sinclair stood by the police car. He had put on gray gloves and he had a long, narrow black book open on the hood. Beyond him cars streamed by in the open lane and a few people in them glanced out idly. The Negroes were climbing back into their truck.

"Come over here and sign this," Mr. Sinclair told Lee.

Lee walked over and looked. It was a form, perforated to be torn out, and across the top was printed: "For Professional Services Rendered to the County of Franklin." Typed underneath was: "For one spearing at crossroads—$30.00."

"I don't get this," Lee said. "I don't like it."

Mr. Sinclair cocked his head like a robin. "You like money, don't you?" he asked dryly. "We can't send you a check unless you sign. Right here."

He pointed with a pen and then held it out. Lee took it, shook his head, and signed.

"It's not much. The fees should be readjusted," Mr. Sinclair said apologetically. "We'll have to deduct for that hammer, too."

"I don't get it," Lee said. "Are we all crazy?"

"You're just young. You'll get the knack of it," Mr. Sinclair said. He put the pen and book into a large Manila envelope. "I expect you'll be out quite often now, being the only one," he said. He stripped off his gloves, put them into the envelope too, and sealed it. "Some of the other services bring higher fees," he said.

"Get in the car, we'll take you home," Mr. Duffy said at Lee's elbow.

Lee rode alone in the back again. The car took the right turn-off for Roseglen and Lee decided they must know where he lived. They did. They pulled up in front of Lee's car at the curb, and he knew Marie was home. Lee got out, the question ready to burst inside him, and clutched his briefcase to his chest. Mr. Duffy had his right elbow casually out the open window and his cigar was about half-smoked. Lee felt more sure of himself in front of his own home.

"Damn it, you've got to tell me what this is all about," he told Mr. Duffy. "Either you're all crazy, or I am."

"You're young and we're not," Mr. Duffy rumbled. "Don't let it throw you. Clancy's a good fellow, ordinarily. He was just pushed for time."

"You're all crazy," Lee said.

Mr. Duffy smiled. "Be seeing you," he said.

He raised his hand, holding the cigar, and the police car pulled away. Lee turned and ran shakily to his front door. He closed it behind him and saw Marie come out of the kitchen. She still had on her black town dress and excitement and concern played over her darkly pretty face. She came toward him across the living room.

"Stop!" Lee said.

She stopped, one hand to her cheek and her eyes inquiring. "You've heard," she said.

"Heard what?" he asked. "Don't touch me, Marie. I think I have to take a bath before anybody can touch me."

"Then you haven't heard." She nodded slowly. "I'll make us a drink while you shower. Then I'll tell you."

"First I'm going to phone Dad," Lee said grimly. "He's got to tell me something."

He started across to the phone.

"Wait, Lee!" she cried.

He held the phone like a club in his left hand and looked around at her. She had her hands clasped together at her breast and her face was all concern now.

"That's what I have to tell you," she said rapidly. "You see, you can't call your father any more."

Keith Laumer is a quiet, tight-lipped, gray-eyed chap who knows exactly what he wants and does not stand in need of much criticism; he comes to the Conference for camaraderie and market news. At the workshop in which this story was entered, we got quite excited about it and suggested several ingenious new plot twists to make it even better. Then Keith told us he had already sold it to Analog.

— *Keith Laumer*

THE LAST COMMAND

I come to awareness, sensing a residual oscillation traversing my hull from an arbitrarily designated heading of 035. From the damping rate I compute that the shock was of intensity 8.7, emanating from a source within the limits 72 meters/46 meters. I activate my primary screens, trigger a return salvo. There is no response. I engage reserve energy cells, bring my secondary battery to bear—futilely. It is apparent that I have been ranged by the Enemy and severely damaged.

My positional sensors indicate that I am resting at an angle of 13 degrees 14 seconds, deflected from a base line at 21 points from median. I attempt to right myself, but encounter massive resistance. I activate my forward scanners, shunt power to my IR microstrobes. Not a flicker illuminates my surroundings. I am encased in utter blackness.

Now a secondary shock wave approaches, rocks me with an intensity of 8.2. It is apparent that I must withdraw from my position—but my drive trains remain inert under full thrust. I shift to base emergency power, try again. Pressure mounts; I sense my awareness fading under the intolerable strain; then, abruptly, resistance falls off and I am in motion.

It is not the swift maneuvering of full drive, however; I inch forward, as if restrained by massive barriers. Again I attempt to penetrate the surrounding darkness, and this time perceive great irregular outlines shot through with fracture planes. I probe cautiously, then more vigorously, encountering incredible densities.

I channel all available power to a single ranging pulse, direct it upward. The indication is so at variance with all experience that I repeat the test at a new angle. Now I must accept the fact: I am buried under 207.6 meters of solid rock!

I direct my attention to an effort to orient myself to my uniquely desperate situation. I run through an action-status checklist of thirty thousand items, feel dismay at the extent of power loss. My main cells are almost completely drained, my reserve units at no more than .4 charge. Thus my sluggishness is explained. I review the tactical situation, recall the triumphant announcement from my commander that the Enemy forces are annihilated, that all resistance has ceased. In memory, I review the formal procession; in company with my comrades of the Dinochrome Brigade, many of us deeply scarred by Enemy action, we parade before the Grand Commandant, then assemble on the depot ramp. At command, we bring our music storage cells into phase and display our Battle Anthem. The nearby star radiates over a full spectrum, unfiltered by atmospheric haze. It is a moment of glorious triumph. Then the final command is given—

The rest is darkness. But it is apparent that the victory celebration was premature. The Enemy has counterattacked with a force that has come near to immobilizing me. The realization is shocking, but the .1 second of leisurely introspection has clarified my position. At once, I broadcast a call on Brigade Action wavelength:

"Unit LNE to Command, requesting permission to file VSR."

I wait, sense no response, call again, using full power. I sweep the enclosing volume of rock with an emergency alert warning. I tune to the all-units band, await the replies of my comrades of the Brigade. None answers. Now I must face the reality: I alone have survived the assault.

I channel my remaining power to my drive and detect a channel of reduced density. I press for it and the broken rock around me yields reluctantly. Slowly, I move forward and upward. My pain circuitry shocks my awareness center with emergency signals; I am doing irreparable damage to my overloaded neural systems, but my duty is clear: I must seek and engage the Enemy.

Emerging from behind the blast barrier, Chief Engineer Pete Reynolds of the New Devonshire Port Authority pulled off his rock mask and spat grit from his mouth.

"That's the last one; we've bottomed out at just over two hundred yards. Must have hit a hard stratum down there."

"It's almost sundown," the paunchy man beside him said shortly. "You're a day and a half behind schedule."

"We'll start backfilling now, Mr. Mayor. I'll have pilings poured by oh-nine hundred tomorrow, and with any luck the first section of pad will be in place in time for the rally."

"I'm . . ." The mayor broke off, looked startled. "I thought you told me that was the last charge to be fired . . ."

Reynolds frowned. A small but distinct tremor had shaken the ground underfoot. A few feet away, a small pebble balanced atop another toppled and fell with a faint clatter.

"Probably a big rock fragment falling," he said. At that moment, a second vibration shook the earth, stronger this time. Reynolds heard a rumble and a distant impact as rock fell from the side of the newly blasted excavation. He whirled to the control shed as the door swung back and Second Engineer Mayfield appeared.

"Take a look at this, Pete!" Reynolds went across to the hut, stepped inside. Mayfield was bending over the profiling table.

"What do you make of it?" he pointed. Superimposed on the heavy red contour representing the detonation of the shaped charge that had completed the drilling of the final pile core were two other traces, weak but distinct.

"About .1 intensity," Mayfield looked puzzled. "What . . ."

The tracking needle dipped suddenly, swept up the screen to peak at .21, dropped back. The hut trembled. A stylus fell from the edge of the table. The red face of Mayor Daugherty burst through the door.

"Reynolds, have you lost your mind? What's the idea of blasting while I'm standing out in the open? I might have been killed!"

"I'm not blasting," Reynolds snapped. "Jim, get Eaton on the line, see if they know anything." He stepped to the door, shouted.

A heavyset man in sweat-darkened coveralls swung down from the seat of a cable-lift rig. "Boss, what goes on?" he called as he came up. "Damn near shook me out of my seat!"

"I don't know. You haven't set any trim charges?"

"No, boss. I wouldn't set no charges without your say-so."

"Come on." Reynolds started out across the rubble-littered stretch of barren ground selected by the Authority as the site of the new spaceport. Halfway to the open mouth of the newly blasted pit, the ground under his feet rocked violently enough to make him stumble. A gout of dust rose from the excavation ahead. Loose rock danced on the ground. Beside him, the drilling chief grabbed his arm.

"Boss, we better get back!"

Reynolds shook him off, kept going. The drill chief swore and followed. The shaking of the ground went on, a sharp series of thumps interrupting a steady trembling.

"It's a quake!" Reynolds yelled over the low rumbling sound. He and the chief were at the rim of the core now.

"It can't be a quake, boss," the latter shouted. "Not in these formations!"

"Tell it to the geologists . . ." The rock slab they were standing on rose a foot, dropped back. Both men fell. The slab bucked like a small boat in choppy water.

"Let's get out of here!" Reynolds was up and running. Ahead, a fissure opened, gaped a foot wide. He jumped it, caught a glimpse of black depths, a glint of wet clay twenty feet below—

A hoarse scream stopped him in his tracks. He spun, saw the drill chief down, a heavy splinter of rock across his legs. He jumped to him, heaved at the rock. There was blood on the man's shirt. The chief's hands beat the dusty rock before him. Then other men were there, grunting, sweaty hands gripping beside Reynolds'. The ground rocked. The roar from under the earth had risen to a deep, steady rumble. They lifted the rock aside, picked up the injured man and stumbled with him to the aid shack.

The mayor was there, white-faced.

"What is it, Reynolds? If you're responsible—"

"Shut up!" Reynolds brushed him aside, grabbed the phone, punched keys.

"Eaton! What have you got on this temblor?"

"Temblor, hell." The small face on the four-inch screen looked like a ruffled hen. "What in the name of Order are you doing out there? I'm reading a whole series of displacements originating from that last core of yours! What did you do, leave a pile of trim charges lying around?"

"It's a quake. Trim charges, hell! This thing's broken up two hundred yards of surface rock. It seems to be traveling north-northeast—"

"I see that; a traveling earthquake!" Eaton flapped his arms, a tiny and ridiculous figure against a background of wall charts and framed diplomas. "Well . . . do something, Reynolds! Where's Mayor Daugherty?"

"Underfoot!" Reynolds snapped, and cut off.

Outside, a layer of sunset-stained dust obscured the sweep of level plain. A rock-dozer rumbled up, ground to a halt by Reynolds. A man jumped down.

"I got the boys moving equipment out," he panted. "The thing's cutting a trail straight as a rule for the highway!" He pointed to a raised roadbed a quarter-mile away.

"How fast is it moving?"

"She's done a hundred yards; it hasn't been ten minutes yet!"

"If it keeps up another twenty minutes, it'll be into the Intermix!"

"Scratch a few million cees and six months' work then, Pete!"

"And Southside Mall's a couple miles farther."

"Hell, it'll damp out before then!"

"Maybe. Grab a field car, Dan."

"Pete!" Mayfield came up at a trot. "This thing's building! The centroid's moving on a heading of 022—"

"How far subsurface?"

"It's rising; started at two-twenty yards, and it's up to one-eighty!"

"What have we stirred up?" Reynolds stared at Mayfield as the field car skidded to a stop beside them.

"Stay with it, Jim. Give me anything new. We're taking a closer look." He climbed into the rugged vehicle.

"Take a blast truck—"

"No time!" He waved and the car gunned away into the pall of dust.

The rock car pulled to a stop at the crest of the three-level Intermix on a lay-by designed to permit tourists to enjoy the view of the site of the proposed port, a hundred feet below. Reynolds studied the progress of the quake through field glasses. From this vantage point, the path of the phenomenon was a clearly defined trail of tilted and broken rock, some of the slabs twenty feet across. As he watched, the fissure lengthened.

"It looks like a mole's trail." Reynolds handed the glasses to his companion, thumbed the Send key on the car radio.

"Jim, get Eaton and tell him to divert all traffic from the Circular south of Zone Nine. Cars are already clogging the right-of-way. The dust is visible from a mile away, and when the word gets out there's something going on, we'll be swamped."

"I'll tell him, but he won't like it!"

"This isn't politics! This thing will be into the outer pad area in another twenty minutes!"

"It won't last—"

"How deep does it read now?"

"One-five!" There was a moment's silence. "Pete, if it stays on course, it'll surface at about where you're parked!"

"Uh-huh. It looks like you can scratch one Intermix. Better tell Eaton to get a story ready for the press."

"Pete—talking about newshounds," Dan said beside him. Reynolds switched off, turned to see a man in a gay-colored driving outfit coming across from a battered Monojag sportster which had pulled up behind the rock car. A big camera case was slung across his shoulder.

"Say, what's going on down there?" he called.

"Rock slide," Reynolds said shortly. "I'll have to ask you to drive on. The road's closed . . ."

"Who're you?" The man looked belligerent.

"I'm the engineer in charge. Now pull out, brother." He turned back to the radio. "Jim, get every piece of heavy equipment we own over here, on the double." He paused, feeling a minute trembling in the car. "The Intermix is beginning to feel it," he went on. "I'm afraid we're in for it. Whatever that thing is, it acts like a solid body boring its way through the ground. Maybe we can barricade it."

"Barricade an earthquake?"

"Yeah . . . I know how it sounds . . . but it's the only idea I've got."

"Hey . . . what's that about an earthquake?" The man in the colored suit was still there. "By gosh, I can feel it—the whole bridge is shaking!"

"Off, mister—now!" Reynolds jerked a thumb at the traffic lanes where a steady stream of cars was hurtling past. "Dan, take us over to the main track. We'll have to warn this traffic off . . ."

"Hold on, fellow," the man unlimbered his camera. "I represent the New Devon *Scope*. I have a few questions—"

"I don't have the answers," Pete cut him off as the car pulled away.

"Hah!" the man who had questioned Reynolds yelled after him. "Big shot! Think you can . . ." His voice was lost behind them.

In a modest retirees' apartment block in the coast town of Idle-breeze, forty miles from the scene of the freak quake, an old man sat in a reclining chair, half dozing before a yammering Tri-D tank.

". . . Grandpa," a sharp-voiced young woman was saying. "It's time for you to go in to bed."

"Bed? Why do I want to go to bed? Can't sleep anyway . . ." He stirred, made a pretense of sitting up, showing an interest in the Tri-D. "I'm watching this show."

"It's not a show, it's the news," a fattish boy said disgustedly. "Ma, can I switch channels—"

"Leave it alone, Bennie," the old man said. On the screen, a panoramic scene spread out, a stretch of barren ground across which a furrow showed. As he watched, it lengthened.

". . . Up here at the Intermix we have a fine view of the whole curious business, lazangemmun," the announcer chattered. "And in our opinion it's some sort of publicity stunt staged by the Port Authority to publicize their controversial Port project—"

"Ma, can I change channels?"

"Go ahead, Bennie—"

"Don't touch it," the old man said. The fattish boy reached for the control, but something in the old man's eye stopped him.

"The traffic's still piling up here," Reynolds said into the phone. "Damn it, Jim, we'll have a major jam on our hands—"

"He won't do it, Pete! You know the Circular was his baby—the super all-weather pike that nothing could shut down. He says you'll have to handle this in the field—"

"Handle, hell! I'm talking about preventing a major disaster! And in a matter of minutes, at that!"

"I'll try again—"

"If he says no, divert a couple of the big ten-yard graders and block it off yourself. Set up field 'arcs, and keep any cars from getting in from either direction."

"Pete, that's outside your authority!"

"You heard me!"

Ten minutes later, back at ground level, Reynolds watched the boom-mounted polyarcs swinging into position at the two road-blocks a quarter of a mile apart, cutting off the threatened section of the raised expressway. A hundred yards from where he stood on the rear cargo deck of a light grader rig, a section of rock fifty feet wide rose slowly, split, fell back with a ponderous impact. One corner of it struck the massive pier supporting the extended shelf of the lay-by above. A twenty-foot splinter fell away, expos-ing the reinforcing-rod core.

"How deep, Jim?" Reynolds spoke over the roaring sound coming from the disturbed area.

"Just subsurface now, Pete! It ought to break through—" His voice was drowned in a rumble as the damaged pier shivered, rose up, buckled at its midpoint and collapsed, bringing down with it a large chunk of pavement and guard rail, and a single still-glowing light pole. A small car that had been parked on the doomed section was visible for an instant just before the immense slab struck. Reynolds saw it bounce aside, then disappear under an avalanche of broken concrete.

"My God, Pete—" Dan blurted. "That damned fool news-hound—!"

"Look!" As the two men watched, a second pier swayed, fell backward into the shadow of the span above. The roadway sagged, and two more piers snapped. With a bellow like a burst dam, a hundred-foot stretch of the road fell into the roiling dust cloud.

"Pete!" Mayfield's voice burst from the car radio. "Get out of there! I threw a reader on that thing and it's chattering . . . !"

Among the piled fragments, something stirred, heaved, rising up, lifting multi-ton pieces of the broken road, thrusting them aside like so many potato chips. A dull blue radiance broke through from the broached earth, threw an eerie light on the shattered structure above. A massive, ponderously irresistible shape thrust forward through the ruins. Reynolds saw a great blue-glowing profile emerge from the rubble like a surfacing submarine, shedding a burden of broken stone, saw immense treads ten feet wide claw for purchase, saw the mighty flank brush a still standing pier, send it crashing aside.

"Pete . . . what . . . what is it—?"

"I don't know." Reynolds broke the paralysis that had gripped him. "Get us out of here, Dan, fast! Whatever it is, it's headed straight for the city!"

I emerge at last from the trap into which I had fallen, and at once encounter defensive works of considerable strength. My scanners are dulled from lack of power, but I am able to perceive open ground beyond the barrier, and farther still, at a distance of 5.7 kilometers, massive walls. Once more I transmit the Brigade Rally signal; but as before, there is no reply. I am truly alone.

I scan the surrounding area for the emanations of Enemy drive units, monitor the EM spectrum for their communications. I detect nothing; either my circuitry is badly damaged, or their shielding is superb.

I must now make a decision as to possible courses of action. Since all my comrades of the Brigade have fallen, I compute that the walls before me must be held by Enemy forces. I direct probing signals at the defenses, discover them to be of unfamiliar construction, and less formidable than they appear. I am aware of the possibility that this may be a trick of the Enemy; but my course is clear.

I re-engage my driving engines and advance on the Enemy fortress.

"You're out of your mind, Father," the stout man said. "At your age—"

"At your age, I got my nose smashed in a brawl in a bar on Aldo," the old man cut him off. "But I won the fight."

"James, you can't go out at this time of night . . ." an elderly woman wailed.

"Tell them to go home." The old man walked painfully toward his bedroom door. "I've seen enough of them for today."

"Mother, you won't let him do anything foolish?"

"He'll forget about it in a few minutes; but maybe you'd better go now and let him settle down."

"Mother . . . I really think a home is the best solution."

"Yes, Grandma," the young woman nodded agreement. "After all, he's past ninety—and he has his veteran's retirement . . ."

Inside his room, the old man listened as they departed. He went to the closet, took out clothes, began dressing.

City Engineer Eaton's face was chalk-white on the screen.

"No one can blame me," he said. "How could I have known—"

"Your office ran the surveys and gave the PA the green light," Mayor Daugherty yelled.

"All the survey charts showed was 'Disposal Area.'" Eaton threw out his hands. "I assumed—"

"As City Engineer, you're not paid to make assumptions! Ten minutes' research would have told you that was a 'Y' category area!"

"What's 'Y' category mean?" Mayfield asked Reynolds. They were standing by the field Comm center, listening to the dispute. Nearby, boom-mounted Tri-D cameras hummed, recording the progress of the immense machine, its upper turret rearing forty-five feet into the air, as it ground slowly forward across smooth ground toward the city, dragging behind it a trailing festoon of twisted reinforcing iron crusted with broken concrete.

"Half-life over one hundred years," Reynolds answered shortly. "The last skirmish of the war was fought near here. Apparently this is where they buried the radioactive equipment left over from the battle."

"But that was more than seventy years ago—"

"There's still enough residual radiation to contaminate anything inside a quarter mile radius."

"They must have used some hellish stuff." Mayfield stared at the dull shine half a mile distant.

"Reynolds, how are you going to stop this thing?" The mayor had turned on the PA Engineer.

"Me stop it? You saw what it did to my heaviest rigs: flattened them like pancakes. You'll have to call out the military on this one, Mr. Mayor."

"Call in Federation forces? Have them meddling in civic affairs?"

"The station's only sixty-five miles from here. I think you'd better call them fast. It's only moving at about three miles per hour but it will reach the south edge of the Mall in another forty-five minutes."

"Can't you mine it? Blast a trap in its path?"

"You saw it claw its way up from six hundred feet down. I checked the specs; it followed the old excavation tunnel out. It was rubble-filled and capped with twenty-inch compressed concrete."

"It's incredible," Eaton said from the screen. "The entire machine was encased in a ten-foot shell of reinforced armocrete. It had to break out of that before it could move a foot!"

"That was just a radiation shield; it wasn't intended to restrain a Bolo Combat Unit."

"What *was*, may I inquire?" the mayor glared.

"The units were deactivated before being buried," Eaton spoke up, as if he were eager to talk. "Their circuits were fused. It's all in the report—"

"The report you should have read somewhat sooner," the mayor snapped.

"What . . . what started it up?" Mayfield looked bewildered. "For seventy years it was down there, and nothing happened!"

"Our blasting must have jarred something," Reynolds said

shortly. "Maybe closed a relay that started up the old battle reflex circuit."

"You know something about these machines?" the mayor asked.

"I've read a little."

"Then speak up, man. I'll call the station, if you feel I must. What measures should I request?"

"I don't know, Mr. Mayor. As far as I know, nothing on New Devon can stop that machine now."

The mayor's mouth opened and closed. He whirled to the screen, blanked Eaton's agonized face, punched in the code for the Federation Station.

"Colonel Blane!" he blurted as a stern face came onto the screen. "We have a major emergency on our hands! I'll need everything you've got! This is the situation—"

I encounter no resistance other than the flimsy barrier, but my progress is slow. Grievous damage has been done to my main-drive sector due to overload during my escape from the trap; and the failure of my sensing circuitry has deprived me of a major portion of my external receptivity. Now my pain circuits project a continuous signal to my awareness center; but it is my duty to my commander and to my fallen comrades of the Brigade to press forward at my best speed; but my performance is a poor shadow of my former ability.

And now at last the Enemy comes into action! I sense aerial units closing at supersonic velocities; I lock my lateral batteries to them and direct salvo fire; but I sense that the arming mechanisms clatter harmlessly. The craft sweep over me, and my impotent guns elevate, track them as they release detonants that spread out in an envelopmental pattern which I, with my reduced capabilities, am powerless to avoid. The missiles strike; I sense their detonations all about me; but I suffer only trivial damage. The enemy has blundered if he thought to neutralize a Mark XXVIII Combat Unit with mere chemical explosives! But I weaken with each meter gained.

THE LAST COMMAND   229

Now there is no doubt as to my course. I must press the charge and carry the walls before my reserve cells are exhausted.

From a vantage point atop a bucket rig four hundred yards from the position the great fighting machine had now reached, Pete Reynolds studied it through night glasses. A battery of beamed polyarcs pinned the giant hulk, scarred and rust-scaled, in a pool of blue-white light. A mile and a half beyond it, the walls of the Mall rose sheer from the garden setting.

"The bombers slowed it some," he reported to Eaton via scope. "But it's still making better than two miles per hour. I'd say another twenty-five minutes before it hits the main ringwall. How's the evacuation going?"

"Badly! I get no cooperation! You'll be my witness, Reynolds, I did all I could—"

"How about the mobile batteries; how long before they'll be in position?" Reynolds cut him off.

"I've heard nothing from Federation Central—typical militaristic arrogance, not keeping me informed—but I have them on my screens. They're two miles out—say three minutes."

"I hope you made your point about N-heads."

"That's outside my province!" Eaton said sharply. "It's up to Brand to carry out this portion of the operation!"

"The HE missiles didn't do much more than clear away the junk it was dragging," Reynolds' voice was sharp.

"I wash my hands of responsibility for civilian lives," Eaton was saying when Reynolds shut him off, changed channels.

"Jim, I'm going to try to divert it," he said crisply. "Eaton's sitting on his political fence; the Feds are bringing artillery up, but I don't expect much from it. Technically, Brand needs Sector OK to use nuclear stuff, and he's not the boy to stick his neck out—"

"Divert it how? Pete, don't take any chances—"

Reynolds laughed shortly. "I'm going to get around it and drop a shaped drilling charge in its path. Maybe I can knock a tread off. With luck, I might get its attention on me, and draw it away from the Mall. There are still a few thousand people over there, glued to their Tri-D's. They think it's all a swell show."

"Pete, you can't walk up on that thing! It's hot . . ." He broke off. "Pete—there's some kind of nut here—he claims he has to talk to you; says he knows something about that damned juggernaut. Shall I send . . . ?"

Reynolds paused with his hand on the cut-off switch. "Put him on," he snapped. Mayfield's face moved aside and an ancient, bleary-eyed visage stared out at him. The tip of the old man's tongue touched his dry lips.

"Son, I tried to tell this boy here, but he wouldn't listen—"

"What have you got, old-timer?" Pete cut in. "Make it fast."

"My name's Sanders. James Sanders. I'm . . . I was with the Planetary Volunteer Scouts, back in '71—"

"Sure, dad," Pete said gently. "I'm sorry, I've got a little errand to run—"

"Wait . . ." The old man's face worked. "I'm old, son—too damned old. I know. But bear with me. I'll try to say it straight. I was with Hayle's squadron at Toledo. Then afterwards, they shipped us . . . but hell, you don't care about that! I keep wandering, son; can't help it. What I mean to say is—I was in on that last scrap, right here at New Devon—only we didn't call it New Devon then. Called it Hellport. Nothing but bare rock and Enemy emplacements . . ."

"You were talking about the battle, Mr. Sanders," Pete said tensely. "Go on with that part."

"Lieutenant Sanders," the oldster said. "Sure, I was Acting Brigade Commander. See, our major was hit at Toledo—and after Tommy Chee stopped a sidewinder . . ."

"Stick to the point, Lieutenant!"

"Yes, sir!" the old man pulled himself together with an obvious effort. "I took the Brigade in; put out flankers, and ran the Enemy into the ground. We mopped 'em up in a thirty-three-hour running fight that took us from over by Crater Bay all the way down here to Hellport. When it was over, I'd lost six units, but the

Enemy was done. They gave us Brigade Honors for that action. And then . . ."

"Then what?"

"Then the triple-dyed yellow-bottoms at Headquarters put out the order the Brigade was to be scrapped; said they were too hot to make decon practical. Cost too much, they said! So after the final review . . ." He gulped, blinked. "They planted 'em deep, two hundred meters, and poured in special High-R concrete."

"And packed rubble in behind them," Reynolds finished for him. "All right, Lieutenant, I believe you! But what started that machine on a rampage?"

"Should have known they couldn't hold down a Bolo Mark XXVIII!" The old man's eyes lit up. "Take more than a few million tons of rock to stop Lenny when his battle board was lit!"

"Lenny?"

"That's my old Command Unit out there, son. I saw the markings on the 3-D. Unit LNE of the Dinochrome Brigade!"

"Listen!" Reynolds snapped out. "Here's what I intend to try . . ." He outlined his plan.

"Ha!" Sanders snorted. "It's quite a notion, mister, but Lenny won't give it a sneeze."

"You didn't come here to tell me we were licked," Reynolds cut in. "How about Brand's batteries?"

"Hell, son, Lenny stood up to point-blank Hellbore fire on Toledo, and—"

"Are you telling me there's nothing we can do?"

"What's that? No, son, that's not what I'm saying . . ."

"Then what!"

"Just tell these johnnies to get out of my way, mister. I think I can handle him."

At the field Comm hut, Pete Reynolds watched as the man who had been Lieutenant Sanders of the Volunteer Scouts pulled shiny black boots over his thin ankles, and stood. The blouse and trousers of royal blue polyon hung on his spare frame like wash on a line. He grinned, a skull's grin.

"It doesn't fit like it used to, but Lenny will recognize it. It'll help. Now, if you've got that power pack ready . . ."

Mayfield handed over the old-fashioned field instrument Sanders had brought in with him.

"It's operating, sir—but I've already tried everything I've got on that infernal machine; I didn't get a peep out of it."

Sanders winked at him. "Maybe I know a couple of tricks you boys haven't heard about." He slung the strap over his bony shoulder and turned to Reynolds.

"Guess we better get going, mister. He's getting close."

In the rock car Sanders leaned close to Reynolds' ear. "Told you those Federal guns wouldn't scratch Lenny. They're wasting their time."

Reynolds pulled the car to a stop at the crest of the road, from which point he had a view of the sweep of ground leading across to the city's edge. Lights sparkled all across the towers of New Devon. Close to the walls, the converging fire of the ranked batteries of infinite repeaters drove into the glowing bulk of the machine, which plowed on, undeterred. As he watched, the firing ceased.

"Now, let's get in there, before they get some other scheme going," Sanders said.

The rock car crossed the rough ground, swung wide to come up on the Bolo from the left side. Behind the hastily rigged radiation cover, Reynolds watched the immense silhouette grow before him.

"I knew they were big," he said. "But to see one up close like this—" He pulled to a stop a hundred feet from the Bolo.

"Look at the side ports," Sanders said, his voice crisper now. "He's firing anti-personnel charges—only his plates are flat. If they weren't, we wouldn't have gotten within half a mile." He unclipped the microphone and spoke into it:

"Unit LNE, break off action and retire to ten-mile line!"

Reynolds' head jerked around to stare at the old man. His voice had rung with vigor and authority as he spoke the command.

The Bolo ground slowly ahead. Sanders shook his head, tried again.

"No answer, like that fella said. He must be running on nothing but memories now . . ." He reattached the microphone and before Reynolds could put out a hand, had lifted the anti-R cover and stepped off on the ground.

"Sanders—get back in here!" Reynolds yelled.

"Never mind, son. I've got to get in close. Contact induction." He started toward the giant machine. Frantically, Reynolds started the car, slammed it into gear, pulled forward.

"Better stay back," Sanders' voice came from his field radio. "This close, that screening won't do you much good."

"Get in the car!" Reynolds roared. "That's hard radiation!"

"Sure; feels funny, like a sunburn, about an hour after you come in from the beach and start to think maybe you got a little too much." He laughed. "But I'll get to him . . ."

Reynolds braked to a stop, watched the shrunken figure in the baggy uniform as it slogged forward, leaning as against a sleet-storm.

"I'm up beside him," Sanders' voice came through faintly on the field radio. "I'm going to try to swing up on his side. Don't feel like trying to chase him any farther."

Through the glasses, Reynolds watched the small figure, dwarfed by the immense bulk of the fighting machine as he tried, stumbled, tried again, swung up on the flange running across the rear quarter inside the churning bogie wheel.

"He's up," he reported. "Damned wonder the track didn't get him before . . ."

Clinging to the side of the machine, Sanders lay for a moment, bent forward across the flange. Then he pulled himself up, wormed his way forward to the base of the rear quarter turret, wedged himself against it. He unslung the communicator, removed a small black unit, clipped it to the armor; it clung, held by a magnet. He brought the microphone up to his face.

234   KEITH LAUMER

In the Comm shack Mayfield leaned toward the screen, his eyes squinted in tension. Across the field Reynolds held the glasses fixed on the man lying across the flank of the Bolo. They waited.

The walls are before me, and I ready myself for a final effort, but suddenly I am aware of trickle currents flowing over my outer surface. Is this some new trick of the Enemy? I tune to the wave-energies, trace the source. They originate at a point in contact with my aft port armor. I sense modulation, match receptivity to a computed pattern. And I hear a voice:

"Unit LNE, break it off, Lenny. We're pulling back now, boy! This is Command to LNE; pull back to ten miles. If you read me, Lenny, swing to port and halt."

I am not fooled by the deception. The order appears correct, but the voice is not that of my Commander. Briefly I regret that I cannot spare energy to direct a neutralizing power flow at the device the Enemy has attached to me. I continue my charge.

"Unit LNE! Listen to me, boy; maybe you don't recognize my voice, but it's me! You see—some time has passed. I've gotten old. My voice has changed some, maybe. But it's me! Make a port turn, Lenny. Make it now!"

I am tempted to respond to the trick, for something in the false command seems to awaken secondary circuits which I sense have been long stilled. But I must not be swayed by the cleverness of the Enemy. My sensing circuitry has faded further as my energy cells drain; but I know where the Enemy lies. I move forward, but I am filled with agony, and only the memory of my comrades drives me on.

"Lenny, answer me. Transmit on the old private band—the one we agreed on. Nobody but me knows it, remember?"

Thus the Enemy seeks to beguile me into diverting precious power. But I will not listen.

"Lenny—not much time left. Another minute and you'll be into the walls. People are going to die. Got to stop you, Lenny. Hot here. My God, I'm hot. Not breathing too well, now. I can feel it; cutting through me like knives. You took a load of Enemy power, Lenny; and now I'm getting my share. Answer me, Lenny. Over to you . . ."

It will require only a tiny allocation of power to activate a communication circuit. I realize that it is only an Enemy trick, but I compute that by pretending to be deceived, I may achieve some trivial advantage. I adjust circuitry accordingly, and transmit:

"Unit LNE to Command. Contact with Enemy defensive line imminent. Request supporting fire!"

"Lenny . . . you can hear me! Good boy, Lenny! Now make a turn, to port. Walls . . . close . . ."

"Unit LNE to Command. Request positive identification; transmit code 685749."

"Lenny—I can't . . . I don't have code blanks. But it's me . . ."

"In absence of recognition code, your transmission disregarded." *I send. And now the walls loom high above me. There are many lights, but I see them only vaguely. I am nearly blind now.*

"Lenny—less'n two hundred feet to go. Listen, Lenny. I'm climbing down. I'm going to jump down, Lenny, and get around under your force scanner pickup. You'll see me, Lenny. You'll know me then."

The false transmission ceases. I sense a body moving across my side. The gap closes. I detect movement before me, and in automatic reflex fire anti-P charges before I recall that I am unarmed.

A small object has moved out before me, and taken up a position between me and the wall behind which the Enemy conceal themselves. It is dim, but appears to have the shape of a man . . .

I am uncertain. My alert center attempts to engage inhibitory circuitry which will force me to halt, but it lacks power. I can override it. But still I am unsure. Now I must take a last risk, I must shunt power to my forward scanner to examine this obstacle more closely. I do so, and it leaps into greater clarity. It is indeed a man—and it is enclothed in regulation blues of the Volunteers.

*Now, closer, I see the face, and through the pain of my great
effort I study it . . .*

"He's backed against the wall," Reynolds said hoarsely. "It's
still coming. Fifty feet to go—"

"You were a fool, Reynolds!" the mayor barked. "A fool to stake
everything on that old dotard's crazy ideas!"

"Hold it!" As Reynolds watched, the mighty machine slowed,
halted, ten feet from the sheer wall before it. For a moment it sat,
as though puzzled. Then it backed, halted again, pivoted ponderously to the left and came about.

On its side, a small figure crept up, fell across the lower gun
deck. The Bolo surged into motion, retracing its route across the
artillery-scarred gardens.

"He's turned it," Reynolds let his breath out with a shuddering
sigh. "It's headed out for open desert. It might get twenty miles
before it finally runs out of steam."

The strange voice that was the Bolo's came from the big panel
before Mayfield:

*"Command . . . Unit LNE reports main power cells drained,
secondary cells drained; now operating at .037 percent efficiency,
using Final Emergency Power. Request advice as to range to be
covered before relief maintenance available."*

"It's a long, long way, Lenny . . ." Sanders' voice was a bare
whisper. *"But I'm coming with you . . ."*

Then there was only the crackle of static. Ponderously, like a
great, mortally stricken animal, the Bolo moved through the ruins
of the fallen roadway, heading for the open desert.

"That damned machine," the mayor said in a hoarse voice.
"You'd almost think it was alive."

"You would at that," Pete Reynolds said.

Carol Emshwiller and her husband Ed came to the first Conference but didn't feel they really belonged, and had to be reassured that it was all right for them to stay. Since then they have been here every year, and we have watched Carol grow as a writer until she overshadows the rest of us, while Ed, formerly a science fiction illustrator, has become a famous avant-garde filmmaker. Carol, who was born in the Year of the Mouse, barely said a word for the first three or four years. Then she discovered her voice, and now nobody can shout her down.

A couple of years ago Carol brought a story to the workshop in two versions. In one, an important character was male; in the other, female. It did not occur to her to warn us about this. When the story came up for discussion, Piers Anthony, who had read version "B," began talking about the protagonist's "wife." Harlan Ellison, who had read version "A," leaped up with a strangled scream and ran into the kitchen. He came back in a few moments with a flyswatter quivering in his hand. Later he said: "All I could think was Kill! Kill!"

———————————————————— *Carol Emshwiller*

PELT

She was a white dog with a wide face and eager eyes, and this was the planet, Jaxa, in winter.

She trotted well ahead of the master, sometimes nose to ground, sometimes sniffing the air, and she didn't care if they were being watched or not. She knew that strange things skulked behind iced trees, but strangeness was her job. She had been trained for it, and crisp, glitering Jaxa was, she felt, exactly what she *had* been trained for, *born* for.

I love it, I love it . . . that was in her pointing ears, her waving tail . . . I *love* this place.

It was a world of ice, a world with the sound of breaking goblets. Each time the wind blew they came shattering down by the trayful, and each time one branch brushed against another, it was: Skoal, Down the hatch, To the Queen . . . tink, tink, tink. And the sun was reflected as if from a million cut-glass punch bowls under a million crystal chandeliers.

She wore four little black boots, and each step she took sounded like two or three more goblets gone, but the sound was lost in the other tinkling, snapping, cracklings of the silver, frozen forest about her.

She had figured out at last what that hovering scent was. It had been there from the beginning, the landing two days ago, mingling with Jaxa's bitter air and seeming to be just a part of the smell of the place, she found it in crisscrossing trails about the squatting ship, and hanging, heavy and recent, in hollows behind flat-branched, piney-smelling bushes. She thought of honey and fat men and dry fur when she smelled it.

There was something big out there, and more than one of them, more than two. She wasn't sure how many. She had a feeling this was something to tell the master, but what was the signal, the agreed upon noise for: We are being watched? There was a whisper of sound, short and quick, for: Sighted close, come and shoot. And there was a noise for danger (all these through her throat mike to the receiver at the master's ear), a special, howly bark: Awful, awful—there is something awful going to happen. There was even a noise, a low rumble of sound for: Wonderful, wonderful fur—drop everything and come after *this* one. (And she knew a good fur when she saw one. She had been trained to know.) But there was no sign for: We are being watched.

She'd whined and barked when she was sure about it, but that had got her a pat on the head and a rumpling of the neck fur. "You're doing fine, Baby. This world is our oyster, all ours. All we got to do is pick up the pearls. Jaxa's what we've been waiting for." And Jaxa was, so she did her work and didn't try to tell him any more, for what was one more strange thing in one more strange world?

She was on the trail of something now, and the master was behind her, out of sight. He'd better hurry. He'd better hurry or there'll be waiting to do, watching the thing, whatever it is, steady on until he comes, holding tight back, and that will be hard. Hurry, hurry.

She could hear the whispered whistle of a tune through the receiver at her ear and she knew he was not hurrying but just being happy. She ran on, eager, curious. She did not give the signal for hurry, but she made a hurry sound of her own, and she heard him stop whistling and whisper back into the mike, "So, so, Queen of Venus. The furs are waiting to be picked. No hurry, Baby." But morning was to her for hurry. There was time later to be tired and slow.

That fat-man honeyish smell was about, closer and strong. Her curiosity became two pronged—this smell or that? What *is* the big thing that watches? She kept to the trail she was on, though. Better to be sure, and this thing was not so elusive, not twisting and doubling back, but up ahead and going where it was going.

She topped a rise and half slid, on thick furred rump, down the other side, splattering ice. She snuffled at the bottom to be sure of the smell again, and then, nose to ground, trotted past a thick and tangled hedgerow.

She was thinking through her nose now. The world was all smell, crisp air and sour ice and turpentine pine . . . and this animal, a urine and brown grass thing . . . and then, strong in front of her, honey-furry-fat man.

She felt it looming before she raised her head to look, and there it was, the smell in person, some taller than the master and twice as wide. Counting his doubled suit and all, twice as wide.

This was a fur! Wonderful, wonderful. But she just stood, looking up, mouth open and lips pulled back, the fur on the back of her neck rising more from the suddenness than from fear.

It was silver and black, a tiger-striped thing, and the whitish parts glistened and caught the light as the ice of Jaxa did, and sparkled and dazzled in the same way. And there, in the center of the face, was a large and terrible orange eye, rimmed in black with black radiating lines crossing the forehead and rounding the head. That spot of orange dominated the whole figure, but it was a flat, blind eye, unreal, grown out of fur. At first she saw only that spot of color, but then she noticed under it two small, red glinting eyes and they were kind, not terrible.

This was the time for the call: Come, come and get the great fur, the huge-price-tag fur for the richest lady on earth to wear and be dazzling in and most of all to pay for. But there was something about the flat, black nose and the tender, bow-shaped lips and those kind eyes that stopped her from calling. Something masterlike. She was full of wondering and indecision and she made no sound at all.

The thing spoke to her then, and its voice was a deep lullaby sound of buzzing cellos. It gestured with a thick, fur-backed hand. It promised, offered, and asked; and she listened, knowing and not knowing.

The words came slowly. *This . . . is . . . world.*

Here is the sky, the earth, the ice. The heavy arms moved. The hands pointed.

We have watched you, little slave. What have you done that is free today? Take the liberty. Here is the earth for your four shoed feet, the sky of stars, the ice to drink. Do something free today. Do, do.

Nice voice, she thought, nice thing. It gives and gives . . . something.

Her ears pointed forward, then to the side, one and then the other, and then forward again. She cocked her head, but the real meaning would not come clear. She poked at the air with her nose. Say that again, her whole body said. I almost have it.

I *feel* it. Say it once more and maybe then the sense of it will come.

But the creature turned and started away quickly, very quickly for such a big thing, and disappeared behind the trees and bushes. It seemed to shimmer itself away until the glitter was only the glitter of the ice and the black was only the thick, flat branches.

The master was close. She could hear his crackling steps coming up behind her.

She whined softly, more to herself than to him.

"Ho, the Queen, Aloora. Have you lost it?" She sniffed the ground again. The honey-furry smell was strong. She sniffed beyond, zigzagging. The trail was there. "Go to it, Baby." She loped off to a sound like Chinese wind chimes, businesslike again. Her tail hung guiltily, though, and she kept her head low. She had missed an important signal. She'd waited until it was too late. But was the thing a man, a master? Or a fur? She wanted to do the right thing. She always tried and tried for that, but now she was confused.

She was getting close to whatever it was she trailed, but the hovering smell was still there too, though not close. She thought of gifts. She knew that much from the slow, lullaby words, and gifts made her think of bones and meat, not the dry fishy biscuit she always got on trips like this. A trickle of drool flowed from the side of her mouth and froze in a silver thread across her shoulder.

She slowed. The thing she trailed must be there, just behind the next row of trees. She made a sound in her throat . . . ready, steady . . . and she advanced until she was sure. She sensed the shape. She didn't really see it . . . mostly it was the smell and something more in the tinkling glassware noises. She gave the signal and stood still, a furry, square imitation of a pointer. Come, hurry. This waiting is the hardest part.

He followed, beamed to her radio. "Steady, Baby. Hold that pose. Good girl, good girl." There was only the slightest twitch of her tail as she wagged it, answering him in her mind.

He came up behind her and then passed, crouched, holding

the rifle before him, elbows bent. He knelt then, and waited as if at a point of his own, rifle to shoulder. Slowly he turned with the moving shadow of the beast, and shot, twice in quick succession.

They ran forward then, together, and it was what she had expected—a deerlike thing, dainty hoofs, proud head, and spotted in three colors, large gray-green rounds on tawny yellow, with tufts of that same glittering silver scattered over.

The master took out a sharp, flat-bladed knife. He began to whistle out loud as he cut off the handsome head. His face was flushed.

She sat down near by, mouth open in a kind of smile, and she watched his face as he worked. The warm smell made the drool come at the sides of her mouth and drip out to freeze on the ice and on her paws, but she sat quietly, only watching.

Between the whistlings he grunted and swore and talked to himself, and finally he had the skin and the head in a tight, inside out bundle.

Then he came to her and patted her sides over the ribs with the flat, slap sound, and he scratched behind her ears and held a biscuit to her on his thick-gloved palm. She swallowed it whole and then watched him as he squatted on his heels and himself ate one almost like it.

Then he got up and slung the bundle of skin and head across his back. "I'll take this one, Baby. Come on, let's get one more something before lunch." He waved her to the right. "We'll make a big circle," he said.

She trotted out, glad she was not carrying anything. She found a strong smell at a patch of discolored ice and urinated on it. She sniffed and growled at a furry, mammal-smelling bird that landed in the trees above her and sent down a shower of ice slivers on her head. She zigzagged and then turned and bit, lips drawn back in mock rage, at a branch that scraped her side.

She followed for a while the chattery sound of water streaming along under the ice, and left it where an oily, lambish smell crossed. Almost immediately she came upon them—six small, greenish balls of wool with floppy, woolly feet. The honey-fat man smell was strong here too, but she signaled for the lambs, the come and shoot sound, and she stood again waiting for the master. "*Good* girl!" His voice had a special praise. "By God, this place is a gold mine. Hold it, Queen of Venus. Whatever it is, don't let go."

There was a fifty-yard clear view here and she stood in plain sight of the little creatures, but they didn't notice. The master came slowly and cautiously, and knelt beside her. Just as he did, there appeared at the far end of the clearing a glittering, silver and black tiger-striped man.

She heard the sharp inward breath of the master and she felt the tenseness come to him. There was a new, faint whiff of sour sweat, a stiff silence and a special way of breathing. What she felt from him made the fur rise along her back with a mixture of excitement and fear.

The tiger thing held a small packet in one hand and was peering into it and pulling at the opening in it with a blunt finger. Suddenly there was a sweep of motion beside her and five fast, frantic shots sounded sharp in her ear. Two came after the honey-fat man had already fallen and lay like a huge decorated sack.

The master ran forward and she came at his heels. They stopped, not too close, and she watched the master looking at the big, dead tiger head with the terrible eye. The master was breathing hard and seemed hot. His face was red and puffy looking, but his lips made a hard whitish line. He didn't whistle or talk. After a time he took out his knife. He tested the blade, making a small, bloody thread of a mark on his left thumb. Then he walked closer and she stood and watched him and whispered a questioning whine.

He stooped by the honey-fat man and it was that small, partly opened packet that he cut viciously through the center. Small round chunks fell out, bite-sized chunks of dried meat and a cheesy substance and some broken bits of clear, bluish ice.

The master kicked at them. His face was not red any more,

but olive-pale. His thin mouth was open in a grin that was not a grin. He went about the skinning then.

He did not keep the flat-faced, heavy head nor the blunt-fingered hands.

The man had to make a sliding thing of two of the widest kind of flat branches to carry the new heavy fur, as well as the head and the skin of the deer. Then he started directly for the ship.

It was past eating time but she looked at his restless eyes and did not ask about it. She walked before him, staying close. She looked back often, watching him pull the sled thing by the string across his shoulder and she knew, by the way he held the rifle before him in both hands, that she should be wary.

Sometimes the damp-looking, inside-out bundle hooked on things, and the master would curse in a whisper and pull at it. She could see the bundle made him tired, and she wished he would stop for a rest and food as they usually did long before this time.

They went slowly, and the smell of honey-fat man hovered as it had from the beginning. They crossed the trails of many animals. They even saw another deer run off, but she knew that it was not a time for chasing.

Then another big silver and black tiger stood exactly before them. It appeared suddenly, as if actually it had been standing there all the time, and they had not been near enough to see it, to pick it out from its glistening background.

It just stood and looked and dared, and the master held his gun with both hands and looked too, and she stood between them glancing from one face to the other. She knew, after a moment, that the master would not shoot, and it seemed the tiger thing knew too, for it turned to look at her and it raised its arms and spread its fingers as if grasping at the forest on each side. It swayed a bit, like bigness off balance, and then it spoke in its tight-strung, cello tones. The words and the tone seemed the same as before.

Little slave, what have you done that is free today? Remember this is world. Do something free today. Do, do.

She knew that what it said was important to it, something she should understand, a giving and a taking away. It watched her, and she looked back with wide, innocent eyes, wanting to do the right thing, but not knowing what.

The tiger-fat man turned then, this time slowly, and left a wide back for the master and her to see, and then it half turned, throwing a quick glance over the heavy humped shoulder at the two of them. Then it moved slowly away into the trees and ice, and the master still held the gun with two hands and did not move.

The evening wind began to blow, and there sounded about them that sound of a million chandeliers tinkling and clinking like gigantic wind chimes. A furry bird, the size of a shrew and as fast, flew by between them with a miniature shriek.

She watched the master's face, and when he was ready she went along beside him. The soft sounds the honey-fat man had made echoed in her mind but had no meaning.

That night the master stretched the big skin on a frame and afterward he watched the dazzle of it. He didn't talk to her. She watched him a while and then she turned around three times on her rug and lay down to sleep.

The next morning the master was slow, reluctant to go out. He studied charts of other places, round or hourglass-shaped maps with yellow dots and labels, and he drank his coffee standing up looking at them. But finally they did go out, squinting into the ringing air.

It was her world. More each day, she felt it was so, right feel, right temperature, lovely smells. She darted on ahead as usual, yet not too far today, and sometimes she stopped and waited and looked at the master's face as he came up. And sometimes she would whine a question before she went on . . . Why don't you walk brisk, brisk, and call me Queen of Venus, Aloora, Galaxa, or Bitch of Betelgeuse? Why don't you sniff like

I do? Sniff, and you will be happy with this place . . . And she would run on again.

Trails were easy to find, and once more she found the oily lamb smell, and once more came upon them quickly. The master strode up beside her and raised his gun . . . but a moment later he turned, carelessly, letting himself make a loud noise, and the lambs ran. He made a face, and spit upon the ice. "Come on, Queen. Let's get out of here. I'm sick of this place."

He turned and made the signal to go back, pointing with his thumb above his head in two jerks of motion.

But why, why? This is morning now and our world. She wagged her tail and gave a short bark, and looked at him, dancing a little on her back paws, begging with her whole body. "Come on," he said.

She turned then, and took her place at his heel, head low, but eyes looking up at him, wondering if she had done something wrong, and wanting to be right and noticed and loved because he was troubled and preoccupied.

They'd gone only a few minutes on the way back when he stopped suddenly in the middle of a step, slowly put both feet flat upon the ground and stood like a soldier at a stiff, off-balance attention. There, lying in the way before them, was the huge, orange-eyed head and in front of it, as if at the end of outstretched arms, lay two leathery hands, the hairless palms up.

She made a growl deep in her throat and the master made a noise almost exactly like hers, but more a groan. She waited for him, standing as he stood, not moving, feeling his tenseness coming in to her. Yet it was just a head and two hands of no value, old ones they had had before and thrown away.

He turned and she saw a wild look in his eyes. He walked with deliberate steps, and she followed, in a wide circle about the spot. When they had skirted the place, he began to walk very fast.

They were not far from the ship. She could see its flat blackness as they drew nearer to the clearing where it was, the burned, iceless pit of spewed and blackened earth. And then she saw that the silver tiger men were there, nine of them in a wide circle, each with the honey-damp fur smell, but each with a separate particular sweetness.

The master was still walking very fast, eyes down to watch his footing, and he did not see them until he was there in the circle before them all, standing there like nine upright bears in tiger suits.

He stopped and made a whisper of a groan, and he let the gun fall low in one hand so that it hung loose with the muzzle almost touching the ground. He looked from one to the other and she looked at him, watching his pale eyes move along the circle.

"Stay," he said, and then he began to go toward the ship at an awkward limp, running and walking at the same time, banging the gun handle against the air lock as he entered.

He had said, Stay. She sat watching the ship door and moving her front paws up and down because she wanted to be walking after him. He was gone only a few minutes, though, and when he came back it was without the gun and he was holding the great fur with cut pieces of thongs dangling like ribbons along its edges where it had been tied to the stretching frame. He went at that same run-walk, unbalanced by the heavy bundle, to one of them along the circle. Three gathered together before him and refused to take it back. They pushed it, bunched loosely, back across his arms again and to it they added another large and heavy package in a parchment bag, and the master stood, with his legs wide to hold it all.

Then one honey-fat man motioned with a fur-backed hand to the ship and the bundles, and then to the ship and the master, and then to the sky. He made two sharp sounds once, and then again. And another made two different sounds, and she felt the feeling of them . . . Take your things and go home. Take them, these and these, and go.

They turned to her then and one spoke and made a wide gesture. *This is world. The sky, the earth, the ice.*

They wanted her to stay. They gave her . . . was it their world? But what good was a world?

She wagged her tail hesitantly, lowered her head and looked up at them . . . I do want to do right, to please everybody, everybody, but . . . Then she followed the master into the ship.

The locks rumbled shut. "Let's get out of here," he said. She took her place, flat on her side, take-off position. The master snapped the flat plastic sheet over her, covering head and all and, in a few minutes, they roared off.

Afterward he opened the parchment bag. She knew what was in it. She knew he knew too, but she knew by the smell. He opened it and dumped out the head and the hands. His face was tight and his mouth stiff.

She saw him almost put the big head out the waste chute, but he didn't. He took it in to the place where he kept good heads and some odd paws or hoofs, and he put it by the others there.

Even she knew this head was different. The others were all slant-browed like she was and most had jutting snouts. This one seemed bigger than the big ones, with its heavy, ruffed fur and huge eye staring, and more grand than any of them, more terrible . . . and yet a flat face, with a delicate, black nose and tender lips.

The tenderest lips of all.

Ted Thomas, a stalwart in these sessions from the first, has pointed out that very often we see a story heavily criticized in the workshop, many good suggestions made, and the author busily taking notes . . . and four or five months later the story comes out in a magazine, without a word changed.

I think this is understandable. For one thing, even if a story is not sold by the time we workshop it, it may be out to market. This was the case with "Masks," a costive, difficult story written over a period of three years. I got a full load of criticisms from the workshop, including three or four that I thought were worth taking seriously, but the story was out to *Playboy* and if they wanted it as it was, I was not about to tinker with it. A week or two later I got a list of suggested changes from *Playboy*. They were the same ones the workshop people had proposed; so I tinkered.

Other years, from the criticisms of my stories and more especially of other people's, I've learned not so much how to write *that* story better—because by then it's usually too late—but how to write the next one better; and I think that's the point.

MASKS

The eight pens danced against the moving strip of paper, like the nervous claws of some mechanical lobster. Roberts, the technician, frowned over the tracings while the other two watched.

"Here's the wake-up impulse," he said, pointing with a skinny finger. "Then here, look, seventeen seconds more, still dreaming."

"Delayed response," said Babcock, the project director. His heavy face was flushed and he was sweating. "Nothing to worry about."

"OK, delayed response, but look at the difference in the tracings.

Still dreaming, after the wake-up impulse, but the peaks are closer together. Not the same dream. More anxiety, more motor pulses."

"Why does he have to sleep at all?" asked Sinescu, the man from Washington. He was dark, narrow-faced. "You flush the fatigue poisons out, don't you? So what is it, something psychological?

"He needs to dream," said Babcock. "It's true he has no physiological need for sleep, but he's got to dream. If he didn't, he'd start to hallucinate, maybe go psychotic."

"Psychotic," said Sinescu. "Well—that's the question, isn't it? How long has he been doing this?"

"About six months."

"In other words, about the time he got his new body—and started wearing a mask?"

"About that. Look, let me tell you something: he's rational. Every test—"

"Yes, OK, I know about tests. Well—so he's awake now?"

The technician glanced at the monitor board. "He's up. Sam and Irma are with him." He hunched his shoulders, staring at the EEG tracings again. "I don't know why it should bother me. It stands to reason, if he has dream needs of his own that we're not satisfying with the programmed stuff, this is where he gets them in." His face hardened. "I don't know. Something about those peaks I don't like."

Sinescu raised his eyebrows. "You program his dreams?"

"Not program," said Babcock impatiently. "A routine suggestion to dream the sort of thing we tell him to. Somatic stuff, sex, exercise, sport."

"And whose idea was that?"

"Psych section. He was doing fine neurologically, every other way, but he was withdrawing. Psych decided he needed that somatic input in some form, we had to keep him in touch. He's alive, he's functioning, everything works. But don't forget, he spent forty-three years in a normal human body."

In the hush of the elevator, Sinescu said, "Washington."

Swaying, Babcock said, "I'm sorry; what?"

"You look a little rocky. Getting any sleep?"

"Not lately. What did you say before?"

"I said they're not happy with your reports in Washington."

"Goddamn it, I know that." The elevator door silently opened. A tiny foyer, green carpet, gray walls. There were three doors, one metal, two heavy glass. Cool, stale air. "This way."

Sinescu paused at the glass door, glanced through: a gray-carpeted living room, empty. "I don't see him."

"Around the el. Getting his morning checkup."

The door opened against slight pressure; a battery of ceiling lights went on as they entered. "Don't look up," said Babcock. "Ultraviolet." A faint hissing sound stopped when the door closed.

"And positive pressure in here? To keep out germs? Whose idea was that?"

"His." Babcock opened a chrome box on the wall and took out two surgical masks. "Here, put this on."

Voices came muffled from around the bend of the room. Sinescu looked with distaste at the white mask, then slowly put it over his head.

They stared at each other. "Germs," said Sinescu through the mask. "Is that rational?"

"All right, he can't catch a cold, or what have you, but think about it a minute. There are just two things now that could kill him. One is a prosthetic failure, and we guard against that; we've got five hundred people here, we check him out like an airplane. That leaves a cerebrospinal infection. Don't go in there with a closed mind."

The room was large, part living room, part library, part workshop. Here was a cluster of Swedish-modern chairs, a sofa, coffee table; here a workbench with a metal lathe, electric crucible, drill press, parts bins, tools on wallboards; here a drafting table; here a free-standing wall of bookshelves that Sinescu fingered curiously as they passed. Bound volumes of project reports, technical journals, reference books; no fiction, except for *Fire* and *Storm* by George Stewart and *The Wizard of Oz* in a worn blue binding. Behind the bookshelves, set into a little alcove, was a glass door through which they glimpsed another living room, differently furnished: upholstered chairs, a tall philodendron in a ceramic pot. "There's Sam," Babcock said.

A man had appeared in the other room. He saw them, turned to call to someone they could not see, then came forward, smiling. He was bald and stocky, deeply tanned. Behind him, a small pretty woman hurried up. She crowded through after her husband, leaving the door open. Neither of them wore a mask.

"Sam and Irma have the next suite," Babcock said. "Company for him; he's got to have somebody around. Sam is an old Air Force buddy of his and, besides, he's got a tin arm."

The stocky man shook hands, grinning. His grip was firm and warm. "Want to guess which one?" He wore a flowered sport shirt. Both arms were brown, muscular and hairy; but when Sinescu looked more closely, he saw that the right one was a slightly different color, not quite authentic.

Embarrassed, he said, "The left, I guess."

"Nope." Grinning wider, the stocky man pulled back his right sleeve to show the straps.

"One of the spin-offs from the project," said Babcock. "Myo-electric, servo-controlled, weighs the same as the other one. Sam, they about through in there?"

"Maybe so. Let's take a peek. Honey, you think you could rustle up some coffee for the gentlemen?"

"Oh, why, sure." The little woman turned and darted back through the open doorway.

The far wall was glass, covered by a translucent white curtain. They turned the corner. The next bay was full of medical and electronic equipment, some built into the walls, some in tall black cabinets on wheels. Four men in white coats were gathered around what looked like an astronaut's couch. Sinescu could see someone lying on it: feet in Mexican woven-leather shoes, dark socks, gray slacks. A mutter of voices.

"Not through yet," Babcock said. "Must have found something else they didn't like. Let's go out onto the patio a minute."

"Thought they checked him at night—when they exchange his blood, and so on . . . ?"

"They do," Babcock said. "And in the morning, too." He turned and pushed open the heavy glass door. Outside, the roof was paved with cut stone, enclosed by a green-plastic canopy and tinted-glass walls. Here and there were concrete basins, empty. "Idea was to have a roof garden out here, something green, but he didn't want it. We had to take all the plants out, glass the whole thing in."

Sam pulled out metal chairs around a white table and they all sat down. "How is he, Sam?" asked Babcock.

He grinned and ducked his head. "Mean in the mornings."

"Talk to you much? Play any chess?"

"Not too much. Works, mostly. Reads some, watches the box a little." His smile was forced; his heavy fingers were clasped together and Sinescu saw now that the fingertips of one hand had turned darker, the others not. He looked away.

"You're from Washington, that right?" Sam asked politely. "First time here? Hold on." He was out of his chair. Vague upright shapes were passing behind the curtained glass door. "Looks like they're through. If you gentlemen would just wait here a minute, till I see." He strode across the roof. The two men sat in silence. Babcock had pulled down his surgical mask; Sinescu noticed and did the same.

"Sam's wife is a problem," Babcock said, leaning nearer. "It seemed like a good idea at the time, but she's lonely here, doesn't like it—no kids—"

The door opened again and Sam appeared. He had a mask on, but it was hanging under his chin. "If you gentlemen would come in now."

In the living area, the little woman, also with a mask hanging around her neck, was pouring coffee from a flowered ceramic jug. She was smiling brightly but looked unhappy. Opposite her sat someone tall, in gray shirt and slacks, leaning back, legs out, arms on the arms of his chair, motionless. Something was wrong with his face.

"Well, now," said Sam heartily. His wife looked up at him with an agonized smile.

The tall figure turned its head and Sinescu saw with an icy shock that its face was silver, a mask of metal with oblong slits for eyes, no nose or mouth, only curves that were faired into each other. "Project," said an inhuman voice.

Sinescu found himself half bent over a chair. He sat down. They were all looking at him. The voice resumed. "I said, are you here to pull the plug on the project." It was unaccented, indifferent.

"Have some coffee." The woman pushed a cup toward him.

Sinescu reached for it, but his hand was trembling and he drew it back. "Just a fact-finding expedition," he said.

"Bull. Who sent you—Senator Hinkel."

"That's right."

"Bull. He's been here himself; why send you. If you are going to pull the plug, might as well tell me." The face behind the mask did not move when he spoke, the voice did not seem to come from it.

"He's just looking around, Jim," said Babcock.

"Two hundred million a year," said the voice, "to keep one man alive. Doesn't make much sense, does it. Go on, drink your coffee."

Sinescu realized that Sam and his wife had already finished theirs and that they had pulled up their masks. He reached for his cup hastily.

"Hundred percent disability in my grade is thirty thousand a year. I could get along on that easy. For almost an hour and a half."

"There's no intention of terminating the project," Sinescu said.

"Phasing it out, though. Would you say phasing it out."

"Manners, Jim," said Babcock.

"OK. My worst fault. What do you want to know."

Sinescu sipped his coffee. His hands were still trembling. "That mask you're wearing," he started.

"Not for discussion. No comment, no comment. Sorry about

that; don't mean to be rude; a personal matter. Ask me something—" Without warning, he stood up, blaring, "Get that damn thing out of here!" Sam's wife's cup smashed, coffee brown across the table. A fawn-colored puppy was sitting in the middle of the carpet, cocking its head, bright-eyed, tongue out.

The table tipped, Sam's wife struggled up behind it. Her face was pink, dripping with tears. She scooped up the puppy without pausing and ran out. "I better go with her," Sam said, getting up.

"Go on; and, Sam, take a holiday. Drive her into Winnemucca, see a movie."

"Yeah, guess I will." He disappeared behind the bookshelf wall.

The tall figure sat down again, moving like a man; it leaned back in the same posture, arms on the arms of the chair. It was still. The hands gripping the wood were shapely and perfect but unreal: there was something wrong about the fingernails. The brown, well-combed hair above the mask was a wig; the ears were wax. Sinescu nervously fumbled his surgical mask over his mouth and nose. "Might as well get along," he said, and stood up.

"That's right, I want to take you over to Engineering and R and D," said Babcock. "Jim, I'll be back in a little while. Want to talk to you."

"Sure," said the motionless figure.

Babcock had had a shower, but sweat was soaking through the armpits of his shirt again. The silent elevator, the green carpet, a little blurred. The air cool, stale. Seven years, blood and money, five hundred good men. Psych section, Cosmetic Engineering, R and D, Medical, Immunology, Supply, Serology, Administration. The glass doors. Sam's apartment empty, gone to Winnemucca with Irma. Psych. Good men, but were they the best? Three of the best had turned it down. Buried in the files. *Not like an ordinary amputation, this man has had everything cut off.*

The tall figure had not moved. Babcock sat down. The silver mask looked back at him.

"Jim, let's level with each other."

"Bad, huh?"

"Sure it's bad. I left him in his room with a bottle. I'll see him again before he leaves, but God knows what he'll say in Washington. Listen, do me a favor, take that thing off."

"Sure." The hand rose, plucked at the edge of the silver mask, lifted it away. Under it, the tan-pink face, sculptured nose and lips, eyebrows, eyelashes, not handsome but good-looking, normal-looking. Only the eyes wrong, pupils too big. And the lips that did not open or move when it spoke. "I can take anything off. What does that prove."

"Jim, Cosmetic spent eight and a half months on that model and the first thing you do is slap a mask over it. We've asked you what's wrong, offered to make any changes you want."

"No comment."

"You talked about phasing out the project. Did you think you were kidding?"

A pause. "Not kidding."

"All right, then open up, Jim, tell me; I have to know. They won't shut the project down; they'll keep you alive, but that's all. There are seven hundred on the volunteer list, including two U. S. Senators. Suppose one of them gets pulled out of an auto wreck tomorrow. We can't wait till then to decide; we've got to know now. Whether to let the next one die or put him into a TP body like yours. So talk to me."

"Suppose I tell you something, but it isn't the truth."

"Why would you lie?"

"Why do you lie to a cancer patient."

"I don't get it. Come on, Jim."

"OK, try this. Do I look like a man to you."

"Sure."

"Bull. Look at this face." Calm and perfect. Beyond the fake irises, a wink of metal. "Suppose we had all the other problems solved and I could go into Winnemucca tomorrow; can you see me walking down the street—going into a bar—taking a taxi?"

"Is that all it is?" Babcock drew a deep breath. "Jim, sure there's a difference, but for Christ's sake, it's like any other prosthesis—people get used to it. Like that arm of Sam's. You see it, but after a while you forget it, you don't notice."

"Bull. You pretend not to notice. Because it would embarrass the cripple."

Babcock looked down at his clasped hands. "Sorry for yourself?"

"Don't give me that," the voice blared. The tall figure was standing. The hands slowly came up, the fists clenched. "I'm in this thing. I've been in it for two years. I'm in it when I go to sleep, and when I wake up, I'm still in it."

Babcock looked up at him. "What do you want, facial mobility? Give us twenty years, maybe ten, we'll lick it."

"I want you to close down Cosmetic."

"But that's—"

"Just listen. The first model looked like a tailor's dummy, so you spent eight months and came up with this one, and it looks like a corpse. The whole idea was to make me look like a man, the first model pretty good, the second model better, until you've got something that can smoke cigars and joke with women and go bowling and nobody will know the difference. You can't do it, and if you could what for."

"I don't— Let me think about this. What do you mean, a metal—"

"Metal, sure, but what difference does that make. I'm talking about shape. Function. Wait a minute." The tall figure strode across the room, unlocked a cabinet, came back with rolled sheets of paper. "Look at this."

The drawing showed an oblong metal box on four jointed legs. From one end protruded a tiny mushroom-shaped head on a jointed stem and a cluster of arms ending in probes, drills, grapples. "For moon prospecting."

"Too many limbs," said Babcock after a moment. "How would you—"

"With the facial nerves. Plenty of them left over. Or here." Another drawing. "A module plugged into the control system of a spaceship. That's where I belong, in space. Sterile environment, low grav, I can go where a man can't go and do what a man can't do. I can be an asset, not a goddamn billion-dollar liability."

Babcock rubbed his eyes. "Why didn't you say anything before?"

"You were all hipped on prosthetics. You would have told me to tend my knitting."

Babcock's hands were shaking as he rolled up the drawings. "Well, by God, this just may do it. It just might." He stood up and turned toward the door. "Keep your—" He cleared his throat. "I mean, hang tight, Jim."

"I'll do that."

When he was alone, he put on his mask again and stood motionless a moment, eye shutters closed. Inside, he was running clean and cool; he could feel the faint reassuring hum of pumps, click of valves and relays. They had given him that: cleaned out all the offal, replaced it with machinery that did not bleed, ooze or suppurate. He thought of the lie he had told Babcock. *Why do you lie to a cancer patient?* But they would never get it, never understand.

He sat down at the drafting table, clipped a sheet of paper to it and with a pencil began to sketch a rendering of the moon-prospector design. When he had blocked in the prospector itself, he began to draw the background of craters. His pencil moved more slowly and stopped; he put it down with a click.

No more adrenal glands to pump adrenaline into his blood, so he could not feel fright or rage. They had released him from all that—love, hate, the whole sloppy mess—but they had forgotten there was still one emotion he could feel.

Sinescu, with the black bristles of his beard sprouting through his oily skin. A whitehead ripe in the crease beside his nostril.

Moon landscape, clean and cold. He picked up the pencil again.

Babcock, with his broad pink nose shining with grease, crusts of white matter in the corners of his eyes. Food mortar between his teeth.

Sam's wife, with raspberry-colored paste on her mouth. Face

smeared with tears, a bright bubble in one nostril. And the damn dog, shiny nose, wet eyes . . .

He turned. The dog was there, sitting on the carpet, wet red tongue out *left the door open again* dripping, wagged its tail twice, then started to get up. He reached for the metal T square, leaned back, swinging it like an ax, and the dog yelped once as metal sheared bone, one eye spouting red, writhing on its back, dark stain of piss across the carpet and he hit it again, hit it again.

The body lay twisted on the carpet, fouled with blood, ragged black lips drawn back from teeth. He wiped off the T square with a paper towel, then scrubbed it in the sink with soap and steel wool, dried it and hung it up. He got a sheet of drafting paper, laid it on the floor, rolled the body over onto it without spilling any blood on the carpet. He lifted the body in the paper, carried it out onto the patio, then onto the unroofed section, opening the doors with his shoulder. He looked over the wall. Two stories down, concrete roof, vents sticking out of it, nobody watching. He held the dog out, let it slide off the paper, twisting as it fell. It struck one of the vents, bounced, a red smear. He carried the paper back inside, poured the blood down the drain, then put the paper into the incinerator chute.

Splashes of blood were on the carpet, the feet of the drafting table, the cabinet, his trouser legs. He sponged them all up with paper towels and warm water. He took off his clothing, examined it minutely, scrubbed it in the sink, then put it in the washer. He washed the sink, rubbed himself down with disinfectant and dressed again. He walked through into Sam's silent apartment, closing the glass door behind him. Past the potted philodendron, overstuffed furniture, red-and-yellow painting on the wall, out onto the roof, leaving the door ajar. Then back through the patio, closing doors.

Too bad. How about some goldfish.

He sat down at the drafting table. He was running clean and cool. The dream this morning came back to his mind, the last one, as he was struggling up out of sleep: *slithery kidneys burst gray lungs blood and hair ropes of guts covered with yellow fat oozing*

and sliding and oh god the stink like the breath of an outmouth no
sound nowhere he was putting a yellow stream down the slide of
the dunghole and

He began to ink in the drawing, first with a fine steel pen,
then with a nylon brush. *His heel slid and he was falling could not*
stop himself falling into slimy bulging softness higher than his
chin, higher and he could not move paralyzed and he tried to
scream tried to scream tried to scream.

The prospector was climbing a crater slope with its handling
members retracted and its head tilted up. Behind it the distant
ringwall and the horizon, the black sky, the pinpoint stars. And
he was there, and it was not far enough, not yet, for the Earth
hung overhead like a rotten fruit, blue with mold, crawling,
wrinkling, purulent and alive.

Avram Davidson once planned to reform sheep raising in Israel by persuading the shepherds to milk the sheep from the side instead of from the rear, thus keeping the sheep-shit out of the milk. Failing in this, he became a writer.

Once during the Conference he went into the river in his B.V.D.'s, which turned transparent when wet; he acquired an interested female audience, stayed in the water a long while, humming nonchalantly, and finally came out with a flower tucked behind his ear.

————————————————————— Avram Davidson

THE SOURCES OF THE NILE

It was in the Rutherford office on Lexington that Bob Rosen met Peter ("Old Pete"—"Sneaky Pete"—"Poor Pete": take your pick) Martens for the first and almost last time. One of those tall, cool buildings on Lexington with the tall, cool office girls it was; and because Bob felt quite sure he wasn't and damned well never was going to be tall or cool enough for him to mean anything to them, he was able to sit back and just enjoy the scenery. Even the magazines on the table were cool: Spectator, Botteghe Oscuro, and Journal of the New York State Geographical Society. He picked up the last and began to leaf through "Demographic Study of The Jackson Whites."

He was trying to make some sense out of a mass of statistics relating to albinism among that curious tribe (descended from Tuscorora Indians, Hessian deserters, London street women, and fugitive slaves), when one of the girls—delightfully tall, deliciously cool—came to usher him in to Tressling's office. He laid the magazine face down on the low table and followed her. The old man with the portfolio, who was the only other person waiting, got up just then, and Bob noticed the spot of blood in his eye as he passed by. They were prominent eyes, yellowed, reticulated with tiny red veins, and in the corner of one of them was a bright red blot. For a moment it made Rosen feel uneasy, but he had no time to think about it.

"Delightful story," said Joe Tressling, referring to the piece which had gotten Rosen the interview, through his agent. The story had won first prize in a contest, and the agent had thought that Tressling . . . if Tressling . . . maybe Tressling . . .

"Of course, we can't touch it because of the theme," said Tressling.

"Why, what's wrong with the Civil War as a theme?" Rosen said.

Tressling smiled. "As far as Aunt Carrie's Country Cheese is concerned," he said, "the South *won* the Civil War. At least, it's not up to Us to tell Them differently. It might annoy Them. The North doesn't *care*. But write another story for us. The Aunt Carrie Hour is always on the lookout for new dramatic material."

"Like for instance?" Bob Rosen asked.

"What the great cheese-eating American public wants is a story of resolved conflict, concerning young contemporary American couples earning over ten thousand dollars a year. But nothing sordid, controversial, outré, or passé."

Rosen was pleased to be able to see Joseph Tressling, who was the J. Oscar Rutherford Company's man in charge of scripts for the Aunt Carrie Hour. The *Mené Mené* of the short story was said that year to be on the wall, the magazines were dying like mayflies, and the sensible thing for anyone to do who hoped to make a living writing (he told himself) was to get into television. But he really didn't expect he was going to make the transition, and the realization that he didn't really know any contemporary Americans—young, old, married, single—who were earning over ten thousand dollars a year seemed to prophesy that he was never going to earn it himself.

"And nothing avant-garde," said Tressling.

The young woman returned and smiled a tall, cool smile at them. Tressling got up. So did Bob. "Mr. Martens is still outside," she murmured.

"Oh, I'm afraid I won't be able to see him today," said Joe Tressling. "Mr. Rosen has been so fascinating that the time seems to have run over, and then some. . . . Great old boy," he said, smiling at Bob and shaking his hand. "Really one of the veterans of advertising, you know. Used to write copy for Mrs. Winslow's Soothing Syrup. Tells some fascinating yarns. Too bad I haven't the time to listen. I expect to see you back here soon, Mr. Rosen," he said, still holding Bob's hand as they walked to the door, "with another one of your lovely stories. One that we can feel delighted to buy. No costume dramas, no foreign settings, nothing outré, passé, or avant-garde, and above all—nothing controversial or sordid. You're not going to be one of those *hungry* writers, are you?"

Even before he answered, Rosen observed Tressling's eyes dismiss him; and he resolved to start work immediately on an outré, controversial, sordid costume drama with a foreign setting, etc., if it killed him.

He made the wrong turn for the elevator and on coming back he came face to face with the old man. "'Demography of the Jackson Whites,'" the old man said, feigning amazement. "What do you care about those poor suckers for? They don't buy, they don't sell, they don't start fashion, they don't follow fashion. Just poach, fornicate, and produce oh-point-four hydrocephalic albinoes per hundred. Or something."

The elevator came and they got in together. The old man stared at him, his yellow-bloody eye like a fertilized egg. "Not that I blame them," he went on. "If I'd had any sense I'd've become a Jackson White instead of an advertising man. The least you can do," he said, without any transition, "is to buy me a drink. Since Truthful Tressling blames it onto you that he can't see me, the lying bugger. Why, for crying out loud!" he cried. "What I've got here in this little old portfolio—why, it's worth more to those men on Madison, Lexington, Park—if they only—"

"Let me buy you a drink," said Rosen, resignedly. The streets were hot, and he hoped the bar would be cool.

"A ball of Bushmill," said old Peter Martens.

The bar *was* cool. Bob had stopped listening to his guest's monologue about what he had in his little old portfolio (something about spotting fashion trends way in advance) and had begun talking about his own concerns. By and by the old man, who was experienced beyond the norm in not being listened to, had begun to listen to *him*.

"This was when everybody was reading *Aku-Aku*," Bob said. "So I thought for sure that mine would go over good because it was about Rapa Nui—Easter Island—and Peruvian blackbirders and hints of great legends of the past and all that."

"And?"

"And it didn't. The publisher, the only one who showed any interest at all, I mean, *that* publisher, he said *he* liked the writing but the public wouldn't buy it. He advised me to study carefully the other paperbacks on the stands. See what they're like, go thou and do likewise. So I did. You know the stuff. On even-numbered pages the heroine gets her brassiere ripped off while she cries, *'Yes! Yes! Now! Oh!'*"

He was not aware of signaling, but from time to time a hand appeared and renewed their glasses. Old Martens asked, "Does she cry 'rapturously'—or 'joyously'?"

"Rapturously *and* joyously. What's the matter, you think she's frigid?"

Martens perished the thought. At a nearby table a large blonde said lugubriously, "You know, Harold, it's a lucky thing the Good Lord didn't give me any children or I would of wasted my life on them like I did on my rotten stepchildren." Martens asked what happened on the odd-numbered children.

"I mean, 'pages,'" he corrected himself, after a moment.

The right side of Bob Rosen's face was going numb. The left

side started tingling. He interrupted a little tune he was humming and said, "Oh, the equation is invariable: On odd-numbered pages the hero either clonks some bastard bloodily on the noggin with a roscoe, or kicks him in the collions and *then* clonks him, or else he's engaged—with his shirt off, you're not allowed to say what gives with the pants, which are so much more important: presumably they melt or something—he's engaged, shirtless, in arching his lean and muscular flanks over some bimbo, *not* the heroine, because these aren't her pages, some other female in whose pelvis he reads strange mysteries. . . ." He was silent for a moment, brooding.

"How could it fail, then?" asked the old man, in his husky voice. "I've seen the public taste change, let me tell you, my boy, from A Girl of the Limberlost (which was so pure that nuns could read it) to stuff which makes stevedores blench: so I am moved to inquire, How could the work you are describing to me fail?"

The young man shrugged. "The nuns were making a comeback. Movies about nuns, books about nuns, nuns on TV, westerns . . . So the publisher said public taste had changed, and could I maybe do him a life of St. Teresa?"

"Coo."

"So I spent three months doing a life of St. Teresa at a furious pace, and when I finished it turned out I'd done the wrong saint. The simple slob had no idea there was any more than one of the name, and I never thought to ask did he mean the Spanish St. Teresa or the French one? D'Ávila or The Little Flower?"

"Saints preserve us . . . Say, do you know that wonderful old Irish toast? 'Here's to the Council of Trent, that put the fasting on the meat and not on the drink'?"

Bob gestured to the barkeeper. "But I didn't understand why if one St. Teresa could be sold, the other one couldn't. So I tried another publisher, and all *he* said was, public taste had changed, and could I do him anything with a background of juvenile delinquency? After that I took a job for a while selling frozen custard in a penny arcade and all my friends said, BOB! You with *your talent?* HOW COULD YOU?"

The large blonde put down a jungle-green drink and looked at her companion. "What you mean, they love me? If they love me why are they going to Connecticut? You don't go to Connecticut if you love a person," she pointed out.

Old Martens cleared his throat. "My suggestion would be that you combine all three of your mysteriously unsalable novels. The hero sails on a Peruvian blackbirder to raid Easter Island, the inhabitants whereof he kicks in the collions, if male, or arches his loins over, if female; until he gets converted by a vision of both St. Teresas who tell him their life stories—as a result of which he takes a job selling frozen custard in a penny arcade in order to help the juvenile delinquents who frequent the place."

Bob grunted. "Depend on it, with my luck I would get it down just in time to see public taste change again. The publishers would want a pocket treasury of the McGuffey Readers, or else the memoirs of Constantine Porphyrogenetus. I could freeze my arse climbing the Himalayas only to descend, manuscript in hand, to find everybody on Publishers' Row vicariously donning goggles and spearing fish on the bottom of the Erythrean Sea. . . . Only thing is, I never was sure to what degree public taste changed by itself or how big a part the publishers play in changing it. . . ."

The air, cool though he knew it was, seemed to shimmer in front of him, and through the shimmer he saw Peter Martens sitting up straight and leaning over at him, his seamed and ancient face suddenly eager and alive. "And would you like to be sure?" old Martens asked. "Would you like to be able to know, really to *know?*"

"What? How?" Bob was startled. The old man's eyes looked almost all blood by now.

"Because," Martens said, "*I* can tell you what. *I* can tell you how. Nobody else. Only *me*. And not just about books, about everything. Because—"

There was an odd sort of noise, like the distant sussuration of wind in dry grass, and Rosen looked around and he saw that a man was standing by them and laughing. This man wore a pale brown suit and had a pale brown complexion, he was very tall and very thin and had a very small head and slouched somewhat. He looked like a mantis, and a mustache like an inverted V was cropped out of the broad blue surface of his upper lip.

"Still dreaming your dreams, Martens?" this man asked, still wheezing his dry whispery laugh. "Gates of Horn, or Gates of Ivory?"

"Get the hell away from me, Shadwell," said Martens.

Shadwell turned his tiny little head to Rosen and grinned. "He been telling you about how he worked on old Mrs. Winslow's Soothing Syrup Account? Too bad the Harrison Narcotics Act killed that business! He tell you how he worked on the old Sapolio account? The old Stanley Steamer account?" ("Shove off, Shadwell," Martens ordered, planting his elbows on the table and opening his mouth at Bob again.) "Or has he been muttering away like an old Zambezi hand who claims to know the location of the Elephants' Graveyard? Tell me, where is fashion bred?" he intoned. "In the bottle—or in Martens' head?"

Martens' head, thinly covered with yellowish-white hair, jerked in the direction of the new arrival. "This, my boy, is T. Pettys Shadwell, the most despicable of living men. He runs—out of his pocket, because no one will sell him a hat on credit—he runs a so-called market research business. Though who in blazes would hire him since Polly Adler went respectable beats the hell out of me. I'm warning you, Shadwell," he said, "take off. I've had my fill of you. I'm not giving you any more information." And with a further graphic description of what else he would *not* give T. Pettys Shadwell if the latter was dying of thirst, he folded his arms and fell silent.

The most despicable of living men chuckled, poked a bone-thin hand into a pocket, plucked out a packet of white flaps of cardboard, one of which he tore along a perforated line and handed to Bob. "My card, sir. My operation, true, is not large, but it is Ever Growing. Don't take Mr. Martens too seriously. And don't buy him too many drinks. His health is not as good as it used to be—but then, it never was." And with a final laugh, like the rustling of dried corn-shucks, he angled away.

Martens sighed, lapped the last few dewy drops of Bushmill's off a molten ice-cube. "I live in mortal fear that some day I'll have the money to buy all the booze I want and wake up finding I have spilled the beans to that cockatrice who just walked out. Can you imagine anyone having business cards printed to be torn off of perforated pads? Keeps them from getting loose and wrinkled, is his reason. Such a man has no right, under natural or civil law, to live."

In the buzzing coolness of the barroom Bob Rosen tried to catch hold of a thought which was coyly hiding behind a corner in his mind. His mind otherwise, he felt, was lucid as never before. But somehow he lost the thought, found he was telling himself a funny story in French and—although he had never got more than an 80 in the course, back in high school—marveled at the purity of his accent and then chuckled at the punch-line.

"'Never mind about black neglijays,'" the stout blonde was saying. "'If you want to keep your husband's affections,' I said to her, 'then listen to me—'"

The errant thought came trotting back for reasons of its own, and jumped into Bob's lap. "'Spill the beans'?" he quoted, questioningly. "Spill *what* beans? To Shadwell, I mean."

"Most despicable of living men," said old Martens, mechanically. Then a most curious expression washed over his antique countenance: proud, cunning, fearful . . .

"Would you like to know the sources of the Nile?" he asked. "Would you?"

"'Let him *go* to Maine,' I said. 'Let him paint rocks all day,' I said. 'Only for heaven's sake, keep him the hell off of Fire Island,' I said. And was I right, Harold?" demanded the large blonde.

Pete Martens was whispering something, Bob realized. By the look on his face it must have been important, so the young man tried to hear the words over the buzzing, and thought to himself in a fuddled fashion that they ought to be taken down on a steno pad, or something of that sort . . . *want to know, really know, where it begins and how, and how often?* But no; what do I know? For years I've been Clara the rotten step-mother, and now I'm Clara the rotten mother-in-law. *Are there such in every generation? Must be . . . known for years . . . known for years . . . only, Who?—and Where?—searched and sought, like Livingston and all the others searching and seeking, enduring privation, looking for the sources of the Nile . . .*

Someone, it must have been Clara, gave a long, shuddering cry; and then for a while there was nothing but the buzzing, buzzing, buzzing, in Bob Rosen's head; while old Martens lolled back in the chair, regarding him silently and sardonically with his blood-red eye, over which the lid slowly, slowly drooped: but old Martens never said a word more.

It was one genuine horror of a hangover, subsiding slowly under (or perhaps despite) every remedy Bob's aching brain could think of: black coffee, strong tea, chocolate milk, raw-egg-red-pepper-worcestershire sauce. At least, he thought gratefully after a while, he was spared the dry heaves. At least he had all the fixings in his apartment and didn't have to go out. It was a pivotal neighborhood, and he lived right in the pivot, a block where lox and bagels beat a slow retreat before the advance of hog maw and chitterlings on the one hand and *bodegas, comidas criollas,* on the other; swarms of noisy kids running between the trucks and buses, the jackhammers forever wounding the streets.

It took him a moment to realize that the noise he was hearing now was not the muffled echo of the drills, but a tapping on his door. Unsteadily, he tottered over and opened it. He would have been not in the least surprised to find a raven there, but instead it was a tall man, rather stooping, with a tiny head, hands folded mantis-like at his bosom.

After a few dry, futile clickings, Bob's throat essayed the name "Shadburn?"

"Shadwell," he was corrected, softly. "T. Pettys Shadwell . . . I'm afraid you're not well, Mr. Rosen. . . ."

Bob clutched the doorpost, moaned softly. Shadwell's hands unfolded, revealed—not a smaller man at whom he'd been nibbling, but a paper bag, soon opened.

". . . so I thought I'd take the liberty of bringing you some hot chicken broth."

It was gratefully warm, had both body and savor. Bob lapped at it, croaked his thanks. "Not at all, not-a-tall," Shadwell waved. "Glad to be of some small help." A silence fell, relieved only by weak, gulping noises. "Too bad about old Martens. Of course, he *was* old. Still, a shocking thing to happen to you. A stroke, I'm told. I, uh, trust the police gave you no trouble?"

A wave of mild strength seemed to flow into Bob from the hot broth. "No, they were very nice," he said. "The sergeant called me 'son.' They brought me back here."

"Ah." Shadwell was reflective. "He had no family. I know that for a fact."

"Mmm."

"But—assume he left a few dollars. Unlikely, but— And assume he'd willed the few dollars to someone or some charity, perhaps. Never mind. Doesn't concern us. He wouldn't bother to will his papers . . . scrapbooks of old copy he'd written, so forth. That's of no interest to people in general. Just be thrown out or burned. But it would be of interest to *me*. I mean, I've been in advertising all my life, you know. Oh, yes. Used to distribute handbills when I was a boy. Fact."

Bob tried to visualize T. Pettys Shadwell as a boy, failed, drank soup. "Good soup," he said. "Thanks. Very kind of you."

Shadwell urged him strongly not to mention it. He chuckled. "Old Pete used to lug around some of the darndest stuff in that portfolio of his," he said. "In fact, some of it referred to a scheme we were once trying to work out together. Nothing came of it, however, and the old fellow was inclined to be a bit testy about that, still—I believe you'd find it interesting. May I show you?"

Bob still felt rotten, but the death wish had departed. "Sure," he said. Shadwell looked around the room, then at Bob, expectantly. After a minute he said, "Where is it?" "Where is what?" "The portfolio. Old Martens'."

They stared at each other. The phone rang. With a wince and a groan, Bob answered. It was Noreen, a girl with pretensions to stagecraft and literature, with whom he had been furtively lecherous on an off-and-on basis, the off periods' commencements being signaled by the presence in Noreen's apartment of Noreen's mother (knitting, middleclass morality and all), when Bob came, intent on venery.

"I've got a terrible hangover," he said, answering her first (guarded and conventional) question; "and the place is a mess."

"See what happens if I turn my back on you for a minute?" Noreen clucked, happily. "Luckily, I have neither work nor social obligations planned for the day, so I'll be right over."

Bob said, "Crazy!", hung up, and turned to face Shadwell, who had been nibbling the tips of his prehensile fingers. "Thanks for the soup," he said, in tones of some finality.

"But the portfolio?" "I haven't got it." "It was leaning against the old man's chair when I saw the two of you in the bar." "Then maybe it's still *in* the bar. Or in the hospital. Or maybe the cops have it. But—" "It isn't. They don't." "But *I* haven't got it. Honest, Mr. Shadwell, I appreciate the soup, but I don't know where the hell—"

Shadwell rubbed his tiny, sharp mustache, like a ∧-mark pointing to his tiny, sharp nose. He rose. "This is really too bad. Those papers referring to the business old Peter and I had been mutually engaged in—really, I have as much right to them as . . . But look here. Perhaps he may have spoken to you about it. He always did when he'd been drinking and usually did even when he wasn't. What he liked to refer to as, 'The sources of the Nile'? Hmm?" The phrase climbed the belfry and rang bells audible, or at least apparent, to Shadwell. He seemed to leap forward, long fingers resting on Bob's shoulders.

"You do know what I mean. Look. You: Are a writer. The old man's ideas aren't in your line. I: Am an advertising man. They are in my line. For the contents of his portfolio—as I've explained, they are rightfully mine—I will give: One thousand:

Dollars. In fact: For the opportunity of merely *looking* through it: I will give: One *hundred*. Dollars."

As Bob reflected that his last check had been for $17.72 (Monegasque rights to a detective story), and as he heard these vasty sums bandied about, his eyes grew large, and he strove hard to recall what the hell *had* happened to the portfolio—but in vain.

Shadwell's dry, whispery voice took on a pleading note. "I'm even willing to pay you for the privilege of discussing your conversation with the old f— the old gentleman. Here—" And he reached into his pocket. Bob wavered. Then he recalled that Noreen was even now on her way uptown and crosstown, doubtless bearing with her, as usual, in addition to her own taut charms, various tokens of exotic victualry to which she—turning her back on the veal chops and green peas of childhood and suburbia—was given: such as Shashlik makings, *lokoumi*, wines of the warm south, *baklava, provolone,* and other living witnesses to the glory that was Greece and the grandeur that was Rome.

Various hungers, thus stimulated, began to rise and clamor, and he steeled himself against Shadwell's possibly unethical and certainly inconveniently timed offers.

"Not now," he said. Then, throwing delicacy to the winds, "I'm expecting a girl friend. Beat it. Another time."

Annoyance and chagrin on Shadwell's small face, succeeded by an exceedingly disgusting leer. "Why, of *course,*" he said. "Another time? Cer-tain-ly. My card—" He hauled out the perforated pack. "I already got one," Bob said. "Goodbye."

He made haste to throw off the noisome clothes in which he had been first hot, then drunk, then comatose; to take a shower, comb his mouse-colored hair, shave the pink bristles whose odious tint alone prevented him from growing a beard, to spray and anoint himself with various nostra which T. Pettys Shadwell's more successful colleagues in advertising had convinced him (by a thousand ways, both blunt and subtle) were essential to his acceptance by good society; then to dress and await with unconcealed anticipation the advent of the unchaste Noreen.

She came, she kissed him, she prepared food for him; ancient duties of women, any neglect of which is a sure and certain sign of cultural decadence and retrogression. Then she read everything he had written since their last juncture, and here she had some fault to find.

"You waste too much time at the beginning, in description," she said, with the certainty possible to those who have never sold a single manuscript. "You've got to make your characters come *alive*—in the very first sentence."

"'Marley was dead, to begin with,'" muttered Bob.

"What?" murmured Noreen, vaguely, feigning not to hear. Her eye, avoiding lover boy, lit on something else. "What's this?" she asked. "You have so much money you just leave it lying around? I thought you said you were broke." And Bob followed her pointing and encarnadined fingertip to where lay two crisp twenty-dollar bills, folded lengthwise, on the table next the door.

"Shadwell!" he said, instantly. And, in response to her arched brows (which would have looked much better unplucked, but who can hold what will away?), he said, "A real rat of a guy— a louse, a boor—who had some crumby proposal."

"And who also has," said Noreen, going straight to the heart of the matter, "money." Bob resolved never to introduce the two of them, if he could help it. "Anyway," she continued, laying aside Bob's manuscript, "now you can take me out somewhere." Feebly he argued the food then cooking; she turned off the gas and thrust the pots incontinently into the ice-box, rose, and indicated she was now ready to leave. He had other objections to leaving just then, which it would have been impolitic to mention, for in Noreen's scheme of morality each episode of passion was a sealed incident once it was over, and constituted no promise of any other yet to come.

With resignation tempered by the reflection that Shadwell's four sawbucks couldn't last forever, and that there was never so long-drawn-out an evening but would wind up eventually back in his apartment, Bob accompanied her out the door.

And so it was. The next day, following Noreen's departure in mid-morning, found Bob in excellent spirit but flat-broke. He was reviewing the possibilities of getting an advance from his agent, Stuart Emmanuel, a tiny, dapper man whose eyes behind double lenses were like great black shoe-buttons, when the phone rang. ESP or no ESP, it was Stuart himself, with an invitation to lunch.

"I'm glad *some* of your clients are making money," said Bob, most ungraciously.

"Oh, it's not my money," said Stuart. "It's J. Oscar Rutherford's. One of his top men—no, it's not Joe Tressling, I know you saw him the day before yesterday, yes, I know nothing came of it, this is a different fellow altogether. Phillips Anhalt. I want you to come."

So Bob left yesterday's half-cooked chow in the ice-box and, very little loath, set out to meet Stuart and Phillips Anhalt, of whom he had never heard before. The first rendezvous was for a drink at a bar whose name also meant nothing to him, though as soon as he walked in he recognized it as the one where he had been the day before yesterday, and this made him uneasy—doubly so, for he had callously almost forgotten what had happened there. The bartender, it was at once evident, had not. His wary glance at the three of them must have convinced him that they were reasonably good insurance risks, however, for he made no comment.

Anhalt was a middle-sized man with a rather sweet and slightly baffled face and iron-grey hair cut *en brosse*. "I enjoyed your story very much," he told Bob—thus breaking in at once upon the shallow slumber of the little scold who boarded in Bob's Writer's Consciousness. Of *course* (it shrilled) I know *exactly* the one you mean, after all, I've written only *one* story in my entire *life* so "*your story*" is the only identification it needs. I liked your *novel*, Mr. Hemingway. I enjoyed your *play*, Mr. Kaufman.

Stuart Emmanuel, who knew the labyrinthine ways of writers' minds as he knew the figures in his bank statement, said smoothly, "I expect Mr. Anhalt refers to *Unvexed to the Sea.*"

With firm politeness Mr. Anhalt disappointed this expectation.

"I know that's the prize-winner," he said, "and I mean to read it, but the one I referred to was *The Green Wall*." Now, as it happened, this very short little story had been bounced thirteen times before its purchase for a negligible sum by a low-grade salvage market of a magazine; but it was one of Bob's favorites. He smiled at Phillips Anhalt, Anhalt smiled at him, Stuart beamed and ordered drinks.

The waiter passed a folded slip of paper to Bob Rosen when he came with the popskull. "The lady left it," he said. "What lady?" "The blonde lady." Agent and ad man smiled, made appropriate remarks while Bob scanned the note, recognized it as being in his own handwriting, failed to make it out, crammed it in his pocket.

"Mr. Anhalt," said Stuart, turning dark, large-pupiled eyes on his client, "is a very important man at Rutherford's: he has a corner office." A gentle, somewhat tired smile from Anhalt, who gave the conversation a turn and talked about his home in Darien, and the work he was doing on it, by himself. Thus they got through the round of drinks, then walked a few blocks to the restaurant.

Here Bob was infinitely relieved that Anhalt did not order poached egg on creamed spinach, corned beef hash, or something equally simple, wholesome, and disgusting, and tending to inhibit Bob's own wide-ranging tastes: Anhalt ordered duckling, Stuart had mutton chops, and Bob chose tripe and onions.

"Joe Tressling tells me that you're going to write something for the cheese show," said Anhalt, as they disarranged the pickle plate. Bob half-lifted his eyebrows, smiled. Stuart gazed broodingly into the innards of a sour tomato as if he might be saying to himself, "Ten percent of $17.72, Monegasque rights to a detective story."

"More cheese is being eaten today in the United States than twenty-five years ago," Anhalt continued. "Much, much more . . . Is it the result of advertising? Such as the Aunt Carrie Hour? Has that changed public taste? Or—has public taste changed for, say, other reasons, and are we just riding the wave?"

"The man who could have answered that question," Bob said, "died the day before yesterday."

Anhalt let out his breath. "How do you know he could have?"

"He said so."

Anhalt, who'd had a half-eaten dilled cucumber in his hand, carefully laid it in the ash-tray, and leaned forward. "What else did he say? Old Martens, I mean. You *do* mean Old Martens, don't you?"

Bob said that was right, and added, with unintentional untruthfulness, that he'd been offered a thousand dollars for that information, and had turned it down. Before he could correct himself, Anhalt, customary faint pink face gone almost red, and Stuart Emmanuel, eyes glittering hugely, said with one voice, "*Who* offered—?"

"What comes out of a chimney?"

Stuart, recovering first (Anhalt continued to stare, said nothing, while the color receded), said, "Bob, this is not a joke. That is the reason we have this appointment. An awful lot of money is involved—for you, for me, for Phil Anhalt, for, well, for everybody. For just everybody. So—"

It slipped out. "For T. Pettys Shadwell?" Bob asked.

The effect, as they used to say in pre-atomic days, was electrical. Stuart made a noise, between a moan and a hiss, rather like a man who, having trustingly lowered his breeches, sits all unawares upon an icicle. He clutched Bob's hand. "You didn't godforbid *sign* anything?" he wailed. Anhalt, who had gone red before, went white this time around, but still retained diffidence enough to place his hand merely upon Bob's jacket-cuff.

"He's a cad!" he said, in trembling tones. "A swine, Mr. Rosen!"

"'The most despicable of living men,'" quoted Mr. Rosen. ("Exactly," said Anhalt.)

"Bob, you didn't *sign* anything, godforbid?"

"No. No. No. But I feel as if I've had all the mystery I

intend to have. And unless I get Information, why, gents, I shan't undo one button." The waiter arrived with the food and, according to the rules and customs of the Waiters' Union, gave everybody the wrong orders. When this was straightened out, Stuart said, confidently, "Why, of course, Bob: Information: Why, certainly. There is nothing to conceal. Not from *you*," he said, chuckling. "Go ahead, start eating. I'll eat and talk, you just eat and listen."

And so, as he tucked away the tripe and onions, Bob heard Stuart recount, through a slight barrier of masticated mutton-chop, a most astonishing tale. In every generation (Stuart said) there were leaders of fashon, arbiters of style. At Nero's court, Petronius. In Regency England, Beau Brummel. At present and for some time past, everyone knew about the Paris designers and their influence. And in the literary field ("Ahah!" muttered Bob, staring darkly at his forkful of stewed ox-paunch)—in the literary field, said Stuart, swallowing in haste for greater clarity, they all knew what effect a review by any one of A Certain Few Names, on the front page of the Sunday Times book section, could have upon the work of even an absolute unknown.

"It will sky-rocket it to Fame and Fortune with the speed of light," said Stuart.

"Come to the point." But Stuart, now grinding away on a chunk of grilled sheep, could only gurgle, wave his fork, and raise his eyebrows. Anhalt stopped his moody task of reducing the duckling to a mass of orange-flavored fibers, and turned to take the words, as it were, from Stuart's mutton-filled mouth.

"The point, Mr. Rosen, is that poor old Martens went up and down Madison Avenue for years claiming he had found a way of predicting fashions and styles, and nobody believed him. Frankly, *I* didn't. But I do now. What caused me to change my mind was this: When I heard, day before yesterday, that he had died so suddenly, I had a feeling that I *had* something of his, something that he'd left for me to look at once, something I'd taken just to get rid of him. And, oh, perhaps I was feeling a bit guilty, certainly a bit sorry, so I asked my secretary to get it for me. Well, you know, with the J. Oscar Rutherford people, as with Nature, nothing is ever lost—" Phillips Anhalt smiled his rather shy, rather sweet and slightly baffled smile— "so she got it for me and I took a look at it. . . . I was . . ." he paused, hesitated for the *mot juste*.

Stuart, with a masterful swallow, leaped into the breach, claymore in hand. "He was flabbergasted!"

Astounded, amended Anhalt. He was astounded.

There, in an envelope addressed to Peter Martens, and postmarked November 10, 1945, was a color snapshot of a young man wearing a fancy weskit.

"Now, you know, Mr. Rosen, no one in 1945 was wearing fancy weskits. They didn't come in till some years later. How did Marten *know* they were going to come in? And there was another snapshot of a young man in a charcoal suit and a pink shirt. Nobody was wearing that outfit in '45 . . . I checked the records, you see, and the old gentleman had left the things for me in December of that year. I'm ashamed to say that I had the receptionist put him off when he called again. . . . But just think of it: fancy weskits, charcoal suits, pink shirts, in 1945." He brooded. Bob asked if there was anything about grey flannel suits in the envelope, and Anhalt smiled a faint and fleeting smile.

"Ah, Bob, now, Bob," Stuart pursed his mouth in mild (and greasy) reproof. "You still don't seem to realize that this is S*E*R*I*O*U*S*."

"Indeed it is," said P. Anhalt. "As soon as I told Mac about it, do you know what he said, Stu? He said, 'Phil, don't spare the horses.'" And they nodded soberly, as those who have received wisdom from on high.

"Who," Bob asked, "is Mac?"

Shocked looks. Mac, he was told, the older men speaking both tandem and *au pair*, was Robert R. Mac Ian, head of the happy J. Oscar Rutherford corporate family.

"Of course, Phil," Stuart observed, picking slyly at his baked potato, "I won't ask why it took you till this morning to get in touch with me. With some other outfit, I might maybe suspect that they were trying to see what they could locate for themselves without having to cut our boy, here, in for a slice of the pie. He being the old man's confidante and moral heir, anyway, so to speak." (Bob stared at this description, said nothing. Let the thing develop as far as it would by itself, he reflected.) "But not the Rutherford outfit. It's too big, too ethical, for things like that." Anhalt didn't answer.

After a second, Stuart went on, "Yes, Bob, this is really something big. If the late old Mr. Martens' ideas can be successfully developed—and I'm sure Phil, here, will not expect you to divulge until we are ready to talk Terms—they will be really invaluable to people like manufacturers, fashion editors, designers, merchants, and, last but not least—advertising men. Fortunes can literally be made, and saved. No wonder that a dirty dog like this guy Shadwell is trying to horn in on it. Why listen—but I'm afraid we'll have to terminate this enchanting conversation. Bob has to go home and get the material in order—" (What material? Bob wondered. Oh, well, so far: $40 from Shadwell and a free lunch from Anhalt.)—"and you and I, Phil, will discuss those horses Mac said not to spare."

Anhalt nodded. It seemed obvious to Rosen that the ad man was unhappy, unhappy about having given Peter Martens the brushoff while he was alive, unhappy about being numbered among the vultures now that he was dead. And, so thinking, Bob realized with more than a touch of shame, that he himself was now numbered among the vultures; and he asked about funeral arrangements. But it seemed that the Masonic order was taking care of that: the late Peter Martens was already on his way back to his native town of Marietta, Ohio, where his lodge brothers would give him a formal farewell: aprons, sprigs of acacia, and all the ritual appurtenances. And Bob thought, why not? And was feeling somehow, very much relieved.

On the uptown bus which he had chosen over the swifter, hotter, dingier subway, he tried to collect his thoughts. What on earth could he ever hope to remember about a drunken conversation, which would make any sense to anybody, let alone be worth money? "The Sources of the Nile," the old man had said, glaring at him with bloody eye. Well, Shadwell knew the phrase, too. Maybe Shadwell knew what it meant, exactly what it meant, because he, Bob Rosen, sure as hell didn't. But the phrase did catch at the imagination. Martens had spent years—who knew how many?—seeking the sources of his particular Nile, the great river of fashion, as Mungo Park, Livingstone, Speke, and other half-forgotten explorers, had spent years in search of theirs. They had all endured privation, anguish, rebuffs, hostility . . . and in the end, just as the quest had killed Mungo Park, Livingstone, Speke, the other quest had killed old Peter Martens.

But, aside from insisting that there *was* a source or sources, and that he knew *where*, what had Pete said? Why hadn't Bob stayed sober? Probably the fat blonde at the next table, she of the poisonously green drink and the rotten step-children, probably she retained more of the old man's tale, picked up by intertable osmosis, than did Bob himself.

And with that he heard the voice of the waiter at the bar that noon: *The lady left it . . . What lady? . . . The blonde lady* . . . Bob scrabbled in his pocket and came up with the note. On the sweaty, crumpled bit of paper, scrawled in his own writing, or a cruel semblance of it, he read: *Ditx sags su Bimsoh oh—*

"What the hell!" he muttered, and fell to, with furrowed face, to make out what evidently owed more to Bushmill's than to Eberhard Faber. At length he decided that the note read, *Peter says, see Bensons on Purchase Place, the Bronx, if I don't believe him. Peter says, write it down.*

"It must mean something," he said, half-aloud, staring absently from Fifth Avenue to Central Park, as the bus roared and rattled between opulence and greenery. "It has to mean something."

"Well, what a shame," said Mr. Benson. "But how nice it was of you to come and tell us." His wavy gray hair was cut evenly around in soupbowl style, and as there was no white skin at the back of his neck, had evidently been so cut for some time. "Would you like some iced tea?"

"Still, he Went Quickly," said Mrs. Benson, who, at the business of being a woman, was in rather a large way of business. "I don't think there's any iced tea, Daddy. When I have to go, that's the way I want to go. Lemonade, maybe?"

"There isn't any lemonade if what Kitty was drinking was the last of the lemonade. The Masons give you a nice funeral. A real nice funeral. I used to think about joining up, but I never seem to get around to it. I think there's some gin. Isn't there some gin, Mommy? How about a nice cool glass of gin-and-cider, Bob? Kit will make us some, by and by."

Bob said, softly, that that sounded nice. He sat half-sunken in a canvas chair in the large, cool living-room. A quarter of an hour ago, having found out with little difficulty *which* house on Purchase Place was the Bensons', he had approached with something close to fear and trembling. Certainly, he had been sweating in profusion. The not-too-recently painted wooden house was just a blind, he told himself. Inside there would be banks of noiseless machines into which cards were fed and from which tapes rolled in smooth continuity. And a large broad-shouldered young man whose hair was cut so close to the skull that the scars underneath were plain to see, this young man would bar Bob's way and, with cold, calm, confidence, say, "Yes?"

"Er, um, Mr. Martens told me to see Mr. Benson."

"There is no Mr. Martens connected with our organization and Mr. Benson has gone to Washington. I'm afraid you can't come in: everything here is Classified."

And Bob would slink away, feeling Shoulders' scornful glance in the small of his shrinking, sweaty back.

But it hadn't been like that at all. Not anything like that at all.

Mr. Benson waved an envelope at Bob. "Here's a connivo, if you like," he said. "Fooled I don't know how many honest collectors, and dealers, too: Prince Abu-Somebody flies over here from Pseudo-Arabia without an expense account. Gets in with some crooked dealers, *I* could name them, but I won't, prints off this *en—tire* issue of airmails, pre-cancelled. Made a mint. Flies back to Pseudo-Arabia, *whomp!* they cut off his head!" And he chuckled richly at the thought of this prompt and summary vengeance. Plainly, in Mr. Benson's eyes, it had been done in the name of philatelic ethics; no considerations of dynastic intrigues among the petrol pashas entered his mind.

"Kitty, are you going to make us some cold drinks?" Mrs. B. inquired. "Poor old Pete, he used to be here for Sunday dinner on and off, oh, for just years. Is that Bentley coming?"

Bob just sat and sucked in the coolness and the calm and stared at Kitty. Kitty had a tiny stencil cut in the design of a star and she was carefully lacquering her toenails with it. He could hardly believe she was for real. "Ethereal" was the word for her beauty, and "ethereal" was the only word for it. Long, long hair of an indescribable gold fell over her heart-shaped face as she bent forward towards each perfectly formed toe. And she was wearing a dress like that of a child in a Kate Greenaway book.

"Oh, Bentley," said B., Senior. "What do you think has happened? Uncle Peter Martens passed away, all of a sudden, day before yesterday, and this gentleman is a friend of his and came to tell us about it; isn't that thoughtful?"

Bentley said, "Ahhh." Bentley was a mid-teener who wore jeans cut off at the knees and sneakers with the toes, insteps, and heels removed. He was naked to the waist and across his suntanned and hairless chest, a neat curve commencing just above his left nipple and terminating just under his right nipple, was the word *VIPERS* stenciled in red paint.

"*Ahhh,*" said Bentley Benson. "Any Pepsies?"

"Well, I'd asked you to bring some," his mother said, mildly. "Make a nice, big pitcher of gin-and-cider, Bentley, please, but only a *little* gin for yourself, in a separate glass, remember, now." Bentley said, "Ahhh," and departed, scratching on his chest right over the bright, red S.

Bob's relaxed gaze took in, one by one, the pictures on the mantelpiece. He sat up a bit, pointed. "Who is that?" he asked. The young man looked something like Bentley and something like Bentley's father.

"That's my oldest boy, Barton, Junior," said Mother B. "You see that nice vest he's wearing? Well, right after the War, Bart, he was in the Navy then, picked up a piece of lovely brocade over in Japan, and he sent it back home. I thought of making a nice bed-jacket out of it, but there wasn't enough material. So I made it into a nice vest, instead. Poor old Uncle Peter, he liked that vest, took a picture of Bart in it. Well, what do you know, a few years later fancy vests became quite popular, and, of course, by that time Bart was tired of his ("Of course," Bob murmured), so he sold it to a college boy who had a summer job at Little and Harpey's. Got $25 for it, and we all went out to dinner down town that night."

Kitty delicately stenciled another star on her toenails.

"I see," Bob said. After a moment, "Little and Harpey's?" he repeated.

Yes, that same. The publishers. Bart, and his younger brother Alton, were publishers' readers. Alt had been with Little and Harpey but was now with Scribbley's Sons; Bart had worked for Scribbley's at one time, too. "They've been with *all* the biggest publishing houses," their mother said, proudly. "Oh, *they* aren't any of your stick-in-the-muds, no sirree." Her hands had been fiddling with a piece of bright cloth, and then, suddenly, cloth and hands went up to her head, her fingers flashed, and—complete, perfect—she was wearing an intricately folded turban.

Bentley came in carrying a pitcher of drink in one hand and five glasses—one to each finger—in the other. "I told you to mix yours separately, I think," his mother said. Taking no notice of her youngest's *Ahhh*, she turned to Bob. "I have a whole basket of these pieces of madras," she said, "some silk, some cotton . . . and it's been on my mind all day. Now, if I just remember the way those old women from the West Indies used to tie them on their heads when I was a girl . . . and now, sure enough, it just came back to me! How does it look?" she asked.

"Looks very nice, Mommy," said Bart, Sr. And added, "I bet it would cover up the curlers better than those babushkas the women wear, you know?"

Bob Rosen bet it would, too.

So here it was and this was it. The sources of the Nile. How old Peter Martens had discovered it, Bob did not know. By and by, he supposed, he would find out. How did they *do* it, was it that they had a *panache—?* or was it a "wild talent," like telepathy, second sight, and calling dice or balls? He did not know.

"Bart said he was reading a real nice manuscript that came in just the other day," observed Mrs. Benson, dreamily, over her glass. "About South America. He says he thinks that South America has been neglected, and that there is going to be a revival of interest in non-fiction about South America."

"No more Bushmen?" Barton, Sr., asked.

"No, Bart says he thinks the public is getting tired of Bushmen. He says he only gives Bushmen another three months and then— poo—you won't be able to *give* the books away." Bob asked what Alton thought. "Well, Alton is reading fiction now, you know. He thinks the public is getting tired of novels about murder and sex and funny war experiences. Alt thinks they're about ready for some novels about ministers. He said to one of the writers that Scribbley's publishes, 'Why don't you do a novel about a minister?' he said. And the man said he thought it was a good idea."

There was a long, comfortable silence.

There was no doubt about it. *How* the Bensons did it, Bob still didn't know. But they did do it. With absolute unconsciousness and with absolute accuracy, they were able to predict future trends in fashion. It was marvelous. It was uncanny. It—

Kitty lifted her lovely head and looked at Bob through the long, silken skein of hair, then brushed it aside. "Do you ever have any money?" she asked. It was like the sound of small silver bells, her voice. Where, compared to this, were the flat Long Island vocables of, say, Noreen? Nowhere at all.

"Why, Kitty Benson, what a question," her mother said, reaching out her glass for Bentley to refill. "Poor Peter Martens, just to think—a little more, Bentley, don't think you're going to drink what's left, young man."

"Because if you ever have any money," said the voice like the Horns of Elfland, "we could go out somewhere together. Some boys don't ever have any money," it concluded, with infinitely loving melancholy.

"I'm going to have some money," Bob said at once. "Absolutely. Uh—when could—"

She smiled an absolute enchantment of a smile. "Not tonight," she said, "because I have a date. And not tomorrow night, because I have a date. But the day after tomorrow night, because then I don't have a date."

A little voice in one corner of Bob's mind said, "This girl has a brain about the size of a small split pea; you know that, don't you?" And another voice, much less little, in the opposite corner, shrieked, "Who *cares?* Who *cares?*" Furthermore, Noreen had made a faint but definite beginning on an extra chin, and her bosom tended (unless artfully and artificially supported) to droop. Neither was true of Kitty at all, at all.

"The day after tomorrow night, then," he said. "It's a date."

All that night he wrestled with his angel. "You can't expose these people to the sordid glare of modern commerce," the angel said, throwing him with a half-nelson. "They'd wither and die. Look at the dodo—look at the buffalo. Will you *look?*" *"You* look," growled Bob, breaking the hold, and seizing the angel in a scissors-lock. "I'm not going to let any damned account executives get their chicken-plucking hands on the Bensons. It'll all be done through me, see? Through *me!*" And with that he pinned the angel's shoulders to the mat. "And besides," he said, clenching his teeth, "I need the money . . ."

Next morning he called up his agent. "Here's just a few samples to toss Mr. Phillips Anhalt's way," he said grandiosely. "Write 'em down. Soupbowl haircuts for men. *That's* what I said. They can get a sunlamp treatment for the backs of their necks in the barber-shops. Listen. Women will stencil stars on their toe-nails with nail polish. Kate Greenaway style dresses for women are going to come in. Huh? Well, you bet your butt that Anhalt will know what Kate Greenaway means. Also, what smart women will wear will be madras kerchiefs tied up in the old West Indian way. This is very complicated, so I guess they'll have to be prefolded and pre-stitched. Silks and cottons . . . You writing this down? Okay.

"Teen-agers will wear, summer-time, I mean, they'll wear shorts made out of cut-down blue jeans. And sandals made out of cut-down sneakers. No shirts or undershirts—barechested, and—What? NO, for cry-sake, just the *boys!*"

And he gave Stuart the rest of it, books and all, and he demanded and got an advance. Next day Stuart reported that Anhalt reported that Mac Ian was quite excited. Mac had said—did Bob know what Phil said Mac said? Well, Mac said, "Let's not spoil the ship for a penny's worth of tar, Phil."

Bob demanded and received another advance. When Noreen called, he was brusque.

The late morning of his date-day he called to confirm it. That is, he tried to. The operator said that she was sorry, but that number had been disconnected. He made it up to the Bronx by taxi. The house was empty. It was not only empty of people, it was empty of everything. The wallpaper had been left, but that was all.

Many years earlier, about the time of his first cigarette, Bob had been led by a friend in the dead of night (say, half-past ten) along a quiet suburban street, pledged to confidence by the most frightful vows. Propped against the wall of a garage was a ladder —it did not go all the way to the roof: Bob and friend had pulled themselves up with effort which, in another context, would have won the full approval of their gym teacher. The roof made an excellent post to observe the going-to-bed preparations of a young woman who had seemingly never learned that window shades could be pulled down. Suddenly lights went on in another house, illuminating the roof of the garage; the young woman had seen the two and yelled; and Bob, holding onto the parapet with sweating hands and reaching for the ladder with sweating feet, had discovered that the ladder was no longer there. . . .

He felt the same way now.

Besides feeling stunned, incredulous, and panicky, he also felt annoyed. This was because he acutely realized that he was acting out an old moving picture scene. The scene would have been closer to the (film) realities had he been wearing a tattered uniform, and in a way he wanted to giggle, and in a way he wanted to cry. Only through obligation to the script did he carry the farce farther: wandering in and out of empty rooms, calling out names, asking if anyone was there.

No one was. And there were no notes or messages, not even *Croatan* carved on a doorpost. Once, in the gathering shadows, he thought he heard a noise, and he whirled around, half-expecting to see an enfeebled Mr. Benson with a bacon-fat lamp in one hand, or an elderly Negro, perhaps, who would say, tearfully, "Marse Bob, dem Yankees done burn all de cotton . . ." But there was nothing.

He trod the stairs to the next house and addressed inquiries to an old lady in a rocking-chair. "Well, I'm sure that I don't know," she said, in a paper-thin and fretful voice. "I saw them, all dressed up, getting to the car, and I said, 'Why, where are you all *going*, Hazel?' ("Hazel?" "Hazel Benson. I thought you said you *knew* them, young man?" "Oh, yes. Yes, of course. Please go on.") Well, I said, 'Where are you all *going*, Hazel?' And she said, 'It's time for a change, Mrs. Machen.' And they all laughed and they waved and they drove away. And then some men came and packed everything up and took it away in trucks. Well! 'Where did they all *go*?' I asked them. 'Where did they all *go*?' But do you think they'd have the common decency to *tell* me, after I've lived here for fifty-four years? Not-a-word. Oh—"

Feeling himself infinitely cunning, Bob said, offhandedly, "Yes, I know just the outfit you mean. O'Brien Movers."

"I do *not* mean O'Brien Movers. Whatever gave you such an idea? It was the Seven Sebastian Sisters."

And this was the most that Bob Rosen could learn. Inquiries at other houses either drew blanks or produced such probably significant items as, "Kitty said, 'Here are your curlers, because I won't need them anymore'"; "Yes, just the other day I was talking to Bart, Senior, and he said, 'You know, you don't realize that you're in a rut until you have to look up to see the sky.' Well, those

Bensons always talked a little crazy, and so I thought nothing of it, until—"; and, "I said to Bentley, 'Vipe, how about tomorrow we go over to Williamsbridge and pass the chicks there in review?' and he said, 'No, Vipe, I can't make that scene tomorrow, my ancients put another poster on the billboard.' So I said, 'Ay-las,' and next thing I knew—"

"His who did what?"

"Fellow, you don't wot this Viper talk one note, do you? His *family*, see, they had made other plans. They really cut loose, didn't they?"

They really did. So there Bob was, neat and trim and sweet-smelling, and nowhere to go, and with a pocketful of money. He looked around the tree-lined street and two blocks away, on the corner, he saw a neon sign. *Harry's*, it flashed (green). *Bar and Grill* (red).

"Where's Harry?" he asked the middle-aged woman behind the bar.

"Lodge meeting," she said. "He'll be back soon. They aren't doing any labor tonight, just business. Waddle ya have?"

"A ball of Bushmill," he said. He wondered where he had heard that, last. It was cool in the bar. And then he remembered, and then he shuddered.

"Oh, that's bad," Stuart Emmanuel moaned. "That sounds very bad . . . And you shouldn't've gone to the moving van people yourself. Now you probably muddied the waters."

Bob hung his head. His efforts to extract information from the Seven Sebastian Sisters—apparently they were septuplets, and all had grey mustaches—had certainly failed wretchedly. And he kept seeing Kitty Benson's face, framed in her golden hair like a sun-lit nimbus, kept hearing Kitty Benson's golden voice.

"Well," Stuart said, "I'll do my damndest." And no doubt he did, but it wasn't enough. He was forced to come clean with Anhalt. And Anhalt, after puttering around, his sweet smile more baffled than ever, told Mac everything. Mac put the entire *force majeure* of the T. Oscar Rutherford organization behind the search. And they came up with two items.

Item. The Seven Sebastian Sisters had no other address than the one on Purchase Place, and all the furniture was in their fireproof warehouse, with two years' storage paid in advance.

Item. The owner of the house on Purchase Place said, "I told them I'd had an offer to buy the house, but I wouldn't, if they'd agree to a rent increase. And the next thing I knew, the keys came in the mail."

Little and Harpey, as well as Scribbley's Sons, reported only that Alt and Bart, Junior, had said they were leaving, but hadn't said where they were going.

"Maybe they've gone on a trip somewhere," Stuart suggested. "Maybe they'll come back before long. Anhalt has ears in all the publishing houses, maybe he'll hear something."

But before Anhalt heard anything, Mac decided that there was no longer anything to hear. "I wash my hands of it all," he declared. "It's a wild goose chase. Where did you ever pick up this crackpot idea in the first place?" And Phillips Anhalt's smile faded away. Weeks passed, and months.

But Bob Rosen has never abandoned hope. He has checked with the Board of Education about Bentley's records, to see if they know anything about a transcript or transfer. He has haunted Nassau Street, bothering—in particular—dealers specializing in Pseudo-Arabian air mail issues, in hopes that Mr. Benson has made his whereabouts known to them. He has hocked his watch to buy hamburgers and pizzas for the Vipers, and innumerable Scotches on innumerable rocks for the trim young men and the girls fresh out of Bennington who staff the offices of our leading publishers. He—

In short, he has taken up the search of Peter Martens (Old Pete, Sneaky Pete). He is looking for the sources of the Nile. Has he *ever* found *anything*? Well, yes, as a matter of fact, he has.

The strange nature of cyclical coincidences has been summed up, somewhere, in the classical remark that one can go for years without seeing a one-legged man wearing a baseball cap; and then, in a single afternoon, one will see three of them. So it happened with Bob Rosen.

One day, feeling dull and heavy, and finding that the elfin notes of Kitty Benson's voice seemed to be growing fainter in his mind, Bob called up her old landlord.

"No," said the old landlord, "I never heard another word from them. And I'll tell you who else I never heard from, either. The fellow who offered to buy the house. He never came around and when I called his office, he just laughed at me. Fine way to do business."

"What's his name?" Bob asked, listlessly.

"Funny name," said the old landlord. "E. Peters Shadwall? Something like that. The hell with him, anyway."

Bob tore his rooms apart looking for the card with the perforated top edge which Shadwell had—it seemed so very long ago—torn off his little book and given him. Also, it struck him, neither could he find the piece of paper on which he had scribbled Old Martens' last message, with the Bensons' name and street on it. He fumbled through the Yellow Book, but couldn't seem to locate the proper category for the mantis-man's business. And he gave up on the regular directory, what with Shad, Shadd, -wel, -well, -welle, etc.

He would, he decided, go and ask Stuart Emmanuel. The dapper little agent had taken the loss of the Bensons so hard ("It was a beauty of a deal," he'd all but wept) that he might also advance a small sum of money for the sake of the Quest. Bob was in the upper East 40s when he passed a bar where he had once taken Noreen for cocktails—a mistake, for it had advanced her already expensive tastes another notch—and this reminded him that he had not heard from her in some time. He was trying to calculate just how much time, and if he ought to do something about it, when he saw the third one-legged man in the baseball cap.

That is to say, speaking non-metaphorically, he had turned to cross a street in the middle of a block, and was halted by the absence of any gap between the two vehicles (part of a traffic jam caused by a long-unclosed incision in the street) directly in front of him. Reading from right to left, the vehicles consisted of an Eleanor-blue truck reading *Grandma Goldberg's Yum-Yum*

Borsht, and an obscene-pink Jaguar containing T. Pettys Shadwell and Noreen.

It was the Moment of the Shock of Recognition. He understood everything.

Without his making a sound, they turned together and saw him, mouth open, everything written on his face. And they knew that he knew.

"Why, Bob," said Noreen. "Ah, Rosen," said Shadwell.

"I'm sorry that we weren't able to have you at the *wedding,*" she said. "But everything happened so *quickly.* Peter just swept me off my feet."

Bob said, "I'll bet."

She said, "Don't be bitter"—seeing that he was, and enjoying it. Horns sounded, voices cursed, but the line of cars didn't move.

"You did it," Bob said, coming close. Shadwell's hands left the wheel and came together at his chest, fingers down. "*You* saw that crisp green money he left and you saw his card and got in touch with him and *you* came in and took the note and— *Where are they?*" he shouted, taking hold of the small car and shaking it. "I don't give a damn about the money, just tell me where they are! Just let me see the girl!"

But T. Pettys Shadwell just laughed and laughed, his voice like the whisper of the wind in the dry leaves. "Why *Bob,*" said Noreen, bugging her eyes and flashing her large, coarse gems, and giving the scene all she had, "why, Bob, was there a *girl?* You never told *me.*"

Bob abandoned his anger, disclaimed all interest in the commercial aspect of the Bensons, offered to execute bonds and sign paper in blood, if only he were allowed to see Kitty. Shadwell, fingering his tiny carat of a mustache, shrugged. "Write the girl a letter," he said, smirking. "I assure you, all mail will be forwarded." And then the traffic jam broke and the Jag zoomed off, Noreen's scarlet lips pursed in blowing a kiss.

"Write?" Why, bless you, of course Bob wrote. Every day and often twice a day for weeks. But never a reply did he get. And on realizing that his letters probably went no farther than Noreen

(Mrs. T. Pettys) Shadwell, who doubtless gloated and sneered in the midst of her luxury, he fell into despair, and ceased. Where is Kitty of the heart-shaped face, Kitty of the light-gold hair, Kitty of the elfin voice? Where are her mother and father and her three brothers? Where now are the sources of the Nile? Ah, where?

So there you are. One can hardly suppose that Shadwell has perforce kidnapped the entire Benson family, but the fact is that they have disappeared almost entirely without trace, and the slight trace which remains leads directly to and only to the door of T. Pettys Shadwell Associates, Market Research Advisors. Has he whisked them all away to some sylvan retreat in the remote recesses of the Great Smoky Mountains? Are they even now pursuing their prophetic ways in one of the ever-burgeoning, endlessly proliferating suburbs of the City of the Angels? Or has he, with genius diabolical, located them so near to hand that far-sighted vision must needs forever miss them?

In deepest Brooklyn, perhaps, amongst whose labyrinthine ways an army of surveyors could scarce find their own stakes?—or in fathomless Queens, red brick and yellow brick, world without end, where the questing heart grows sick and faint?

Rosen does not know, but he has not ceased to care. He writes to live, but he lives to look, now selling, now searching, famine succeeding feast, but hope never failing.

Phillips Anhalt, however, has not continued so successfully. He has not Bob's hopes. Anhalt continues, it is true, with the T. Oscar Rutherford people, but no longer has his corner office, or any private office at all. Anhalt failed: Anhalt now has a desk in the bullpen with the other failures and the new apprentices.

And while Bob ceaselessly searches the streets—for who knows in which place he may find the springs bubbling and welling?— and while Anhalt drinks bitter tea and toils like a slave in a salt mine, that swine, that cad, that most despicable of living men, T. Pettys Shadwell, has three full floors in a new building of steel, aluminum, and blue-green glass a block from the Cathedral; he has a box at the Met, a house in Bucks County, a place on the

Vineyard, an apartment in Beekman Place, a Caddy, a Bentley, *two* Jaguars, a yacht that sleeps ten, and one of the choicest small (but ever-growing) collection of Renoirs in private hands today. . . .